Lainey Cash

Book 1

FROM THE SERIES
FIFTEEN THOUSAND TIMES
FOR FIFTY YEARS

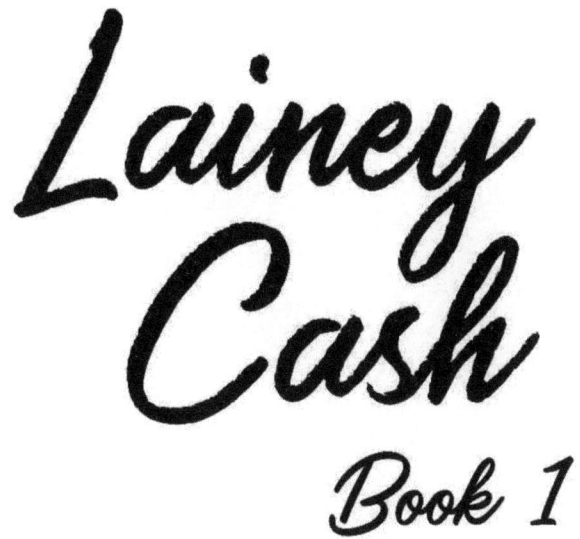

TRILOGY BY
CLARE CINNAMON

MILL CITY PRESS

Mill City Press, Inc.
2301 Lucien Way #415
Maitland, FL 32751
407.339.4217
www.millcitypress.net

© 2019 by Clare Cinnamon

All rights reserved. No part of this publication may be reproduced, stored in a retrieval system, or transmitted, in any form or by any means, electronic, mechanical, photocopying, recording, or otherwise, without the prior written permission of the author.

Printed in the United States of America

LCCN : 2019-917885

ISBN-13: 978-1-5456-7616-5

From the series
Fifteen Thousand Times for Fifty Years

Lainey Cash, Book One
Lainey and Jed, Book Two
Delaina, Book Three – Coming soon!

Others coming up in the series:

Asunder
A Town Called Lake
Ayla From Atlanta
Sunshine and Lev

*For Christopher Cinnamon (wink) –
If you think it's you and me, it is.
The rest is 'write what you know.'
Thank you for both.*

Table of Contents

Introduction: A Few Years Ago ix

One: Today 1
Two: Tonight 20
Three: Mouths 36
Four: Ears 50
Five: Eyes 67
Six: The River 83
Seven: The Dance 102
Eight: Mercy 108
Nine: Solemnity 116
Ten: Questions 132
Eleven: Plans 143
Twelve: April Fool's Day 158
Thirteen: In Lust 175
Fourteen: In Love 188
Fifteen: Novelty 206
Sixteen: Privacy 223
Seventeen: Realization 239
Eighteen: Straight Talk 252
Nineteen: Sweet Talk 260
Twenty: Pillow Talk 268
Twenty-one: Broken 286

About the Author 289

Introduction

A Few Years Ago

Whatever that thing is some men have, they're just born with it.

It's in the looks, the walk, the voice, the attitude. There was no doubt about the authenticity of this one. He had the face, the body, the backdrop, and the money. More importantly, he had that thing most of them aren't born with. A disregard for all of it.

It sold, as sure as Marlboro sells cigarettes. To every single female in Mallard, Mississippi.

His name was Jed McCrae, and tonight, he lingered alone on a balcony, black iron and vines and shadowy, atop a narrow lane between historic homes. Returned to his humdrum Mississippi hometown for the past eight months offered enough motivation for this weekend jaunt to New Orleans. In his late twenties, Jed already realized what brought him pleasure in life. Foremost, land, owning it and watching things grow. Travel, mostly for the feelings of leaving and coming back home. Women, or more precisely, putting his hands on the right woman at the right time.

Jed's current situation offered two out of three. He felt rusty, or maybe too evolved, too everything adult for this place. He knew two people, kind of. Cabot Hartley, hometown banker's son who invited him and Jenna Lee Lester, who seemed to have set her sights on him. Cabot, the only Mallard guy in his league so to speak; thus, when Jed moved home, they naturally hung out. Cabot, as aimless as would be expected. Too rich to work, too young to care, too spoiled to know anything but keeping up his fraternity brother status long after college days. His parents' getaway home, about two blocks from the French Quarter, provided a supreme chance for Cabot to pretend he was still twenty-one, in the frat house, unaccountable. Jed didn't like him, but what else was there, so far, back home?

Jed had been to New Orleans before. Spent nights, did a ghost tour, street festivals, beignets, coffee, riverboats, streetcars, and/or jazz. Those trips had been with his mama years ago, a different NOLA, a different Jed. She told him, when they drank coffee before he left this morning, to enjoy the food, music, architecture. His mama wasn't wrong about much, and she wasn't wrong about New Orleans. She was dead wrong about here. This was Mardi Gras, boys with money and time. Sex, drugs, rock and roll.

The party took place below. Shallow women and drunk males filled the small square, an unblemished rose garden with ornate tables and chairs. The sole modern amenity, a built-in oversized outdoor kitchen. Throwback 90s alternative hits, The Smashing Pumpkins, Nirvana, Pearl Jam blared over the hum of laughter, loud voices, and an occasional jazz note drifting from clubs closer to the river. Lights peaked and dimmed, partiers streaming in and out the door. Cell phone flashes, never-ending. Pot smoke pervaded. Outside opened to a sensational interior; Jed saw it when he arrived. A tapestry of monochromatic fabrics, elegant paint colors, and impressive artwork had been purposefully chosen and appointed. A long marble island between the kitchen and living room stood out with a lavish bar hanging from the ceiling overhead and mirrored shelves in the corner full of expensive bottles of alcohol. Dozens of wineglasses, shot glasses, Champagne flutes, and ballers. The Hartley weekend manor, a gray three-story mansion in the heart of Southern-French-Spanish classic nostalgia, at first glance may've seemed an improper venue for their carousing. In actuality, it was perfect.

New Orleans, city of stories, keeper of secrets within old walls and pretty courtyards.

Single and seasoned, Jed's life experiences should've prepared him. They didn't. He had tried drugs, if smoking marijuana maybe five times as a high school senior and college freshman counted. He'd been in a house where people were doing cocaine, if once as a college senior at a grad party, and hightailing out, counted. He could hang in there with most anybody, no collar to blue collar to white collar. This was not his scene.

First weekend in March felt damned cold to sit outside in darkness. He smoked a lone Marlboro, habit he picked up from his stepfather. It would take him a week to smoke a pack at the height of nicotine binges. Since he moved back to Mississippi, he'd been storing one at a time in his pocket. Rationing, an effort to quit. Right now, he smoked gladly and wondered over the definition of prostitution.

Hometown girls straight out of community college. Mallard born and raised, a town of ten thousand. Attractive and relatively smart females. No pedigree, no depth. A decent education, a decent job, a decent house, a halfway decent husband were the goals of their raising. Plucked with precision and hired to work at Mallard First Financial, the bank Cabot would eventually inherit, then enticed by his wealth, gluttony, and the naive notion of a better future. They cooperated willingly, advanced sparingly, hung on, and didn't care about much of anything in the present setting.

Jenna Lee seemed different. Not much different. Different enough to consider. Shapely, prissy, physically perfected, the given characteristics of Cabot's girls, she possessed. She came across as slightly more interesting, totally most pretty. Not five minutes ago, Cabot had hollered up for Jed to come down. Jed answered that he would, when he finished his cigarette. He figured Cabot neither cared nor would he remember if he came down. Jenna Lee would.

"Got a light?" Speak of the devil. Jenna Lee with her slinky red top, spiky heels, feline eyes.

"Yep." They'd done this before, a time or three. Cabot held camp house parties, deep in Mallard's woods, at his parents' place on Big Sunflower River. Rural Mississippi-type parties. Playing cards, pool table, football game watching on the big screen, beer, girls, barbecue. Jenna Lee noticed Jed, the few parties he attended, or he noticed her. Whichever. She liked to single him out and make small talk. He had obliged her out of boredom. In Mallard, he could flirt, be nice, and exit. Not now and here. Stuck with Jenna Lee, the least of a half-dozen evils.

He leaned over and flicked his lighter. She lit her cigarette. His, gone. "Got a cigarette?"

"If you like slims."

Hell no, he didn't. "Never mind." She smoked a minute. He grinned with, "Who drew your name tonight?" Partner swapping, at home and here, was obvious. From lack of options or morals, no one thought about or cared, except Jed. He'd seen better, known better, lived more.

...Jenna Lee Lester knew what she wanted. Dang, if it hadn't taken more than six months so far. Jed McCrae. Black hair, blue eyes, over six feet tall, tantalizing. What else did a woman need to know? Stylish, nice, educated, a traveler, rumored wealthy, a lot of great bonuses. "You."

Jed raised his eyebrows. His shock, not fake. Rusty he felt, for sure, because her one word caught him off guard.

The thing was, he didn't have to hook up with a female every weekend. The thing was, he liked substance. He liked decency. He liked...class. The hell of it, where were those women? Not a single night with anyone in his hometown. First several weeks there, he made trips to Atlanta, ex-sex with Mallory, until they, too, felt incomplete. He didn't want to put down roots in the big city. Mallory sure as heck wasn't settling in measly Mallard. For three months, he'd been womanless. His longest break since...well, his first time, before he could drive. "Lucky us." He winked. He thought he felt Jenna Lee's heart flutter from three feet away.

She sat on the chair across from his, took time inhaling and blowing smoke, crossed her lethal legs. "I know a lot about you, Jed McCrae."

He heard that one before. "Most of it isn't true."

"Try me."

"Go ahead."

"You don't own your daddy's land yet."

Ouch. "Okay, try again."

"The cabin you're buildin' on the river is really nice." How did she know? Miles from town, back of a field, down a dirt road, hidden in trees purposely. "It'll be finished by midsummer," she added.

"All right, Jenna Lee. Three for three." Jed reached forward, took her cigarette, dragged. "How do you know about my cabin?"

"Girls talk about you. Wanna know more." He got a lightbulb smile from Miss Jenna Lee. "You're interesting. I had a thing with David Jake Jones, too."

Jed's house builder. Ah, the beauty of small-town living. Everybody knew everything about everybody, one way or another. Or thought they did. The truth became whatever got said and spread. Jed didn't know *that*, though. David Jake and Jenna Lee, destined from the Lord above. Not keen on toying with his contractor's girlfriend, he questioned, "When's the last time David Jake had your thing?" Jed grinned the grin that ladies forgave.

She twisted in her seat with a guilty little laugh. "*Stop it*. We're done. DJ's not the settling down type."

He would be, in a couple years or so. Those two would settle right on down. Jed was certain of it.

"You know I lost my virginity to your first cousin."

Jed didn't flinch; she used a common ploy. He had three first cousins. His mama, from Baton Rouge, had no siblings. His Mallard-born father, a lower-class farmhand, eventually big-time farmer, had one sister who married their best worker and bore three sons. Ben and Bryan settled down with high school sweethearts. "Boone." Wild and careless, he favored Jed in an unrefined way.

"Yes, sir." She narrowed her eyes on the last intake of her shortened cig. "I'm not the only Mallard County High School cheerleader who went after Boone when we couldn't turn your head."

Jed raised his eyebrows. His shock, not fake. He had no memory of Jenna Lee Lester prior to months ago. "I...think I graduated before you got to high school."

She shook her head no. "Freshman when you were a senior. Shay Morris had her hands on your heart back then."

Her hands on his balls, more likely. Below, a female laughed too loudly. Jed needed good conversation, motivation, adults. Jenna Lee looked prettier at closer range, a rarity among females. "What do you wanna do with your life, Jenna Lee?"

She made a face, looked around. "This?" Bless her. He must've made a face. She edited, "Or maybe travel, a master's degree, or something? I mean, until Mr. Right comes along." She put out her cigarette.

He tried, "Where would you travel first?"

"Uhm." Never thought about it, he could tell. "I've been to Alabama, Florida, and here, so..." She smiled. "Got suggestions? You and I could do a fun weekend."

"Yeah, anywhere but here."

She laughed and tossed glistening straight hair over one shoulder. More laughter below too, to the tune of "Heart-Shaped Box" and Mary Jane smells. He leaned back, spread his arms on the balcony rails, nowhere to escape. "What're you lookin' for in Mr. Right?"

"Unlike those fools..." She motioned to the party. "Not Cabot."

"Hard to believe."

"I mean, he's interesting and entertaining." More of her shifting and smiling, giving Jed ample cleavage, apple-like breasts. "I'm glad for my job, but..." She shrugged. "I don't do drugs. Besides, they're stupid to think they're gonna be the one." Her smile widened. She turned secretive. "Everybody knows the truth, right?"

What, that Cabot took advantage of a pack of wannabes? Jed, kind enough not to say it, waited.

"He's gonna marry Lainey Cash."

Had she said Cabot was gay, Jed would've been no more stunned. He tried to hide it, irritated somehow. "She's a kid, barely drivin'..."

"Drivin' a Range Rover or Porsche or something, I'm sure. Cabot jokes about marrying her all the time."

"They drive American." Chevy 4X4 SUV. Jed knew what she drove; he knew what everybody at Cash Way drove. Where they banked. Their property lines. How they farmed. Who they screwed and screwed over. By necessity. Jed got interested in Jenna Lee mighty fast. "He brags about it, huh?" What a match. "She wouldn't give him the time of day." Or Jed, for that matter.

A slow perusal from pretty Jenna Lee. "You seem aggravated. Sorry. I know y'all's families hate each other bad."

"Ah, it's all right." He was aggravated. This weekend, supposed to be a getaway, no thought of home or farming or Cashes. Jenna Lee shivered in her skimpy top. She had to be cold. Jed was cold. He shrugged off his coat. "Here." Vaguely, he noticed the party had gone inside.

Faraway jazz, dim streetlights, and cold. Cabot Hartley and Delaina Cash, the duo shook him. Jenna Lee, winter wind blowing in her hair, glanced inside. Jed asked, "Where do you like to go in New Orleans?" Mardi Gras had no closing time. He'd take her anywhere to get away from hos and blows and overage frat bros.

"Uhm, here?"

Pitiful. He descended the winding outer staircase. She followed. He looked around the courtyard, glimpsed the French doors to inside. She said, "Come on," and wound her way through the kitchen-living-dining area. People danced, made out, did lines, unnoticing. Rootless and high, another bank teller walked around in a black bra and jeans with smeared eye makeup. Jenna Lee reached a downstairs bedroom. A sherbet orange coverlet draped the queen-size bed framed by a white iron headboard. Tall windows bordered each side. A brightly colored jute rug accented honey oak floor. Jed closed the door behind him. A fireplace straddled the opposing wall. Burning candles lined the mantle. A partially opened door revealed an updated bathroom with a glitzy built-in bar. She stepped in toward shelves of plush bath towels, robes, oils, uppity bath salts and a Jacuzzi tub. All in all, perfect. Too perfect, like a honeymoon hideaway. Jed saw a gleaming streetcar through the darkened window.

Being rich had a lot of perks. He enticed her out the window and to the lane. He enticed the streetcar operator to drive them around alone, for a considerable tip. They sat in back. The wood seat, the fuel smell, emitted potent heat. Jenna Lee, enthralled and seduced, kept saying, "How romantic." Jed gave her what she wanted in rear of a NOLA streetcar until something more intriguing came along.

LAINEY CASH

~ ~ ~

I should've seen it
then again
how do you see when you're not looking

I expected magic

Echoing waterfalls
Glittering raindrops
splashing joyfully against my face

a symphony of songs
like trade winds
swishing gleefully across the air

a scurry of love birds
like reverse snowflakes
bursting suddenly through the sky

that moment
I expected magic
some whimsical current

I found you
I know love for the first time

~ ~ ~

ONE

Today

There was nothing extraordinary about today. Things buzzed; stuff budded; wind blew the newness and anticipation of spring to Mississippi.

For two decades, Jed McCrae had done his best to ignore the daughter of Tory Cash, largest landowner in Mallard County by a thousand acres. Seven miles from town, traveling south on the only major highway, a turn onto Cash-McCrae Road proved every precious, fertile acre for miles on both sides belonged to one of them, all the way to Big Sunflower River. Their time and season and place traditionally defined, today local farmers had begun to turn the soil. Some went for broke and put seed in broke ground. Good Friday a week away and a warm winter, good enough reasons to jump the gun and get on with it.

Jed knelt on the front porch of his riverside cabin to scratch behind the ears of his faithful red-haired mutt Lucy. Finished planting for today, he wore ragged button-fly blue jeans, dirty work boots, and a smile intended for Lucy, not the other female standing next to them. On rare occasion did Lucy acknowledge anyone but Jed with more than a bored glance. Now, no exception. Once Jed got on his feet, eye level with Holland Sommers, she said regretfully, "Better run. It'll take ten minutes to get to town. Things at the bank demanding my attention." Jed smelled like sweat, the rough edges smoothed by woodsy deodorant, finished off in a layer of fine dust. It was a dirtiness a woman grew accustomed to, looked forward to, produced from field work. She breathed in. "I could come back," she purred. "Tonight."

Holland charmed. Jed would give her that much. Every inch feminine, skin soaked in floral perfume, makeup plastered flawlessly, she would be suited for pawning cosmetics at a ritzy department store. Chestnut-auburn hair hung stick straight across the tops of her breasts. Arched eyebrows framed almond-shaped Hershey eyes. Her cheeks were rosy and her lips glossy red against an olive complexion. Nearly as tall as Jed and full-figured, she had breasts like cantaloupes. He stifled the observation. They'd known each other since babyhood and never crossed the line. "No time to play around here." Thunder rumbled.

Holland nodded. "Yes, Jed, be certain to stay a step ahead of your neighbor. Wouldn't want a female to outdo you." A name wasn't necessary. Delaina Cash, known as Lainey. Not the first time Holland had picked him about her, for some damn reason. He craned his neck out to check on a drab sky. Sturdy border trees swayed, fencing his possessions from the world. A good shower was on the way.

Holland did her best to expand the conversation as she ran a finger down his bare torso. "I run into Lainey at the bank often. Cute girl. Friendly. Makes it difficult to believe she comes from such bad blood or holds grudges. Maybe she's not like previous Cashes."

Jed could not recall a single spoken word that had come from Delaina's silver-spoon-fed mouth. In trucks or tractors, they passed and repassed regularly on the winding dirt roads and field rows dividing land they worked. They went months without seeing one another in close flesh. Jed's facial expression said his feeling on the subject was nonnegotiable, and he'd reveal no details of the legendary feuding between their families.

Holland didn't press, inched her skirt up, and cleared her throat. Jed's head tilted from the sky to her smooth legs. She wore white lace thong underwear. A little bit prissy for him and a lot too innocent for her. She tossed them on the porch. "A souvenir... so you don't forget about me. Hope to see you tonight." Holland darted to her car, a sunshine-yellow convertible. She cranked the engine and whirled around, throwing dust behind her, barreling down the gravel path at a speed more suitable for the interstate than a backwoods lane.

Jed ambled across the porch. Thunder boomed. He mentally patted himself on the back for getting seed planted in the ground that morning. He cast another glance across the place, like a parent who knows his child is okay but needs a reassuring look. Keeper of the land bestowed certain characteristics upon him. A sharp eye, brisk mind, and strong back had been genetic. Patience and intuition grew up with him. He had learned to carry heavy burdens without it showing on his face other than the slightest lines etched on the outside corners of his eyes, and those lines, according to ladies, were traces of character.

He strolled inside. Lucy followed. Jed sat on a barstool in his kitchen facing the den and tossed part of his sandwich on the floor. "Miss Holland used a lot of mayo, but you might like it." Lucy gobbled, licked her mouth, and sniffed for more.

Holland mentioning Delaina Cash, perhaps a cause for concern. Suspicion motivated Jed to ponder the history of Cash-McCrae Road. Delaina's ancestors had maintained their land through respectable and scandalous methods. Regardless of their business habits or moral character, they set an unbending precedent. They held on to it, every inch. Until it passed to the last remaining male member, Delaina's father Victor Kelly Cash, better known as Tory.

Tory, like Cash men before, had immense pride for his heritage and unyielding determination to keep the land alive. He also inherited the Cash inclination for less-than-pristine business deals and immorality. He had not inherited the usual Cash trait of spinning those plates with the grace of a practiced magician. Hard-core living came to bite Tory Cash in the butt and left a lasting scar.

James Ed McCrae, Jed's father, began work out of high school as a laborer for Tory over forty years ago. While Tory partied like hell and went from woman to woman, James Ed worked diligently, saving money and renting parcels. After an unusually stressful farming season, Tory was unable to make all his loan payments. James Ed bought acreage under tense circumstances. Steadfastly, he acquired more and married comfortably rich Cassandra Jane Darrah from Baton Rouge. By then, he had overtaken a third of the Cash land. Land belonging to Tory Cash's family since the declaration of the state of Mississippi.

James Evan Darrah (Jed) McCrae was born before his parents celebrated their first anniversary, and ten months later, his father, also a hobby pilot, died in a plane crash. James Ed McCrae left his baby boy Jed and Jed's mother Cassie Jane alone with thousands of acres to tend and few laborers. She remarried quickly to save the land her husband had worked tediously to acquire from falling back into Cash hands. Jed was never particularly pleased with her choice of Attorney Fain Kendall. Fain didn't know much about farming and less about being a father.

The universe grabbed the reigns on Jed's thoughts. His spot on the globe combusted and dumped him into an uncharted place. *Delaina Cash.* His phone blinked and displayed her name, first time ever. This ought to be good.

He read, *Need a wrench fast. Otw. Thanks, Delaina*

Surely she was not asking him for a wrench. Granted, she could fix things. Delaina Cash had never asked him for anything. Nor would he give her anything. The universe shoved him. Jed typed, *Okay.*

Jed remembered precisely the last time he saw her months ago at MacHenry's, the local bar and grill.

She was on the arm of Cabot Hartley.

Jed had weighed the outcome of their alliance, and its occupational effect on him, almost daily since. Cabot Hartley and Lainey Cash were, for all practical purposes, a match made in heaven. Or hell. Cabot, the town's most eligible bachelor, the prince of Mallard, an equal in arrogant stupidity. Lainey, the town's reigning debutante with a sixty-five-hundred-acre dowry although Jed doubted Mallard would see her newspaper picture in a frothy white evening gown at a "Coming Out" ball. Nevertheless, she was the town's princess, run through the washing machine on a spin cycle. Jed predicted their relationship would lead them to a royal wedding by year's end. The earth-splitting, muck-throwing divorce would follow soon after when the princess realized her frog-turned-prince-turned-frog crawled on a high-class whore as often as she climbed on a green tractor.

Mallard, Mississippi, might as well be renamed Hartleyville. Located near Jackson and near enough to New Orleans, their town could be found on a map by a single natural wonder. Big Sunflower River, a shallow, watery bed of flat rocks. Twenty or so buildings stacked along Main and Commerce Streets in a two-block stretch with the First United Methodist and First Baptist Churches as bookends comprised town. Not a single business operated without Hartley approval or backing. Thus, the town and its citizens hadn't flourished or progressed in fifty years keeping the Hartleys in their desired position as Mallard's First Family. Town had a community college on the east side. The county had a logging company on the north side, and the area's soil proved ripe for farming. A man couldn't make much of a living at either. A handful of farms made of several hundred acres each hit a plateau in recent years. No one could get their hands on significant plots with Hartleys controlling the town's financing and real estate. Lainey Cash and Jed McCrae held firmly in their clutches the most fertile property for a twenty-mile stretch, their rich land on Mallard's south side originally all Cash-owned. In recent years, Mallard County, as much as any place in the farming-dependent South, had taken a bankrupting agricultural plunge. Not so on Cash-McCrae Road; these were large, diversified operations. McCrae Farms and Cash Way spread gambles over more than cotton. Hay, timber, cattle, corn, soybeans, wheat, poultry, rice, and pecans blended into an exact science, made inexact only by severe drought or massive flooding. Jed and Delaina had experienced neither.

Jed's mind shifted to that night at MacHenry's, first time he saw her with Cabot Hartley, last November during Thanksgiving weekend. She faintly nodded at Jed from a distance. He was half willingly entangled by heavily perfumed, slow-talkin', fast-movin' Samantha Hensley, though he didn't know why he'd fooled with her now. Delaina sent a costly, tremendous, fantastic flower arrangement to Jed's mother's funeral in December. Nice gesture for a spoiled rotten little girl. Crackling gravel outside broke up his thoughts. She had arrived, not exactly a queen in a carriage.

Jed strutted onto the porch, a bloodhound sniffing its next capture, Lucy close behind. Lainey noticed neither. She had screeched to a halt, parked her shiny black SUV, and leapt to the ground in fluid motion. "Sorry to bother you," she called out, not looking at him as she pointed to the sky. "We've been plantin' seed at Farm 130 all mornin', runnin' around like lost angels in hell, tryin' to beat that big-ass cloud. Less than fifteen acres to go and the damn tractor broke down right here. I thought you'd be home for lunch. Your cabin's a lot closer than our workshop."

"You learn that kind of talk in Sunday School, little girl?" Jed stood on the top step and watched her. Again, she didn't notice, watching the sky while simultaneously walking forward. Jed had never *really* looked at her before. She was ten years his junior.

She stopped and made eye contact. Thunder echoed. "Excuse me, sir. I'm just flustered, uhm...Mr. McCrae."

"Call me Jed. I'm not much older than you."

"But you called me a little girl," she huffed.

"All grown-up, no doubt about it."

Delaina looked down to find her braless breasts detectable through her grimy T-shirt. Bleu Cotton jeans rode low on her hips, filthy and ragged, a nice match to Jed's. Wearing three-hundred-dollar-plus denims to work in should've been Jed's first sign he was in trouble with her. He figured they were the only two real farmers in Mississippi who *worked* in the pricey, well-cut jeans. The Baton Rouge clothing company, started by the legitimate, prestigious Calhoun farming family, marketed the agricultural aspect, as did a lot of industries, to sell their stuff. Generally, a male or female would be spotted in the threads at a concert in Nashville, a ballgame in Tuscaloosa, a restaurant in Atlanta. Her worn-out, $$$ work boots were a nice match to his, too.

He took in details, as he did to any woman, with the sweep of his eyes.

Her hair was thin and straight, probably shoulder length when hanging loose, and currently looped in a messy, girlish ponytail, inexplicably, as appealing as sin. No makeup other than lip gloss.

Her eyelashes were thick and her eyebrows thin, both browner than her honey hair. She had wide eyes as green as emeralds, which sparked gold with mischief, and topped a rather sharp nose. Her lips pouted enough to be dangerously kissable. Hers was not the exotic face of Holland Sommers. Delaina Cash would turn any man's head. Fresher, more all-American, more real. She stood a foot shy of Jed's 6'3" frame. Softly muscled shoulders evidenced exhausting work she committed herself to since her father's debilitating illness. Her breasts were adequate, the size of peaches, Jed would guess. Her tiny waist swelled into slim hips. She came in a mighty small, mighty nice package for a twenty-year-old college girl. And, no, ma'am, Jed McCrae didn't like her one bit. His dislike, not all because she was a Cash. Not all because she presumed herself better than him. More because he found it difficult not to like a pretty, authentic Southern female. Because she aroused him like a woman should and worked like a man should. Because he would work like a slave the rest of his life, like his father did, to hold on to the land he knew she could take back. And mostly because she wore her stringy pair of jeans like Bleu Cotton's founder, his Uncle John Talbot Calhoun III, used her ass and hips for the pattern. "It's rainin' at Farm 130," Jed stated, sure of himself, pointing northward. "Glad I got my seed in the ground." He turned and walked inside.

Out of breath, mouth hanging open, Lainey stared at the deserted doorway. She had risked her pride, sincerely apologizing, and simply asked for a stupid wrench. Jed McCrae had a chip on his shoulder. She flared her nostrils. Not a chip. A cement block! How dare *he* stop *her* in her tracks! Did he think she'd be too proud to follow him in? Misting rain began as she stood in the grass. She didn't need the wrench now and could've driven to her own shop in the time she wasted. Lainey marched toward the porch. She would get his wrench, by God, and she didn't care if basketball-size hail were falling from the sky at Farm 130. The mutt on the top step blocked her from going farther. Her eyes darted to the dog's face, to a wagging tail. Rain started to drench her hair and clothes. She stepped under the porch awning. The dog rubbed against her.

In her scurry, Lainey had hardly noticed Jed's abode. She'd never been this far down the dirt trail. Quite conservative for a man of his supposed material assets. A bachelor's pad, square as a box, metal roof and weathered wood, two front windows and a door trimmed in green-black. From where she stood, she could see the gravel driveway continued around back, probably where his truck was parked. She decided the clearing that Jed had chosen for his cabin appeared phenomenal, really. Funneling from his biggest wide-open field on a short road into a patch of sinfully green grass trimmed in trees as solid as bones with the river running down one side, the landscape itself was as much a part of their everyday lives as it would be off-grid and astonishing to most of humanity. Private and completely hidden, it screamed, *Mine, all mine*, for no one could find it without directions or enter without permission.

She lifted her hand to knock on the door. His porch, undecorated except for two wooden rocking chairs and a pair of lacy underwear. At first the underwear shocked her, then embarrassed her, then angered her. Did Jed have a woman in his house waiting with her legs sprawled? Her own body shivered, and not from the rain. She didn't care how good he looked. He was Mallard County's famously uncommitted guy. Come to think of it, the fly of his Bleu Cotton jeans wasn't completely buttoned. Why the heck did he work in Bleu Cotton? How…annoying. Unnecessary. Ironic. She didn't know much about Jed McCrae. What she did know, she didn't like. Mainly because strange sensations swelled in her reliably practical body.

He had a fit build and sported a year-round tan from working outside. His hair, loose-chunky black with brown sun streaks, capped a face etched prominently in high cheek bones and blood-red lips with eyes as dusty blue as his unbuttoned denim jeans. His legs were long but not lanky like most tall men. She couldn't help but notice how his jeans molded to his crotch and his cute butt when he sauntered around on the porch, a suspicious lion protecting its den.

He had that outdoors essence, nearly extinct in its truest form. It swept over a woman, like winds of a hurricane, while simultaneously sucking her in, like the funnel of a tornado, then spit her out like old chewing gum. Leaving her groping for her origin, searching through wreckage for what was left. Yet he seemed unpretentiously subtle, blending into the landscape, as at home in the woods as a deer or raccoon, unaware anyone felt amazed and lost in his presence. His every move broadcast him native to the masculine tribe. As basic and powerful as earth and sky.

Okay, so he was sexy. Downright breathtaking.

James Ed McCrae's son, she promptly reminded herself, and her only competition, all she could attribute to gaining or losing an inch of land from the highway to Big Sunflower River. Land rightfully hers. She could hear the river flowing but could hardly see it through brush woods from where she stood. Startled by his truck engine, she jumped. Rain spilled off the metal roof and formed puddles in the dirt. She leaned out and watched Jed back up in his black Chevy pickup. What annoyed her further, the truck was plain for a Mallard country boy. He left the tires and rims like they came from the factory, no extra side-stripe detailing or silver trim or fancy rails on every other truck in the county, many mortgaged to the radio. His truck had options necessary for his work. How humble...she rolled her eyes. She knew he realized she stood watching. He didn't look her way. No female in the truck, she noted in relief.

Jed meticulously aligned his truck with the side opening of the porch as if it were a drive-through service window and she, the server. Ha! She snickered at the thought of serving Jed McCrae. He let down the window and commented, "Make yourself at home, wouldn't wanna mess up your hair." Jed threw a judgmental look at her floppy ponytail. "Besides you might melt." He chuckled. "See ya, girl," he said to his dog. "Gonna see if we got this downpour everywhere."

"I wanna go," Lainey blurted. Oh Lord, she didn't say that, did she? Maybe she merely thought it. Nope, from the look on his face, she said it aloud. Oh, hell's bells. They locked eyes. Heat seared through her like charcoal on a grill. What was wrong with her? Jed McCrae represented everything bad in her life, her daddy's failures.

Only son Tory Cash had been a raging alcoholic and woman-user all Lainey's life. On the contrary, Jed's father had been a responsible worker and devoted husband in his short life, so the story went. Lainey knew she'd have to stay on the farm and work hard to maintain Cash Way or marry someone who could do it for her. A recognizable pang thumped her stomach. Cabot Hartley didn't care a bit about farming her land.

"Are you gonna stand there?"

Lainey, not sure if he meant her or the dog hunched against her, jiggled her leg, in case he meant the dog, then reconsidered her choices in case he meant her. She hated to admit it could be a rare opportunity to get into Jed's mind. The mind of the best farmer in Mallard County. Perhaps Mississippi. Everyone knew he served on state and federal ag committees, won soil and water conservation awards, did research projects with universities. She might learn something. "I wouldn't miss it." Jed bristled with amusement. Lainey looked over at the underwear in a superior way. "Are we leavin' her behind?" She slid into the passenger's seat and shut the door. "I'm surprised a gal wearin' *those* could find this place."

Well, she hit that on the bull's eye. "Precisely the point when I built it," Jed said and held up his phone. "Thanks, modern technology."

Led Zeppelin, her daddy's favorite, played from Jed's Bluetooth. She looked over at him holding his phone. "Oh." He didn't want anybody coming out here. She pressed her lips together. "Sorry." She reached for the door handle.

"I wasn't talkin' about..." *you*, he didn't get to say.

"Congrats." Pushing on the door to get out, "There won't be a woman in sight."

Jed gave her a calculating once-over. "You're right. Not a woman in sight, little girl."

He used that inaccurate nickname again. She slammed the door and stayed in the truck. His remark burned Lainey to the core, not lust this time. She met Jed McCrae on the road frequently at dawn, at dusk, and in between. Her situation since she graduated high school had been tough. Accepted at Ole Miss, set on attaining her goal of a career in politics after university... Her daddy made it clear she'd have to come to Cash Way someday to run the place or provide a husband for the job.

She hadn't planned on returning so soon.

One week after she settled in, eager to experience college life, she got the call. Tory Cash, a stubborn, vital man, had suffered a stroke and was disabled. Maydell Smith, the farm assistant's wife and Cash Way's housekeeper, broke the news and assured her that her husband Moll and their sons Rhett and Eli, both Cash Way workers, could handle the farm. Smack-dab in the middle of harvest season, Lainey wasn't satisfied. Because she was his only choice, her father had exposed her to aspects of business and record keeping. She loved driving tractors, digging in the dirt, tending cattle, cruising timber. That night in the solitude of her dorm room, Delaina Cash made a life-changing decision. Cash Way needed her more than she needed a university degree. She moved home and enrolled in Mallard Community College primarily online. She visited her father at the nursing home often to confer about plans. Sometimes he'd nod if he agreed or grimace if he didn't. Commonly, he wasn't up to communicating. She saved Cash Way. It was in her blood to be on the land, in her boiling blood. She exploded with gunshot force, months of stress, struggle, and sacrifice culminated into a bullet of a statement. "Of all people, you should know I'm not a little girl! It takes grown, mature men to run an operation the size of Cash Way, but I'm doing it. You haven't always slaved on the farm, frat boy. Didn't you get called home by your *stepfather Fain Kendall* during medical school to run *his* farm?" Jed didn't answer. The wipers on the windshield swished back and forth in the ensuing silence. Little droplets of water ran down Delaina's face. He was vexed and intrigued that being soaking wet didn't seem to bother this female or take away from her prettiness. She seethed from his lack of interest or sympathy. "I don't need you to pat me on the back. In fact, I don't need anything of yours. What a huge mistake! To think we could develop mutual respect. Might possibly lend each other a wrench. You've proven to me in ten minutes what I've heard. You're a self-serving son of a bitch."

"I am." Jed had also been rained on getting into his truck. Food for his soul, Lainey guessed. "If you wanna play in the big league, develop a similar approach." He shrugged. "Let's ride. Our property lines are tiger stripes."

Every bone in her body, and every muscle, played cheerleader for her to stay in his truck. Self-serving, huh? It would start this minute. She'd dig for information about the farm to use it to her advantage. She ignored the more pressing purpose it would serve. To fill her sudden need to be close to Jed McCrae. Using a dab of reverse psychology, Lainey swallowed her pride and spoke in a voice as sweet as southern iced tea. "Sorry about the insults. My mouth tends to get away from me."

Jed cracked a demonic smile. "No problem. I've heard about your mouth." His comment was meant to scathe. She didn't get the implication. He wore no shirt until that moment, when he plucked one from the backseat. Not before she watched beads of water on the taut brown skin of his chest. He wouldn't let it pass. "What's the matter, little girl? Don't tell me you've never been in a truck with a man 'cause I know better." Big smile and his eyes gleamed steel gray with sapphire flecks and a hint of excitement.

She had no idea what Jed hinted. The insinuation, along with his now wearing *The Original* Bleu Cotton T-shirt, worn slap out, words *Cotton to the Core* peeling off, pushed her to move on to business. She tilted her head toward the gravel path. "Let's check Farm 130, biggest plot for us." Who, besides her, farmed in a $95 T-shirt? She wore the newest one, words *Grown Locally* across her chest.

Rain had slackened. Dark clouds and semi-cool air directed the mood. Jed drove past her SUV onto a dirt path winding through woods. Trees cleared into a field row angled left and right. To the left was Jed's two-hundred-acre spread of freshly planted seed. To the right were Delaina's 185 acres of planted ground and fifteen acres unplanted. The four-hundred-acre plot had a strip wide enough for a tractor running down the middle to the main road. Towering across the field stood the new irrigation unit Jed and Lainey shared since winter, her bold and unprecedented move to add that equipment to the parcel. Determined to replace the old irrigation system after last growing season, she had enough operating capital to consider an upgrade. It required an expensive well. The irrigation specialist had pointed out, as he surveyed and drew up estimates, the economic desirability of using the well for one enormous unit over the entire place. She claimed it wasn't an option to share. Citing profitability and sensibility, the specialist encouraged her to talk to Jed. She thought about it for days, deemed little risk, and drafted a letter to Jed stating her interest in the new system and her willingness to split the cost of the well, irrigation, and future repairs. Neither planned to sell their half of Farm 130; if one did, logically, the other would buy it. Jed had his senior farmhand Dale Barlow call and tell her they were interested. Her accountant handled financing and Moll Smith, her senior farmhand, handled practicalities. Jed and Lainey hadn't met or talked during the deal although cell phone numbers were exchanged. She assumed Dale and Moll never disagreed on their orders of system maintenance.

Jed decided to compliment her, rare for him. He didn't talk to women much. Most were eager to skip talk and get in his pants, except for ex-fiancé Laureth. *Look where that got him...* He brushed Delaina's hand on the middle console. "Hey, your irrigation plan was a good one. Hope we continue to agree." She pulled her hand away. An atmosphere of heat and energy hung over them as present and threatening as the thunderstorm had been. Humidness glued damp tendrils of hair to her face. Any other time, the humidity would have been unbearable. Her clothes and hair sticking to her added to the intensity. She cursed her silliness. Jed didn't feel it, appearing as cool as a drink of creek water. Everyone said he was a player. Either he didn't know or chose not to acknowledge the extent of the vicious spell he flung on a female. Waiting for her response, he had stopped the truck in the middle field row. A catty one, he predicted.

She didn't reply and pressed her lips together, drawing Jed's eyes to her mouth. To her shiny lips. He had the urge to kiss her. What the hell for? Locked in the wonder of what it would feel like to touch the enemy, they stared. Neither wanted it to last a moment longer although they were drawn to each other by a force outside themselves. Low thunder shook Lainey to sense. "Not my idea," she muttered. "Roy Lowndes, the irrigation specialist, suggested we share a well."

Jed watched her mouth intently as she talked, unable to pull himself out of his primary thoughts. He managed to remark, "You wanna use my tools?"

She laughed nervously. Her chin went to her chest. Her eyes glittered gold. "That was a good one."

With a lead-heavy body, Jed drew himself into his seat. It took a fair amount of mental coaxing to remain obscure. He hadn't meant for his question to have a double meaning. Delaina looked cute playing flattered innocence. He left it at that. For an inestimable time, Jed looked out his window. She looked out hers. He looked at his side of the field; she looked at hers. Both contemplated advantages of rain at this stage. Good farmers were a dwindling breed. Each year, many gambled their last wager and lost. This year seemed pivotal for anyone in the game. To know about crops other than cotton. To know what to do mechanically and financially. Jed planned to have his hands and eyes and mind involved in every procedure. "It's only mistin'. I'll help you fix the tractor."

Jed offered to help her? With humility. The right step, Lainey thought. *Or was it?* There were certainly valid reasons why their fathers never tried this approach after the fallout. There had been occasions when it would have been more convenient to work together, or at least be amicable, right? They never were. She recalled the most recent piece of Mallard gossip, often centered around Hartleys, Cashes, Jed, or a combo. No one else in town was rich or scandalous enough to be worthy. She heard that Jed's mother Cass willed her land to Fain Kendall, Jed's stepfather, when Jed was a child, and it had never been changed. If true, Jed didn't own land yet, except parts he bought on his own like Farm 130 and the woods around his cabin. Lainey had considered purchasing land from Fain Kendall. Everybody knew he and Jed were at odds all the time anyway. "I don't know if I should accept your help, Jed. We've never needed each other before." The broken-down tractor, in plain view. Moll, Eli, and Rhett Smith, her best workers, had deserted the place for a rainy afternoon break.

Today

"Hey, you came to me, cupcake."

Her mouth formed an -O. *Cupcake?* Worse than little girl. "Only because I was tryin' to beat the rain. Irrelevant now."

"Uh, huh." Jed appeared a tad sulky.

"I can fix the tractor by myself. I'm not a little girl or a *cupcake*."

"Uh, huh," he repeated. "It'll take two people. Who's gonna help? Looks like Moll and sons have split. Probably downin' liquor and chasin' skirts at MacHenry's." Flashy white smile. "I apologize for the name callin'." There was nothing sincere about it. "You're kind of..." His eyes went over her, dicing her insides. "...small."

He would *not* get away with that. "Huh, well. You're kind of..." Her eyes went over him boldly. "Large. Doesn't mean it's right for me to call you..." Her hands went up. "Big Guy or..." She hunted for an insult. "Pound cake." She sneered self-importantly.

Jed laughed. Beer, he needed one, or something quick since Delaina Cash calling him Big Guy did something internally it shouldn't do. He reached for bottled water in a vinyl cooler on the backseat. "Want one? I'm sorry it's not beer." He cast her a downward glance. "Never mind. You're not legal."

Lainey spoke before she should've. "So? Nothing you've done lately has been legal. I know about the marijuana bust at the party on Mill's Pond, about the weed found in your truck. I've heard about your whores in New Orleans. How do you know I'm not twenty-one?"

"'Cause you were born on my tenth birthday. I'm thirty." He commented as if it weren't an extraordinary coincidence. Lainey forced herself not to say Really? and opted instead for, "Oh." On a light smile, "I'm sorry for the mudslinging. I tend to have a smart mouth."

Jed pounced like a fat tomcat to a baby bird. "No offense taken. Boone told me about your oral talents."

She gasped aloud. It did have a hidden meaning! Jed tossed her the water and drank a significant portion of his. "I don't know what to say." She had one hand on her forehead, mouth open.

"Your expression says everything. To think, a teenager granting sexual favors less than a hundred yards from my back steps, and she chose my first cousin Boone Barlow over me. What a cryin' shame." Jed finished his water. "You gonna drink that?"

"No." She sat up in her seat. "You can help me fix the tractor, you jerk. You owe me after that rude remark."

Jed shrugged. "I guess Boone or maybe Cabot Hartley has told you." He served another compliment. "You're sexy when you're mad, Delaina."

Ooh, he used her name. Her full name, the one she tried to get everyone else to use. It was an adult name, specifically why *she* used it when she texted him about the wrench. It's the way she signed her name, and often she would refer to herself as Delaina, hoping maybe. But after she'd been Lainey, The Lainey Cash, all her life in a small town, Delaina never did catch on. It rolled off his tongue like melted ice cream, liquid and sweet. It made her feel older and more competent coming from his close-to-perfect mouth. "I don't need your help."

Jed raised one eyebrow. "Changed your mind again? That's the problem with you...females. Never know what you want. Fine, I'll take your skinny butt to your car."

Although she was much younger without experience in relationships, Delaina had a feeling his sarcastic spill of words wasn't for her. Probably aimed at Laureth Andrews, *almost McCrae*, Stevens. About a year ago, Jed and Laureth were to be married at the First United Methodist Church in downtown Mallard. Invitations sent, dresses bought, the whole shebang. Laureth, a blonde bombshell, could've passed for a saucy Playboy bunny or a doting elementary school teacher on the same day. Five-ish years older than Delaina and respected, she was the school superintendent's daughter. Everyone questioned the quick wedding. The two dated less than a month when Jed proposed, wedding to follow in weeks. Laureth broke it off days beforehand, resigned from her school system job, and left town. Rumors flew related to Jed's character. Had she caught him in bed with someone else having a fling before married life set in? Was he selling something besides cotton, corn, and cattle off his fertile land, like rumors in the past? Months later, he did get caught with marijuana at the party on Mill's Pond. Explanation for Laureth's hasty departure came as a social media birth announcement. Laureth Andrews *Stevens* and her ex-boyfriend then new husband Mark Stevens had delivered a healthy baby boy. She obviously never stopped seeing him, perhaps got engaged to Jed to cause jealousy, to compel Mark to marry her. Being with Jed now, Delaina was surprised he fell for it. She could've called him on his comment and rubbed Laureth in his face. She changed the subject. "Where's the pot? I've been all over this place, and I've never seen marijuana growing."

"That makes two of us," Jed said, his voice even and honest. Delaina looked into his eyes, sinless blue, and instantly believed him. He had been blamed at the Mill's Pond party. Nothing was done about it. The bags of grass were found in the open back of his truck.

"Everyone thinks you're gettin' rich on something besides cotton and cattle."

"Why did you ask about the marijuana? It's not what we were talkin' about."

"Guess I was trying to get off the subject of us complicated females."

He reached between her legs for the unopened bottle. She flinched. "Relax. All I want is something to drink."

The sun had opened its eyes and stretched its arms, a sticky heat for late March. Delaina glanced at the dashboard clock. Working alone, she might repair the tractor before sundown. Maybe the field would dry out, and she could finish planting tomorrow. "Jed, I do need your wrench."

"Okay." He turned the steering wheel to whip around, pushing his outstretched arm across her seat. He brushed Delaina's shoulder accidentally with the back of his hand. The almost nonexistent contact sent pulsing heat through him. He admonished himself for acting like a pathetic schoolboy. A damned interesting package but she was Lainey Cash, and he'd never trust her. Jed drove the truck toward the cabin, taking his time, thinking of a way to end this meeting for good. Last thing he needed was lust for Tory Cash's daughter. Delaina peered out the window at her world; he recognized the look. Pride bottled in protection, a look reserved for landowners. Jed judged every bodily feature for all its worth. Not a little girl anymore. Heck, she probably tumbled in Cabot Hartley's sheets nightly. How convenient for both, and Jed couldn't blame a man for trying, nightly, with her. He fought the shot of arousal headed from his dirty mind to its forever destination with annoyance.

Quietly she asked, never bringing her gaze from the woods, "Why are you lookin' at me?"

"Just tryin' to figure you out."

"Give it up, Jed McCrae."

"What size wrench do you need?"

"Fifteen-sixteenths."

He parked the truck. They got out. Jed opened the toolbox on the back end. He reached in and retrieved the right wrench. Things had turned solemn. None of the stirring remarks or ugly putdowns. Jed didn't like the courteous silence and would do something to get her gone.

Delaina walked up behind him. The rim of his boxer briefs peeked over the waistband of his jeans while he leaned over his truck. A back strapped with muscles and broad shoulders, Jed outlined what a man should be. All natural, built and bred from pure hard work. Jed turned to give her the wrench and caught her appreciating him. She batted her eyelashes blamelessly. "Thank you."

"Uh, huh."

"I'll bring it back when I'm done."

Jed didn't like her tone. It made him primitively uncomfortable. "You can leave it on the porch."

"Yeah, that seems to be your philosophy, Jed," she cracked. "Leave it on the porch." She tilted her head toward the underwear bunched on wooden planks. She flirted now, with danger.

"You can leave yours, too, if you want," he said to gauge her response.

Oh heavens. Delaina tried to appear unaffected. "Sorry. I'm not wearing any." Thinking she aced him, she opened her door.

Jed wanted to believe they met up by chance, and now Delaina felt truly attracted to him. He had experience with Cabot Hartley and Tory Cash. The meeting and dialogue could be deliberate. If he had his way, she wouldn't be back. "That's a first," he commented casually.

"First what?" She turned to look at him. His back was to her. He opened his truck door.

"First time a female has left me not satisfied."

Delaina nearly jumped from his blatancy. "You're not exactly right."

"Oh yeah?" Jed couldn't wait to hear it.

"This is a first for you, not me. I'm leaving here very satisfied, and you haven't touched me."

Jed didn't react.

Today, everything changed.

Two

Tonight

The nerve of that man! Jed McCrae had the sexual discretion of a bull and the sexual conduct of a monkey. Somehow, he pulled it off with a dose of sheer sexual appeal. It was more than that. Lainey had a compulsion to be Delaina, to try that adultlike name evolution, along with an impulsive desire to know everything about Jed. She wanted to talk to him for hours, laugh together over silly private jokes, hold his hand. To share ice cream cones, read to each other, and take long walks.

Good gracious, what kind of storm had he pounded her with?

Moll, Rhett, and Eli worked on the tractor throughout afternoon. They hadn't needed the wrench. Moll brought tools. Delaina helped then drove along Farm 130 toward Cash-McCrae Road away from Jed's cabin. She could think of a dozen reasons to take the wrench now and only one reason to wait. She wanted to see him again, preferably alone and after dark. She disliked his crude sense of humor, his crass indifference toward her, everything. She had to get one more look, up close and personal.

A yellow convertible turned in front of her and went left. She caught glimpse of the driver's profile, suspicion confirmed. Oh

God! Holland Sommers, Cabot's personal assistant at the bank, undoubtedly driving to Jed's cabin. Everything clicked in Delaina's head. Jealousy and fury sprinted to squeeze her heart, and fury won.

Jed swapped rainy day bed favors for information about Cash Way. Information that Holland would have. Damn him. Damn Holland; she owed loyalty to the bank. Cabot wouldn't believe it.

"Self-serving," she repeated and gripped the wrench lying in the passenger's seat. It had been fated to go to his cabin to piece this together. Now she was supposed to use the wrench to knock Jed McCrae's handsome head off his shoulders. Stepping on the accelerator, she started toward the bank to inform Cabot. He was vice president; he'd be president soon. He could tell Holland to go back to wherever she came from or go to hell!

Delaina pulled into the parking lot of Mallard First Financial, Cabot's foreign SUV the only car there. She walked to the palatial-style foyer and squinted through glass. Cabot came out. "Lainey, what a nice surprise. You look like you've been rolling in a cow pasture." Timidly, Cabot put a kiss on her nose, the one clean spot on her face.

She pulled back. "I'm here on business."

He had been guiding Lainey on business for months. His forehead creased. "Do we need to go inside?"

"No, let's go someplace more relaxing."

Cabot watched her. A smart girl, wise beyond her years in some ways. She turned in front of her SUV. "You drive."

Cabot couldn't tell if she acted mad at him or simply mad. They had been seeing each other about four months. Technically, it began when she sought his guidance after returning home to run Cash Way, a professional relationship then. Last autumn, Cabot began finding excuses for her to come to the bank, began "running into her" around town. He casually asked her out in November. People were talking about what a good match they were. Their fathers had been close associates. Cabot had done his share of playing around. Still did some. Twenty-six years of age seemed old enough to give up public bachelorhood. What he did in private, no one had to know. Sweet Lainey, smart, naive, and financially well-off, exactly what he needed in a wife. A merger, not a marriage, between the bank and the largest landowner in Mallard County, he aimed for a midsummer spontaneous wedding and planned to use the most insurable method of influence. Fear.

Cabot's father, Joe Cabot Hartley, breathed down his neck, devising ways to entrap Lainey. Joe Cabot didn't play by the rules and encouraged his son to participate in underhanded schemes, which Cabot did, for the right money. Joe Cabot Hartley hadn't turned over the bank to Cabot completely because he realized and made it clear that Cabot needed grooming. Joe Cabot advised Cabot to learn to think through possible outcomes before acting. The mere thought of his father's merciless criticism made Cabot's stomach acid rise to his throat. Cabot had a surprise brewing, plans of his own for her. It would be a success story. Time drew near.

When car doors shut, Delaina said, "I've got a problem only you can solve."

"Do you want to go to my place?"

"Okay. Fine." She cut through small talk. "Cabot, I know you like Holland."

"As an employee, yes. She's...an achiever."

She shook her head no. "Cabot, you can't trust her. She's divulging bank secrets."

"Where did you hear this, Lainey? Bank matters are strictly confidential." He seemed more adamant than ever. She considered Cabot's profile. Sandy blond hair and brown eyes, an odd but alluring combo. Nice-looking and preppy, the typical fraternity brother, he had aristocratic manners and a pedigree to match. She understood life with him meant she would be responsible for farm work. He didn't know how to do manual labor and didn't own work boots. She did not love him. Cash Way held importance over a loving marriage. She wasn't sure she could identify love anyway.

"Cabot, I saw Holland driving on Cash-McCrae Road. She turned at Farm 130, the dirt road to Jed McCrae's cabin. Probably her underwear I saw on his porch today. She..."

"What were you doing on Jed McCrae's porch?" He dismissed allegations about Holland with a drilling question.

Anxious to return to her original concern, she frowned. "I needed to borrow a wrench."

"Since when did you start using anything of Jed McCrae's?" Cabot's voice, a decibel below a yell.

"Never. That's not the point. I know Holland's giving him information about my land. Get rid of her. My farm depends on it."

"Whoa! Wait a minute!" Cabot raised the decibel. He drove to the gates of his apartment complex. Hartley Pointe glittered on the gold-lettered entrance sign. He inserted his key card into the security system. Gates opened automatically. He lived in a two-story condo. The winding drive revealed children playing, couples walking, college students gathered. Pavement led across a narrow creek bridge. Trees on both sides of the lane led to his place at the end. "Let's go in and talk rationally." He followed her through the oversized front door. "Sit down. Want a drink?"

"Yes, please. Water." Lainey, too filthy to get comfy on imported leather, sat on the edge of the sofa. Cabot fixed himself a glass of wine and her water at the corner wet bar. He cast a glance at her as if she were too dirty then handed her the drink. He sat at the bar and took a swallow.

"Baby, I understand your concern." Cabot mustered as much sympathy as he could. "I know Holland's not doing anything to jeopardize her job or your farm. You're not giving me much credit. Holland earned her position at the bank." Cabot lowered his voice and shrugged. "She doesn't have any inhibitions. Probably two adults having great sex." He frowned behind his glass. "Something I'm entitled to, by the way." He had major issues with a Holland-Jed alliance, nothing Lainey needed to sense. "Back to your being at Jed's..." *That* worried him tremendously. *That* would be a volatile alliance.

"How do you know Holland doesn't have inhibitions? Did she trade sex for her job promotion?"

"Lainey! This is going nowhere. Here's what I'll do. It's inappropriate to question Holland about her personal life. I'll check on the sly and watch her closely. You're focusing on the wrong person. I don't know what the hell possessed you to go to Jed's!" Cabot fumed. She had no idea such distinct dislike existed between them. He paused and poured wine. "Stay away. He'll screw you. Literally. You're smart. You're no match for him. He's got an agenda, Lainey.

He'd do anything to own everything on Cash-McCrae Road, if he has to get it one inch at a time."

"That makes two of us!" Competitive fire blazed in her eyes. "I can take care of myself. It's what I've done my whole life." Both knew what she meant. Tory Cash had never shown her much love. He wanted an heir, preferably a son, for his adored Cash Way, and he spent enough time with her to begin showing her how the farm operated. Delaina's mother, though not deserving of the relational title, was a money-hungry, white-trash-to-rich snob, according to Mallard tales. Della Mueller, an orphan, then a prostitute, from New Orleans. Tory had met her there on a bar-hopping trip. He claimed love at first sight, got whimsical, married her, and brought her home. No one knew the magnitude of Della's sordid past; Tory blurted the truth to Lainey in a drunken stupor years ago. Della thought she could endure Tory's drinking and affairs in return for newfound wealth. It wasn't enough. She left Lainey, age four. Miss Maydell, Moll's wife, became Lainey's primary caretaker. Delaina had no memory of her mother. Last time her father mentioned her, he said she dropped off the face of the earth.

"Chin up, you're tough," Cabot said as he pressed his fingers under her jaw. "It's Friday night. Want to shower and go out? Or we could shower and...go to bed."

Suggestive talk always fell flat between them. "Don't you have plans?"

"Yeah, with this hot little blonde girl. Freshen up. We'll go out for drinks and dinner." She wasn't the legal drinking age; it didn't matter around Mallard with Cabot Hartley.

"No thanks. It's been a long day. Will you take care of the other for me like you said?"

Cabot glanced. Her breasts made slight imprints on her muddy gray T-shirt. Her jeans hugged her hips. Put her in a soft-colored business suit, style that mop of hair, introduce her to lipstick, and she'd make a man's pants uncomfortable. "Shower here. We'll order takeout." Lainey turned weary eyes at him. He concluded, "Not up for it. My car's at the bank. I'll drive us." He waited a moment, went for a big one. "Why not New Orleans tomorrow?

We could spend the night, come back Sunday morning. You've never seen my family's NOLA house."

"I need to plant seed tomorrow if it's dry enough."

"It'll be wet. Farming can wait until Monday." Cabot used a playfully serious tone. "Your local banker's encouraging you to take the risk. We'll leave before lunchtime."

"Okay. I might as well."

Back at the bank, sitting in Lainey's SUV, Cabot kissed her goodbye on the lips. He forced his tongue in her mouth and swirled. It reminded her of a blender, and her mouth, a stubborn block of ice. She tried to respond and closed her eyes. Jed McCrae eased into her mind. Lounging in his Chevy, his chest naked and wet, his stalwart arm draped behind her seat. Her mouth gave way. Tongues tasted. Cabot withdrew, his eyes glazed, muscles in his face tense. Their most provocative kiss. Too bad it wasn't Cabot she had been with in her mind.

Driving toward Cash-McCrae Road, Delaina couldn't shake her bad feeling about Holland. Jed was sly; he acquired a hundred acres of Cash land since he quit medical school to farm. Jed, an Atlanta-Emory University graduate student? A city-boy doctor? She couldn't picture it. He belonged on land, in wide open space, as much a part of the place as she. For her, the land was her legacy, her heritage. For Jed, his mission, his sustenance. For Delaina, it offered opportunity to prove she could be all her father wanted her to be; for Jed, opportunity to prove he could be all his father never got to be. She enjoyed a spectacular twilight drive. Row upon row, layer upon layer of green streaked brown, splashed on a silver-black canvas. Soft hills rolled into grand fields and disappeared into lush forests. Clean air flowed into her lungs. Her air. Jed's air. For an instant, she connected to him like she'd never been connected to anyone. She felt sorry for him that his stepfather Fain Kendall still owned almost all the land. Rumors claimed Jed had a large bank account from his mother's family money and his father's life insurance. Somehow she knew, he'd trade the cash for the land.

Why did Cabot hate Jed? She remembered overhearing him at a dinner talking in an annoyed tone to someone about Jed and a boat. Jed never banked at Mallard First Financial. Her headlights flashed across glitzy letters. *Cash Way* glowed in the night. Headlights in the opposite direction glowed, too. The cars met and passed, Delaina's SUV and a yellow convertible.

~ ~ ~

A drunk Cabot sat on the sofa in his den, television tuned to a golf match he paid no attention. His phone rang. He followed its ring until he found it on the bar. "Hello."

"Hello," was the cool reply. Cabot knew who it'd be without checking the name. He wasn't ready to talk. "Are you home?" His partner-in-crime, indeed.

"Yeah," Cabot said.

"Is your girlfriend there?" They rarely used real names.

"No."

"Why not?"

"Because she's a cold piece of ass," Cabot remarked.

"We need to wrap this up. You know where she was today?"

"The cabin."

"Uh, huh. Hurry up and rope her in. Get her hitched."

"I'm working on it. She's not exactly an easy bitch."

"I know. You seem tense."

Cabot swallowed wine. "I'm running this goddamn plan while you entertain yourself in a fucking fish hole. Tonight, she confronted me."

"Oh. Why?"

"She's suspicious about something she saw today, leaving the field. I curtailed her. You and I will talk in person on Monday."

"You know, the best way to get a gal like her to commit would be to push toward a more physical relationship to lead into marriage."

"Thanks for unsolicited advice. I don't view you as an authority on marriage." Cabot hung up. He reached for his cigar box, lit a paper roll, and dragged. Sweet marijuana filled his being.

~ ~ ~

Not a light on in the cabin. Music from Jed's phone played through the whole-house system. He lounged on his comfy sofa uncomfortably, dissatisfied by a phone conversation recently finished. Sketchy details and strained dialogue, as usual. Added to that, Holland came back. He sent her on her way in haste. Tonight, he preferred Delaina Cash or nothing. *She's spoiled rotten and you can't trust her.* He couldn't trust anyone. Didn't want to, really. He wanted something certain in life besides taxes and rumors. His father's land is what he wanted. And one day, sooner than later hopefully, a wife...and, hell, why not a couple of kids? If he could find a woman who offered him a challenge, not just sexually but emotionally and intellectually. In other words, he wouldn't be marrying anyone he'd been with so far.

A tap at the door surprised him. Dark and still as thieves outside, he hadn't seen headlights or heard a car engine. Lucy hadn't barked from her pen. He eased up and glanced at the clock on the stovetop, nine-zero-zero enumerated in bright green. He opened a drawer in the side table and pulled out a pistol. Cautiously, as fleet-footed as a fox, he crept to the door and cracked it. Female silhouette, too short to be Holland. Probably a girl from the college hoping for a hookup. What a challenge. He opened the door.

"Hey," Delaina said weakly.

"Jesus, little girl!" Jed boomed. He waved his pistol in front of her. "You almost got your head blown off." He gave her a belligerent look. "Still might." He flipped on a yellow porch light, illuminating her golden hair and dainty-curvy outline. Clean now, she looked like she came fresh from a shower. The thought, a shower with Delaina Cash, sent a surge to his loins. Hair yanked up in another messy ponytail, loose damp clumps framed her face and neck. Her breasts tugged at her clingy Bleu Cotton top, the *It's Better in the Field* one, and worn-out sweatpants graced her hips. "You could get killed. Or raped," he added, fixing a stare on her chest then raking his eyes over her. "...wandering in the woods alone at night."

"I doubt it." Delaina pulled her own small pistol out of the back waistband of her pants.

Jed rubbed his hand across his forehead. "Good Lord, do you know how to fire that weapon?"

She smiled dumbly and responded in a high pitch, "I'm not sure. Maybe I could use you for target practice."

He didn't comment or budge. His massive body blocked the doorway. The only cloth covering that body, a pair of baggy boxers with an elasticized gray waistband. BC underwear. Cotton to the core. Delaina's eyes took an unapologetic tour. Lust, the gracious guide. Jed's left arm propped against the door frame, enhancing full biceps and triceps, cut like an athlete. His pectoral and abdominal muscles, substantially defined, beckoned to be stroked by agile fingers. His boxers held his sex loosely. God outdid Himself with the blessing He bestowed there. The hair on her arms sprang. Her reaction appalled her.

Jed looked at her skin. "It's not cold outside tonight."

You're right. In fact, I'm in the middle of a blinding heat. "Not really, but my hair's wet." She shook her ponytail.

"Right," he said and intentionally cast his eyes upon her crotch.

A crimson stain crawled up her neck and sprawled itself across her face. He was impossible. She'd never been around a man so sexual. And sexy. "You're crude."

"You like me." Rarely crude toward women, he *had* to send this girl packing. Her soft drawl, the real deal. Only a man Southern born and raised appreciated the difference. Not country, not uneducated. Refined syrup. As good as the damp ponytail and bare chest. She burned him up. Did Robert Plant really have to whisper-sing dirty "Custard Pie" right about now? She faintly moved her hips to the words.

"You probably don't wanna hear it, but..." Her hips kept doing that barely moving dance thing. "Daddy is Led Zeppelin's biggest fan. Guess y'all have that in common."

"It's questionable." He watched her. "Whether Tory's their biggest fan. My father did a run of Deep South Led concert road trips, six in one year with Tory, back when they were wild, single best friends forty years ago, before they fell out." His eyebrows raised. *Whatcha gonna say to that, Miss Cash?* The face she made. Butterflies and twenty. She liked it. Damn.

"Too bad I didn't come for a visit since we all love "Custard Pie" and things."

"You sure?" Jed moved in and tilted his head. "You're welcome inside, but I'm warning you." He shot another amusing look at her crotch; again, she felt inexplicable heat. "This could be a dangerous place for you...in your condition." He smiled innocently.

"You have the manners of a tomcat." She walked past him. "Maybe one day you'll learn not to challenge me, Jed McCrae." The porch light cast overgrown shadows on the dark room. Jed's space felt personal, superbly quiet, other than Led Zeppelin singing to her to save a slice. Delaina squinted, an effort to inspect his living quarters, not caring if he saw. The interior structure was as remarkable as the exterior was unremarkable. It seemed, right away, authentically Jed that a person had to be special enough to get inside to be rewarded a first-class picture. The front door opened to a central room, each board on the floor and walls in unmatched reclaimed wood of varied length and color, set off by casual leather furniture, real skin rugs. The biggest whitetail buck shoulder mount she'd seen hung on the far wall. He didn't land those horns in Mississippi. "You hunt?"

"Bow only. Fairer. Dropped him behind the Denton Place."

He killed *that* with a *bow* behind the Denton Place? No way. Why hadn't they run into each other on the trail, going in and out of deer stands? Next he'd claim he carved canoes with Tunicas and danced with black bears.

"You hunt, too."

He knew? Delaina said, "Gun only. Faster. Yours must've been the granddaddy to the whopper nine-point I dropped behind the Denton Place this winter." She had a not-buying-it face and took two steps. At some point, he had flipped on a light. Big beams stretched up the corners, in the middle of the room, over the kitchen at the back, across high ceilings. She decided she might stay awhile and walked herself in. Deep in.

"You hunt sundown. Sunup's better," he said.

Hmm. She'd keep it in mind. The know-it-all ass. Because of his smarty pants and because he watched her, she said, "I'd like to learn bow. Haven't had anybody to, you know..." She did a minor hip motion and pulled her arm back like a bow shot. "Line up behind me and show me the particulars."

Hmm. He'd keep it in mind. That sweet ass. He'd like to line up behind her and show her his particulars.

Delaina turned away. Manly smells mingled. Brewed coffee, barbecued meat, Murphy's oil. An empty water bottle on the hand-hewn coffee table amid his cell phone, a laptop computer, and two books- *Investing in Diamonds, Smart or a Fool's Game?* and *The Subtle Art of Not Giving a F*ck*. She twisted, gave him a bored look. "Conflictive reading, don't you think?"

"Huh?" He gave her an unbored look.

"One who invests in diamonds should indeed give a fuck."

Jed breathed a tight breath. Sweet Jesus. Burnt, he was. More *Drop down* lyrics from Robert Plant. If Jed's blood dropped any lower, conflict would apply to his boxers.

Everywhere Delaina's eyes went topped the last place. Behind the sofa, a dynamic wood and metal staircase with those beams rose straight up, twisted into a partial landing halfway, with a reading nook and shelves in the wall, stacked *full* of books, then turned again, up into presumably Big Guy's bedroom on the top level, open to the bottom by rails and a ledge. She couldn't see it. She would one day. That came out of nowhere and slammed her stomach. Led Zeppelin had moved on, assuring her a stairway to heaven. She nearly took the liberty of defying someday and climbed steps to ecstasy now. Jed stepped in front of her, their bodies less than arm's length apart. "Why did you come here?"

"To bring the wrench."

"The wrench. Yeah, I don't know what I'd do without my wrench tonight. Couldn't possibly wait 'til daylight, could it?" He implied her intentions were less honorable.

"Actually, no, it couldn't wait. I'll be in a hurry. Cabot invited me to his NOLA house." Jed showed no emotion. She felt foolish to think he'd care. He could have practically anyone.

Jed contemplated. Huh... Delaina didn't seem *that way*. He started to say it. '*Invited*' she had said. So, she hadn't been to the NOLA house before. Too...confident for Cabot's scene. And too young for that place. "Do you..." Know about the others? He wanted to ask so damn bad. Aw, well, Tory Cash raised her. Forget it.

"What?" she blurted.

"Nothing."

Her fiery determination surfaced; green irises burned gold. "No, it's something. I wanna know."

One day she'd thank him if she listened to his cue. Jed sniffed obnoxiously. "Is Cabot with you for your generous sexual favors or his interest in Cash Way?"

"Both," she smarted off, concealing hurt with all her might. "I left your wrench on the porch." She turned, head held high, and walked to the door. "Oh, by the way, this is the second time in one day, the same woman has left your house, completely satisfied, no credit to you." She walked out, shaking her hips provocatively. Jed's palm splayed over her back, shoving her harder than he intended across the porch. Lucy barked crazily in the distance. Jed caught Delaina's arm, breaking her fall, and swung her around. His big hands clasped each side of her tiny waist. He shook her gently. "You're out of your league, little girl." *Did she get his implications? Maybe she was part of a bigger plan and played herself off as innocent.*

Delaina's emerald eyes pierced wildly. He had knocked the wind out of her. "The way I...see it, Jed, you're...the one out of your league, no...match for me and...Cabot. I'll own this place before I'm twenty-five."

Jed caught the back of her head in his hands, his fingers pressing her skull. He drew Delaina's face to his and lowered his gaze to her lips. She strained her neck to pull away. He brushed his mouth across hers sideways. His stubble scratched delicate skin on her cheek. Not a kiss. Just a sweeping of lips.

It was enough. Enough to make her sigh suggestively and relax.

This would be for her own good and his. Jed pulled the side of her face to his lips and whispered in a hot caress, "You're not my type."

"From what I've heard, you're not choosy," she responded breathlessly against his cheek.

"You heard wrong." Jed let her go. "What's wrong with me?" she demanded, throwing her arms in front of her, giving herself a favorable survey.

"For starters, you're a Cash and think you have more rights to this place than I do. If I could put that aside..." He talked faster;

words jammed together into one fat insult. "You're too opinionated, too skinny, too short, *way* too young. You talk too much, and you try to get me to talk. Your boobs are too small, your hair is too straight, you know too much about farming, you're too smart in general, and you're capricious. Besides, I don't generally like blondes."

"Since when, Jed? Huh? Since Laureth Andrews. Or should I say, since Laureth *Stevens* dumped you?"

"Go home."

She yelled, "I am home! This land was ours before it was yours. It is not okay for you to push me around, insult me, and kick me out." Her chest rose and fell. She wasn't sure if she was about to laugh or cry. "You need a dose of your own medicine."

"You asked. I answered. I can assure you, you're out of your league despite Cabot's help." His eyes went silver, framed by pure black lashes and brows. "How many of y'all are headed to the NOLA house, huh? He has a closet full of skeletons, you know."

"How many what? Does he really?" Delaina dismissed her own questions. "Never mind, I can handle it. All of it. All of you." She wanted to be strong. One look at Jed McCrae and she felt scared. Scared for herself. Scared for her land. He had become a towering menace, malice seeping through his pores. She struck a nerve, maybe his heart. Must've been the mention of ex-fiancé Laureth and/or the discord with Cabot. She began running.

"What made you come here?"

She looked across the yard. The porch light pitched an inky outline around him on the top step. She didn't think he'd try to kill her. Terrified nonetheless, she had a long walk in the dark to her car. She parked at Farm 130 in case Jed had a girl with him. To abandon the wrench on the porch and exit quietly if she had to. Now, Delaina didn't know whether to go to him and call a truce or bolt in the opposite direction. She stood there, shaking slowly, like a sheet suspended from a clothesline.

Jed made her decision for her. He walked into the house. Seconds passed. His porch went black.

Delaina didn't run. She walked with all the casual aplomb she could manufacture. Trees sneaked out as looming monsters with a spooky mix of cool heat in the nighttime spring air. She held out her cell phone flashlight. Disfigured shadows it created frightened her more than darkness. She turned off the light and took deliberate steps.

She had nobody. Did Jed tell the truth about Cabot? What did he mean about the NOLA house? Or was he trying to break up her only alliance? She didn't know much about Cabot's business deals. He seemed refreshingly strait-laced.

The night nurse at the nursing home called earlier. Her father had been in and out of consciousness, failing. Tory and Lainey never had much relationship, and she had been forced to take over the farm under unexpected circumstances. Her father didn't get to coach her on the crooked ways of businessmen. Tory Cash would be dead soon. Delaina didn't know how much longer she could hold up. Out of necessity, she had built a protective facade, going through motions, like wearing a mask. It wasn't singularly Jed or the farm, more like the glass she had seen her life through, a plain and simple decision in her dorm room, had lots of chips in it, and suddenly, pieces were breaking apart.

Her footsteps crunched in the grass. For nearly two hundred years, Cash land survived war and countless droughts, tornadoes, floods, and innumerable changes in planting and procedure. Cash men who came before her loved it, hated it, watched it, cursed it, used it, abused it, and profited from it. They started here and ended here, in this dirt. Twenty granite headstones at the family cemetery confirmed a never-ending, ever-addictive cycle. The unbroken circle had paused, hitched at the gatepost of Delaina Cash. People knew as soon as Tory died, she'd be the largest landowner in the county with no family, no heirs. Such a tremendous responsibility for a twenty-year-old with competent Jed McCrae as runner-up. She could hardly admit her next thought. *She needed an extra pair of hands to help her hold it together.* If Cabot continued to prove his integrity, she'd push things to the next level. She had no choice.

She got to her car and slid in. A shadow moved out of nowhere, a figure in the passenger's seat. She screamed in recognition of the stark face and reached to draw her gun. Jed's hands cuffed her wrists. She struggled to free herself. "Relax," he said in a benevolent voice. He let her go. Her heart pounded in her chest. On the verge of crying, she concentrated on breathing. "What do you want?" she asked calmly and hysterically.

"To prove to you how foolish you are. You will get raped or killed, roamin' in the dark."

"By you, maybe. You probably want me dead."

"Frankly, I'd choose a permissive form of the other," he stated flatly.

"This is no time for your always inappropriate sexual lingo!" Emotion captured her eyes, her trembling lips, her breath. Her hand gripped tightly on the gearshift.

"It's okay, Delaina." Her name rolled off his tongue. He stroked the top of her hand. "You gotta use your head, little girl."

"Damn you, I am not a little girl!"

"All right. All right." On the cusp of losing control, he said, "Listen to me. I can't believe I'm doing this." *He couldn't, what if she...*

"What? What is it?" She hung on to every word. Her car felt like a cave.

"You and I want the same thing, Delaina."

"*No.* No, we don't." He planted seeds of doubt again without giving her concrete facts.

"Yeah, we do. We want the land. Free and clear and without needless worries." He searched her eyes, hoping for the common denominator, any level at which they could connect. *So he would know she wasn't part of a bigger scheme.*

Delaina plunged her hands through her hair and pulled out the rubber band. Golden tendrils fell around her face and tickled her shoulders. She looked vulnerably beautiful with her hair down. Jed bit his tongue to keep from telling her. Pain filtered through her cracked voice and choppy words. "I... don't know...what I want... and I'm so young to make choices that...I might regret later. So young to...take a path that could lead me to the end. Or a cliff...or a... cage." Tears spilled onto her face. She laid her head against the seat. "I don't know who to trust." Her body stiffened. She linked eyes with his, stoic as a soldier in battle. "I trust no one."

The answer Jed wanted, she wasn't scheming with Cabot, and he believed her. Her hand rested on the gearshift again. His slipped over it and squeezed. She turned her palm. Her fingers curled into his. He faced forward, watching darkness. Waiting, but she had finished. Straight as arrows, they stared into night. Neither moved. Breathing was questionable. Time stood still and moved at lightning speed while Jed McCrae and Delaina Cash held hands and stared at dark Farm 130.

Perhaps angels spoke in unison, granting them permission to break their truce. They simultaneously broke their hands apart. Jed pushed on the door and looked at her. She let her eyes catch his. He opened his mouth to speak then thought better of it. He couldn't let himself find what he wanted in her. Not Delaina Cash. He closed the door behind him, not looking back.

Three

Mouths

The clock struck midnight.

Fain Kendall, a short, serious man with white hair and black wire glasses, wrote furiously. He hunched in a ladder-back chair and had trouble sorting thoughts. Prioritizing thoughts. The doctor's words echoed. One month to live. Pancreatic cancer, no cure. Fain had been an attorney for thirty-seven years. He had drawn up wills for so many people he lost count, seen them to completion, seen them carried out, seen them contested, seen them tear families apart and bring families together. Drafting his own could be his rectification.

A fiercely determined man, Fain put himself through college, raising himself out of poverty. He had acquired a sizable estate, much of his wealth directly from marriage to Cassandra Jane Darrah McCrae. Jed's mother deserved more credit than gossips gave her. She did not *leave* the entire McCrae land to Fain Kendall. It was already his, deeded to him years ago with the logical understanding that Jed would inherit a lot of it. Fain had saved James Ed McCrae's land from ruin, giving Cass knowledge she needed to make decisions, and expanded, taking more from Tory Cash. As a local attorney privy to vital information, he steered Cass away from Mallard First Financial Bank and the greedy ways of Joe Cabot Hartley. Fain penned every legal document for the farm to ensure confidentiality. He banked through associates in Texas and Georgia. His guidance, the main reason they thrived. That and senior farmhand, Jed's uncle Dale Barlow by marriage to James Ed's sister Caroline McCrae, and sons Ben, Bryan, and Boone were key factors. James Ed had been generous in giving his poor sister's family a better life and opportunity. They worked hard, especially during years Jed went away to college. When Jed came back, it had been his decision.

Jed was a wealthy man. His father had cash and life insurance when he died, and Cass had family money. Cass and Fain combined it in a trust when Jed was a toddler to be accessed when he turned twenty-five. Jed continued to invest and had an impressive portfolio. The original McCrae land belonged to Fain Kendall for as long as he lived.

Jed and Fain's relationship had been rocky. Fain was a bad father, a staunch career man thrown into a paternal role. As Jed grew, Fain wanted a child of his own flesh and blood, not Jed, the replica of Cass's first husband's positive attributes. Cass wouldn't hear of it; in her eyes, Jed was all they needed. A wedge grew larger between Fain and Cass, and Fain and Jed. Fain and Jed went months without talking. Fain's conversation with Jed earlier tonight had been their first since Cass's death in December. Fain had asked Jed to meet him at the homeplace Monday morning before work.

For now, Fain had another person to see and share his devastating news. He pushed his chair from the desk, buried his head in his hands, and cried. Cried for time he lost and time he wasted. Cried for things he'd done and hadn't done. Cried for things he said and hadn't said. With at least one person, there would be no closure.

~ ~ ~

"I miss you sooo much, Butterscotch." Cabot Hartley's lover gazed into his eyes. She twirled her flaming red hair around her manicured finger. "I go on for days without so much as a hidden glance down at the bank. It's tough the way you carry on with the others."

"It's you that I want; that's why I'm careful." If Cabot gave the notion of marrying for love a consideration, the nude, strawberry-topped, freckle-faced country bumpkin sucking on his big toe would be his first choice. He believed every person, no matter how smart, good-looking, wealthy, or refined, had a weakness. His, this twenty-two-year-old bank teller who talked like Minnie Pearl and looked like Strawberry Shortcake. Any grooming and refining had been at his persuasion. She was pretty, in a look-twice-but-you're-not-sure-why way. Not smart in common sense or bookish but a born actress who loved local drama, and Cabot used that advantageously on more than one occasion. He already explained that he planned to marry Lainey. She said she understood business. This little sweetie not only deserved a big house and a nice car, things she never had, she also deserved a good man. Maybe one day... Who was Cabot fooling? His mother would choke him, and his father would kill him after they disowned him. Who, besides the woman next to him, would believe the Prince of Mallard wanted a girl who barely finished high school, lived in a concrete block cottage on Fourth Street with her parents and three brothers, and drove a ten-year-old car painted kiwi green and hot pink? He laughed thinking about her cruising through town with the windows rolled down and Patsy Cline turned up.

"What's tickled you?"

"You."

"Am I that funny-lookin'?" Her turquoise eyes sparkled.

"You're fine enough for me," Cabot answered huskily.

"Which means I'm pretty dang fine." She giggled and licked his thigh.

"And you're good in bed." He reached and squeezed her breasts, watching his hands form globes. "The flame between your legs brings me back, Red."

Her breath caught audibly. "That, from Cabot Hartley? If I did tell our secret affair, no one would believe me."

"I'm the only one that matters."

"Yeah, for over a year now. I got to hurry, Butterscotch. I'm supposed to count money at the bank this mornin'." She licked her tongue down his hairy leg to the knee. "Wouldn't want my boss to fire me."

In a groan, Cabot replied, "No need to worry about that, Red."

"Ain't no need to worry 'bout much of nothing so long as you meet me at your camp house every Saturday mornin' at four." She slipped on her jeans and sweater and slicked her hair into a headband.

"Remember, I'll be in New Orleans today and tomorrow with Lainey. Don't call or text me."

"I know it. That don't mean I like it," she said in a huff.

"I'm taking you somewhere luxurious someday, Red."

"I ain't holdin' my breath. I do want more of that rich-smellin' perfume."

~ ~ ~

Sunlight peeked into Delaina's room. Gauzy curtains swayed. She stretched on her bed and rose. She had a lot to do before she left town. She heard Miss Maydell rambling downstairs in the kitchen. The house was too much for a lone twenty-year-old resident. Miss Maydell and Moll insisted on moving into the adjoining guest house when Delaina returned early from college. For years, they had rented a farmhouse on an obscure part of Cash Way. Now their sons Rhett and Eli lived there.

She dreamed about Cabot, Jed, her father, her mother, and Cash Way all night long. She tossed and turned and decided in her restless contemplation. She would go to New Orleans with Cabot to search for clues that he was anything but honest. If he proved himself, she would push toward marriage, a mutually beneficial partnership. The more she analyzed her dialogue with Jed, the more she believed he tried to break her alliance. Cash Way, an easier target without Cabot Hartley. She might surprise Cabot tonight...

Eager to feel hot water running over her muscles, Delaina stepped in the shower. She rolled her head to release tension. Jed came knocking again on her mind's door. She tried to lock him out or let in Cabot. Just Jed, standing on his front porch in his boxer shorts. The subtle brush of his lips. Their hands intertwined at Farm 130. Passion rose like a cresting wave. She opened her eyes. Foam dissipated, tossing her ashore, steeped in a haunting, taunting reality as itchy and irritating as wet sand. Jed McCrae, the devil in disguise, sent to destroy every shred of willpower she had.

Breakfast smelled good. Hoping for bacon and eggs, Delaina hurried downstairs. "Miss Maydell?"

"Lainey, honey. Good mornin'."

"Good mornin'." Delaina darted into the kitchen. Her girly nickname grated; perhaps she wouldn't correct anyone. It could be Jed's special name for her.

"Bacon and eggs, Lainey, your favorite."

"Great." Delaina hugged Miss Maydell. Jed's special name for her? He didn't even know it was special.

Maydell stiffened. "We got to have us a serious girl talk." Delaina braced herself. Last time Miss Maydell approached her like this, she explained benefits of tampons over pads in gory detail. *Yikes.*

"You've been dating the Hartley boy for some time. You're like a daughter to me. I must meddle. Gonna tell you the same thing I told them sons of mine. Girls keepin' their virginity for their husbands ain't popular like when me and Moll was courtin'. I believe with all my Christian heart that's the way the Good Lord intended it. It makes for a mighty special thing between man and wife. Me and Moll waited. Not easy, 'specially for a horny teenage boy." Delaina's preparations fell short; she blushed. Miss Maydell, a stout woman, round and soft, wore glasses and bright makeup. Her hair, salt-and-pepper gray, stayed wrapped in a bun. She wore solid-colored elastic pants and button-up blouses, tucked in. The highlight of her day meant deciding whether to serve iced tea or lemonade at supper. She didn't know better and wouldn't change upon enlightenment. "Anyhow, girls spread their legs fast nowadays." Maydell shook her head in disgrace. "Moll and I seen to it you went to church every Sunday; you know better. Still, I ain't crawled out from a cabbage leaf yesterday. I know what you kids are probably doing when you say you're headin' to New Orleans overnight. Givin' the devil an upper hand, is all." She smacked her lips and viewed Delaina skeptically. "This trip is sure to tempt you. Like Moll told our boys when they was old enough to start takin' girls out, 'If you're thinkin' about playin' in the rain, have the sense to wear a raincoat.'" Maydell took a breath. "In other words, carry you some condoms, dear."

"Yes, ma'am." Delaina smiled. Miss Maydell had good intentions. "Yummy," she said, eager to break up the lecture.

~ ~ ~

On the drive to the nursing home, Delaina thought about her father, an aggressive man disintegrated into a crippled mute. She hated the nursing home smell, like existing in a hospital perpetually. She held her breath when she entered and reached his room. A nurse was taking his pulse. Her father's eyes were closed, like most days lately.

The nurse said, "Miss Cash, your father has taken a turn."

Delaina's hand flew to her mouth. She sank into the nearest chair. "My father's dying?"

"Stroke patients can go on like this indefinitely. However, many follow the pattern of your father shortly before death. I'll give you time alone." Delaina walked over to him, held out her hand to touch him but didn't. This corpse of a man wasn't Mallard County's notorious Tory Cash. Scaly skin, snowy hair, a colorless face, dead by his standards and hers. Anger overtook her. He lived for himself and made a grave error in judgment believing himself invincible. No one expected the turn his life had taken. The day of the stroke, he leisurely golfed with buddies, Joe Cabot Hartley among them. Tory was as drunk as a broom-beaten dog, the only way he'd play golf. He teed off. His ball fell short, landing in a pond. He hurled a golf club and cussed. Seconds later, he suffered a stroke. The beginning of the end. Delaina sat and watched monitors for an hour. "Daddy?" No response. "Victor Kelly Cash?" Nothing. "Tory?" Silence. She continued like he could hear her. "Thank you, Daddy, for staying with me when Mama didn't." Delaina cried softly. "Thank you for holding on to the land. I forgive you for your shortcomings. I'll make you proud, somehow. Daddy? *Daddy.*"

Delaina dropped her head. Monitors continued, the only proof he was alive.

Returning to the front desk, Delaina spoke to the receptionist. "Excuse me. When will Dr. Rainwater be in?"

"He doesn't make rounds on Saturday, but I'm sure he'd come for you. Want to see him?"

"Yes, ma'am, please. I'll wait." Delaina sat, mentally exhausted, and dug in her purse for her phone. She called Cabot.

"Good morning," Cabot answered pleasantly. "Are you getting ready for the time of your life?"

"Not exactly. I have bad news. Daddy's taken a turn for the worse."

"Lainey, I'm sorry. What can I do?"

"There's nothing anyone can do. I'm waiting to talk to the doctor."

"Okay...I'm here if you need me, and I love you."

Delaina couldn't believe her ears. She didn't love Cabot. At least she thought love should be stronger than what she felt. She called Miss Maydell to tell her about Tory.

~ ~ ~

Cabot held the phone in his hands, trying to comprehend that Tory was going to die now. He had to rethink his strategy. He made a call to his partner.

"What is it?"

"Good and bad news. Tory's about to croak."

"Shoot. What are you going to do about it?"

"I'm going to marry the bitch," Cabot answered. "More quickly than planned."

"I'm not totally convinced marriage is the most surefire way to get her land. Your girl will play hell for every inch of it."

"We'll get the land." Cabot smiled smugly. "That's where Step Two comes in. We meet Monday."

~ ~ ~

The doctor had a grim face as he approached Delaina. "Good morning."

"Good mornin', Dr. Rainwater." Delaina stood to greet him. He hugged her. "I won't take much of your time. I'm wondering is there anything I can do for him? Is he in pain?"

"No and no."

Delaina nodded. "How much longer?"

"Hard to say, maybe two days. He's shutting down. I don't expect him to be conscious again. There's nothing you can do. I'm so sorry, Lainey."

"Thank you. Should I stay by his side?" Her voice quivered. She didn't want to. Too sterile, too lonely a room.

"Personal choice, but I'd go home and rest. It'll be a lot for you. A public event, his funeral. Our staff is highly trained for end of life."

"Yes, sir. Thank you for everything. Daddy thought highly of you." They hugged again.

Driving home, as Delaina turned onto Cash-McCrae Road, she met Boone Barlow, son of Jed's senior farmhand and uncle by marriage. In his truck, headed toward town. She waved. He wiggled fingers in her direction.

Passing him reignited Delaina's humiliation because Boone told Jed what happened. The summer she graduated high school, the summer she left for college at Ole Miss, almost three years ago. She had limited experience with boys. She'd been kissed, sneaked out once, made out with a few guys. Nothing substantial. After graduation, she contemplated whether she wanted to go to college inexperienced. Growing up without a loving father or female role models left her wary of waiting for the right man to come along and sweep her off her feet. Miss Maydell's dragging her to church every time the doors opened sparked curiosity and the belief that sex should be special. She looked for someone nice and quiet to be with, someone mature, to decide if she should shed her virginity or at least get a grip on her fear of intimacy. Son of Dale and Caroline (McCrae) Barlow, Boone worked and lived on McCrae land all his life. Tall and ruggedly attractive, Boone stood out with his Jed-black, rock star hair and topaz eyes and elusive McCrae countenance.

One hot day, she jogged alongside the road as he drove by. She motioned to stop, and they flirted. He arranged a time to go fishing on the creek. Boone was known throughout Mississippi for his fishing expertise, participating in tournaments. By July, they secretly saw each other daily. She asked him not to tell, blaming it on the age difference and that he worked on McCrae land, saying Tory would kill him. Boone didn't doubt it. Delaina had a feeling he also knew he wasn't in the right social class. She didn't think of herself as a snob. The relationship would have been a public atrocity.

Delaina wasn't in love with Boone. She did enjoy his company. They told jokes, played cards, and fished. One night, when they went parking behind Farm 130 on the McCrae side, Delaina whispered she was ready. He slid his pants down. He took off her pants but seemed uncertain about completely undressing her. She gripped her shirt front, so he left it on. Boone fumbled with a condom. When it was secure, he lowered himself on top of her on the back seat. She held her legs together tightly. Her stomach churned, not from desire but a gross feeling like she drank spoiled milk. The scene spoiled as quickly. She didn't consider herself terribly old-fashioned; something didn't feel right.

"Stop," she muttered. Boone frowned. "What is it?" He had her pinned down. She didn't answer. He sat up and rolled his shoulders. She felt sorry for him and offered, "I don't like the condom. It seems impersonal."

"You're not on the Pill. I'm not doin' it without the rubber with Tory Cash's daughter. Hell no."

"I don't want to anyway."

Boone tossed the condom out the window and jerked up his jeans. Delaina pulled her pants on awkwardly. She hadn't meant to hurt Boone or lead him on. They'd become good friends. "I'm sorry." Delaina forced herself to be casual and accommodating. She kissed his neck, his chest, his stomach. She moved inside his jeans and paused. Then licked, pretending she licked a Popsicle. In seconds, it was over. Delaina coiled in her seat like a provoked snake. "Boone?"

"Uh, huh?" He looked unable to move.

"Please, *please*, don't tell anyone. I felt sorry for you."

"I won't tell. Your daddy would castrate me."

"If I hear you've told anyone, I'll tell my daddy myself. Don't depend on me for these, uh, services. A one-time thing. I leave for college next week. I thought I was ready."

Boone held up his hand. "I think I know what happened."

Being closed in a ragged truck that smelled of sweat and sex made Delaina nauseated. When she thought of what she had done, she almost gagged. "Are you mad?"

"Forget it and consider yourself lucky, Lainey." He pointed in the general direction of Jed McCrae's cabin. "I don't know anyone else you could've used who would be so understanding."

That night at home, Delaina panicked. What if Boone told? What about how mad her daddy would be? She called him at sunrise and asked to meet at Carr's Creek. He was waiting when she got there. She didn't waste time, felt a thousand eyes staring through tree trunks. She held out three hundred-dollar bills. "I'll pay you not to tell."

Boone glared and marched away. "God dang, this gets worse." He yelled, "You'll pay me? I thought we were friends...and more! Keep your money! I'd rather park cars for crooks in a filthy big city than take money from Lainey Cash. You're spoiled rotten."

Delaina went to college, returning to Mallard County in a short week. She had not spoken to Boone since. She nodded or waved each time she saw him. Their one episode inhibited her love life as much as coming to terms with her mother's prostitution had.

Enveloped in the memory, Delaina drove past the gated, tree-lined entrance to Cash Way. Realizing what she'd done, she turned around in the driveway leading to Jed's workshop. She circled through the empty place and drove toward the main road. She met Jed, head-on, on the narrow strip of asphalt. "Oh shoot," she stammered.

His windows were down, his hair wandering breezily. He pulled off the asphalt into the grass parallel with her SUV. She parked and gave him a questioning look. Jed spoke through his open window, tanned arm propped on it. "There are more inconspicuous ways to gather information about the competition."

Delaina was improving at his game. "Sure. Like sex with the bank vice president's secretary."

Jed shrugged. "Or the bank vice president himself."

"Go to hell."

"Ladies first." He allowed a peek at a pearly smile. It vanished. "Look, I just wanted to say I heard about your old man. He could be a pompous, backstabbing, crooked son of a bitch, but..."

Delaina erupted in a fit. "How dare you? My father's been crippled and mute and is about to die. You stop me to say he's a crooked S.O.B.? You are unbelievable, Jed McCrae. You're the crook! Selling dope. Soliciting prostitutes. Stealing land. I'm leaving!"

Jed had abandoned his truck to stalk toward her like an ominous storm. He covered her open window with his grand form. She felt his hot breath. He spoke without raising his voice. "Would you, for once, shut up? I wasn't finished. Damn. Damn you." His eyes cut through her like serrated slivers of blue ice.

Delaina gripped her fingers on the wheel. "This is useless. These little chance meetings are futile." She pursed her lips together as she talked, shaking her head. "There's too much water under the bridge as the saying goes."

"Is it yours or mine?"

"Is what yours or mine?"

"The water under the bridge." Jed motioned toward Carr's Creek, a slinky strip in the distance.

Delaina rested her elbow on the steering wheel and shoved her palm against her forehead. Her eyes closed. "We share it, don't we? It's beneficial to both of us." Her voice dripped haughty sarcasm.

Jed backed off and looked at sunshine bright enough to blind, a breeze easy enough to make the most work-minded man stop and think of taking a long lunch on the riverbank or a passionate tumble in the wheat pasture. Like an injection of black coffee, Delaina Cash made him hot with the clear picture of stripping her clothes off amidst tall grass and dandelions. Pouting and red-faced, she stared out her windshield. He could get addicted to these mental wars, her tantrums. She smelled like sea-scented soap, looked fresh as dawn. She wore a dressy shirt today and her I-don't-care-what-you-think ponytail. He waged his next attack. If forced to admit it, his words came out of guidance. "It's dry enough to plant seed."

Delaina knew what he insinuated. She had no business going to New Orleans with Cabot. "Moll can do it."

"Uh, huh. Usually a man's job anyway." Jed knew that stung.

She appeared unscathed. "I farm as competently as the best of you."

"I know you do."

With Jed's head turned toward the road, Delaina seized the opportunity to look. Skin damp from a barely broken sweat with dust in the creases, untucked shirt, stringy Bleu Cottons, suede work boots. His rugged appeal couldn't be imitated, the one-of-a-kind image that Levi, Dodge, Winston cigarettes and countless others worked tediously to capture and paid for. The epitome of it, close enough to touch. She shivered. "Glad to see you know how to wear a shirt."

"Glad to see you know how to wear a bra."

"Are you?" Her question hung in the air more like a proposition.

Jed jammed his arm in the window and coiled it around the back of her neck, fast as the strike of a snake. "No." He looked into her eyes. Delaina held his stare, squinting at him against the light of day. He tilted his head and leaned in, watching sun reflect golden in her eyes, or maybe her eyes reflected golden in sun. They inhaled. She raised up to accommodate him. Jed jerked his head out the window and squeezed his eyes shut. Like someone pushed him, he came back through. His lips were on hers before she knew what happened. He attacked her mouth with tongue and teeth gnashing roughly. Jed needed Delaina Cash's lips on his more than his next meal. She pushed, pulled, and suddenly went pliant, giving it back to him good. They kissed and kissed, hard and deep. To slow it down, with all the reserve Jed could gather, he rested his mouth on hers sensually. Delaina clamped her arms around his neck to ensure he wouldn't tug away. She pulled her head back and parted her lips, giving a nice close view. Intentionally, she slid her tongue past her teeth. Jed watched with ill-restrained hunger. She gently licked her lips. He touched his lips to her tongue and caught it. The next kiss was everything the last one wasn't. Paced, planned, easy. She felt smooth and wet and tasted like peppermint. Jed's mouth stayed inside hers to savor her sweetness. She wanted more. He knew it; she confirmed it by lifting closer to him. He licked and tasted lazily, the corner of her mouth, her cheek, her earlobe. He relaxed his grip; she relaxed her grip around his neck. One of his hands pulled her ponytail loose. Strands tickled her neck as they fell. Returning to her mouth deliberately, Jed's kissing went on and on. She melted in his mouth as his hands became controlled, like he had settled in for the afternoon.

Like she was had.

No. She would give him an overdue dose of his own medicine, the smug jerk. Arrogantly, deliberately, she slid her tongue into his mouth, plunged deeply and flicked across the inside once, then retreated, sucking his bottom lip, pulling it with her teeth as she broke free.

They split apart defensively like a referee blew the shrill parting whistle on a personal foul. Delaina's face flushed, cheeks pink from desire. She could feel something, perhaps raw dirty lust, not blood, pumping through her body. She pressed her knees together instinctively to relieve pressure between her legs. Jed saw it, and she would have felt embarrassingly exposed were he recovering any better.

He was not.

He plowed his hands through his hair anxiously and furiously while he ground his teeth together. Expletives exploding under his breath, he began pacing, the bulge in his pants obvious. Both breathed heavily through swollen, puckered, red mouths. "That was a mistake," he admitted.

"That was a kiss." Delaina smiled deliciously.

"No. Hell no, it wasn't." Jed gave her a hard look. "*That* was an invitation."

Delaina gave him no answer either way, daring him to come back and find out. Jed hissed, "Go spend the night with Cabot Hartley while you think about me." He got in his truck and drove forward.

Delaina sat there for more than a minute, defying his command, then drove away. She burned like incense on the way home from a new high that inevitably had a gut-wrenching low. Jed McCrae, a potent drug. Once he injected his tongue into a mouth, the patient would never recover. She'd need more and more in larger doses to survive. Already in withdrawal, Delaina felt tempted past common sense to turn around and get another shot. She forced herself to pick up her phone and dial, shaking with her drug-induced need. "Hi, Cabot," she quaked.

"How're things? I thought I'd hear from you by now."

"Yeah, well, something else came up." *I kissed Jed McCrae, and I've never felt better.* His kissing tormented her. She couldn't get rid of the desire for more if someone removed her brain with a pair of pliers. "Dr. Rainwater expects Daddy to pass away soon," she rambled. "There's nothing I can do. I said my goodbyes. He's comatose. Miss Maydell is going every few hours 'til it's over."

"I'm sorry. I'm truly sorry."

"I know you are, Cabot. You were close to my father long before you knew me."

"On the contrary. I've had my eye on you for a long time." She was putty in his hands today. "The best thing you can do is come to New Orleans with me."

"I am. I'll be at your apartment in less than an hour." This trip would serve a purpose for Delaina. Cabot had been steadfast in convincing her of his genuineness. Delaina might be young and blonde; she was smarter than Jed McCrae thought. Their kissing, no matter how good, meant nothing to him. If it had, he wouldn't have had the will to leave her. Jed knew Delaina stood perilously close to inheriting the Cash land. He thought if he challenged her to go with Cabot, she wouldn't go. He probably even thought she'd speed down Jed's driveway and beg him to take her to bed. Jed knew he appealed to her and used himself as a weapon because she and Cabot were a threatening alliance. Maybe she wished the kiss meant more. Maybe she wanted to be a Jed-McCrae addict. Cabot Hartley would have to rehabilitate her. Suck it up and self-serve, she told herself. Delaina packed her things and left, not before checking with Moll, Miss Maydell, and the nursing home, confirming she left her farm, her house, and her father in good hands.

Four

Ears

MacHenry's, the local bar and grill, hummed with gossip as usual.

Moll slid in a booth with a farmer-turned-lumber-worker. "Hey there, Billy Dean. What's the story 'round here today?" Billy gulped his tea and made room. Rhett and Eli slid in on the other side. "I don't reckon y'all've heard." Billy looked more depressed than usual. "Clyde Burns put a bullet through his head this mornin'. One of his workers found him spread out in a fresh-plowed field, bits of brain scattered in front of him."

Moll shook his head. "Well, things is gettin' tougher every year. I'm not surprised. I heard Clyde didn't make nothin' off cotton last season."

"Naw, he ain't made nothin' in two or three seasons. Had debts piled high as horse hockey. Y'all might as well put your application in over at the lumber yard. I'm tellin' ya..." He pointed his finger at Moll's sons. "...all of farmin' is going the way mine did. Belly up quick."

Moll chewed on his lip. "Cash Way's different, Billy Dean. We got ours spread out. If one thing gets bad, something else makes up. It's like a...what's the word...corporation."

Billy laughed. "That don't make a damn if the Hartleys don't lend you the money to go another year. It's what happened to me and Clyde; Hartley set us up. He knew we'd never clear the money we owed their god dang bank. Who would've thought my acres would become a fancy apartment complex for a bunch of college students and Joe Cabot Hartley's squirty son?" Billy sipped on his iced tea like bitter whiskey. "I reckon Clyde couldn't bear to see his land become retail store lots."

~ ~ ~

"Let's go," Cabot said. "My bag's loaded. I'll get yours."

"Brought a duffel and a hanging bag," Delaina remarked. They hurried down the staircase into the garage.

"You pack light."

"Yeah, I'm not your typical female."

Cabot patted her hip. "I agree." Delaina felt nothing. She had blocked memories of Jed's venomous kisses all the way to town; they came rushing in. She wanted to love Cabot or more accurately to prove him worthy of her trust. She sighed. Cabot loaded her bags, came to her, and lifted her chin to meet his face. "What is it?"

"Huh? Oh, it's my father," Delaina lied. *She'd probably go to hell for using a dying man for an excuse.* "Should I leave town?"

"You should. The nursing home has your number. So does Maydell. It's an easy drive. If you want to come back, I'll gladly drive you." They got in the car and left.

"Forgive my somber mood." Delaina needed this opportunity. "I've never been to New Orleans."

Cabot tilted his head toward her. "Really? What a shame. Why?"

Uh, because I had no family, no raising, few vacations, no real boyfriends, and because of my mother. "I don't know. Farming's demanding." Delaina felt a tinge of guilt. Not out of Mallard County yet, already she spoke dishonestly twice. If she expected trust, she should give Cabot the same. "The truth is my biological mother grew up there."

Cabot halfway listened as he changed lanes and tapped out a drum pattern on his steering wheel. "You don't see her much."

"No, not one time since she left."

"Can't imagine. I talk to my parents every day and my sister weekly. How old were you? When she left."

"Age four."

"I don't mean to pry, but why?"

"My father was a violent, raging..."

"I know, but what about you?"

"What about me? I didn't matter obviously." Delaina faked a smile. "Enough about my screwed-up family. Tell me what you have planned."

"A surprise." Cabot squeezed Delaina's thigh. She jerked. He thought she seemed edgier than usual. Probably because of her father's pending death. "You'll like it."

"I'm sure." Cabot didn't seem to mind silence. He certainly wasn't dying to know more about her. Looking ever-the-prep wearing a yellow golf shirt and smelling of crisp cologne, he hummed to music. No conversation stretched several miles. Delaina sipped bottled water then dove into her reason for coming. "People are talkin' about us..."

"Are they?" Cabot feigned surprise.

"Sayin' we're the perfect match."

"Do you agree?" Cabot watched her crystal green eyes for emotion. Delaina blinked. "I told you how I felt this morning." Cabot ran one finger down her bare arm. "Remember? I told you I love you."

She squirmed uncomfortably. She remembered something her father once said when he raged about her mother. *Saying "I love you" brings down shields, leaves you exposed. Your mother was a paid whore from a trashy ghetto when she lived in New Orleans, Lainey, but wouldn't let her heart be naked. She never told me she loved me.* Delaina found her own reliable shield and managed to remark, "You're very sweet."

"I meant it."

"I wouldn't want you to say it otherwise. Cabot, you said last night that I should avoid Jed McCrae."

"Like herpes," Cabot stated, wondering how they went from the subject of love to Jed McCrae.

"I understand he's a hard man to trust, but I think you know something specific." Cabot answered cautiously, "I know generals and specifics. Generally, he's selfish and suspiciously private, especially with women. Specifically, we've done business. I'm not impressed. His name's been linked to illegal acts." Cabot added with daring contempt, "He'd love to get his hands on you. Like trespassing on Cash Way."

"Where does he bank?" *Was Cabot right?* He would be furious if he knew she went against his wishes and saw Jed again twice. What would he do if he knew she had Jed's tongue in her mouth? Hers in his. Sensation crawled over Delaina's skin. Against her better judgment, she had a feeling she wouldn't be posting "Private Property" signs anytime soon. "I don't know where he banks, but I'm working on it," Cabot said.

"How will you find out? Why is it important?"

"Let me worry about how, and it's good business, that's why."

"I have enough to worry about anyway." Trying to be nonchalant, Delaina played songs. They rode for twenty miles. Shouldn't they have more to talk about on their first trip alone together? Delaina went for it. "What do you think I should do? After my father's death, I mean."

Cabot anticipated the question. He prepared himself months ago on how to answer. Lainey valued self-sufficiency. "Depends on how you feel about the land."

"Isn't it apparent? I want every square inch of it. It's tremendous work, though."

"Yes, it's hard work." Cabot walked this tightrope rehearsed. "You're young. Need to relax, take trips, hang out with friends. Maybe you should look for a good manager. Hire more help. Of course, a good businessman...or woman considers *every* option. I mean, hey..." He played casual. "You may decide to bite the bullet and sell it." He squeezed her leg. "It would bring an unbelievable price." Cabot paused. She didn't seem offended. "Up to you. I'm here to bounce ideas. You know I'll help any way I can."

Delaina felt super-impressed. He couldn't have answered more appropriately if she wrote a perfect response. Tonight would be their night.

~ ~ ~

Holland Sommers drove through the field to Jed McCrae's cabin at a snail's pace. Jed, not nearly as easy to understand as Cabot Hartley had been. What could he want mid-Saturday afternoon? No way he had proof she switched sides. If things got touchy, she'd lead his mind elsewhere. Under her dress, she wore frilly thongs and a matching push-up bra. Holland had inherited her father's hunger for power and intuitive ability to sniff out a rat. These weren't rats. They were powerful men. Certainly, Jed or Cabot should not be provoked.

Jed sat in a rocker on the front porch with his legs thrown up and crossed, feet resting on a rail. Late-day sun ribbons did nothing to soften his features. A broody face, lips clamped tight, and eyes two shades stormier than the blue spring sky, he could've been Marlboro Man, absolutely. Today he had the trademark cigarette to match. His red mutt napped on the porch floor.

Holland aimed for lively and light. "Hey, Jed!" She pranced across the grass. He didn't acknowledge her. Neither did Lucy. "I didn't know you smoke." She closed in, smiling cheerfully.

"I don't."

"Anyway..." Holland paused. "I'm glad you called." She stretched her arms. Her breasts jutted forward, playing tug-of-war with the buttonholes on her dress. "You seem aloof lately. Maybe you need to relax." She watched a cigarette roll between his lips. "I could use a beer."

"Don't have any." Jed's lips curled. "How 'bout tequila?"

She had a bad feeling he knew something. Holland watched him reach for the brown bag on the plank floor. "I don't think I'll take a... swig," she said, rather demurely.

Jed looked toward her. Makeup thick as icing, she wore a flirty black dress and heeled sandals and smelled like a side street flower shop. Lush green trees projected majestic subtlety in blinding contrast, like a strip club's lap dancer dumped in the wilderness. "Take a swig. It's good." Jed shoved the bottle outward. "Garrick Sommers' daughter is too sophisticated for liquor, huh?"

"I'm not thirsty." *Where was this headed?* she wondered.

"You've acquired a taste for the irreplaceable chardonnay."

Cabot's drink of choice. Holland refused to reply. Jed smashed his shortening cigarette into the chair arm. She treaded against a swift current to question him without revealing her recent actions. She risked it. "Okay, let's talk." Holland sat in the opposite rocker. "I guess you heard about Clyde Burns' suicide."

Jed nodded. "Hate it for Clyde's family. That's what he gets for bankin' with Hartley. No way to win. It's why I brought you here."

She dodged with, "In your opinion, what does the future of farming look like?"

Jed lowered his eyebrows. "Farmin's fine. A daily picnic in the park." He stood, towered. "Come on in. We're definitely going to talk." She followed him inside. Holland liked the obnoxious masculinity of Jed's place, no effort to add anything to accommodate a woman's tastes or needs. A bachelor pad fully equipped with a bedroom loft and hot tub, from what she could see of it below. They always met at his office at the farm shop. She'd been inside here a couple times. Made him a sandwich yesterday, trying to be more personal.

Jed pulled out a chair at his table, in the open space in front of his kitchen, and sat. A fine table, handmade chunky wood with matching heavy chairs. Holland sat. Both looked out the window wall. His view couldn't be ignored. Big Sunflower River flowed peacefully fifty yards away, semi-masked by unbothered timber—ash, oak, pine, sweet gums, older than Jed and Holland combined. Delta National Forest thrived not far from Cash-McCrae Road. From inside his cabin, one would swear Jed lived smack-dab in the middle of the preservation. Nervous, Holland relied on her preferred direct method. "How often do you run into Lainey Cash?"

Jed noted this was the second time she mentioned Delaina in a day. "Matter of fact, I talked to her this mornin'." *Right before she rammed her silky, minty tongue down my throat.* "I can't help but run into her. Property lines on this place are as jumbled as Atlanta's godforsaken sidewalks."

Holland felt on the verge of getting information. "Lainey's not a snobby bitch. So nice when she comes to the bank to see Cabot."

She picked him, and he knew it. Jed had become suspicious lately. Holland hadn't been supplying information like she once did. She was a tough cookie. They'd known each other as business associates and friends, family connections since diapers. "Sure, she's nice to Cabot. She's exchanging her pretty crotch for low interest loans." Jed wore a white oxford, untucked, mostly unbuttoned, sleeves rolled up, and good jeans. Barefoot with messy hair, he smelled like nature and tequila.

Holland watched him, affected and astonished. "You're in a foul mood."

Jed leaned in his chair carelessly. "I told you not to fuck with Cabot. Literally and figuratively." Holland's mouth matched her eyes, stuck in permanent wideness. "I knew he'd come on to you hard. He's a damn man whore, Holland. I thought you could hang in there and stay professional. You know how men are, as much as you've spread yourself around." He leveled her. "I'm still thinkin' about how I'm gonna handle you." He sniffed. "Here's what I don't want." He came forward on the table, intimidating and gorgeous in a word. Holland was in trouble. Big trouble. Jed McCrae invested a lot of money in deals with her prudish-in-business father. "I don't want you showin' up here to make sandwiches or to leave prissy panties meant for Cabot on my porch. Won't work with me. You've switched sides, and you thought you could butter me up or play us both." Another leveling look. "Wrong. I'll come to you." His tone alone threatened. "When I'm ready." He didn't mean sex.

"I'm sorry." Holland stood, struggled to balance, ready to go. She made ungraceful-for-her steps through the center room. She glanced up the splendid staircase, saw books stacked on the shelves halfway up. "Is this where you sleep?" Her head went backward, viewing rails at the top. She tried to take the heat off her poor decision-making.

Call him sentimental, selfish, or plain private, Jed had not taken a woman to his bedroom since he had the cabin built. He used the bedroom downstairs for guests. "Uh, huh."

"You're not with Samantha anymore."

"Nope. Not since Thanksgiving." A fact jolted Jed. He had sex with one woman, one time, since he saw Delaina and Cabot together the first time. "My mother was too sick for me to concentrate on anything or anybody else."

"And since she passed away?" She continued looking toward his landing and loft.

"This is your business, why?" Jed stood close behind, corralling her toward his front door.

"Because you seem defensive about Lainey."

Holland was good. It's why Jed brought her to Mallard. "Look…" He kept going toward the door. "Delaina and I are the rightful owners to everything between here and the highway. Her father's about to die, making us also the only heirs. We might fight, backstab, sell out to each other, or choose to get along. But the fact remains, and she and I've talked and agreed: Nobody else will get this land. That was your purpose, to clue me in to Cabot's schemes." On the porch, in the setting sun, Jed stepped in front of her. Holland, again, got caught up in his view. Far from mankind, far from Atlanta. She felt like a trespasser on God. He spoke, "You've breached part of our agreement."

She had been physical with Cabot. "It meant nothing. A long time ago."

"Yeah, I bet. What, a few hours? Is that why you've been mentioning Delaina? You're jealous." Jed sat in his rocker, swished tequila, and commented as an afterthought, "Jealous, huh? He does it with you but dates her."

"No," Holland answered weakly. Jed *always* called her Delaina. Nobody else did. Hmm.

"How do you feel, knowin' he has sex with everybody down there? Have you been upstairs to his bank teller penthouse? What's Cabot got, a big dry erase board of employee names? Today it's your turn to fuck me." Holland took a huge breath. "Have you been to his NOLA house, where Delaina is? How many gals went this weekend?"

"I've been to the top of the bank, honestly." She shrugged. "Only heard rumors about his New Orleans house. Hard to believe, despite my…indiscretions." Humbly, she stared. "A lot of girl gossip at the bank about NOLA. You never know who wants to be noticed or promoted." She made a dire face. "Cabot and Lainey went alone. Lainey seems too nice. Too secure for him."

That Holland appeared certain they went alone should have made Jed feel better. It bothered the everliving hell out of him. "You're right about Delaina. She has more land, clout, and confidence than you and me and Cabot combined." The purpose of their conversation was complete.

"Jed, I couldn't have achieved the level of trust you wanted me to have with Cabot without being sexual." She made an unconcerned face. "Just business."

"Yet you've given me next to nothing to go on, and now he's all up in Lainey Cash." Saying that aloud amplified Jed to pure temper. "Their alliance isn't in my best interest." Some reasons of which he cared not to admit, even to himself. "If you stay here, and I haven't decided you will, you need a boyfriend. He'll cheat on her plenty. Not with you." Jed got up, letting her know they were done. "I'm coming to see you soon. Be ready." He walked inside his forest fortress.

~ ~ ~

Fain Kendall sipped on a cappuccino and stared at the waterfront. For years, he'd been meeting the woman beside him at this sidewalk shop for coffee, drinks, talks, kisses, and walks. Not once had she shed a tear. Today, his bedmate, his helpmate, his other half sniffled yet remained remarkably composed. He had less than a month to live. A sparkling teardrop spilled from her jade-colored eye. Fain felt numb. He wondered if she felt the same.

Finally, he spoke, "I'm here until tomorrow night. I'll come later in the week. If you want me to."

"I do." She stared wildly into his eyes, studying his wrinkled face, memorizing weary creases and lines, knowing she put most of them there. "I want to be with you every moment until the end."

"Will you marry me?"

"I thought you'd never ask. I'll gladly marry you."

"When?" Fain reached for her hand.

"As soon as possible," she responded.

"I love you."

"I know you do." Several breathless moments later, she whispered, "I...love you. I always have. Always will."

~ ~ ~

Delaina's first impression of New Orleans wasn't exactly what she expected. She witnessed a drug swap, homeless junkies, and a prostitute solicited. Thirty years ago, that would have been her mother.

Cabot assaulted traffic like he owned the road. He probably did. He drove down a narrow lane between historic homes and motioned to a gray three-story mansion. "There she is. A beauty, huh?" He parked in an alley. The majesty of the home interested Delaina. He elaborated, "Reworked. Immense care taken to preserve valuable elements." "Extraordinary," she complimented. Cabot pressed the latch on an iron gate. Inside she saw a small courtyard, an unblemished rose garden with ornate tables and chairs and a built-in oversized outdoor kitchen. A worn brick path led to the service entry. He fumbled for the key. "This way." Outside opened to a sensational interior. A tapestry of monochromatic fabrics, elegant paint colors, and impressive artwork had been purposefully chosen and appointed. A long marble island between the kitchen and living room stood out with a lavish bar hanging from the ceiling overhead and mirrored shelves in the corner full of pretty bottles of alcohol. Dozens of wineglasses, shot glasses, Champagne flutes, and ballers.

"Pretty nice, huh?" Cabot turned and caught Delaina's wrist. "For a pretty nice lady." He kissed her. "Why don't you go to the master bedroom and lie down?" He pointed. "I'll wake you in time to get dressed for dinner."

Tired, Delaina didn't argue. She wound her way beyond the kitchen-living-dining area. A sherbet orange coverlet draped the queen-size bed framed by a white iron headboard. Tall windows bordered each side. A brightly colored jute rug accented the honey oak floors. A fireplace straddled the opposing wall, a mantle lined with candlesticks, burned-down candles in them. A partially opened door revealed a modern bathroom with a glitzy built-in bar. She stepped in to see shelves of plush bath towels, robes, oils, candles, and uppity bath salts on each side of a Jacuzzi tub. All in all, perfect. A little too perfect, like a...honeymoon hideaway. Did Joe Cabot and Claudia entertain dozens of people in the house? Did they come in here, get drunk in the Jacuzzi, and have sex in this bed? She couldn't imagine. Did they really need twenty towels and six robes? Oh well. Being rich had a lot of perks. Delaina climbed on the bed and fell asleep.

Cabot slipped out to the courtyard and hastily dialed. "Yeah?" his partner answered.

"Don't sound so excited. Who were you expecting?"

"No one."

Cabot continued, "Things are smooth as silk here."

"Uh, huh. Somehow I can imagine."

"I won't call you again 'til we get back to Mallard."

"Busy wrinkling the sheets."

"Soon. Any news there?" Cabot asked.

"Yeah, about Holland Sommers. It can wait 'til we meet Monday. Have yourself a good time. Someone needs to."

"I plan to." Smiling boastfully, Cabot hung up.

~ ~ ~

Jed sat on the couch in his cabin in semi-darkness. His mind wandered for the hundredth time. He believed, after being with Delaina in her SUV last night, she had not been roped into Cabot's plans, and they weren't involved in a scheme against him. For how long? He also believed Delaina had no idea Holland was one of Cabot's current lovers or the extent of his cheating. Delaina seemed too self-assured to tolerate any infidelity, and unless he misjudged her by a mile, she didn't know about, nor would she participate in, his pussy parties. Jed felt a strange compulsion to tell her. Everything. She wouldn't believe him. Forget it. A big girl now, she'd land on her feet. Hopefully not in a death plunge.

Headlights flashed across the window. A tipsy brunette barged in. "Hi! Remember me?" She held a wine cooler. He vaguely recalled the stringy hair, the high-pitched voice. Katie? Taylor? He couldn't remember on a good day, much less when he drowned himself in tequila, poisoned by Delaina Cash.

"I'm happy you don't have company." She giggled and let out a burp. "Oops! Up for an overnight?"

"I'll stumble to bed soon."

"Wanna take me?" She twirled around in her denim skirt, cowboy boots, and tight top.

Hell no, he didn't. "You go to the community college?" They all did, the ones who showed up like this. They got the same runaround.

"Yeah, when I go." She laughed with her big mouth open, looking like a better version of Miss Piggy. "It's hard to make it to class with parties and boys, and the, like, girls' nights and stuff."

"Can't imagine." Jed didn't attempt interest. "How old are you?" "Twenty." "Do you work?"

"Are you kiddin'? I mean, like, when would I go out? I'm doing things I can't in five years. Play, party, you know."

Jed thought of Delaina. She'd never known this freedom. She and this girl, the same age. No comparison in their manner, their looks, their appeal. "Look, Katie. I have a headache." True, tonight. Forlorn, she corrected him. "I'm Kaylor with a K-."

"Excuse me, Kaylor with a K-." Jed forced a sympathetic smile. He saw double. Two Kaylors were worse than one. "I've had a long day."

"Remember the Christmas parade? I flirted my way into your truck then out here. You got a call to the farm." Jed remembered a silly she-cat in heat, and he faked a farm emergency. "I'm here to finish what we started. I'll…"

"Doesn't a girl like you have a boyfriend?"

"I do." She giggled. Jed looked away. She had good breasts like oranges and pretty eyes. But no. Hell no. "Go home to your boyfriend. Whatever it is you think I can do, teach him to do it."

She sighed. "He doesn't have your equipment."

Jed walked out the back door and waited for her to leave through the front to save further embarrassment. He leaned his head against the wall. Two women plus Delaina in one day. None left happy. Neither was he. He scanned the land and listened to the water flow, black-as-sin coffee sprinkled with moonlit sugar. Delaina Cash, as much a part of his identity as Big Sunflower River.

~ ~ ~

"Wake up, Cinderella." Delaina rolled to one side. "Come on," Cabot urged.

"Jed."

Cabot flinched. She yawned and stretched. "Lainey, get up." He shook her.

His impervious tone caused Delaina to raise her head. "What's wrong?"

"Nothing."

"No, it's something…"

"Jed. You said Jed's name."

Delaina's wide eyes widened. "I had a strange dream." A sequence of dreams. Each started with a wedding in a sunny garden park, breeze blowing. She the bride, alone with a faceless groom, except for a pastor. When her groom kissed his bride, the dream became novel. Delaina and Jed kissed passionately everywhere. His truck. The cabin. On the front porch at Cash Way. Standing in dirt at Farm 130. Jed chanted huskily, "Do you want me to get Cabot Hartley? Do you want him to finish this?" Over and over, her groom kissed his bride, Delaina and Jed kissed, and Jed chanted.

Cabot knew what he heard. "When you went to his place yesterday, was it the first time?"

"Yes."

"The last?"

"Uh, yes." If Cabot noticed her hesitation, he ignored it. "You better keep it that way."

"I can't imagine anything I'll need Jed McCrae for, except to sign papers every time I purchase his land." Delaina stood beside the bed, fluffing decorative pillows and straightening them.

"Let's get moving. We have reservations."

She disappeared into the bathroom and got in the shower. Boggled by how much transpired since yesterday's thunderstorm, Delaina decided she'd been overanalyzing. She had a man most women would die for and a night in a mansion with him. Why wait? She used a luxurious towel to dry off and reprimanded herself for supplying an answer. The wrong answer. She dressed, dotted on mascara and pink gloss, put her hair into an airy twist. She glanced in an antique mirror. Hopefully, Cabot would be impressed. As he entered her mind, he entered the room.

"My, my..." His eyes wandered. "I've lost my appetite, for food. You're beautiful when you're dressed up."

"I didn't appeal to you yesterday in my worn-out clothes with a dirty face?"

"I like a woman who dresses, and undresses, well."

Delaina attempted to flirt and poked him. "You don't look bad yourself." Decked in an expensive gray suit, he reminded her of a male model, the wholesome kind strategically placed behind a woman, admiring her beauty from afar like a scene in women's fashion photos and brides' magazines. "Let's go." Cabot cupped her elbow.

~ ~ ~

Holland Sommers flubbed up with Jed. He brought her to Mallard for a purpose, and she switched her allegiance to Cabot after they had sex. She was ethical enough not to share anything she knew about Jed with Cabot and smart enough to know it was time to destroy evidence of her work. Jed never asked her to do anything illegal. Cabot had. Minor things. She left bad things to him and his cronies.

She sipped on sweet iced tea while she flipped through notes scattered on the desk in her apartment. Biographical information for everyone who worked or lived on Cash-McCrae Road, aerial photo maps of land, transcripts of important conversations between herself and Jed, Cabot and Delaina, Jed and Cabot, and others. All of it would go through the paper shredder at the bank Monday morning before anyone got there. Holland eyed her cluttered apartment. Stress from work caused her to forego doing ordinary tasks. She wanted to get away. She missed parties and cocktails and girl talks and pursuing men. A vivacious woman should not sit at home on Saturday night. She freshened up and walked out the door.

~ ~ ~

Eli Smith sat in a corner booth at MacHenry's. He drank a beer and chomped chicken wings. He didn't have any freakin' luck with females, had spent too much time in the sun rakin' dung and pullin' weeds for Tory Cash. It got to his pea for a brain. Thirty-seven years old, never married, he cursed his luck and his life.

Fortunate that he took Cabot Hartley's offer, with farmin' the way it was. A man had to have back-up means. Then and there, Eli promised to dress better and get a newer used truck. He'd go to Jackson next weekend, dressed like a country music legend in a glossy red truck, and he'd come home with a fine woman, if he had to pay her what Cabot Hartley paid him. Forget his excuse-for-a-girlfriend Marigold Shanks. She deserted him tonight, mad as a wet hen. "She ain't worth it," he muttered.

"Hello." Eli looked up to see Holland Sommers directed her greeting at him. "I'm Holland, in case you forgot."

"I ain't forgot," he drawled, touring her body.

"I didn't know. It's been some time since I, uh, needed any... uh, you know."

"Grass for Cabot," Eli finished. "It's been longer than a month of Sundays since I've seen your smile. Have a seat, Miss Holland." Eli and Rhett Smith had been growing containers of marijuana at the secluded farmhouse they rented from Lainey since their parents moved to the guest suite at Cash Way. Cabot Hartley was their best customer. He never bought it himself.

"You're Eli?" Holland guessed. He nodded. Fifty-fifty odds, she guessed correctly. She thought she remembered Eli as more handsome than his brother Rhett. Sun-baked skin, silky brown hair, hazel eyes. "Are you expecting someone?"

"No, ma'am." Eli frowned. "She got pissed as a drenched goat and left."

"Who?" Holland asked, crunching on a celery stick.

"My *ex*-girlfriend, Marigold."

"What happened?"

"She's a goody-goody." He shrugged, not caring. "Started askin' a bunch of questions about a rumor she heard this afternoon. Always breathin' down my neck, tellin' me what to do. Typical female."

"Insecure women are like that."

"Yeah, plus I've been with her 'bout two years too long."

"Oh really? How long had you been together?"

Eli cracked a good ole boy smile. "Two years." Holland laughed and reached for a chicken wing. "I bet you ain't like most of 'em." He sized her up.

"Me? No. I prefer the masculine approach. No silly worries. Good conversation, good food, good sex, and I'm satisfied."

Eli chuckled and flipped his hand through his hair. "Has the food been good?"

"Yes, it's so nice of you to share."

"Has the conversation been good?" Eli leaned across the table.

"Yes, so far." Holland smiled, anticipating the next statement.

"The sex will be good."

Holland's eyes shined. "I'm sure, Eli. I'm sure. Your place or mine?"

"Yours is closer."

"What about Marigold?"

Eli put his arm through Holland's as they crossed the open room. "What about her?"

"I like you. I like your style."

Eli winked. "Honey, you ain't seen nothin' yet."

~ ~ ~

Maybe it was the neighborhood. New Orleans proved captivating at dusk, the street's illicitness hidden in blackness, replaced by scores of pedestrians taking in sights and sounds along overlapped sidewalks. Neon signs enticed customers through claims of fresh gumbo and crawfish, free drinks and strippers. Familiar and not-so-familiar jazz tunes glided through open doorways of cafes and clubs. Cabot suggested they walk to the restaurant. Delaina enjoyed night air and happy spirits. "The view is wonderful," she claimed when they were seated. Her sparkly eyes followed a chugging tugboat in the water below the window.

"Nice, isn't it." Cabot poured wine into his glass.

She smiled shyly. "I'd like a glass."

"You're not legal. I don't want any grief in an important place like this."

She looked away. He sighed, slid his glass toward her. She held it. "I always toast."

"Let me." She looked better with her hair pulled away from her face, Cabot decided. "To a very pretty woman who has given me the immense pleasure of her company." Delaina blushed, lifted the glass, and gulped nervously. Cabot took it away. "I'm falling in love with you." A baby step in his big agenda.

"Oh gosh." She tilted the bottle to pour more into his glass. Cabot cautioned, "Stop. I'll do it. Be discreet." She took two gulps before he took it away again. "How do you feel about me?" he probed. Delaina watched his wineglass like it could grow a mouth and answer. "An appetizer for the miss." A server in black tie appeared. "One for you, Mr. Hartley."

Delaina assumed the interruption capped the question. Cabot resumed his pensive gaze. She took a bite of lobster. "Very nice." Cabot waited patiently. Delaina sucked in breath louder than intended and spoke on the exhale, "I'm no good with words. I was not taught to verbalize feelings. I depend on myself for what I need, but..." She reached deep inside and found a shield, the calm, controlling one. "I'll show you how I feel later tonight."

"Words really aren't necessary, are they? When two people love each other."

"I wouldn't know." Delaina realized he took her comment personally. "I'm sorry," she stuttered. "I, uh, should clarify. I meant, uh, I've never been in love until..." Delaina's head spun. She couldn't focus, couldn't speak. Images of Jed. Jed? ...He spawned infatuation, lust, a diabolical spell, or a drug in his saliva, of which she exchanged plenty, but not love. Her mind and her heart approached the ring, ready to box it out. Her mind fought that she was crazy and unrealistic. Her heart fought that she knew Jed, understood him better than anyone. She twirled her fork in one hand. It banged against her plate. Other patrons looked around to find the noise. Her mind won, knocking her heart out of commission. Eyes squinting, Cabot shook his head negatively. "This is very new to me," Delaina continued, overcome by her need to save Cash Way. "I...I'll...tonight...I do...I care...I, uh...deeply...and I'll...be with you tonight."

Cabot breathed relief, not from her admission but that she had finished the sentence. Maybe she'd be better at making love than communicating it.

Five

Eyes

Holland and Eli had their legs and arms wound through each other like caged snakes, letting their debauchment soak in.

"That was good. Very good, but I want a shower. Care to stay the night?"

Eli stretched. "I'll go." He nipped her shoulder. "Call me."

"I will. Goodbye, Eli." He watched Holland slink to the bathroom.

Fully dressed, he stood at the door of the apartment then turned around, reconsidering her offer to stay the night. Holland's desk papers caught his eye. He walked over for a closer look at an aerial photo map of land tracts. Shocked by what he found, he thoroughly examined the contents and left when he no longer heard running water.

~ ~ ~

"I'd love to give him a squeeze." Two attractive women in their mid-twenties drank margaritas at a round table in a corner at MacHenry's.

"I already have!"

"Nealy, no, you're kiddin'."

"Yeah, I really did. One time. Several weeks ago." Nealy lowered her voice on a sneaky smile. "He's really not the player everyone thinks. He put me off, dealing with his mother's death, very sincere and distracted. We went out a few times before it happened. Even then, truth be known, I pushed myself on him."

"How was it?"

"Look at him. More specifically, his strong hands, soft crystal eyes, broad chest, the crotch of his finely fitting jeans. How do ya think it was?"

Jed McCrae, straddling a stool, talked to Joe Mac Henry, a stout man, fiftyish, with a receding hairline. One of Mallard's most popular citizens, he had the friendly bartender look.

"So, Joe Mac, anything interesting happenin' around here tonight?"

"It depends."

"On what?"

"On whether ya think Holland Sommers is interesting."

"She was," Jed answered.

"Before you banged her?"

"She's a fine woman." Jed never appeared too interested. "Just easy as first grade math."

Joe Mac wiped down the bar. "Uh, Jed, who ain't, for you?" Jed had an answer he didn't share. "Tonight, you're as grumpy as my ole lady on the rag," Joe Mac joked. "Want the regular?"

"No, I want vodka and ice."

"Drownin' your sorrows, huh? Miss Holland's seeing Moll's boy, and you don't like it."

"What?"

Joe Mac poured the drink and raised his eyebrows as he slid it toward him. "Don't you know?"

"No, Joe Mac, but you're gonna tell me, I'm sure."

Gossip garnished the business for Joe Mac Henry, a willing propagandist. "Eli came in with his girlfriend. She got mad and left. Holland came in shortly after and took to him like fish to worm." Joe Mac stopped, smirked and leaned in. "They weren't here ten minutes. Left hangin' on each other." He watched Jed's face. Emotionless, as usual. "I don't know, Jed, but I kinda thought you were courtin' Holland. Seen y'all in here a time or two."

"I guess not."

"Ah, well, no need for you to be exclusive."

"Damn straight." Jed sensed rumblings of a tequila-vodka headache coming on. "As long as they'll put up with my roamin' eye."

"Speaking of roamin' eyes, those gals over there've been watching you since you walked in." Jed finished off his vodka. "What're you gonna do about it?" Joe Mac challenged.

"Go for a threesome?" Jed slugged him on the arm and laughed.

"Hell, go for it." Joe Mac rubbed his forehead. "Only threesome I'll get is my wife snorin' with the dog between us."

"You need to do something about that, Joe Mac."

"Tell me 'bout it."

Jed put money on the counter. "Thanks for the company," he called back as he walked out the door without looking at the two ladies looking at him.

~ ~ ~

Cabot and Delaina returned to the house after eleven o'clock. Walking through the courtyard, Delaina swayed, giggled, and gripped Cabot's arm.

"Remind me not to let you drink from four glasses of my chardonnay again. You went from demure lady to giggling schoolgirl."

Delaina burst out laughing. "It'll work to your advantage." Thank God, she consumed wine at dinner. Cabot looked cuter and sexier. She couldn't think rationally enough to analyze. "I'll be legal soon."

"Twenty-one, I know. I know when your birthday is."

"When?" she flirted.

"July twenty-second."

"Bonk. I'm sorry, Mr. Hartley. The correct answer is May twenty-second." Delaina twirled around then stumbled. "I have a nice consolation prize."

Cabot seemed unamused. "I thought July."

"No, Daddy's is July twenty-second. Hey! Don't look so shocked. You have time to buy me something nice and expensive." She patted him on the back. "Right?"

"Yes, right." Cabot needed to make a call. They had less time than he thought. Tory Cash's will, unbendingly specific, yet unknown to her. For six months, Cabot worked on this plan, believing her birthday to be in July. If Tory Cash died before Lainey turned twenty-five, she had to name a farm manager, an agent to make all financial decisions until her twenty-fifth birthday, unless she was married. If she married *before* age twenty-one and Tory died, her husband became automatic manager. Cabot had to marry her, it's what his parents wanted anyway, and he had to get it done before she turned twenty-one. He'd been courting her like a lovesick fool even though she acted frigid and screwed-up. Her birthday, seven weeks away? His head spun possibilities. He would get Cash Way one way or another.

"Cabot? Cabot?"

"Huh? Look, I have a lot on my mind, the bank and business. You go in. I'll be there in a minute."

Delaina bounced around seductively. "I have to change into something more suitable." Cabot handed her the key and waited until she left. "Christ!" His seemingly small-scale scheme grew larger and larger. He didn't mind marrying Lainey. Marriage, inevitable at some point, would probably cause his father to retire and make him bank president. But all these unexpected details popped up. He dialed the number. It rang once, twice, three, four, five times. Cabot went to his SUV, reached underneath the seat, got weed, and smoked.

As soon as Delaina got inside, she went to the liquor cabinet. She needed something strong to dull her urge to run and pulled down a bottle of vermouth. She sniffed. "Whew! Oh well. Cheers!" She gulped. It tasted terrible and stung her throat. She turned up the bottle. Her head spun. She felt ridiculously giddy. "Okay." She staggered toward the bedroom. "I can do this. To hell with love and romance. I'm gonna make you proud, Daddy."

~ ~ ~

Holland rubbed her eyes and reached for her ringing phone. "What?" The clock on her table read 12:01.

"It's Jed. Let me in."

She'd known Jed since he toddled and shouldn't be afraid. She'd never been on the other side. "What do you want?" "Let me in." "I'll have to punch in the security code." Holland got to her feet and slid on a T-shirt over her lacy panties. She finger-brushed her hair. Holding a pistol, she waited by the door when he tapped on it. She opened with a pressed-on smile.

Jed sensed her anxiousness. "Are you alone?" "Yes." He pushed past her. "You'd have a better chance of hitting me over the head with that than hitting a vital organ."

"You don't have a heart these days. What do you want?" Holland set the pistol on the edge of her desk.

"The truth."

"About what?"

"Everything." Jed slid a pack of cigarettes out of his pocket and lit one. He inhaled deeply. "I don't play, Holland, when it comes to business. You know me. You should've picked up on that important fact."

Holland would've preferred raking coals for the devil. "Oh Jed, we go way back. Lighten up."

"You're Garrick Sommers' daughter. You've been taught to use sex like a handshake to seal the deal. Too bad for you and your old man, I'm not whipped. But Cabot…you gave allegiance to him, didn't you?"

She bit her lower lip. "Yes."

"How long?"

"About a month ago. I haven't told him anything about you. Cabot recognized a sharp tack." Jed blew smoke. She kept on, "He said I'm unusually intuitive. He doesn't know you brought me here to give you an inside track at his bank or that you do business with my father in Atlanta. My work for him isn't about you. It's about other things he's into, and I've been careful. I'm a go-between and he pays me exceptionally well. I haven't shared anything notable with you behind his back, as you've figured out."

"Does Garrick know?" "No." "He will." "Jed, don't. This is between you and me."

"Not anymore. You gave up our deal. Now it's between you and me and Cabot." Jed sat on her sofa. Faint light from the bedroom shone down the hall. "Eli Smith, huh? What deal were you sealin' tonight, Holland?"

Her mouth gaped. "How in the world do you know?"

"We're not in Atlanta, honey. News travels mighty fast. Whatever you do, I'll know. Was it planned?"

Holland closed her eyes. "Yes and no."

"You think Eli knows something. About Cabot."

"Yes."

"What would you do with such information?"

"Depends on what he knows."

"Liar." Jed shot to his feet, the first bolt of lightning in a threatening atmosphere, and thundered, "I'm not playin' around here." He took a breath. "You've got a plan, so does Cabot, and so do I. Can you run with big dogs, Holland? We don't sit around and chew bones. It's teeth and blood." Jed lowered his voice. "You can get out now. I'll double what Cabot's paid you up-to-date for you to leave and go back to Atlanta."

"Any other offers?"

"I'll quadruple what's he's paid you for you to swing to my side and stay and play along with his deal, but you'll have to tell me everything you know and everything he asks you to do, about me or not, and show me files, texts, and transcripts to back it up. I'll know if you're lying. I have sources, like I knew about you and Eli tonight. You swing to my side and screw up again, and I'll tell your father, the very honorable Garrick Sommers, you sold out on me, and I'll pull out of every investment you two get rich on. Hell, I could contact a few men and give you and your father a business reputation that would have them drop out like flies."

"Don't bring my father into this."

"You have until Monday. Three choices: Stay with Cabot and risk the unknown. Go home. Or come clean and deal with me. You know I'm not involved in anything criminal, and I've never asked you to do anything criminal." Jed headed for the door. "Regardless, there's one more thing." He picked up Holland's pistol and twirled it in his hand like a pinwheel. "Is Delaina Cash in danger?"

"Why do you ask? You must have plans for Cash Way."

"Answer me, or I'll give you a fourth, very quick option." He stopped the twirling.

"Whether or not Lain...Delaina is in danger depends on your definition of danger."

"That's what I thought." Jed opened the door. "If I don't hear from you, I'll assume you chose the first option. If you do stay with Cabot and I find out you've divulged our conversations or if Delaina is physically harmed, I'll inform Garrick, and you'll be ATL bound and broke. Sleep tight, Holland. Big dogs get an early start."

~ ~ ~

Cabot sneaked in. He stayed outside longer than a minute. He went to the guest room where he respectfully deposited his luggage when they arrived. Mellow from wine and marijuana, he stripped out of his clothes to his silk boxers. "Lainey?"

"In here! Come on in," she announced like a cheesy game show host calling a new contestant from the audience. Cabot didn't have to be asked twice to come to a drunk bitch's bedroom, especially in this house. "Hi there, you little studdy muffin!" she slurred, clinging to the door frame. Her hair looked like a bird's nest. She'd taken it out of the twist but hadn't bothered to brush it. She wore a knee-length silk gown and feet bare. Cabot expected a full get-up. White lace teddy, garter belts, high heels and thong panties. Maybe she wasn't a virgin. Hell, she could be a dripping whore. "Well, well. What do we have here?"

"Me. Ha! Ha! Ha! Wanting cute, hunky you." Delaina laughed loudly. "Oh, call me Delaina, would you? It's sexy." Cabot knew a hammered drunk when he saw one. Evidently, Delaina Cash took after her father. "What are we waiting for?" he asked. Delaina came to him at the foot of the bed. Their eyes locked. She panicked. "Excuse me, I need a drink...a drink of water. I'll be right back." "I'll get it," Cabot offered. "You need to sit down."

"No! Let me. You stay here." She went into the kitchen. She'd stashed the bottle of vermouth in a desk drawer. She downed another significant swallow. Then another. She reached for her purse on the desktop, retrieved a piece of peppermint, and chewed it to pieces. *I'll make you proud, Daddy. I'll show you, Mother. I can be like you. And I'll show you, Jed McCrae.* Delaina tripped as she turned to the bedroom. She grabbed hold of a table. "You ready, Joe Cabot Hartley Jr.?"

"I'm waiting."

Swinging her arms clumsily, she stalked toward him. "You've waited long enough, sweetie angel pie."

"I agree. Are you worth the wait?"

"Who knows?" She threw her arms out beside her. "I'm a virgin. Congratulations, Mr. Hartley." She had adopted the game show host voice again. "You won the prize. Come on down and claim it."

Cabot plunged toward her. "I plan to. Lain...uh, I mean, Delaina, you're sure?"

"Yep, far as I know. Unless I was seduced in my sleep." Her previous dreams of Jed seeped into her drunk head. "Which is a possibility..." She cackled ungracefully. "Don't tell me you're gonna turn me down."

Cabot squeezed her upper arm and pushed one strap off her shoulder to reveal her breast. "I told you this morning. I love you."

Daggers pierced Delaina's conscience. Her heartbeat pounded through her thin gown. She wanted to bolt out of the house. She dug her heels in the floor for Cash Way. She swallowed the last bits of peppermint. Her tongue stuck in her throat.

Cabot pulled her to him. His erection speared into her stomach. He planted his moist lips on hers, parting them. Delaina put her coveted shield into place, over her heart this time, to keep it from shattering. Sliding her tongue in Cabot's mouth, she became stone. She rubbed her body against his. He hastily slid off her straps. Her gown landed on the floor. Again, he felt disappointed. No lacy panties or racy thongs to play with, naked Lainey Cash trembled like a baby bird fallen from the nest. Only her face stayed resolute. Small muscles in her arms and shoulders, breasts in proportion to her body, enough to fill a wineglass. Her waist curved in daintily. Her hips curved out nicely to graceful legs. "You're quite a woman, Lainey."

Delaina had hoped against hope the alcohol would get her through. She gave up. She would feel every sensation, hear every word, and respond as a woman should. "Prove it."

Cabot guided her toward the bed, to soft white sheets. A single candle flickered on the bedside table. Delaina chose a design on the sherbet orange coverlet and focused on it. The thoughts she fought desperately eased into her mind. A few hours ago, she dreamed of Jed while she slept there. Self-serving? She could do it. Here it is, Delaina screamed silently, I'm taking your advice, Jed McCrae. I'm spending the night with Cabot Hartley, but God knows, I can't do it without thinking about you.

~ ~ ~

Jed woke from a dream, a bad one. He jerked covers back and stood. His head ached from the alcohol he consumed throughout the day. He felt like he'd been poked and prodded and slapped and slugged. From the dream, not the alcohol. Acquainted with that venomous snake of a female for about thirty-six hours and already he kissed her like a sex-starved fool, threatened Holland if she were hurt, and now he dreamt of fighting Cabot Hartley. In a dark bedroom with Delaina sprawled over the bed whispering, "I'm all yours," Cabot and Jed stood on the bed's mattress. They yelled obscenities and bounced back and forth.

Damn it to hell. Inexplicable and crazy. Eyes wide open, body throbbing from a pain-like pulse, Jed fell back across the bed. He reached for his phone, scrolled to her name. *Delaina Cash*. Text her or call her and say what? No need to worry about having the nightmare again. He lost that fight. Surely Delaina snuggled like a bug in a rug, curled beside or beneath Cabot Hartley tonight.

~ ~ ~

Cabot sprawled over Delaina, lying horizontally across the bed. Dropping kisses on her body, he didn't seem to expect any response. Eventually kneeling at her feet, he circled fingers on her ankles and pulled her legs apart. She suppressed the reflex to close her knees together as he climbed up her legs. He slid his finger inside her body. Delaina lurched across the bed. He laid his left arm over her stomach to pin her down. He kissed her mouth. "Relax. I'll go easy." *What a fool*. She hadn't flinched because of a finger. She flinched because of *his* finger. The alcohol closed in. She might vomit. She clenched balls of coverlet in her hands and swallowed recklessly. Cabot, unnoticing, turned away. He pulled a condom out of a nightstand drawer full of condoms. Delaina felt unpleasantly drunk, tremendously dreadful, yet something didn't set right. She couldn't quite connect the dots. She hadn't liked the condom with Boone either; maybe that was it. Cabot held up the package. "You want me to use this?" he asked, unromantic and brusque.

"Doesn't matter." Delaina closed her eyes and prayed. *Dear God, Show me the way. Send me a sign. Help me know what to do.* Instantaneously, Cabot brushed against her, unprotected. Was this her sign? To allow him inside.

This would hurt in a whole host of ways.

Cabot looked at her face carefully. He had planned this act and gloated in his sensitivity. His approach might lead them to a marriage bed soon. She seemed uncertain, or maybe she would be pathetic always. "Do you wanna wait 'til we're married?" A seed of their future, he planted. "I will, if it matters." Her crotch was worth any wait, priceless. It would be fake for him, plenty of gals to fill up his "waiting" time.

Delaina shook her head no; she couldn't comprehend their marriage and wanted this night over fast. She closed her eyes, allowing images of Jed- his coolness, his sexiness, the way he watched her and listened- to pour like rain off the roof on a dry summer's day. He rescued her. She relaxed her legs and waited for the plunge.

Her cell phone rang in the next room. Startled, Cabot leaned back on his knees. Delaina sat up for the second ring. It came. Cabot crawled over her. "We'll let it go to voicemail."

"No! Could be Miss Maydell or Daddy's nurse. Get it."

Cabot shrugged on his shorts. Delaina couldn't have pulled herself off the bed with the help of a tow truck. Her body carried the immeasurable weight of the burden she almost bore. She sighed loudly, thanking God for her reprieve. Momentarily, Cabot returned. His face was grim. Her father was dead. She knew it. He didn't have to say it.

"No!" she screamed and buried her head in the pillow. This wasn't what she wanted. Had she been granted freedom from Cabot Hartley's body in exchange for her father's life? Despair paralyzed her. Cabot covered her in a blanket, put his arms around her, and for a fraction of a second, he felt sorry for her. Then greed kicked him swiftly, and jubilance clutched him permanently. His time had come.

~ ~ ~

Night sky painted a dismal ride to Mallard, no blacker than Delaina's heart. She insisted on returning to Cash Way. She and Cabot didn't mutter ten words from the moment the phone rang until they arrived at the gates. Nor had Delaina shed tears. She climbed in her shell and closed it shut. Cabot didn't know what to say, so he said nothing. Tears trickling down her face, her eyes glistening as a beacon in the darkness, Miss Maydell stood on the porch. "Oh, Lainey honey." She opened her arms. Delaina fell into them and let Miss Maydell bear her weight. Awkwardly, Cabot stood. "Come on in, Mr. Hartley. Would you like a glass of water or a cup of coffee?"

"No. Thank you, ma'am."

"I know you're exhausted. It's four a.m. Tomorrow's gonna be a wallop. Lainey, why don't you let Mr. Hartley take you up to your room? You two need sleep."

"No," Delaina practically yelled. She cut her eyes at Cabot like he was a newly identified serial killer.

"I'll leave."

Delaina rolled her shoulders. "I'm sorry. Stay." They climbed the stairs together. Delaina paused at the top to consider the portrait of herself and her father. About six years old and wearing a white ankle-length dress, she kneeled over a patch of yellow wildflowers, eyeing the one she'd pick, her hand extended, her straight honey hair spilling along her profile. Her father was bent down to her level anticipating the flower as his gift. Beautifully captured, a touching moment between father and daughter. In Delaina's mind, it never existed. Not once in his life had Tory Cash told her that he loved her. Delaina clutched her stomach from painful grief and a sickening hangover. Cabot covered her hand with his and squeezed it. She bristled and continued to her room. She climbed in her sheets wearing T-shirt and jeans. She fell asleep hovering under the covers. Cabot slept on top, fully dressed.

Morning absorbed Delaina in dread so consuming she couldn't lift her head from the pillow. Cabot attempted to coax her, to no avail. Miss Maydell came in and encouraged her to get up and get dressed. "Honey, I know you're hurtin', but folks'll start comin' soon. Come on and make yourself pretty." Despondent, she asked them to leave. As soon as they were gone, she sobbed. Delaina despised self-pity, never allowing it. For having a poor, socially inept whore for a mother or for never having a mother at all. For having a nasty drunk for a father, for having no brothers or sisters to share hell. She had sucked it up, looked for the good in life, thanked God for her material blessings, and moved forward with unshakable courage.

This time she grieved for herself. For the parental love she never had and never would. For innocent childhood and liberating adulthood she never had and never would. For the chance to know a man she couldn't have and never would. As if someone stepped inside and turned off the switch that opened the flood gates, the pity party concluded. She became Delaina Tory Cash again, a lady dressed beyond her years in classy black. The lady everyone knew and expected to greet them this morning at the front door of Cash Way. Her home.

Like a broken record, the scene played over and over. Food trays arrived every few minutes, and flowers were delivered on Sunday by the dozens. People filed in offering identical messages of sympathy and hope, a dozen before the morning's church services and two hundred after. Delaina felt physically and emotionally exhausted. She reached deep into her soul that morning and plucked the proper shield, a somber but appreciative daughter mask pasted securely to her face. Cabot remained near, making small talk with visitors, shaking hands and setting golf dates with the town's prominent men, hugging each prim lady. Delaina, classy in black and he, as slick as a groomed politician and equally charismatic. They made the perfect match, the talk among Mallard gossips. "What a darling pair." "Just what she needs." "Meant for each other." Delaina resorted to the front porch swing by five o'clock. Cabot had disappeared inside with two local accountants. Once again, the monotonous movie replayed. The florist's van barreled down the driveway. Delaina wondered where they could cram another floral arrangement or plant. Nance Mathis, the florist, stepped out. "Hi again, Lainey. A few more." She held tall baskets of peace lilies in each arm as she headed toward the front door.

Delaina stepped in front of her to open the door. "Thanks, Nance."

"Sure, I don't mind, but I have stopped taking orders for the day. I was in Jackson early this morning to get what I'd need for these deliveries. I'm tired."

"I appreciate your many trips out here. The flowers help. They let us know how many people really care," Delaina lied. She doubted a single arrangement out of true sympathy. Mallard knew Tory Cash for what he was, never one to put on niceties for anyone's sake. Flowers, food, and visits came from a sense of obligation or because it gave folks something to do and a chance to get an inside look at a grand historical home. Nance set the plants on each side of the archway to the dining room. "One more in the van. It's enormous. I'll be right back."

Delaina raised her eyebrows watching Nance stagger up the porch steps. "For you specifically, I was told," she said through flower stems. The style and color of the flowers seemed oddly familiar. Realization came to Delaina like she pulled at a box on a high shelf. It gave way and knocked her square in the head. "Jed," she mumbled aloud. The flowers were an exact match to the ones she sent when Jed's mother died three months ago.

Nance watched Delaina with keen interest. "You're right. From Jed...McCrae. You sent something almost identical when Mrs. Kendall died. Considering the bad history between your families, it's good that you make the effort to be cordial. A nice gesture."

Sure, they were cordial. Cordial enough to accommodate each other's lusty tongues. "Yes, a nice gesture." Delaina plunked the big thing down by the front door. When Nance left, she slid the card from the prongs. Jed put no thought into this "nice gesture." He simply asked for whatever Delaina previously ordered, insincerity blatant. She glanced at the envelope. *Delaina,* not in Nance's handwriting but a somewhat neat, masculine scribble. At least the arrogant jerk had gone to the shop himself instead of calling to order. Delaina's hand covered her mouth when she opened the sealed miniature envelope and read words on the card. *You're a good kisser.* No signature.

"Sorry about your father, Delaina." She looked up to find Holland Sommers standing in front of her. Delaina; she had called her Delaina. That came from being around Jed. So, yes, they talked about Delaina. More precisely, about her land. Delaina stuffed the card in her pocket. His compliment disintegrated. Looking as exotic as a Hawaiian orchid, hand-plucked and treated with utmost care, Holland wore a gauzy dress. The stretchy bodice accented her more-than-ample cleavage. Delaina felt a knife pierce her heart, not because Holland was Cabot's personal assistant. Because she was Jed's lover.

"Hello," Delaina said coolly. "Thank you for coming."

"Certainly. I'll go in and speak to the others."

Delaina sank on the swing only to rise again. Jed's "nice gesture" unnerved her. She trotted down the steps onto the grass, perused her home. More pretentious than the Mississippi governor's mansion, too much house and land for one person. She doubted Cabot would agree to live there if they got married. She didn't have to decide anything today. Strolling through the side yard, she heard trailing voices.

"From now on, I'm planning to keep my distance. He's a tough man."

"Regardless, I've got Jed where I want him."

"Don't underestimate his abilities, Cabot."

"It's under control. This isn't the place for this conversation."

Though she couldn't see faces, Delaina knew it was Cabot and Holland talking about Jed.

"I'm leaving," Holland said.

"Follow me into town. I haven't been home yet. Lainey's SUV is still in town at my place. You can help me switch the cars."

Delaina dashed around to the porch, settling herself before they came through the door. Cabot came out first. "Lainey honey, I need to go home. I can come back and stay overnight if you need me."

"No. I'm tired. I think I'll go in and take a shower, go to bed."

"I'm riding into town with Holland. We'll straighten out the car situation."

"Cabot, take your car. I won't be going anywhere. Miss Maydell's car is here anyway."

Cabot kissed Delaina on the forehead. "Okay, I'll get your car out here by morning. Mr. Lowery, the funeral director, will ask you to come view your father tomorrow. I'll go with you."

Delaina dreaded tomorrow. "Can you get away from the office?"

"I'll be here as soon as you need me."

"Thank you, Cabot."

Cabot stroked her hair away from her face. "I want to be here for you."

Delaina retrenched, glad to see Holland come out. "Oh. What amazing flowers," she said, eyeing the exquisite arrangement by the front door. "Exceptionally nice," Cabot added. "Who's it from? State Capitol."

Delaina waited until both looked her in the face. "They're from Jed McCrae."

Holland raised her eyebrows; her chin slid downward. Cabot glanced at the flowers, looked sourly at Delaina. "We don't spare any expense, do we?"

Delaina shrugged. "Good business, don't you know?"

Cabot shook his head in disagreement. "Good business is a donation to a charitable organization. Flowers this extravagant are showmanship or friendship or love." Holland nodded with Cabot's statement.

"I guess I'm as much of a show-off as Jed is." Delaina swung around and opened her gargantuan front door. "I sent the same thing to him when Cass Kendall died in December. Bye, y'all."

Delaina passed through the grand entry foyer and went into the kitchen. Miss Maydell slid a tray of sandwiches into the refrigerator. "Miss Maydell?"

"What do you need, sweetie? You want a bite to eat?"

"No, I'm not hungry, thanks. Visitors have left. Moll and the boys are in the den watchin' a game. I'm stir-crazy. I think I'll change clothes and go for a ride on my four-wheeler before dark." Delaina walked over and hugged Miss Maydell. "I couldn't do this without you."

"I'm always here for you. Be careful and don't be late. You've got another long day ahead."

~ ~ ~

Eli Smith knew Holland saw him when she stepped into the den to offer condolences to him, Rhett, and Moll. Eli had nodded his head then smiled secretively at her. No response and she hadn't acknowledged him when he got up and followed her to the back porch where Cabot stood.

Was she too good for Eli Smith in daylight?

Maybe he needed to remind her of last night. He had discovered disturbing information on her desktop. He could tell her what he saw or tell someone else. "I'm going into town. Looks like we've seen the last guests," Eli told Moll and Rhett. Hartley Pointe Apartments was his destination.

Six

The River

It had been a particularly long Sunday. Jed hadn't slept last night.

He took a swallow of tequila from the bottle. Hard liquor was not a habit or the cigarette hanging from his lips. Inhaling on it, he peered at the river rushing across the rocks. He closed his eyes to savor the freedom of being on his land.

The low rumble of an engine hummed over music coming from his truck. Jed cursed. He didn't want to be bothered by his Uncle Dale or cousins Ben or Bryan and sure as hell not Boone. He took another swig as the rumble drew nearer. Maybe the intruder would meander past his spot. The engine's hum ceased. Someone had stopped for a view of the river farther south on the Cash land.

Jed mumbled along to a song, a Canadian guy reminiscing about the last summer of the 1960s, and quit when he heard the crunch of footsteps on grass behind him. He kept his gaze steady on the river. *Take a hint.*

"That's his best song." Her voice tiptoed over and capered down his spine. Hotter than four hundred hells.

"Uh, huh." Jed watched a bobbing turtle. She stopped short, close enough to touch. Neither moved for several seconds. Delaina broke the silence. "I take it you want to be alone."

"Uh, huh." *With you.*

"Me too. That's why I came to the river. For peace."

"This is McCrae land, isn't it?"

"I parked my four-wheeler at our boat landing, not to be accused of trespassing." She laughed softly. "Good music, so I..."

"Interrupted this romantic evening I'm having with Lucy." Jed hadn't turned to look at her. Delaina seized the option of giving him a thorough perusal. His virile form proved something to behold, any styling of his hair left to Zeus. His upper body filled his white T-shirt. Bleu Cottons graced his butt and legs like they'd been painted on by a talented artist. Delaina tingled. She'd love to paint the lower half of his body, with her tongue. Her gut twisted when his statement sank in. "Lucy?" She glanced around.

Jed motioned to the truck. The red mutt hung over the back. She wagged her tail and barked when Delaina looked in her direction. Delaina responded, "Oh, hey, girl," repressing the urge to go over and give her an affectionate pat. She walked toward the trail to leave instead. "Sorry I interrupted. Thanks for the damned spiteful flowers."

Jed flicked his cigarette over the edge and turned to face her back. "I wasn't tryin' to be..." No sooner had he spoken, he regretted his decision to look at her. Dressed in a thin white sweater. Probably nothing underneath because he could see the outline of her shoulder blades. Hair snatched up in a ponytail, more strands hanging loose than captured. Dark denim Bleu Cotton swept over those fine little hips as she swung them innocently. No cell phone in the back pocket. Red canvas sneakers and no socks. It was over before it started for Jed.

Delaina pivoted slowly. "I didn't know you smoke. What a nasty habit."

"Not a habit." He looked over the edge. "And I just quit."

She smiled. Jed didn't. She faced him now. The sweater, a cardigan haphazardly pulled across her upper body, only the two middle buttons fastened. The curves of her breasts exposed more silhouette than flesh. Her lean, lightly tanned tummy partly hidden, her navel played peek-a-boo for Jed's eyes. His sexuality went fully alert and made him thankful he'd never been one to tuck his shirt.

She was about to leave.

Jed said the first thing he thought of. "You like tequila?" She cocked her head to one side. He held out the bottle. She frowned and took a backward step. A long shot and probably an insult to a lady, but he went for it. "Oysters?" He motioned toward a cooler on his truck.

Delaina smiled delightfully. "Oh, I love 'em!" She'd been eating raw oysters as long as she could remember. Sitting on the back porch at dusk on Sunday nights, she'd crack them open for her father while he drank beer and munched soda crackers. "Not without beer and crackers."

Jed laughed. A real laugh. "I've got you covered."

"Really?" Her eyes lit up like fireflies.

He focused on a pile of logs. "Heck yeah, the only way I'll eat 'em. These aren't on the half shell. In other words, if you want 'em, you'll have to shuck 'em."

Delaina pranced past him and plopped on a tree stump. "I'm takin' that as an invitation to dinner."

"Call it whatever you want. I'm gonna call it a date. Where'd you learn?"

A date? Oh, sweet God. She tried to remember the question. "Uh, one of few things my father taught me besides cussin' and farmin'."

Jed walked to the truck, opened the cooler, and lifted a bowl of cold oysters and beer. "I didn't bring folding chairs."

She patted the stump. "This seems more appropriate for the occasion." For their *date*.

He grinned as he opened a beer and handed it to her. "You forgot something," she taunted, looked to the trail and sighed, like she would leave if he didn't get it right. Jed stepped about, raked his fingers through his hair. He flipped his palms. "What'd I forget?"

If Delaina could've allowed herself the flattery, she would've thought Jed was nervous. *That* made her nervous. "Crackers."

"Yeah, you're right. Crackers." He put his hands in front of his chest as if to freeze her. "Hold on, I've got 'em." Jed went to the truck. He let the tailgate down so Lucy could roam the woods. She leapt eagerly and ran to Delaina, plopping at her feet. Jed pretended not to notice. He reached in the cab to retrieve a brown paper grocery sack then leaned into the back seat and pulled out a bed sheet. Returning, he set the bag down by Delaina and spread the sheet on the ground. He placed the bowl of oysters at her feet. "I only brought one pair of tongs."

"It's okay. We can share," she said, toeing her shoes off. Jed sat on the sheet, watching her pretty feet curl up in the fabric. He could almost feel them, curling in the hairs of his legs. "Are you sure we can share?" he huskily questioned.

"It'll probably cause a big fight and one of us will stomp away pissed off, but I'll try if you will." Delaina tossed her head back. Gold cross earrings dangled while she laughed a laugh that made Jed want to laugh with her, among other things. She straightened and made a serious face. "Hmm...okay, we have to toast. I *always* toast when I drink. Even if it's longneck bottles and oysters with Jed McCrae." She laughed aloud again. Jed couldn't tear his eyes away and held out his bottle. "Cheers," she announced, bumping hers against his. She put the longneck to her lips and took a slow swallow. Jed got on his feet and basically sprinted to his truck to rummage in his toolbox. He needed a moment to wipe the latest image from his nasty mind.

Dusk crept in, a ruby-orange sun splashed against cotton candy clouds. A full moon hung in the distance. Air, turning chilly, brought the scent of river foliage. "I'll use this. You can have the tongs." Jed came forward, screwdriver in hand, as Delaina pulled a box out of his grocery sack. She read the words, "Ultra Thin for him. Ribbed for her." She quit before reading aloud, Large and Lubricated. "These aren't crackers."

Jed didn't have a comeback and, uncharacteristically, groped for an explanation. "Several things in the bag. My week's groceries."

"A twelve-count of these is essential to your week?" She tossed the box in the bag and pulled out another object. "Clear gel stick. High endurance." She waited for his response.

He had one. "It takes a good deodorant to use up so many condoms."

She laughed truly. "Good one. If I keep digging, I'll learn all your secrets."

"Uh, no, I think that's it. Besides crackers and Lucy's bones." He sat on the sheet, close and facing her.

She peeked in. "And chocolate chip cookies?"

"Uh, oh yeah. Chocolate chip cookies." With a boyish grin, Jed rubbed his stubbly chin.

Delaina felt a momentary gust of wind. In her lungs. "Your favorite?"

"Uh, huh."

She let out a giggle.

"What's funny about my affection for chocolate chip cookies?"

"I don't know. Makes you seem nice."

Jed looked into her eyes. "I am nice."

"Not to me."

"Oh, and you're sugar-sweet to me."

Delaina huffed a breath. "Well, no. But at least I tried the other day. With the wrench."

He scoffed. "That was you, when you're nice?"

"Yeah..." She tossed her head; gold crosses jigged. "Sort of. Oh, I don't know. Forget it."

"Wish I could." His steely eyes found hers.

Yearning shot through Delaina's body, Jed's drug again. She ached for a second dose and decided to stick to their merciless teasing. "Do you always keep a sheet in your truck or are you expectin' someone tonight?" She glanced at the paper sack in insinuation.

He shrugged. "You should always keep a sheet in the truck and a pocketful of condoms. Never know when you might get the urge for a quickie." He raised his eyebrows up and down mischievously.

"You're a disgrace. Holland doesn't seem like the outdoorsy, do-it-in-the-dirt type."

"Who said Holland? I'm open to options."

Whew. Had he aimed that *at her*? No, of course not. He said options. Plural. He, as rumors suggested, aimed it at the female population of Planet Earth. Delaina glared disgustingly and stood to leave.

"Come on, little girl. You brought this on yourself. I was kiddin'." Standing, he gripped her wrist. "Delaina." Her name hung in the air. *Oh, he said it again.* She felt light-headed. Her eyes flickered 14K gold. They stood like that for seconds. Delaina pulled away, Lucy at her feet. "How'd you come up with Lucy?"

Jed's eyebrows crunched. "Found her on the roadside as a pup." Delaina clarified, "I mean her name. Why *Lucy*?" Jed answered on a throat-clearing, "She has red hair like Lucille Ball. Used to watch it with my mom." Delaina bottled giggles and repeated, "Lucille Ball?"

Jed's hands came to his waist. He towered over her. "Yeah, from "I Love Lucy." You're way too young to know anything about that, I guess." Bending, he started in a coaxing tone. "Yeah, girl. Found you just in time. The dirt road by the pecan orchards. She had fallen into the ditch between our fields." Delaina nodded her head and swallowed her shock, watching rough-tough Jed McCrae take on over an abandoned mutt. "Lucky for her, I found her before that unexpected sleet storm last February." Jed's words came together to solve a puzzle.

Delaina gasped, squealed, jumped up, bent down and squeezed the dog. She knocked Jed out of the way. "My God! Thank goodness. Oh Jed, thank you." He frowned in confusion then bewilderment as her arms left the dog and came around his neck. She exclaimed, "You rescued her! You rescued my Ariel." Her arms tightened around Jed's neck; her torso plastered to him. His body alerted him in lower regions. "Ariel?" he slurred.

Delaina plunged herself into Lucy. "Yes!" She bounded into explanation. "Dr. Yarborough, our cattle vet, gave her to me as an orphaned only-child puppy. Doc didn't have time to bottle-feed a mutt." She paused on the forbidden word. "Look at this princess!" She scratched behind her ears, puffed her lips, talking baby talk. "She rode the tractor with me. We finished near dark. I opened the door and Ariel..."

"Lucy," Jed clarified, a goading smile on his face.

"No, she's like Ariel the mermaid, my fave princess and the red hair, and Ariel has red..." They looked at each other. They'd almost forgotten who they were. Where they were. Delaina blinked and looked toward the dusky horizon. "Anyway, she bolted. I called her, but Ariel kept runnin'."

"I'd run too, from a name like Ariel."

Delaina's eyes narrowed. "She probably needed to poop. I gave up after the sleet, never dreamed I'd get her back." Delaina watched Lucy go back and forth between them and stay with Jed. He reached for tequila. Delaina's eyes stayed on her dog. "I've never tried tequila. Wouldn't think it goes with oysters. In fact, I don't think it'd go with much of anything." Jed took a swallow, put the bottle on the ground, and stayed at the embankment. Delaina opened the box of bones and crouched level with the dog. "Wow, these are gourmet. You're taken care of." Her voice was thick. "Here, Lucy." The dog took the bone and walked off to enjoy it in private.

Oyster tongs in hand, Delaina sat on the stump. Her arms rested on her thighs. Neither acknowledged the other for a span after Jed sat on the sheet again. River sounds filled the air.

He noticed her buffed, short nails. He'd noticed them before. "I like your nails."

She looked at her hands. "Nail polish, long hair, and social media. Things a real farmer has no time for." She smiled, reached into the bowl, dug an oyster out, and cracked it. She scooped the inside out with her tongue, slurped it, and swallowed. Jed became entranced. *Christ.* He'd never seen a woman crack open an oyster, much less between her legs straddling a stump. Not proper at best, Delaina pulled it off as steamy foreplay, and the little priss didn't know it. What she did to his mind felt awful, while what she did for his cock felt, well...petrifaction came next. Jed hadn't eaten a single oyster. Didn't want to. He wanted to watch. She swallowed three oysters off the shell, *have mercy,* ate four soda crackers and took two sips of beer before he forced a cracker in his mouth to prevent telling her what he wanted to do. He decided limbs dangling from a tree were for him to look at, not the inner square of fabric where the legs of her jeans joined together.

"What's the matter, Jed?" she whispered. "Never seen a gal slurp oysters?"

"The way you're straddling that stump got to me," he admitted, his voice openly thick. Delaina closed her legs, suddenly keenly aware of how slutty she must look. She put the tongs in the bowl.

"Don't stop," Jed commanded like she'd gone cold in the middle of making out.

"I'm full."

"I'm not."

Tingly as red wine, blood trickled through Delaina's heart. Jed can't be trusted, her mind told her. "I'll leave cheap thrills to Holland and your other *options*." She wasn't his type; he made that clear. His intentions couldn't possibly be good. Distantly, she realized he responded. "Did you say something?"

Jed nodded, his eyes glassy diamonds. "Yes, I did."

"Well, repeat it. God knows, it's such a rare thing for you to talk. I'm sorry I wasn't listening."

Jed moved in on her, breathing against her face. "I said I'd rather watch you shell oysters than have sex with Holland Sommers if those are my options."

Delaina flinched on the stump and nearly fell off. He gripped her arm. She couldn't speak with him so close, talking so dirty. Her mouth longed to be filled with his like yesterday. Jed pushed her legs apart and placed the tongs in her hands. "Proceed," he said as he undressed her body with his eyes. "...with caution."

She wanted to strip off his clothes article by article, skim her hands over his great chest, and grip her fingernails into his back. Delaina curled her index finger, beckoning him. "What?" he whispered, sliding his hips between her legs. She cracked an oyster and used her fingertips to part his lips. She scooped out the contents and dropped it into his mouth. Holding her gaze, Jed swallowed. She dropped the tongs and draped her arms over his shoulders. He gripped her sides, his work-roughened hands brushing against the skin of her tiny waist. Neither moved. They savored the sensational silence, calm before the passion-hailing storm. Jed started to speak. A motor's hum interrupted. They turned their heads to search the water. A lone fisherman hunched in a boat rounded the river bend, a dark form on black water. Moonglow spotlighted their faces, yet he made no attempt to acknowledge them. Their identities, their embrace, and a rapid force invisible reached his vessel and foretold their love story future.

Jed and Delaina scrambled apart and sat on the sheet. In seconds, the boat disappeared around a bend. Maybe a ghost. Tory Cash's apparition sent to break apart the last living Cash and the last living McCrae, to cease Jed's tongue as he was about to ask Delaina Cash to spend the night with him on the sheet under the stars. He wanted to sleep there together, something he'd never asked of a woman. Later, deep in the night, he had thought about waking her, maybe, from sleep to make love to him. If it seemed like the right place, the right time.

Neither knew it, but soon enough, one of them would know. Damage done between their rival families couldn't be patched up, couldn't be consummated by a single act, no matter how intimate. Some things were not meant to be.

~ ~ ~

"It's Eli."

Holland cracked the door and answered wearing a silky robe draped over her sumptuous body. "Hi. How'd you get through the gates?"

"A friend. I wanted to surprise you." Eli gazed over her curvaceous frame.

"I'm surprised! Come in. Cabot and I were going over notes regarding a client. He's not coming to work until tomorrow afternoon because of Tory's death, so he needed to brief me."

Eli stuck his head in the door. Cabot sat at Holland's desk. Shirt unbuttoned, he studied a computer. Eli suspected the worst but hid his fear. Certainly, Holland wouldn't answer the door in the middle of hanky-panky with her boss, also *Lainey's boyfriend*. He played it cool. "I won't bother you. What I want can wait."

"For an hour?" Holland held her mouth open, hinging on his response.

"Only an hour." Eli tilted his head and smiled.

"I'll be here." She shut the door.

Cabot breathed down her neck like a fiery dragon. "What the hell did he want?"

"None of your business." Holland sat on her sofa.

"Are you sleeping with him?"

"Sleep would be a stretch, but yes." She twirled her robe sash. "He's got the do-it-in-a-haystack appeal."

"And the bullshit smell." Cabot's arms came down around her neck. "You work for me. Twenty-four hours a day. I overlooked your flirtations with Jed because I thought it might serve my interests. Having a relationship with Eli Smith is not in my best interest or yours."

"If anything, I'm double-sealing the deal."

A smart woman; he'd hear her out. "Go on." Eli had supplied him with the marijuana he needed for Stage Two of his plan. As far as Cabot knew, Holland didn't realize that.

"I really like Eli. More importantly, he's falling all over me. I know you're using him in some capacity. He'll be more loyal to you now."

"Not bad, Holland, but I already had Eli by the balls. I threatened to turn him in for selling pot to college students if he didn't cooperate. You should've checked with me first."

"When I went to bed with Eli, it was because I wanted to. I like him and he likes me. I refuse to end my personal relationship with him right now."

"I'm warning you to keep business out of this. At any rate, I've got a message for Eli. I'll wait here."

"Suit yourself. I have primping to do." Holland disappeared into the bathroom.

~ ~ ~

The halt in their passion gave Jed a moment to regain his composure. Today, Delaina became the largest landowner in Mallard County, his main competitor; nonetheless, he almost jumped in her pants after one hour together. Unbearably attracted to the mini package of dynamite, he wanted to believe it wasn't a game to her. He needed a better feel for her intentions before she left. He would have to keep his distance and chat, not good at either when it came to Delaina Cash.

Delaina hadn't come to her senses. Engrossed in ardent longing for this man, her caution and ability to reason had gone into the river with his cigarette. Determined to stay tonight, she'd think about consequences later. Jed's question brought her out of fantasy. "Huh?" she asked in a daze.

"Good thing I'm not much of a talker. You don't listen." Jed cocked his head and smiled. They were sitting side by side on the sheet. "What were you plannin' to study at Ole Miss?" he repeated.

"I'm sorry. Political science with a business minor."

"First female president?"

"More like USDA." She shrugged. "I withdrew from classes at Mallard Community last week because of farm obligations and Daddy's failing health." She saw Jed's frown. "I don't regret my decision. I... love this land."

"You'll re-enroll in the fall, I hope."

She nodded yes and dropped her head back. Jed watched Delaina's elegant pose then turned to the sky, animals' calls, gurgling water. She smiled wistfully into the air. "No one can imagine how much this place is a part of me."

"I can." Their eyes met in a blend of compassion and mistrust. Moments passed.

Unexpectedly, Delaina laughed. "Jed, a thought popped in my head. I can't help but think of Daddy since we've been here. He did love this river. I wonder why, after your daddy died, my daddy didn't pursue your mama? I mean, it would've solved everything." Into the night, she laughed again.

"My mama was way too good for your daddy." Jed twisted the top off another beer, gave her one. "Our fathers fought with fists and never spoke again when my daddy left Cash Way. I'm positive being raised by Tory Cash wouldn't have solved anything for me."

And that was why they shouldn't be there together. Delaina felt a tad offended. Tory was her father, after all. "He raised *me*," she couldn't stop. Besides, Tory and James Ed had been best friends and bachelors together before things went bad. Jed's father couldn't have been much better than Tory, for Jed's mother when they met. Jed drank a long swallow. Softer, she added, "He had a lot of help from Miss Maydell." Somebody had sort of pissed somebody off or something. Too touchy. Not meant to be. Delaina started to stand up. Nope. Jed would hear her out. "My daddy was...awful and explosive, but he could be okay." Cricket sounds and river noise sang her into a trance. "Anytime it rained, giving him a brief break from the farm, I could count on him to show up, drinkin' of course, but he'd come flyin' down the driveway to pick me up to go for a ride." She remembered, "Rainy Day Lainey, that's what he called me but only when it rained."

"Rainy Day Lainey," Jed repeated and seemed like he tried to be nice.

"Like oysters on Sunday night, it became a thing. We'd ride and he'd complain about farmin' and we'd play loud music. Daddy loved music..." As if she saw her father for the first time, removed from the living, she cleared her throat and blinked tears. "I know songs from every decade. He gave me that." More recollections bubbled upon her allowance. "He dressed to the nines, so he made sure I had the best clothes. We never went anywhere together much, for me to wear good stuff, but I had random things anyway, like BC jeans showing up as package deliveries from him."

Jed hadn't shared his mother's death with anyone or shared his mother with anyone ever. "Same with my mama," he admitted, not looking at her. Each reflected, together but separately. "If I'm honest, she dressed me, to the nines as you put it, 'til she got sick. She'd insist on takin' me shopping." He kind of laughed in a shrug.

She had been watching, listening, and smiled. "Oh well, it was a random thought."

The back of his hand touched her knee. "I'm sorry."

Her face went to his. "You mean, as in sympathy for me that I just realized he's really dead or because you said you wouldn't wanna be raised by him?"

"Both."

"It's okay." Her smile looked brave. "You wouldn't wanna be raised by him, trust me." She shrugged. "I'm not very sad about his death. He wasn't alive by my standards near the end. He suffered."

"Yeah." Jed had a taut voice. "Same with Mama at the end with cancer. Ready for it to be over."

Delaina angled toward him. "Your mama was too good for him. He was plenty good-lookin' but so selfish and uncouth. Your mama, oh so beautiful, like in a not-Mallard way. Obvious she was a debutante, had seen Paris, rode horses, was true Old South money.

Those sunglasses, too. Like a celebrity. Our own personal queen." She smiled brightly. "I'm surprised Daddy didn't try with her."

Jed conceded, "Now that you say it, for all we know, he might've tried." If for no other reason than to seek revenge toward Jed's dead father.

Another bright giggle. "Maybe he couldn't find her!" She spoke to herself. "*Such* an event to see Cass Kendall. Miss Maydell would announce it because, you know, no one ever saw her. 'Cass Kendall went to the mailbox today.' Or, when we were at the grocery store, and it rarely happened, so she'd be like, 'Cass Kendall is buyin' ice cream!'" She really laughed. "Glamorous in my mind, and nice, your mama. Very nice to me always even though we're all supposed to hate each other." She talked into the air, in the trance. "I'd see her when I rode my bike. She'd be walkin' in the mornings. People said she didn't come out, didn't go anywhere anymore after your father died and how perfectly understandable because who can imagine what it must've been like? But it wasn't true that she 'didn't go out' because I saw her. She went to church every Sunday. On our way to First Baptist, we'd see her going in, up the wide front steps of First Methodist, dressed like Jackie O…" Delaina discontinued. With Jed, with Jed beside her, dressed like…the son of American royalty. The memories became vivid and poignant. She could see Jed at seventeen, at twenty, at twenty-five, walking in. She saw Easter. Last Easter, a year ago. Delaina never stopped riding to church with Miss Maydell; after she started driving, Maydell rode with her. Maydell's words, 'Oh my, look at Cass Kendall's Easter frock this year.' A crystal-clear flash. Jed, striking, in blue long-sleeved dress shirt, navy sports coat on his finger, hung over his back. Brilliant sunlight. He wore sunglasses. His mother's hair in a French twist, she wore a mint green suit, a flawless fit. A part of Delaina's world on Sundays, taken for granted, and now, a sparkling treasure. She expanded to bypass the meaning of it all. "My whole life, Ms. Cass walked every morning down Cash-McCrae Road until she got sick." Delaina reminisced. "I was enchanted by Maydell's spottings and your mama's glamour. I'd plan my bike ride to run into her." She made a face, like she comprehended and remembered at once. "I didn't have a mom." A nonchalant motion with her hand. "It was like we were...meeting, especially when I got older and jogged instead of riding. She'd speak and smile. Once, she told me if she rode a bike, she'd want baby blue like mine, not pink like most girls." Delaina laughed. "Last time I saw her, in summer, she said that when she was young, she liked to wear cutoff shorts with a bikini top like me, and I'd grown into a petite beauty. She wore a pair of those sunglasses. She's the *only* person who called me Delaina, not Lainey..." Delaina's story dropped off. Called her Delaina, like Jed did. She became aware of quietness.

Jed stared outward, tears in his eyes. Surprising from Jed McCrae and not, too. Everyone knew his mama adored him. "Oh goodness. Now, I'm sorry." She stood up to leave. "I'm so, so sorry."

Jed reached from his sitting position and pulled on her arm. "You mean, as in sympathy for me that I just realized she's really dead or that you described her perfectly?"

"Both." She sat down. "Must've been amazing having her for a mama. I bet you were everything."

"Yes, and yes." He shrugged. "She played music a lot. Wore good sunglasses and shoes because, growing up, she'd been to Italy several summers. Taught me an appreciation for nice stuff, for traveling other places. You got oysters on Sunday nights, and I got homemade chocolate chip cookies. Her daily walk was to the cemetery, by the way."

"Oh gosh." Delaina blinked tears. "How sad. How *sweet*." Neither said anything. That part of their reminiscing deserved a moment of silence. Delaina motioned to the land. "They ALL gave us this." She had a couple swallows of beer left; so did he. They tapped bottles and drank.

"So." Jed drew out the word. "You think it would've solved everything if you were my half-sister?"

"Huh?" Delaina's face scrunched. "Oh. *Oh.* Right." She elaborated with her hand. "Our age difference. I would've been Tory and *Cass's* daughter in a hypothetical, and you would've been..."

"Your incestuous big brother, I'm afraid." He grinned like the Devil.

"Hmm. I guess it is still incest..." She smiled angelically. "Even when it's mutual consent."

Jed scrubbed his hand over his face. "I think we've figured out why God knew better than to put your daddy with my mama." He felt mutual *desire* surfacing. The song coming from his truck, a little ditty about two American kids growing up in the heartland, did its best to convince them to go all the way. He tried a new topic. "Tory stayed on the river a lot, like you said. Do you fish?" He pointed to the water.

"Yeah, but..." Delaina pointed over her shoulder. "I prefer the creek since Boone..." She paused. Boone's name had slipped out, and Jed knew about their ordeal. Maybe he wouldn't jump on the opportunity to chastise her. "Ever since Boone started taking me there to fish. We were, uhm, fishin'. Lots of fishin'."

Right on time, *Suckin' on a chili dog outside the Tastee-Freez*, from the little ditty. Jed bit the inside of his cheek and stifled a laugh. "From what I hear, my cousin Boone used a rather large worm for bait."

Delaina groaned. "Oh hell, here we go."

"I couldn't resist." Jed reclined on the sheet and looked at the dusky sky. Moonbeams glittered on water, reflecting in Delaina's hair like golden wheat set afire. Her eyes sparkled Caribbean, matched in depth and intensity. She eased down. Lying on their backs, their bodies brushing here and there trapped them in heat. Jed reached over and flicked his fingers through her hair. "Why Boone? Or is he one of many to receive your oral pleasure?" Her face turned inward. Jed gave her an easy smile.

"Would you like to hear my side of the story?"

His fingers played with her hair. "I'm not sure."

Delaina smoothed his shirt front. "Too bad. I wanna spill it. No telling what kind of dirt Boone conjured up about me."

"He didn't say much. You rode by the workshop one day. Boone turned to me real smug-like and said, 'Can you believe that proper little rich bitch licked my dick like a Popsicle a hundred yards from your cabin?'. I wasn't sure I believed Boone, but I didn't forget it. The look on your face when I mentioned him in my truck let me know there was truth to it." Jed untangled his fingers and turned his attention to the moon, studying it like something new.

"He called me a bitch?"

"Pretty sure he did."

"Did you defend me?"

Jed looked puzzled. "Why would I?"

"I guess he left out the part about comin' all over himself moments after it started."

"After *it* started? So, it's true."

Delaina frowned. "I had to do something to make up for leading him on."

Jed smirked and tugged at the waistband of her jeans. "Do you do that for every man you lead on 'cause I'm hard as a brick, darlin', and..."

"It happened the summer I graduated high school." Jed shut up. He saw the look in her eyes. She felt the need to explain. "I didn't have much experience with guys, you know, a virgin. I wasn't sure I wanted to go to college that way."

Jed nodded sharply and cleared his throat to suppress a laugh. As far as entertainment went, he figured this might be the peak of the evening.

"I, uh, sought out Boone. He seemed nice enough, cute enough, the quiet type, like he wouldn't kiss and tell. We spent a month together. I kept findin' every excuse I could to be with him."

"Whoa, he didn't tell me..."

"No. *I mean* to get to know him. I hadn't done it yet, goodness gracious." She laughed. "One night, a week before I left for college, I went for it."

"Sounds like my kind of girl." Jed laughed.

"Shh, I'm not finished." She jabbed his ribs. "I backed out." Delaina giggled at Jed for laughing at her. "Jed, I said no at the last possible moment."

He filled the night with chuckles. "That is ruthless, little girl."

"It's actually not funny! I got myself in a major predicament. All at once, I was hell-bent not to give it up."

Jed shook his head with more laughing, imagining the scene. "Jesus Christ."

"So, I...did exactly...what Boone told you I did. For like twenty seconds and... Never mind." Wheels spun in her head. "Let's say I barely, uh. You know the rest." Jed held his sides from laughter.

"I shouldn't have told you."

"Glad you did. I haven't laughed this hard in ages. No wonder he called you a bitch." Jed reached for her hand and stroked her fingers. "Your story is unbelievable. Coming from you, it makes sense."

"I'm not going to give in or give up once I get an idea in my head. Is that bad?"

"It is for any man who attempts to have a relationship of any kind with you." Facts ripped Jed. What was he doing with Cabot Hartley's girlfriend, Tory Cash's daughter? "Delaina, we better go..."

"I could do this all night."

He winced. A pang of want and need and who knew what else shot through his body. "No." He sat up.

"It's not late." Delaina ran fingers down his shirted back. "Don't go."

"Does anybody know where you are? Where's your phone tonight? Where's loverboy? Did you two get in a fight over interest rates or something? Besides, tomorrow's a long day for you. Your father's..."

"I don't care." Delaina considered telling Jed what she overheard Holland and Cabot saying at Cash Way. Jed considered telling Delaina that Holland was sexually involved with Cabot, along with about twenty others. Neither said either.

"We have no reason to be here together. You're Cabot's girlfriend."

"And you're Holland's lover or whatever."

"I'm nobody's lover." He glanced at her. "Don't put much insurance into promises about being lovers or being faithful, Delaina." As close as he'd get to telling her about Cabot and Holland.

Delaina took it as the old Jed again, arrogant and defensive. "Since when, Jed? Another lesson you learned from your former fiancé Laureth Stevens?"

"No." Jed inhaled. "Okay, she's part of it. In general, those terms are false security. You need to keep your eyes open to what the other person is capable of." Another hint.

"You're doing yourself a disservice to let Laureth change your mind about being faithful to someone." His hint went over her head. "You wanna talk about it? Any of it?"

She focused on the wrong guy being unfaithful. Oh well, to hell with it. "To Lainey Cash? No thanks."

That hurt. Jed didn't trust her. Didn't even like her. Delaina slid over to put distance between them. He turned on his side and faced her, his head propped on his arm. He felt like the insolent jerk every female expected. Stubborn as sin, she wouldn't look. This time, she studied the moon like a brand-new scientific discovery.

Jed went to his truck. Everybody from Tom Petty to Alabama to Post Malone had been singing about pretty girls, bad boys, and breaking up. He scanned through a playlist for something else. Delaina neared; he could feel her before she touched him, then she did. Leaning in behind him, she put her arms around his torso. Her fingers gripped the hem of his T-shirt. Jed rolled his head on his neck. Her sweet hand caressed his abdomen. She worked his shirt over his head and whispered, "I like you better bare-chested."

His stubborn resistance had been standing on the throes of a wet spot on glazed tile for two days. Now, it decided to try to straddle the damn thing and step over it gracefully, fell miserably short and hit the cold floor facedown, leaving Jed alone with a piercing need. He turned. "I have a feelin' I'd like you better bare-chested." Their shared look lacked defenses. "I want you, Delaina."

Her eyes gleamed in anticipation. "For one night we can forget who we are."

"I know who you are. I want you anyway."

"It'd be better if we forget it tomorrow. I'll agree to it if you will."

"Doesn't work that way, little girl."

"Doesn't it? You said so. There's no such thing as security. It's all just..."

"You don't trust me." Jed watched her eyes. She blinked several times. "*You* don't trust *me*," she retaliated.

"See, baby, not a good idea." Jed's breath fell hot against her face. Trapped between the partially opened door and the seat of the truck, their unfulfilled lust stamped its mark on every breath.

Delaina pushed backward and yelled, "Why am I different than Holland? Laureth? Any of them? I'm asking for...a one-night stand!"

"Delaina, you're confused. You're vulnerable and angry. You're lashing out at your father for dying, and you're ten years younger than I am."

"Age has nothing to do with maturity," she snapped.

Jed walked to the embankment. "What about Cabot?"

Delaina watched the moon cast a glow across his body. This, however good it felt, would only compound their problems. They'd never carve through the hatred and distrust they were conditioned to feel. What about Cabot? Delaina couldn't pinpoint what she felt for Jed or why. She held back nothing, wanted to give all. How could she show him how much it meant to be with him tonight? How could she repay him for listening? For taking her out of her life and into herself. An idea came if she could pull it off.

~ ~ ~

"Two hundred dollars?" Eli Smith repeated in astonishment. He and Cabot stood in the parking lot at Hartley Pointe apartment complex.

"Paid every other week as long as you stay quiet."

"All I have to do is keep what I already know to myself?"

"Which is?" Cabot tested.

"You asked me for a crapload of plants."

"You don't tell anyone, including Holland."

"My name won't be linked to any of this?"

"You must withhold what you know forever. If you come forward, I'll produce evidence on you." Cabot's expression was hard.

"In other words, Cabot Hartley and Eli Smith never had this conversation."

"Or any conversation. I've never purchased marijuana from you for business or pleasure. Not once."

"I'm in, but don't ask me to do anything else. I'm not, by nature, a criminal."

Seven

The Dance

"Jed?"

"What?" He watched Lucy trail a creature and disappear in the dark.

"Turn around." He didn't budge. Resistance had regained consciousness, still inexcusably weak.

Delaina walked up and whispered against his ear. "Please turn around."

Tile was a hard surface to land on. Twice. Jed turned into her arms. "What do you want?"

"To thank you."

"For acting like an ass?"

"No, for listening to me. Showin' me a good time. You're right. We can't be together in any capacity. But for me, tonight felt special. I want to believe you're nice, that you're not out to hurt me. So, for now, allow me to believe it."

"You can believe it from now on." Jed rubbed his hands on the arms of her sweater. "But..." He squeezed his eyes shut. "Yesterday you ran off with Cabot. It makes no sense."

"You're right. I'll leave. Let me leave you with something to remember."

Jed moved away from her. "Hell no. No in-between. Leave things like they are. What are you doing?" Delaina had gone to his truck. Bent inside, she hadn't heard his protest. Jed sat on the sheet. He smiled and frowned. No one rambled in his truck.

"Stay right there. Enjoy our peaceful river." Delaina scrambled through menus on the screen, inspected things in the middle console, got a piece of gum. She looked too cute to stop, scrolling his phone like she owned it. "Your Faves playlist…"

"Uh, yeah. Wait, you know my passcode?" Then, wham. 0522, same birthday. Of course, she knew his passcode. That appealed when it should've appalled.

"Our birthdays, *duh*." Scanning through his song list casually, "These are your favorites besides Led?"

It might've been the most personal thing Jed ever let a woman do. "Uh, yeah."

"Do you have a very favorite?"

"Uhm, not really. I like all of 'em depending on my…"

An excited sound interrupted him. "Ooh, my gosh, good one! I'll surprise you." She tiptoed over and leaned down. Her cheek brushed his. "Guess what."

"You want us to dance before you leave. To one of my favorite songs."

Delaina stepped backward, eyes on his. "Let's say every time you play it, you'll remember that Jed McCrae and Delaina Cash, for one fine night, put their families' expectations, the town's speculations, and their individual reputations aside and lived for themselves."

"Sounds too good to be true."

"It is when the song ends."

"Go ahead. But nothing seductive." Jed lowered his eyes in warning. Delaina pranced to the truck, started the song. A 1970s bird band had a story about a hotel in California. She called out, "Me? Seductive? No lace, perfume, or thongs here. Just Lainey, take it or leave it."

Exactly what scared him.

The song came to life or met its death. He'd never hear it again without thinking about her and this. Her arms hugged herself, and she swirled in slow motion, like smoke, like her DNA was made of music. Facing Jed, Delaina slid downward elegantly, closer to the ground, as she reached for his arms and sang. A ribbon of something irreversible funneled upward, a mystic phoenix between them, and turned each of them into something altogether new. *Jed and Delaina* was born. She had a good voice as did he, and they sang while she swirled, while they watched their mouths and their eyes, lost in a moment ever-theirs and ever-untouchable.

She slinked upward to standing with the same fluidity into full dancing. She unbuttoned her sweater, not mapping moves. "I've got you right where I want you." Delaina dropped to the sheet on all fours and crawled forward.

Jed's eyes darted toward her breasts beneath her open sweater. Yep, the size of peaches. A mouthful of perfection. "Right where you want me, huh?"

"Listening to your favorite song, sitting in your favorite spot, watching your fiercest competitor at her most exposed moment, and there's nothing you can do about it."

"Take away all that, you've still got me right where you want me."

Delaina backed up on all fours. "You're right. If I'm with you, you're where I want you." She stood now, swaying her hips to the lazy beat.

"I wanna touch you."

"Where?" she asked, twirling.

"Anywhere." He gazed over her. "Everywhere."

Sparks flew and set flame to Delaina from head to feet. She knew he got caught up in his notorious, carnal need. Who cared? She forgot an hour ago who she was, who he was. She reached deep inside for a shield, any shield. There were none because this was Delaina. Her hips rolled enticingly to the music. The fingers of her left hand pulled open the left edge of her sweater then the right. As unrepentant as Satan, she let it drop to the ground.

Jed relinquished control to her motion, to her singing, to her face against the moonlight, to her emerald eyes shining. And her chest. There had been no bra, of course. He ached to reach out. To store the feel and taste of her in his memory. The beat played on. Delaina peeled Bleu Cotton over her hips, no panties. Freakin'

Jesus. She stepped out and showed no shame, twirling, twisting, swaying, singing. He rubbed his eyes over her like sandpaper. Grinding them into her body, as if they could feel for him. It wasn't enough. He stalked her. She backed against the side of the truck to avoid his caging arms. He pulled the rubber band from her hair. Lustrous gold locks fell across her face and neck. Jed looked only at her eyes, drowning in their gold-through-green allure.

In them, he saw it. Trust. It might stay there a little while longer.

Music faded to nothing. Delaina wore nothing, save small gold crosses. An old rock ballad began; Slash and Axl didn't want any girls crying tonight. Jed backed up and held her gaze. He reached for the sheet. When he came to her, he raised her arms, watched her eyes, and twirled her into white fabric. "Dance with me..." he whispered against her hair. "And I'll never dance with anyone else again."

She'd given him a dance. He'd give her all his.

~ ~ ~

Moll Smith had the timing of a broken watch. He seemed to know how to find trouble without looking for it, in places as inconspicuous as the Cash boat landing. Over his lifetime, he came to believe the rich folks had a penchant for greed, unfaithfulness, and deceit. He had seen a lot of shocking things, and there was a time when he kept a chronicle. He learned his lesson on that and would take the rest of what he knew to his grave. He'd let the Lord deal with the sins of man and woman. He had thought, had hoped, Lainey would be different, with all he and Maydell had done for her. One last glance, one last confirmation, proved she wasn't. In the arms of Mallard's most infamous bachelor and the farm's biggest threat, she wore a sheet. Moll had been there under a minute. He had seen enough. She was rich and she was a Cash which more than explained her stray from the righteous path. Moll Smith prayed she wouldn't pay the price of her sin with her heart...or her life.

~ ~ ~

Jed slid his arms around Delaina's waist and stroked the small of her back. She reached around his neck and tipped her head until her lips brushed the front of his shoulder. Dancing together came to them as smoothly as breathing. For drawn-out time, they swayed. Her breasts brushed his ribs through the thin sheet. He pressed his lips into her hair. "Delaina," he whispered. He felt, instead of heard, her desperate sigh, for it replaced his own. He wanted more and unwrapped her as gracefully as he had wrapped her. The sheet fell away and left her bare. Jed gave way to a humble urge. To surrender. He laid his head on her shoulder. She stroked the back of his thigh through his jeans with one hand. His fingers skimmed across her back down to her bottom; he pulled her exposed curls toward a hard, denim-covered shaft. They settled into the feel of each other and the song. The long ballad carved deep emotions. The heat that escaped from every brushing combination of skin against skin, skin against mouth, and skin against denim cooled into a sense of satisfaction so pleasurable it comforted them more than a sexual act ever could. They weren't left with wishes or regrets or what-ifs or has-beens. The dance was complete, and trust faded with the music.

March wind sliced like jagged ice through Delaina's nude body. Gurgling river water and the noises of animals and bugs grew louder and louder, a prelude to realization. Becoming aware of her nakedness, Delaina chewed on the inside of her cheek like the forbidden fruit. Jed sensed it and turned to give her privacy. She dressed and ran fast as hell, racing without looking back.

"Delaina," he said and repeated louder, "Delaina!"

Running from herself, she kept going. His arm came down, hammer to wood. Tears blurred her vision. "Don't," she warned.

He went ahead, "Your daddy came to see me more than once when you were a senior in high school. I started to say that to you yesterday at my shop before we kissed, when I called him an S.O.B., but you didn't let me finish. Things were getting better between us before Tory's stroke." He touched her arm. "I'm here if you need me." Jed walked to where their date had happened.

Delaina watched him clean up from a thirty-yard distance. He sensed her presence. He wouldn't look her way again. Looking at her got the whole night started in the first place. In minutes, he felt empty and knew she was gone.

Propped against the door of his truck, Jed surveyed the lot. No laughter or food or litter remained. Everything put in its place. He figured he had imagined it, though it seemed so real. Had it really happened? He opened the truck door but couldn't get in for the tiny mess she made.

Yes, it happened.

He had fallen in love with Lainey Cash.

Eight

Mercy

"So, she said, 'Mama, do they all spew like that when they thaw out?'."

Holland howled at Eli's punch line. "Hilarious! You missed your calling, Cowboy. Should've been a stand-up comedian." They were curled in her rumpled sheets. She ran a red fingernail down his cheek. "Still could be. Even though I like you buck naked, we could dress you up. We could do snakeskin boots, a patchwork shirt, Wranglers, a rope belt. Get an RV and travel the South. You, my country boy, telling those nasty-funny jokes. Me watching the shows then keeping you up at night."

"Are you gonna keep me up tonight?"

"You tell me, Cowboy."

"I'd rather show you," he growled and nibbled her neck.

"My pleasure." She stroked his ribs.

"No, mine." He stroked hers.

"Stop."

"What?" Eli grinned a bad grin.

"*That.*" "Oh, that." "Yes, stop it." "I can't." "Okay, then don't."

He pulled her on top of him and watched her erotic display, a woman knowledgeable in satisfying both partners. While he probed deep inside her, one confessed to the other, "I swear we're sparks to the same fire." In the time to come, neither could recall who said it because both felt it. When Eli fell asleep, Holland slipped into the bathroom. She took a shower and discovered she had run out of birth control pills. One night wouldn't hurt. She'd get them refilled first thing in the morning and take two. She returned to bed happy and fell asleep in the arms of Eli Smith.

~ ~ ~

Not a damn drop of liquor in the house and nowhere to get any on Sunday night. Jed slammed the kitchen cabinet. He needed something to dull his senses. To knock him flat of his back, out cold until morning. He lit a cigarette inside for the first time and reclined on the couch. He watched smoke twirl; Delaina twirled, too, naked and singing.

Torture, it was sheer torture.

Had it been her plan to torture him to death then buy his land? Hoping movement would cause images to cease, he stood up and paced. No such luck. He smashed out the cigarette and played music at a blaring volume to drown her soft singing. No such luck. He turned off lights to go to bed. He'd fall asleep shortly. He hadn't slept the night before because of nightmares about fighting with Cabot over her. He felt weary to the bone.

How unrealistic, unreasonable, and unfathomable that he loved Lainey Cash. He climbed stairs to his loft. 12:30 a.m. He had to sleep. Meeting his stepfather Fain at seven in the morning, he had important things to think about and work to do tomorrow. By one a.m., Jed convinced himself Delaina's visit to the river was intentional, a haphazard scheme to overtake the McCrae land. He tossed and turned and smoked.

By two o'clock, he didn't care if she schemed to destroy him. Hell, he'd give her the land if she'd have sex with him in the process. The thought alone aroused him. He took a cold shower. By three a.m., he didn't want to sleep with her; he just wanted sleep. He sat on the edge of his bed, repented his sins, and begged God to give him peace. He reclined motionless on top of the sheets and closed his eyes. Still and quiet. *Tiptoe, tiptoe.* Delaina's dainty feet crept into his head followed by her nude body.

By four a.m., he sat downstairs, television on, and stared alien-like at sports highlights. Delaina's words and actions played in his mind. She asked him for a one-night stand, made no mention of a relationship, and offered no explanation of Cabot Hartley. Jed logically concluded she couldn't possibly feel anything close to what he felt for her.

At five, he lay in his bed. He married Lainey Cash, a female he had kissed for two minutes and never been to bed with. They jointly owned everything from the highway to Big Sunflower River. He laughed his head off at his absurd notion then sulked. He wanted her in bed, in his bed in the loft. To hold her and sleep. He wanted sleep. By six, he was making coffee in the kitchen. He decided, when he finished meeting his stepfather Fain, he'd cross the road he crossed thousands of times, take Delaina to their spot on the river, and tell her that he was sleep-deprived, possibly losing it, but he had feelings for her. He'd offer to expose anything. Where he banked, what he knew about Cabot, his net worth. Proof that he didn't need or want Cash Way. He'd offer to help her get through her father's death and get her farm organized.

Then he might tell her exactly what he felt: Love. The forever kind.

Or he might do what any lovesick fool does: Wait and worry and smoke.

~ ~ ~

Such a restful slumber.

Delaina never felt better; she couldn't worry about the future for luxuriating in the past. She slept nude in her cool sheets, a first. In seconds, she fell asleep dreaming dreams like quality color photographs swishing through her mind, one at a time, each pose and emotion eloquently harnessed. Two people did everything together. Counting dolphins in Pacific tide. Painting a barn at the farm. Standing before the Eiffel Tower in awe. Having sex in a rainy Manhattan park. A legendary love story of a dream. Sleep, a wonderful thing, where a woman could be anything and have everything and feel perfectly guiltless and ladylike in the morning.

~ ~ ~

By seven o'clock, Jed parked in the driveway of his childhood home. Fain Kendall's home. A traditional, two-story, white farmhouse with a front porch, it rose behind a pecan orchard with a driveway up the center. Across the road from the over-elaborately gated, gaudy Cash Way, the McCrae homeplace showed off as sizable and impacting, not brassy and intimidating. Fain walked out pushing his shirt into his trousers and sloshed coffee from a mug across his hand. "Good morning," he commented tersely.

"Mornin'," Jed replied gruffly and propped against the grill of his truck. One booted foot hooked in the front bumper.

Fain's face seemed especially grim. "I don't have good news, but it's not necessarily bad for you."

"What are you talkin' about?"

"We've never been close."

"That's not news." Jed folded his arms across his chest.

"At any rate, you've proven yourself on this farm. You're a man now. Hell, you've acquired a small fortune in fund investments with Garrick Sommers and other real estate deals."

Jed turned his head to the sky and trailed a plane across the clouds. "Get to the point. I have more important things."

"I have four to six weeks to live."

Jed lost his fascination with the sky. He examined Fain's face. Bloodshot eyes, drawn mouth, yellow skin. "What's the diagnosis?"

"Pancreatic cancer."

"What's the plan?"

Fain made a sound then stopped to mentally organize his thoughts. "I got remarried this weekend."

"Fuck you. You're not givin' my land to a money-hungry bitch."

"Watch your mouth, boy." Fain pointed his finger at Jed. "I'm leaving all my cash assets to her."

"And *my* land to me, like my mother and father intended."

"I'll explain."

"Burn in hell."

Fain's lips made a line. "I'm sure I will. I want to try to make things right in death that I could never make right in life."

Jed pushed away from the truck and walked toward the front porch. He sat on the top step and pulled out a cigarette. "You can forget making anything right with me."

Fain stood at the bottom. They watched the orchard. Morning sun spread cheerfulness across the landscape, a contrast to the claustrophobic blackness hanging over them. "Do you smoke as a habit?"

"The only thing I got from growin' up with you. Thanks." Jed exhaled. "I don't smoke much. Why do you care?"

"I don't. It's your life. I wish now I hadn't smoked so much. Maybe I would've lived longer." He sighed. "You are the rightful owner to your father's land. He owned about a couple thousand acres when he died."

"I know the numbers, Fain."

"I held on to his land these years with the labor of Dale Barlow and his sons and expanded. They've worked hard, Dale, Ben, Bryan, Boone. For over twenty years, I did the figuring, and Dale did the labor. We showed you the way to do honest business. There was a time you wanted no part."

"I wanted to get away from Mallard. Away from you."

"I understand, but I don't plan to hand you everything."

"I've earned it." Jed took a bitter drag. "Twice."

"Do you love Delaina Cash?" Jed wasn't sure he heard correctly, thinking his jumbled thoughts from last night took over again. He looked at Fain like he'd grown horns. "You heard me correctly, Jed." Jed looked across the driveway toward her pretentious plantation.

"I'm taking your silence as a yes. Brace yourself. What I'm about to say isn't easy to stomach."

Fain unveiled a harrowing story from the past. If Jed McCrae had guessed once for every year of his life, he would've guessed thirty times wrong. By the time Fain finished, Jed stormed across the yard and yelled obscenities he was certain could be heard by consoling visitors at Cash Way. Finally, he sat on the porch steps. Implications began to sink in. "You gutless asshole. My mother deserved better. I deserve better. Delaina deserves…"

"That's why I hung on to this farm."

"You've done none of us any favors."

"There's more."

"No, there's not more. I'm going to consult with my attorney in Houston. I'll fight you on this." Jed stood up and jammed his hands in Fain's chest. "You might as well call the fuckin' funeral home and tell 'em not to count on you. You'll be unavailable to die 'til I'm done with your sorry self."

"Jed, my will's been sealed and delivered, incontestable until I'm dead. If I choose to change it, changes wouldn't be in your best interest. Furthermore, and this is a threat: I expect you to carry on like nothing's different until I'm gone. I don't care what you do later. But if you scheme against me, if you tell anyone what I've told you, I'll cut you out completely while I'm alive. More importantly, do not approach Delaina about this."

"Why would you want to hurt Delaina?"

"I absolutely don't. That's why I do not want this information to be common knowledge until I'm dead first. I've wondered how to go about it for years. I was boating on the river last night when I saw you and Delaina deadlocked in a passionate position. Looked unmistakably loving. With your family history...clearly the makings for a lifetime. I'm a dying man, Jed. Gives me perspective, even premonitions."

"You saw me hug her or something." Jed flicked his hand. He would not give Fain any leverage; he wasn't going to run his life this time, with the land, and he wasn't going to ruin it with Delaina. "Big deal."

Fain gave him a stern look. "Don't deny it. You two chose to be together, alone, secretly, with music and probably dancing and whatever else you did, on the night of Tory Cash's death. What I saw is the future of Cash-McCrae Road. What's happening between you is what this goddamn place has needed for forty years. When I got home, I knew how I wanted to proceed with my will. It's obvious you're in love with her from your actions this morning, too. I don't care how far your relationship goes when I'm gone. Hold your dick until then."

"What you just told me knocked our relationship off its ass anyway."

Fain shook his head. "Maybe not. I'll be dead in a month. If you're around her before then, you'll tell her everything because you care about her. That's *why* if anything happens between you while I'm alive, I've instructed my attorney to deliver a letter to Delaina telling her that *you already knew everything to be revealed in my will*. At any point I become suspicious, she'll receive it. I hated Tory Cash and his dirty ways. I'll meet him in hell soon enough for revenge. In the meantime, I have no qualms. Don't do anything to change my mind, and do not tell her what you know. I could sell everything to Cabot Hartley, no need hiding it. Remember, my cash goes to my wife, so I don't think you want me to sell. Play along with me here, Jed, and you'll get your fair share." Fain paused. "I'll be out-of-town quite a lot. I've got eyes in the back of my head. Do I make myself clear?"

"Yes, sir." Jed walked to the truck. He turned to look at pale, shaking Fain Kendall holding on to the banister.

"I'm trying to right my wrongs, Jed."

"Never." Jed cranked the engine and spoke through the window. "If I don't come back here to kill you first, I'll see you in hell, you bastard." He sped off in a funnel of dust across the yard.

~ ~ ~

"Get up, sleepyhead." Eli nudged Holland.

"I'm not a morning person."

"Too bad. The bank expects its people in the morning. You're due there in twenty-two minutes."

"Twenty-two minutes? It takes fifteen minutes to do my eye makeup!" Holland sailed out of bed. "Eli! Why didn't you wake me sooner?"

"I was sleepin'. Hell, you rode the cowboy instead of the bull last night."

Holland scrambled around and came out in ten minutes, rough around the edges for her, finer than other women. "I enjoyed last night. I'll see you later. Bye." She rushed out then knocked. He opened the door. She spoke meekly. "I forgot my keys."

"And this." Eli kissed her.

She smiled a happy smile. "I like you." She sprinted across the sidewalk to her car while Eli watched. All the way to the gates and beyond, till he could no longer see the blur of her yellow car.

~ ~ ~

Delaina woke to the welcoming scent of baked bread, misleading, giving the impression that family would gather at the dining table for a hearty breakfast. Kissing good morning, discussing the day's plans, then bidding fond farewells. A scene never played in this house. Always Delaina, no one else.

Today she felt no different, like yesterday morning, smothered in a thick cloth and unable to lift her head from the pillow. Tory Cash had been to see Jed more than once before his stroke. Baffling. She searched her mind to remember her father's last spoken words to her. Were they words of wisdom? Discipline? Hope? Anger? Delaina couldn't recall. However, she could remember he had not accompanied her to Old Miss when she left. Neither had Delaina seen him the night before. Next time she did see him, he was in the Jackson hospital in a critical care unit, unable to express his thoughts from then on. Whatever he said the last time they spoke seemed inconsequential at the time. Today it seemed monumental. For the rest of her life, she wouldn't remember her father's last spoken words to her or any words from her mother's mouth.

She had slept soundly enveloped in passionate dreams. The last one hailed as the best. The bride and groom stood in that splendid garden. Her dress defined magnificence. The groom was better. She couldn't remember his face, but she felt his love holding her tenderly.

Time to put on her mask, the somber-but-appreciative daughter. Perhaps she'd only dreamt the episode at the river with Jed. It seemed surreal. An enigma of conversations and caresses and smiles and stares bundled together into one word: Impossible.

Nine

Solemnity

Robotic and largely unemotional, Delaina got through the day. She dressed, a modern black pantsuit recently purchased to make a speech in a college class, her hair slicked into a low bun; she ate breakfast; she greeted visitors. Cabot called and offered to take her to the funeral home to pick out her father's casket; Maydell and Moll also offered. She declined on Cabot, took Maydell and Moll. Delaina parked on the street. She stepped out and walked ahead of the Smiths. Rural, meager people, they were always well-meaning but not worldly, not professional, and as much as she loved them, of little wherewithal today. The white wooden door loomed. She smiled and did what she had to do. "Y'all can wait in the foyer." She stepped in, overtaken by a sterile death smell. The funeral director greeted her with utmost respect and led her to a cold room, casket after casket after casket on the floor and suspended on the walls. Tops open, beds empty. Delaina felt alone and forty, not twenty. "Uhm." Tears were close. She couldn't see Moll and Maydell in the foyer from inside the casket room. The funeral director, accustomed to the space and sundry emotions of death, kept walking. Delaina squeezed her eyes shut and played eeny-meeny-miny-moe. "That one," she blurted. Her finger selected a casket, gunpowder gray metal bedded in pale blue silk.

"Are you certain?" the funeral director asked pleasantly. "I haven't told you details of materials, interiors, prices..." "Uhm, positive." Delaina smiled a fleeting smile and backed up. The funeral director told her she wasn't finished; she needed to bring a suit for her father to be buried in, select a floral blanket at the florist, fill out obituary paperwork, and gather pictures for the video tribute. Her world caved in.

On the ride home, she asked Maydell to please call the florist and give suggestions. Maydell spent hours in the rose garden and flower beds of Cash Way; she would come up with something. She asked Moll to write whatever he could remember about Tory's life, names of family, dates, titles, awards, for the obituary. She assured him that 'anything he came up with would be fine.' At home, she got a box of pictures from a shelf in Tory's study. She didn't look at them. There weren't many. There'd been no mother to do sentimental stuff. She climbed the stairs, went in Tory's room for the first time since his stroke. It smelled of dusting polish. She selected his burial suit, a navy wool with a crisp white shirt and devout Republican's red-striped tie. She greeted more visitors. Cabot showed up, and she hurried him away, asking him to take the suit, obituary notes, and pictures to the funeral home; she greeted more visitors; she ate a late lunch. After that, she greeted more visitors. It seemed like everyone who lived in Mallard and several neighboring counties had shown up. It took something out of her to continue being forty, not twenty.

"Lainey?" Delaina sat at the table and picked at chocolate pie on a dessert plate. Maydell appeared. "Funeral home called, honey. Your father is ready, and the video is done. Mr. Lowery said for you to come give your approval and say your final farewell before they open the parlor to visitors."

"I've decided not to see him." She could not go into that freezing, frightful funeral home again, alone. Her strength, as commendable as it had been, was gone. "I said my goodbyes already."

Miss Maydell put her hand on Delaina's shoulder. "I'm afraid you'll live to regret it. When my ma died, I didn't wanna go neither.

Moll talked me into it, claimed it brings a comfort to the livin' to see loved ones at peace. Don't worry about nothin' out here. Moll and the boys have left to get the most pressin' farm work done, and I'll stay and greet folks. Eat you a bite of pie and go on into town. Cabot said he'd meet you if you need him."

Delaina rose. "I'll go." She walked through an empty house, except for two distant Cash cousins, older ladies who'd come to stay until after the funeral. She reached the opulent foyer. They sipped tea in the formal living room. "Sweetheart, was that the funeral director who called?" "Yes, ma'am." Delaina pressed on a smile.

"Oh, bless you." Cousin Matilda Long from Jackson, a virtual stranger, hobbled over gripping her cane. "We'll go, dear."

"No, ma'am. Thank you. Everyone can go later."

"She needs this time to herself, Matilda," Nellie Coleberry, Matilda's sister from Montgomery, said. Delaina swallowed words like a horse's pill. No, she didn't need time to herself. Twenty years, long enough. Tears splashed down her face as she scurried out of their sight to the front door. She gripped the Waterford crystal knob like a lifeline. She bowed her head and prayed.

God had answered once before. She asked for someone to love, for someone to love her in return. A brother or sister. A true friend. A husband. A child. A mother.

She opened the door.

Jed stood there. His hand extended toward the door and dropped to her cheek like an anchor when he looked into her tear-flooded eyes.

"Delaina." Her name rolled like soft waves of the sea at low tide caressing the sand with subtle power. Serenity passed through Delaina with matching delicate grace.

He wore a black shirt, belt, and loafers with his hair brushed, a brown-onyx mane. Stylish gray pants matched clouded gray eyes. Reflexively, he reached for her and pulled her to his body. Heat from his touch warmed her crushed soul. She squeezed her eyes shut to drain remaining tears. He ran his hand down her back and looked into her eyes. "Jed," she said, voice tinged with relief. He let go and reached around behind her to shut the front door. They stood on the porch.

"Difficult day," he said and forced casual remote interest. Delaina shrugged, not one for sympathy. Jed picked up the pace. "I came to find Moll." It was, at least, a half-truth. "I called him, no answer, looked around the farm, decided he must be here. I won't bother you with this."

"What is it?" She couldn't look at him after last night. She didn't know whether to be embarrassed or proud.

"Farm 130. We need to prep the unit. May have to use water to get the seed up, you know." He skimmed the steps. "It can wait if it must."

"Let's go ahead. Can your crew do it?" Delaina sighed. She never depended on anyone to do her work, especially Jed McCrae. "I hate to ask this favor of you."

"Why?" he broke in too anxiously and cursed himself for it.

"I'll reimburse you for whatever."

Jed turned to face her, to tell her it was the least he could do at a time like this, and immediately turned back around. He had complete lack of control in her presence. That must have been her plan. The devious little spite. He'd never look at her again and see clothes. Only bare-naked Delaina swaying in the dark.

"You just missed Moll," she said absently. "They're tryin' to work between spurts of visitors."

He started for the truck, bound and determined to leave fast. What Fain Kendall told him put a hole between him and Delaina the size of the Grand Canyon. He couldn't tell her what he now knew or that he loved her, and his tongue set on doing both. He wouldn't. He'd stay the hell away.

"Jed?" He didn't turn. "No need for the formalities with your Uncle Dale and Moll regarding Farm 130. I'm willing to work with you personally."

"I think it'd be better if Dale and Moll..."

She crept close, too close, behind him. "Why? It's inconvenient. All their checking with us."

"Whatever you think." He could not resist the possibility of seeing her. Delaina jingled her car keys because she was with Jed and because of where she was going. Tears came. "Let me get out of your way." He made up his mind to turn around and tell her goodbye face-to-face like a man. Never mind he'd turned lovesick, keeling over a woman he kissed one afternoon. "See ya later. Delaina?" She wiped her eyes at the corners. Oh God, she hated to let anyone see her cry. She stamped her foot. "It's okay to cry. This is tough," Jed offered. "Has something in particular upset you?"

She sniffed. "I'm on my way to..." She choked up. "I promise I haven't cried today 'til the funeral home called."

"You're going alone."

She leaned against her SUV and looked into his eyes. This female did things to him that weren't textbook, couldn't be documented or explained logically. "Yeah. Who else is there?" She said it without bitterness or self-pity.

"Cabot," Jed suggested and wished he hadn't. It sounded spiteful and questioning.

Delaina sighed. "I don't wanna bother him at work. Besides, it's awkward. His family's perfect, and mine..."

"I went alone."

Delaina looked up when the words registered. His mama's death in December. "I guess you did."

"I'll take you." Any hope of keeping his distance faded in the face of someone so hurt and lonely and lovely.

She declined stubbornly, "No, if you did this, I can."

"It's not a competition, Delaina. To see which one of us is dealt more trials and still comes out fighting."

"Since when did we stop competing?" Silence. "Take me, Jed. I need someone. Might as well be you. You already know I can be vulnerable." Delaina walked toward the passenger's side of his truck. "What a strategy. My daddy would die if he weren't dead."

Jed climbed into the truck and muttered, "Whatever you're doing, it's working."

~ ~ ~

Holland had a lot of decisions to make. Today, Monday, the deadline. At least Jed offered options. She knew which one she should choose, but what about Eli? She really liked him, not ready to leave town. Undoubtedly, Eli was ten floors high with no elevator and Cabot Hartley ready to push him over the edge. If she didn't stay, how could she help? That left her with two choices. Cabot or Jed. One choice, given her objective. She hoped she had the guts and brains and heart to handle it.

~ ~ ~

The man standing beside Fain Kendall struggled to contain his elation. Milking two cows with one hand! Unbelievable his luck with Lainey Cash as the object of his attention.

"I want updates daily." Fain bit on his lip. "I don't want either Jed or Delaina suspicious or harmed. This is not to be revealed to anyone."

"You'll pay me every day 'til you die?" Fain nodded. "You've got yourself a deal. Go on to New Orleans. Life's too short to hang around this hellhole."

Fain responded, "There will be a check in your mail every Monday."

"Thank you, Mr. Fain. I've always liked you. We'll miss you around this place."

~ ~ ~

"What will people think, I mean, if anyone sees us together?" Delaina's question interrupted Jed's thoughts. Pertained to both cases, their trip to the funeral home and the fact that he loved her. His answer pertained to both, too. "I don't care what people think, but I'll do what makes you happy."

"Then go north of town past the railroad tracks."

"The private parking lot around back reserved for funeral services?"

"Yeah, let's avoid anyone seeing us together. This was surely a mistake. After today I'll get my act together and leave you alone except matters of business."

Exactly what he thought she'd say. On both subjects.

Delaina's mind drifted to her father, the last time she'd see him. Jed's mind drifted to last night. This was the last time Delaina would see him privately, not related to business.

"Harder than I thought," she said, wishing for one last word, one last look, from her father.

"I know," Jed answered, wishing for one last dance or laugh or kiss.

"So many things I think about now that I didn't think about before."

"I know." Jed's eyes stung from lack of sleep.

"Things I should've asked. Things I should've said. Things I should've done."

"I know." Fain's declaration put an end to all those for Jed with her.

Delaina patted his leg. "I guess you do know."

Yes, he knew. He knew things he'd never known.

"I'm sorry, Jed. I'm caught up in myself. This can't be easy for you three months after your mama's death. I tend to forget you can be hurt or sad." Her lips curled up a little. "Because you're so strong and silent and...unfeeling."

Unfeeling? Jed gripped the steering wheel and parked. "Go on in."

Delaina had to brace herself. Jed watched her face. *Unfeeling?* Throughout the day, he analyzed his stepfather's words to come up with a favorite solution: Tell Delaina all of it fast. Today, or it was useless. Now his worst suspicion got confirmed. She felt no more than lust. With Tory Cash's death, the timing for telling her what he knew would be terrible, even if they loved each other and trusted one another. Delaina didn't think Jed was *capable* of feelings. He could leave her alone, what she wanted, and spare her further pain. But the provisions in Fain's will...he'd have to figure out how to get his land. Or get over it. And get over her. Delaina had been in his mind for about seventy-six hours. No problem. Officially history. Gone. Forgotten. He existed without her for thirty years. What was seventy-six hours?

He recalled a time and a female ranked at the top. Her name was Lola. His senior graduation trip to Disney World. They met at a concession stand; a girl dressed like Minnie Mouse served their cokes. Jed bought Lola's- a hot-looking girl, beyond her eighteen years. Hair like Marilyn Monroe's and honeydew boobs to match. They rode one roller coaster, laughing. Afterward, she pushed him into a picture booth. They had quick, hot sex in clothes against a life-size statue of Snow White. He struggled to remember how she felt, how their time felt. All at once, Delaina twirled around them, naked and shameless. He swatted at her like a fly in his face. Unshakable, she blocked his view of fine Lola until Jed and Delaina danced alone on a riverbank. "Jed? *Jed.* My goodness, you're deep in thought. I'm sorry I've brought painful memories of your mother's death to the surface."

"My mother? Yes, my mother."

Delaina reached for the door handle. The camisole under her blazer drooped to reveal the cup of her bra. Plain black satin, one of those semi-across-the-boob kinds, no seams or lace. Beautiful.

He read her mind. "You want me to come. You're too stubborn to ask." She nodded, watching sunlight draw silhouettes across his face. He got out to meet her. He scanned the fenced back parking lot, no one anywhere. He wrapped his fingers around her arm. She shuddered. He felt good. It felt right. They slipped in the service entrance to the chapel. Jed led her to an opening at the parlor rooms. "I'll go to the office and tell them I'm here," Delaina whispered. Jed tucked himself in a corner. She returned in seconds. "Daddy's in the room on the left. I asked for privacy."

"Same room as Mama. Come through here." Jed guided her toward a door, to the freezing cold, dimly lit room. The casket glowed like a silver locket against black velvet on the far wall. The small distance from the doorway seemed like an endless trek. Delaina didn't go forward. Christian piano hymns played in synchrony with a flashing video on the wall TV perpendicular to the casket. "I knew I didn't want to do this."

Jed let go of her arm. "I'll wait in the chapel." Lord knows, he needed to be praying and repenting.

She shook her head no in childlike fear. "Come with me."

"You can do it. He might sit up and choke me if I go closer." Delaina smiled shakily. Jed patted her. "Go on. You'll be glad you did."

"Please wait here." She took each step on a tightrope high above concrete and gasped when her father's body came into her realm. "Oh God." She clutched her waist. Jed turned from the sight of her agony. He couldn't stomach another episode of emotional bonding with Lainey Cash. To his dismay, his ears worked properly.

He hadn't predicted hearing, without seeing, might damned well be worse. The sobs, her gentle sobs. Her words, broken whispers. "Daddy. I'm sorry."

Delaina stared at the ghostly image. None of the usual ruby color in his lips, no trademark ruddiness in his cheeks, instead cake-like orange makeup, eyebrows scrunched in a grimace. "Whatever I did, I'm so sorry." Her hand went to his. That hand. Rough and wrinkled from merciless living. It patted the top of her head in approval and rebuke. It slapped her mother's face one too many times. Those fingers. Stubby and relentless. They gripped a shot glass more often than a dollar bill. They latched with hers and led her to the big glass doors of the elementary school, led her to the dance floor for her first-ever dance at a wedding, pointed in her face as he called her mother a trashy whore. "How Great Thou Art" flowed from video speakers. She felt so cold. She glanced sidelong to a flash on the screen. She and Tory stood together on the riverbank. About twelve years old, she held a fish. Delaina gulped and looked to the opposite wall. The elegant arrangement from Jed had been placed center stage on a pedestal surrounded by smaller plants and arrangements. "I will make you proud, Daddy. I swear I will. Whatever it takes. I promise." More soft sniffing.

Jed couldn't stand there any longer. Her words squeezed. He walked over and rested his hand on her shoulder. "Your father was proud of you. Men...most men are...unable to...they are...*unfeeling*. It doesn't mean they, that he...didn't love you."

She nodded, whispered, "You're right," looking at nothing specific in the casket. Light tears rolled on Delaina's cheeks. "Jed..." Under her breath, glancing at him, "I don't think he went to heaven." She looked up susceptibly. "Did he?"

Hell no, probably not, if such a place existed. Jed stared at the female he loved, wearing an admirable outfit and hairstyle today. Neither added a day to her twenty years, at that moment, depending on him for a proper reply. "Delaina, uh..." Her simple gold cross earrings swayed, eager to hear what he could conjure. Tick. Tock. Tick. Tock. His heart hurt for her. Such a great need for peace in those pretty, pure eyes. "He'll be in your heaven if that's what you want when you get there." True love created answers, apparently.

She smiled, sniffing, satisfied. "Sweet. True. Thank you." She looked at nothing specific in the casket again. "Okay, bye, Daddy." She kissed his cheek. It smelled like rubbing alcohol and felt unforgiving. She gagged, turned, and rushed out. She wouldn't let Jed see silly tears again.

Jed drove across town. Right past Mallard First Financial Bank. Mindfully, he cursed Cabot Hartley for being a pathetic excuse of a man. Miles down the highway, Delaina spoke. "Jed, I owe you for this. What do you want? How about an acre of Farm 130?" Some characteristic cheer had returned to her voice.

"No, I owed you."

"Oh? For what?" Delaina watched him, stumped.

"For last night, Delaina."

~ ~ ~

"...You're certain you have no questions and you understand completely," Cabot Hartley confirmed.

"Certain," his accomplice answered.

"Good. Start tonight as planned." Cabot disappeared from their meeting place first. He decided to drive out to Cash Way and surprise Lainey by arriving early. He would offer to escort her to the funeral home, one more way to get into her heart. The doting boyfriend. He had mastered that act. Maybe he would be a doting husband. Nah. What did it matter once he was her husband?

~ ~ ~

Jed kept his eyes on the highway, revealing nothing.

Delaina tingled, thinking about her dancing act. Jed had touched her, all of her, with his eyes. He halted at Cash Way's gates. "You're not exactly wearing walkin' shoes, but I'm not going up to your house again. Like you said, we...don't belong together." Delaina's words, for sure. They sounded a lot different coming out of his mouth. "I'll take care of irrigation. We'll settle later. By the way, I sent my crew to clean up the cemetery."

The family cemetery. She had not given thought to preparations. How considerate. "Oh gosh, thank you. I don't know what to say." "No problem." His distancing tone, blank expression, stormy eyes. Delaina didn't understand the change. She wanted, at least, eye contact. None. She got out and started walking the lane toward home.

Cabot Hartley turned onto Cash-McCrae Road. Out here smelled like money. Really, it smelled like cow patties and pesticides and diesel fuel and dirt *and* money. He thought his heart would explode. Who wouldn't lie, steal, blackmail? Millions of crisp American dollars. Who could fathom the infinite interest or commerce for Mallard County? He would be the king who saved the struggling farm town from becoming a ghost of one. Cash Way Casino, gambling on the riverbank. So much better than the current purpose.

What in the hell? Surely his mind incorrectly identified what his eyes saw. Jed McCrae's truck, perpendicular in front of Cash Way. Cabot pulled over, cut the engine, and got out. To stop was obligatory.

Jed stepped out. Cabot took notice of his clothes. "Not exactly dressed for plowing, are you?" Cabot flashed a president's grin and extended his right hand. Jed shook. If Delaina noticed their meeting, she chose to ignore it as she continued homeward. "So, partner, how're things?"

"Satisfactory," Jed said. "Everything swell with your boats, drugs, and whores?"

Cabot gauged his answer; he and Jed bluffed each other more than once. The boat deal had been Cabot's first attempt to tangle Jed into something illegal. Cabot, involved although no evidence of him in the operation on the Gulf Coast, sold Jed on the idea; they had been in legal, ethical, money-making deals. Jed figured out, before Cabot could nail him, the boats carted more than seafood. Unknown to Cabot, that's when Jed summoned Holland Sommers. To find out why Cabot wanted him jailed or dead. She applied for a teller's job opening at the bank and got it. No prior documentation linked Jed and Holland. She moved up the ladder at Mallard First Financial quicker than predicted. Jed learned little, and now he knew why. She gave her allegiance and her ass to Cabot Hartley. "Come on, Jed. You know I prefer land deals."

Jed tapped his foot on the ground at the Cash Way sign. "Yeah, you're right." He tried to read Cabot's expression, practiced desperado straight.

"Uh, no. I was thinking I might buy...Fain Kendall's farm."

It stung but not much. If Jed lost Fain's land today, he would still have twice as much money in the bank as Cabot's entire family. "Then what brings you to Cash Way?"

"Better yet, why the hell are you here?" Cabot counterattacked.

Jed glanced up the driveway. Cabot followed his gaze. Dressed in a refined black suit and carrying high heels, Delaina walked toward her showplace. Jed didn't fight his smile; Cabot looked awfully confused. Both men fell back a little, strategically planning their next attack.

"Keep your hands off Lainey. We've got a thing going. You know that."

Jed glared. "You have a lot of fuckin' *things* going, Cabot, like Holland Sommers."

"She's your fucking thing, isn't she?" he retorted.

Jed played along, his face champion-Cabot-Hartley straight. "You didn't seem to mind in New Orleans if we shared bed partners." Jed cast his eyes upon Delaina. He hated to put her in such a sordid conversation, the only way to judge Cabot's intentions. He hoped for a break and got it.

"Sharing sluts is one thing. Sharing someone I'm bedding for a specific purpose is quite another. I speak on Tory Cash's behalf. We don't appreciate your coming on this land."

"Tory looked peaceful enough at the funeral home when I took Delaina." Jed got in his truck and left.

"Son of a bitch," Cabot muttered. He drove up the driveway.

Lainey sat on the front porch swing. He'd let her explain. The two-timing whore. Jed was hard to ace. Lainey in collaboration with him would mess up everything. He never considered their possible collusion. It would've killed Tory Cash.

"Hello, Lainey. How are you?" They didn't look at each other. "Okay, I guess."

"Are you ready to go to the funeral home?" "I've already been."

"Why didn't you call me?" He came across edgy.

"I wanted to go alone." "Must've been difficult."

She glanced. "I, uh, didn't go alone. Didn't Jed tell you? Just now."

"I don't like Jed McCrae, and you know it."

"Then what were you sayin' to him?"

"The regular. Being cordial." He mocked Delaina's words. "Good business, you know?"

"Exactly." Delaina had pulled her newest shield into place. The Tory-Cash's-only-heir, self-serving-bitch one. "Good business. Precisely why Jed took me. We share an irrigation unit on Farm 130, but you wouldn't know anything about my actual farmin' procedures, now would you?"

"I've heard you mention it."

"He came to consult with Moll as I was leavin'. We had decisions to make, so I accomplished a few tasks at once. He drove; we talked; I saw Daddy. I'm sorry if it upsets you, but I must, uh, interact with Jed occasionally. A business relationship. Can we leave it at that?"

"No. You're a naive, uninformed female. Jed McCrae sees it. He asked if I'd mind sharing you. Sexually."

Delaina's mouth intended to fall wide open. She clamped her lips tight. How disgusting. For God's sake. Her shield stayed in place. She wouldn't let Cabot see the shock. "I've heard rumors about his lax morals." She shrugged. "Sleepin' with the enemy is supposed to be the ultimate thrill. Maybe he hoped if you agreed, I would."

"Lainey, I'm warning you to stay away. Your father wouldn't like it."

"My father..." Delaina stared coldly. "...is dead. I refuse to explain myself further."

Cabot mumbled, "Jed's a snake in the grass."

"You think I don't know that? He's the reason I work so hard. I wouldn't do anything to jeopardize this land. Let it go, okay?" Her voice cracked in anger.

"Don't give me a reason to bring it up again."

Delaina shut her eyes. Cabot proved Jed to be a vicious jerk with the comment about sharing beds. She felt like she'd been stuck with needles. She'd get to the bottom of the conversation, and she'd choke that conniving prick to death. She remembered

Cabot beside her, realizing how pitifully close she stood to losing her lone ally. Fear, more dreadful than loneliness. "Cabot, forgive me. I'm tired." They swayed in silence until Miss Maydell came out to invite them in for supper.

~ ~ ~

Tory Cash left no instructions for a funeral service. Delaina climbed into the funeral home's gleaming black escort car. Dressed in an unforgettable dark dress and costly heels, hand-delivered on short notice from a boutique owner/friend of the family in Memphis, she rode alone and paid extra to have Maydell and Moll escorted in a matching car behind her. She chose a graveside afternoon service at the family cemetery. Tory wouldn't have wanted anything in the church. She couldn't recall the last time he went to church. She lost her breath when she looked out the window at the end of the driveway. Cars stretched up and down the ditches of Cash-McCrae Road. The escort car weaved through vehicles on the narrow lane. Was there anyone left anywhere else in west Mississippi today? The extensive display of respect overwhelmed her. She could scarcely take in the importance of her father, her importance now. She chose the details; it did not prepare her for the emotion. The line of American flags on columns forming an archway into the cemetery lent reverence, elegance, and care, and created a long walk for her. Even longer because of the profound crowd. 500? 700? Over a thousand? Lines deep and wide, a swamp of black clothes, wealth and prominence interspersed with common Mallard folk. Representatives from government, stores, her church, the college, the bank, loggers, workers. Because she hadn't moved and the service depended on her arrival, the driver said, "Miss Cash, ma'am, Mr. Lowery is waitin' to lead you to your chair. My condolences and my honor to bring you here." Delaina pushed on the door. "I'll be here when you're ready to go."

Delaina said, "Thank you very much." She did the required one more time. Somber, appreciative, classy, alone.

Eli Smith shifted weight from one leg to another and pushed his hands in and out of his pockets. He found being a pallbearer at Tory Cash's graveside service a somewhat uncomfortable position.

Lainey had asked him personally to serve in the honorary capacity. Cabot Hartley had him by the balls when Holland Sommers didn't have her hands on them. He, unlike Cabot, possessed a conscience. He wanted to come clean. The cash stuffed in his wallet was too nice. The good things in life. Tory Cash enjoyed those things, and he didn't get them being a good ole boy. Eli glanced at Lainey as she sniffled. He had a bad feeling she might get hurt. *But* she was born with a silver spoon in her mouth, a spoon put there because Moll Smith and sons worked like slaves. He decided his fortune came overdue.

Delaina stood near her father's coffin, near graves of her paternal grandmother and grandfather and other relatives. She scanned granite headstones without giving the people in the ground any thought, too numb. Her pastor's memoir had reminisced and touched, leaving the crowd with a warm image, an image that existed only on the paper in his hand. One by one, people spoke to Delaina and filed away. She looked for Jed and never saw him, of course. Not one reason on God's green earth for him to be there. Not one reason on God's green earth for her to want him there. She did.

Joe Cabot Hartley and his wife Claudia, the last guests, came to her. Mr. Hartley clasped her hand. "Lainey, your father was a dear friend. His memory will live on in you. If Mrs. Hartley or I can be of assistance, we'll be glad to help."

"Thank you." Delaina nodded. They parted. Joe Cabot looked every ounce the businessman he was. Dressed in a suit, white shirt, striped tie, ever a slight smile on his face, his salt-and-pepper hair meticulously combed. Delaina felt suddenly, uncomfortably, on her own. She spotted Cabot standing among Mallard's few elites on the lawn. He looked perfect. Almost too perfect, Delaina observed for the first time. Straight white teeth, fixed smile, dimples in his cheeks. He politely excused himself and walked briskly toward her. "I apologize. You know, stroking egos. Want me to take you home?"

"I have the driver."

"Lainey, with an estate as big as Cash Way, you need to get legal aspects done as soon as possible." He offered the fixed smile.

"The banker in me. Do you want to meet with Attorney Gage in the morning?"

"I suppose I need to." Lord, more to do. More somber. More appreciative. More thinking and deciding.

"I could go with you."

"Yes." Delaina stared at flat green land over the distant pasture, a McCrae pasture. "Cabot, did you check out what I asked you about Holland?"

"I did." He leaned in and whispered, "Like I thought, she thought she'd enjoy the challenge but called him tough. She'll keep her distance in the future. I guess it played out quickly."

Voluptuous Holland having her hands on Jed made Delaina self-conscious. Her strip show had been a comedy for him. "I'm drained," she complained. "Goodbye."

"Gage's office at eleven."

"I'll be there." Delaina got in the sleek car, scanning the cemetery lot once more. The graves of Jed's parents, separated from the Cash plot by an iron fence, came into view. She sank into the seat. "Take me home, please."

~ ~ ~

As soon as Cabot got to his SUV, he heard the phone ringing. He knew who it was. "What is it?"

"How was the funeral?" his partner queried.

"It was a funeral."

"Are you going to the attorney's office with her?"

"Yes," Cabot answered in a clipped tone.

"We're making progress. I got about a third of my work done last night."

"Good." Cabot had a compulsion to laugh. Their beloved stupid land, officially compromised.

Ten

Questions

Delaina awoke the next morning to sounds of Miss Maydell and Moll telling each other goodbye.

Moll was headed to a field, she heard him say. He called Eli and Rhett before dawn to ask them to go, but neither answered. "Them boys, I swear," Miss Maydell said. "When're they gonna settle down and give me grandkids to spoil?" "Aw, relax, May. They'll be at work by eight. They work long hours for low pay." "You're right." Delaina heard a loud smooch. "Have a good day."

Delaina hoped the will's provisions would give her guidance. She showered and dressed, selecting tailored clothes again, slicked her hair into a low ponytail and wore makeup. Skipping down the steps, she called out, "Miss Maydell?"

"In the dining room, Lainey honey." Delaina rushed in and saw her stooped over the sideboard, restoring silver trays. "I meet with Attorney Gage at eleven."

"Okay, sweetie. Are you comin' home for a bite at lunch?"

"I'll probably go to lunch with Cabot. Bye." Delaina raced to her SUV. She had time to see Jed, to find out for herself what he said to Cabot about sharing her sexually and why. The arrogant bastard. She sped down the road and parked at his shop, scanning the place for his truck. It was there. Her heart did a backwards somersault. She walked toward an enclosed building marked Office. The door opened. Boone Barlow came out, pencil tucked behind his ear, bare-chested, wearing jeans and snakeskin boots. Delaina felt the palest pink blush her cheeks. They hadn't conversed since that morning at Carr's Creek when she offered to pay him not to tell what had happened the night before.

"Sorry about your father."

"Thank you." Delaina looked over the area. "Is Jed here?"

Boone's eyes widened, but as an employee he wasn't privy to question. "Ah yeah, he's here somewhere." He motioned toward an enormous building. "Was workin' on a tractor." Boone closed in, bracing her against the office door, an arm speared on either side of her shoulders. "Something I can help you with?" Delaina stared into his eyes and felt nothing good or bad. He stood inches from her lips.

A shadow jumped across their bodies, Jed emerging from it. His face revealed shock then sour recognition. He wore dusty clothes, a backward cap, and black grease smeared on his arms. "Excuse the piss out of me."

Delaina pushed herself harder against the door. The men stared each other down like alley cats about to fight for a scrap. Jed blinked first. "I need to get in my office," he said in Delaina's direction. "Don't let me interrupt your foreplay." Delaina shuffled out of the way, moving her head back and forth to make eye contact. Jed shut the door behind him.

Holy Christ. Boone felt something akin to a lightning bolt when those two looked at each other. "I'm sorry, Lainey. My fault, and I apologize for Jed. Probably not in his best interest for me to have a thing with you. I mean, with the hard feelings between your families."

"Never mind it, Boone. I had a quick, uh, Farm 130 question for him." Delaina began walking. "No big deal."

Boone shuffled around as she left, decided he might as well get it over with. He stepped tentatively into Jed's utterly immaculate office, expecting a brutal lecture for dallying with Lainey Cash.

Jed washed his arms at an opened half bath in the corner. He dried with a paper towel. "Why don't you ride to the Denton Place, help your father." Boone walked out thinking he got off suspiciously easy.

~ ~ ~

Dumbfounded, Delaina drove into town. Jed must think of her as a manipulative slut. Stripping for him. Spending the night in New Orleans with Cabot. Nearly being kissed by Boone. In four days. Like a fluke Delaina stewed up, part of an underhanded scheme. Cabot warned her about Jed anyway, a devastating blow. But their dance by the river... Jed's eyes pierced her soul when he whispered that he'd never dance with anyone else again. Delaina jammed her fist into the steering wheel. Impossible obstacles between them seemed miniscule when compared to her intense physical need. The core of her womanhood reminded her every time she looked at him. His mere existence unleashed erotica in a woman, even someone with the reservations of Lainey Cash. Now, more than ever, she had to block out her carnal desire for Jed McCrae. After seeing her with Boone, Jed would suspect her motives for throwing herself at him in the past. She wouldn't have any man believe she used her body or appeal for attention or financial gain. She could never be like her mother. Delaina learned a hard lesson in New Orleans with Cabot, but it had been a good one. If she went to bed with Jed McCrae, it would be because he needed her like no woman ever. Delaina knew such a day would never come.

~ ~ ~

Jed picked up a Collector's Edition baseball-themed soda bottle and crashed it into the wall. Shards of glass and syrupy liquid splintered. He believed Delaina Cash was different. A woman who used her natural intellect or strong spirit to get what she wanted. Why hadn't he thought of it before? The reason for her recent interest in Cabot and Jed. Delaina had her own plan. To use men to get where she was going. The manipulative witch. He'd almost fallen for it. If Fain Kendall hadn't revealed his secrets, Jed would've gone to Delaina like a love-hungry fool and offered anything. He would readily admit his hormones did his thinking often. Never in business. He wasn't about to start now with Tory Cash's little girl. Even at the funeral home, she whispered to her dead father that she'd make him proud, whatever it took. Blockheaded Jed, no, dickheaded Jed stood there and listened sympathetically to the masterminded slut. He picked up another valuable bottle and pitched it. "Whore," he muttered as the bottle busted into pieces. He surveyed the damage. His fit had cost him. He called an employee. "Hank?"

"Go ahead, boss."

"There's a mess in my office. Please clean it up ASAP."

"A mess in *your* office, sir?"

Jed looked at the disaster. "Yes. There'll be a bonus in your check."

"Yes, sir. I'll be there in a little while."

Jed picked up another bottle and hurled it. The bottles, painstakingly difficult to obtain, had been lined on a shelf behind his desk. One by one, Jed pitched them, yelling expletives as they fell. He got to the next-to-last bottle. Teams and dates were painted on the sides. He attended that game, like the others. Memories of good baseball. He placed the bottle on the shelf, refusing to look at his wrecked office. He slammed the door behind him, cursing Delaina Cash evermore.

~ ~ ~

Cabot Hartley arrived at the attorney's office twenty minutes ahead to remind Warren Gage of their earlier agreement. Warren, annoyingly strait-laced, might need last-minute coaxing. Cabot swung open the door and found Warren reading the newspaper. He sat in a leather wingback chair and didn't mince words. "Lainey doesn't know I've seen the will, Warren."

"Right."

"Congratulations." Cabot patted his eel skin leather checkbook. "You're the winner in the election this fall if it comes down to campaign funds."

"I have no reservations about what I've done for you. It would please Tory to no end to see Lainey married off to you. You're the obvious choice."

Minutes later, Delaina appeared in the doorway. "Come in. How are you?" Warren greeted her.

"Better today." Delaina sat beside Cabot in a matching leather chair.

"Lainey, Tory's most recent will was drafted the same month you graduated high school and turned eighteen. Everything belongs to you. I'll take care of legal notices. Your father has life insurance to clear outstanding personal debts, also half a million in assets and the house. Some land is owned, free and clear, but there is farm debt, as you know. You'll need a financial expert to handle such a sizable estate. Cabot would be a good choice."

Delaina glanced at him. He nodded in agreement.

"Your father made one stipulation. A stipulation crucial to remain confidential so no one takes advantage of you: You do inherit the cash and you own the land, but you cannot act in a managerial capacity, that is, make financial or legal farm decisions until you are twenty-five. You are to appoint a temporary agent to act on Cash Way's behalf. Your agent will be paid a significant salary for services and has control over Cash Way farms, bound by law to make decisions in the farm's best interest while also showing you more specific details of how to do it on your own. You are to choose this person in consultation with me."

Delaina grimaced. "I've been managing it almost three years."

"Yes, for the most part." Warren rubbed his chin with his hand. "I admire your determination. Your father's illness was unique because you communicated somewhat. Now that he's deceased, we are bound by his will. Your father counted on outliving the provisions, I'm sure. He devised the best plan he could, when you turned eighteen and left for college. You have thirty days to choose a farm manager. Which puts us at…" Warren scanned his desk calendar. "May first. If you had gotten married *before* you turn twenty-one, your husband would automatically be manager until you turn twenty-five. Stipulations for your husband's role are laid out, but we won't discuss that unless, or if, it becomes necessary."

"I'll be twenty-one on May twenty-second. I don't anticipate it, but what if I named a manager then married someone else before I turned twenty-one?"

"Tory came up with a yearly contract for the manager. If a contract had already been signed before the wedding, it would be up to you whether you would want to break the contract and give the position to your husband."

Cabot inserted, "I disagree. You said if she got married before she turned twenty-one, her husband is automatically the manager." He hadn't expected Lainey to ask such a question. Nor had he expected Tory to die yet. They hadn't secured all details when the man croaked. He assumed she'd choose him to manage and to marry. He had bank records to prove Cash Way had been issued lenient capital for years. Lainey wouldn't have a choice.

Warren answered, "You have until May first to name someone. No need for scenarios. I'm available to bounce ideas." Cabot shot Warren a meaningful glance. Warren added, "Your choices are limited, certainly."

Delaina slipped into the memory of the night in her SUV with Jed at Farm 130. 'I don't trust anyone,' she had said. Yet, holding his hand, she'd felt something close. At the river when she shed her clothes and he held her, that was trust, even if it fled. "Moll," she said.

Warren frowned. "He's not...he's never handled finances. He probably wouldn't understand the contract."

Delaina shrugged. "I see stipulations in Tory's will as a paperwork formality. With Moll, it'd essentially be me. We'll do what we've been doing."

"Lainey, you want the hassle?" Cabot interrupted. "Besides, you've been getting by with leniency from me. Technically, farm finances need to be restructured now."

"He's got a point," Warren chimed in. "You've held it together, but your farm manager is more than a formality. This person should be well-versed in business to give you increased training. Moll Smith isn't the man to run your estate. Choose someone educated who could relieve you of the burden."

"Burden?" Delaina shot from her seat. "Cash Way is my focus, my career, my home, my life, my everything. I have no desire to turn it over to anyone. If you're hinting I should sell it, never."

Cabot interrupted again, "Lainey, maybe you could keep the house and..."

"Sell nothing!" she roared. "Moll may not be the one, but we've done well together while I learned as best I could from my father at the nursing home and through community college. *I know a lot about business!*" She reached for her purse.

Warren gave Cabot the she's-a-tough-cookie look. Cabot gave him the you-better-think-of-something look. "What about Cabot?"

He looked as ready to volunteer as the Red Cross. "Cabot, you don't know anything about farming," she answered as she sat again.

"I know agriculture from the standpoint of making loans. I know the language. You and Moll know the workings. I could handle the business. We could work with Moll on the mechanics. A permanent arrangement."

Delaina shook her head negatively. "I don't know. I need time."

Warren sighed. "Farming is unpredictable. I wouldn't amble around."

"Attorney Gage, we are a large, diversified operation. Our profits are cyclical, yes, but quite predictable. I refuse to decide today."

"Damn, Lainey," Cabot spoke up. "You're makin' this hard. We could handle it. You don't have choices."

"More than you think." Delaina looked back and forth between them. "I won't be backed into a corner by any man."

Warren Gage spoke again. "Your father held esteemed positions spelled out here. Hospital board, bank, local ag cooperative, library, and voting member at the insurance bureau. A state ag committee and a federal ag legislative group. They've been held in absentee status during his illness, or temporary arrangements were made."

Delaina had sort of forgotten due to her work and his illness, other than attending a few necessary meetings or when he was honored with a tribute. Her world felt huge and tiny. Tears, the first today, stung her eyes.

Warren sensed her overwhelm. "We can arrange another time to discuss. Unfortunately, you will probably hear from them soon to determine permanent positions. He did give his state ag seat to Jed McCrae a couple months before his stroke, perhaps the only hint he gave anyone that he might've felt ill." Did she gasp aloud?

"He had an understanding with Jed. If you showed interest, it's yours." "I see," she managed. Cabot seemed perfectly fine with such a wild revelation, for some reason.

"He left a letter for the farm manager. It's yours to read and pass along to the person you choose." He handed it to Delaina.

"I'm feeling...a bit wiped out." She stood. "We'll do a second meeting soon." She left with, "Thank you both."

"Warren, I told you she's hardheaded. That's why I needed to get a look at Tory's will," Cabot claimed.

"I had many conversations with Tory. He didn't want to make this hard on her. You don't want to look eager or suspicious, Cabot."

"Eager or suspicious? By May first, I need to be the manager of Cash Way and a married man." He smiled. "But, I'm fine. I know what I'm doing."

~ ~ ~

Delaina drove down Cash-McCrae Road. Attorney Gage was right. Moll encouraged her to make financial decisions with Cabot's help and limited communication with Tory. Moll was good at mechanical things. The explanation of the will alone would make him nervous. She could talk more with Cabot; he had been helpful before. No! He supported selling her land during the meeting. She could take applications for the farm manager's position, but what about trust and privacy and having someone she was certain she could depend on? Her thoughts like speeding cars circling her racetrack of a brain, she struggled to ignore the announcer's voice calling out that Jed McCrae led the race.

In a near out-of-body experience, she found herself driving past Cash Way's entrance. She found herself, in fact, standing at Jed's office door. The door opened. A stout man stepped out, sweat beads shining on his head. He wiped his face with a handkerchief and held a bag of trash. Delaina recognized him as one of Jed's workers.

He made a stunned face. "Uh. Excuse me, Miss Cash."

"Yes, sir. You are?" Delaina slid out of his way as he took a step toward the open-air shelter where equipment was stored. She extended her hand and smiled.

"I am Hank Pitts, an employee of Jed's." "Nice to meet you." Hank wiped his face again. He touched her hand. "If you'll excuse me, I need to rest." He frowned. "Boss went on one heck of a rampage. I was left to clean it up." His shoulders lifted. "Out of character." His head bent to his chest like he was looking in the dirt for an explanation.

Was she the reason for Jed's rampage? Delaina pushed the door open and peeked in. The room was immaculate. Everything carefully filed and organized. A functional gray desk stood in the center. Shelves containing farm records and ag awards surrounded it. The walls, plastered with pictures of tractors and airplanes, were painted white. His bachelor's degree from Baylor University, she noted because she didn't remember his alma mater, hung in a frame along with certificates and acknowledgments. One of those photo app, calendar-type pictures, March, was tacked to a bulletin board of sticky notes. A decadent redhead with balloon-like breasts covered in a green swimsuit top held an oversize glittery-green clover leaf over her crotch, words *May you have the luck of the Irish. Love, Keely* scratched across it in real handwriting. A separate desk and laptop computer covered one side of the room, half bath on the other. Vinyl chairs flanked the main desk. No sign of Jed's earlier tirade. She touched the top of his desk.

"Finding anything to benefit you?"

Delaina jumped like she'd been shot, sending papers flying across the floor. She'd recognize his voice in a howling snowstorm. He inched toward her, glaring. His hands, arms, shirt, and face were dusty-dirty.

"You scared me," Delaina admitted, patting hand over heart. The motion pressed her thin shirt against her bra.

Jed's eyes took in her breasts then her face. "Good."

Delaina walked around behind him and uttered, "I apologize for eavesdropping. I..."

"Eavesdropping?" Jed turned and frowned. "Is that what you call it? I call it trespassing."

"Trespassing?" Delaina raised her voice to a near yell. "You didn't call it trespassing at the river Sunday night!"

"You weren't in my personal office with your hands on my desk."

"No, I wasn't, was I?" She slinked her index finger on his sweaty T-shirt. "I was on your bed sheet with my hands on your condoms."

Jed backed off and snickered. "Too bad I didn't use one on you when I was interested."

"I wouldn't have allowed it. Besides, Cabot refuses to share me sexually." She tilted her head and gave him an accusatory glance.

"What I said to Cabot was for your own good, Delaina. I never said I'd share you with anyone. The ever-slick rich boy twisted my words. I knew he would." Delaina wanted to believe Jed. "And sayin' you wouldn't have allowed it at the river, I beg to differ."

Delaina tossed her head snootily. "That's not all you'd have to beg for."

He let out a nasty laugh. "You're the one who begged me to give you a one-night stand, if I remember right." He bowed his head and looked at the fly of his pants. "...and my dick's tellin' me I do."

She stomped across the room. "You have the instincts of an animal! I've never met a man like you!"

Jed kept his voice calm. "I've never met a female like you." He put his hand up to his eyes, faking a cry. "'I'll make you proud, Daddy.' Yes, I will. I'll use Cabot Hartley for bank favors, I'll use Jed McCrae to gain access to the McCrae land and better farm techniques, and I'll use Boone Barlow to make them jealous. Is that it?" Jed walked right up to her body, pushing her against the wall with his chest. Delaina burned like lit gasoline. "Did I leave someone out, *Lainey*? Eli and Rhett Smith? Uncle Dale and his other sons? Local accountants and attorneys? Hell, Joe Cabot Hartley and Moll? What a dirty way of doing business, little girl. Got any real strategy, any real courage, any real brains? I thought you did."

Delaina sought the vinyl chair. Her mouth hung open in disgust. In embarrassment. Jed entered the half bath, closing the door. She heard water from the faucet. He was washing up. She'd wait. There was only one way out of the room. She adjusted her rubber band, putting her hair into a higher ponytail. She kicked off her high heels and pulled off her blazer, silky camisole underneath.

He came out moving slick as a shark, Delaina his available prey. Intentionally, he kept his attention focused on her, sitting down, rolling the chair back, propping his legs on the desk, crossing them at the ankle. He had shed his dirty shirt and replaced it with a clean one. He stared Delaina down, animosity his emotion.

The atmosphere in the room felt catastrophic. Delaina held his gaze. Time passed. Jed brought his laptop to his central desk, flipped it open, his face covered up to his eyes. He read through material, reached for an ink pen, made notes. Obviously, he planned to work. He'd met his match in stubborn determination. She'd sit in his chair until Judgment Day. She'd be damned if she'd let his arrogant way bully her.

Eleven

Plans

She sat. He read.

Jed finished with his laptop, retrieved a folder, and began again. In the lull, Delaina thought about what she'd say when they did talk. She wanted him to know she wouldn't use her body as a tactic. How could she prove it when she'd thrown herself at him for days?

Midway through, he slapped it shut. Agitated, he came to his feet and snaked around the desk. He leaned in and hissed, "I give up. You win." His lip curled cynically. "Goodbye."

Delaina poked out her bottom lip and blew tendrils of hair out of her eyes. "I'm not through with you yet."

Jed muttered a gutter word then walked the floor. "Let me guess. You wanna seduce me?"

Delaina stood and slid in front of him, bringing his pacing to a halt. "Yes. But that's beside the point."

Jed licked his lips, looked at hers. He remembered how warm they felt, how good her tongue tasted. He backed against the front edge of his desk, pelvis thrust forward. His BC jeans pulled against his manhood. Delaina made a little sound.

"What's wrong, Delaina?" Jed scourged her sensuality with his raspy voice. "You're in control here."

She snapped out of it. "I wanna set the record straight. I'll get what I need the same way I always have. Through honesty, hard work, determination, and careful planning."

Jed slipped his thumbs in the loops of his jeans and jerked his hips suggestively. "Then it'll be worth the wait."

"Uh!" she yelled in frustration. "You have your head in your pants again."

"If I hadn't interrupted, yours would be in Boone's pants again!" Jed yelled for the first time.

"Oh Jesus, Jed, it was a misunderstanding at the door! You really think I'd do that?" she practically screamed.

"I don't know. You tell me."

"I'm not here to explain my love life to you. I didn't realize Boone still worked out here."

"A couple days a week. Most of the time, he's at those fishin' tournaments. Boone's a regular fishin' legend, but I guess you know." Jed stretched his arms out, his pectorals pulled tight on his T-shirt. "Why are you here?"

"To be honest, I need you."

As fast as he'd become angry, he became docile. "I prefer honesty, Delaina." Her name coming from his mouth trickled like massage oil down her spine. She was visibly shaken, visibly aroused. "Want me to be honest with you?"

"Yes," she groaned.

Jed placed his hands on top of her head and swiped down the sides of her face, cupping her chin. "My primary ailment this afternoon is jealousy. Though I have no rights to you, I'm becoming proprietary against my better judgment." His voice strained. "I wanna take you home with me right now. Strip you myself this time. Finish what you started."

"Oh, Jed, me too."

Fain's threats seized his conscience, slicing desire between them. "I have a feeling that's not why you're here."

"No." Delaina struggled to climb out of the rubble she was trapped beneath, not bouncing out of the trance as easily as Jed had. "Not originally, but..."

"But what?" Jed shoved his hands in his pockets.

"Regardless of my intentions, anytime I'm with you, my thoughts become..."

"Sexual," he replied with humility, answering for himself.

"Yes, sexual...and more."

"Same here, cupcake."

"Yes, but your thoughts are merely sexual, and it's any woman you're alone with."

Merely sexual. Any woman. Unfeeling. Insulted, Jed cashed in on his insurable defense mechanism. "I get what I want every time."

"I'm not seducing my way into anything with anyone. I'll prove it."

"How can you prove it when everything you do is seductive?"

"That's your perception because you're hot for me," Delaina said without mock or conceit. Jed scowled. She went on, "I swear that's not my strategy. My mother, she was..."

He sensed something. "What?" "She was a prostitute in New Orleans. As far as I know, Tory never told anyone." She cringed. "He told me in the middle of a drunken tirade." Jed stepped closer. "I was fourteen when Tory began referring to her as a 'fuckin' paid whore' or a 'trashy G.D. prostitute.' It affected me." She didn't look at him as she talked.

"How?" Jed caught her in a loose hug, breathing her soapy-fresh scent.

"I could never use sex to get what I want. Only for its original purpose, to be with someone I care about. Laugh, if you want to. I know you don't believe in such." Jed didn't laugh. *Did that mean she had started to care for him when she asked him for sex at the river? ...So, she cared about Cabot. She spent the night with him in New Orleans. In fact, she'd been with him for months.* "In other words, I'll handle Cash Way on my merit."

"Good. What I wanted to hear." Jed backed off. "For some reason, I wanna believe you're genuine. If you want me, it's gotta be for me, not land or spite or..." Jed quit talking before he said lust. God knows, he didn't understand where his need for lusty sex went. Granted, he would love lusty sex with Delaina. For now, it was championed by a greater need for, heaven forbid, the sappy stuff.

"Since nothing will happen today," Delaina pushed out the words. "Let me explain why I'm here."

~ ~ ~

Cabot motioned for Holland to come in his office when he caught a glimpse of her returning from lunch. She had spent her break with Eli Smith.

"What is it?"

"You're a woman." Cabot smiled chauvinistically. "An unusually fine one."

"Thank you." Holland sat down. She had a feeling she'd be there a while.

He rested his elbows on his desk. "Analyze Lainey for me."

"She's feisty, tomboyish, caring, independent, and kind of naive."

"All true." Cabot sighed. "How do I get a female like her to marry me?"

"Hmm. Well, she's young. It would be tough. My guess is no man has gone to much trouble to make her feel very feminine. You know?"

"I see your point." Cabot shook his head. "Like one of the boys."

"Buy her perfume, send roses, call her by her full name Delaina. Tell her she's pretty and point out specific things you like about her, feminine things."

"What about a card with flowers? Today. Poor Lainey, going through so much. What should I write?" He narrowed his eyes. He slid paper to Holland. She thought briefly, wrote something romantic.

"Got it. How should I propose?"

Holland's face lit up. "I'm in my thirties. I know how I'd like it! A fantastic evening dinner. Spare no expense. A gigantic ring and bunches of flowers. Wine her. Dine her. Tell her there's no one else for you then pop the big question." She giggled. "You do all that, and I'll marry you if she won't."

"Holland, you have incredible intuition. Take tomorrow. Go to the salon. Manicure, pedicure, wax, whatever, on me."

"You don't have to tell this woman twice." When Holland was gone, Cabot dialed the number to Nance Mathis's florist. "Hi, Nance. Cabot Hartley. I'm fine and you?" Cabot scribbled on the scratch paper. "I want you to deliver two dozen white roses to Lainey. Nice card. Something loving. On the inside, write these words." He checked Holland's message. *"To Delaina, my love. One rose for every hour of the day. I think of your beauty as often. I love you, Cabot.* I'll stop by after work and pay twice the going rate if you'll be certain she gets the flowers in person today."

Not a lie, he did think of her beauty at least once an hour. She looked like millions of dollars. Nothing looked prettier.

~ ~ ~

"First, no games and all truth," Delaina vowed. "Can I expect the same?"

"I won't play games or lie. I may selectively leave things unsaid because I do know..." Jed lowered his head. "...things I can't talk about."

"Tell me if I approach shaky ground. Don't deceive me." Delaina sat in the armchair. Jed sauntered past her and propped against the desk. Their legs brushed. Both looked down, looked at each other. Delaina shifted uncomfortably. "Could you get farther away? I need to think about business and concentrate."

Jed brushed his leg against hers again. "Sweetheart, I could back up the length of a football field, and I'd still see you naked and dancin'. You might as well suffer right along with me."

Delaina bit her tongue to keep from lashing out. "I rushed out here, God only knows why, as soon as I left Attorney Gage's office. I don't have anyone who understands my predicament."

"I'm your last resort."

"No, my first choice."

First choice. Jed liked it.

"My father's current will was drafted when I graduated. The cash and house are mine. There's a protective clause on the land. I own it, but I don't have control over it until I'm twenty-five, supposedly meant to help me until I'm older, until I'm done with school." She glanced at him. "I must name a temporary, salary-paid agent as my farm manager within the next thirty days in consultation with Attorney Gage. Oh, another stipulation, my husband would have automatically been the manager if..."

"If what?" He considered each word.

"I happened to be married before my twenty-first birthday when Daddy passed away." Delaina spoke carefully so Jed would get the facts straight.

"And?" Jed remained calm. He'd marry her this minute; it would solve all their problems. Her Preacher Ward lived six miles away in a run-down brick house. They could say their vows on the broken front steps between the pots of fake ivy with his multiple pet poodles barking.

"I came straight to you, Jed. You are it for me."

~ ~ ~

Caught up in his spider web of plans, Cabot almost forgot about Red. He owed her a warning and maybe something he'd never given her. An afternoon with him. He e-mailed her and told her to get the transactions out of the town's ATM machine. He left work and put a note inside the machine.

Meet me at Moon Dog Creek on Kings County side. ASAP Butterscotch

Red felt a rush of adrenaline and love when she found the note. She jetted across town to where Cabot waited, parked in a blue Ford, a loaner from Mallard's car lot, near a clearing on the far side of the creek. Red walked to the bank and heard a whistle. She looked around to find Cabot in a pair of shades.

"Butterscotch!"

"I like when you wear green. Didn't I buy your outfit?"

"And the earrings." She pulled on her mop of wiry curls to reveal pearl studs.

"Come here. Behind this tree." He pulled her to him. "I have news."

She clucked her tongue. "God a' mighty, that don't sound good."

"I'm proposing to Lainey tomorrow night."

"On a Thursday? On April Fool's Day?"

Cabot laughed. "Only you would think of that."

She cackled. "April Fool's Day. Well I'll be a dang rabbit with hiccups."

"I'll spend the afternoon with you now, Red."

"Here?" She looked around. "It ain't that secluded."

"How about an early dinner over in Greenville?"

"Still too risky, ain't it?"

"Dacey, I know a spot. A friend of mine owns land. No one will be there." Cabot wanted to be good to her, but mostly he wanted to be certain she continued to stay quiet about what she knew.

"I'm easy as a dog in heat, Butterscotch, when it comes to you."

"Good. We'll grab takeout, sneak off into the woods, eat naked, and fuck." He patted her back. "Leave your car here; let's go in the Ford. After today..." Cabot looked into her shining turquoise eyes.

She pressed her finger to his lips. "We'll cross that bridge when we get on it."

~ ~ ~

Between odd jobs, Boone Barlow checked the clock on his phone for one hour and forty minutes. That's how long Lainey had been in Jed's office. What in hell did they need to talk about for so long? Nothing. Jed would never stay in such a small space with a gal as hot as Lainey without getting physical. Jed and Lainey? Not possible. Even if Jed wanted her, she wouldn't have him. Imagine what an individual could do with such information. Boone knew undoubtedly what he was required to do with it.

~ ~ ~

"I'm it for you?" Jed couldn't say it without grinning. Hot damn!

Delaina smiled in surprise at his sweet disposition. "No one else understands how important my land is. How vital it is that I make right decisions. You know because you're dealin' with the same thing. Jed, we have so much in common. You know what I need to do."

"Marry me before May twenty-second." There, he said it, since she was having trouble saying it herself.

Delaina's eyes glowed like gold-encrusted emeralds. "You remember my birthday."

"My birthday," he corrected.

"Oh yeah." She looked away shyly. Jed waited for her answer. Her mouth fell open and she started laughing. "Oh my gosh, you're hilarious. Your sense of humor, so dry I almost missed that jab! Marry you, huh?" Delaina pointed at him. "Good one." Her crazy heart did cartwheels at the thought. "I'm thinkin' Moll as manager."

Jed chewed his bottom lip to keep from chewing her out. Damn the bullheaded flirt straight to a black, burning hell. "Isn't Moll the logical choice?"

"I thought so, but Attorney Gage made a good point."

Jed got trampled but would remain helpful. Which, he was sure, lovesick fools did. "What did Gage say?"

"Moll isn't the choice for finances and, you know, managerial capacity. Tory's intention was partly to relieve stress for me and partly to find someone I could learn from."

"Delaina, look at me."

She did. Her breath fell from her chest to the bottom of her stomach. What a beautiful man. Marry him? His humor wasn't very humorous; it had sent her into a tailspin.

"Are you ready to make such a decision? No," Jed answered for her.

"I would if there were someone I trusted."

"But you don't trust anyone," Jed reminded her. "Neither do I." Their eyes met momentarily.

Delaina stood up and walked. "Cabot was there. Gage suggested him."

"What did Cabot say?"

"He seemed eager. I don't think it'll work. Cabot doesn't know anything about farmin'. Heavy decisions would be up to me. Plus, he's so busy, and he actually suggested sellin' Cash Way like it's a burden."

Jed knew how Cabot felt. "Seems like Tory would've had somebody in mind. Or maybe the best plan he could come up with to get something on paper once you were an adult, and he hoped it wouldn't become necessary."

Delaina decided to reveal more. "I have half a million in cash, house is paid for, most land is paid for, miscellaneous debts are owed, four million dollars-ish. We didn't make much last year, Jed. I've made good and bad decisions. Times I should've listened to Moll, times he should've listened to me."

500K. Huh. Jed would've thought more. Like millions more. He had ten times more ready cash than she did. *She* owned five times more land than he did, until he inherited the McCrae land, *if* he inherited it. "I didn't make much last year, the nature of the beast.

If things stay tough in the ag industry, you wouldn't have to start seriously liquidating for..."

"About two more years, I've been thinking."

"Depending on how nice the Hartleys decide to be," Jed warned. Which usually wasn't very nice.

"It's not smart to be dependent on one bank, but..." Delaina didn't have solutions. "This is Cash Way suicide, what I've confided in you." She reached, clasped each hand around his, and rested them on his thighs. She moved between his legs and looked into his gemlike eyes. "Not a soul, living or dead, would believe I came to you for advice. No trick or scheme involved here, Jed. I wanna believe that's the case every time we've been together." Her breath smelled like mint candy; her hair like a sea breeze. One hell of an intoxicating combination. "I'm riskin' everything by seeking your guidance." She hoped for a shield to save her pride. She felt more naked than she'd been at the river. "If you were me, what would you do?" She sat in the chair, crossed her legs, and waited.

Jed fought to keep his mind on business. Her words slurred together with a brand-new fantasy, being seduced atop his desk while carefully filed papers flew around like jets in an air show. "You know, I could give you...bad advice and...screw you in the process." Immediately, he swore. That hadn't come out right.

Delaina's eyes fell to his crotch. "I suppose so."

He paced. "Not what I meant. I could take advantage of this situation from a business standpoint. I won't. This conversation stays here. I don't want anything of yours." He looked at her to seal the verity. Well, he did want a few things of hers, nothing to do with farming. "If I were you, I wouldn't name anyone until the deadline. Not to scare you, someone may want your head on a platter. Keep them guessing. Delaina, keep everyone guessing, okay, baby?" He took her hand, lifted it, almost kissed the top, dropped it. "I'd quietly choose Moll Smith on May first. You two are doing a fine job. Four more years. You've done it nearly three already."

She nodded then frowned. "Moll does mechanical stuff. Finances..."

"When you need anything you or Moll can't handle, ask me like you did today. No one has to know." He looked into her eyes without motive. "That's what I'd do if you can talk Gage into it. You might get married before twenty-five anyway." He stopped. He didn't like to think about Delaina getting married. To anyone else. "Hopefully, you'll marry someone who understands, who'll...be an asset. Think of Moll as a temporary solution. Is it a yearly contract?"

"Yes."

"Perhaps overemphasize Moll's competency and how much you'll lean on Cabot to Attorney Gage and suggest you may find someone better qualified by next year. Take your time; you want to get this right."

"Yes. To avoid a hostile takeover from the competition." Delaina raised her eyebrows at him and looked extra enticing.

Tile had become a recurring place for Jed's resistance to land. "I'm afraid a hostile takeover from the competition is inevitable." He eased his hands around the back of Delaina's head, drew her lips to his, paused. Eye to eye, she gave mute permission. Jed pressed his mouth to hers and kissed her thoroughly but didn't part her lips. "It's been too long," he whispered, overeager to get mere kisses from Lainey Cash after twenty years of living closer to her than any man in Mallard County.

"It's been three days," she said softly, smiling against his lips.

"Too long," he repeated. Their mouths opened. Their tongues touched, engulfing Delaina in his technique and texture. A scrumptious, sensual blend. Rough and smooth. Strong yet soft. Sexual but loving. He made love to her mouth.

Desire slipped out of its cage and wouldn't go back in without a fight.

They broke apart for a split second to change angles and breathe. Jed's hands slid from Delaina's head to stroke the nape of her neck while his lips tugged at hers. She responded with fervor, allowing her kiss to speak for her. Silently but surely, she begged to be possessed by his hands, his being, smothered in his undeniable sexuality. He felt it; she confirmed it with eager brushes of her tongue.

Jed's hands dropped to the straps of her camisole, pulling them down. Seeking, searching, finding the soft fabric of her strapless bra. Plain, pretty, and a front hook; he could have guessed as much.

Gently, he caressed her through the fabric. She moaned against his mouth. Jed had her camisole pushed to her waist with fingers on her bra hook in scant moments. A steady move he perfected from, no doubt, years of practice. The unwelcome thought held Delaina's passion captive against her body's will.

He sensed her hesitation. "What?" he slurred in blazing need.

"I can't." Her face flushed, paralyzed by unfulfilled lust and unwarranted fear.

He plowed ten fingers through his hair. "Okay." Delaina felt certain it took reserve neither knew he had for him to appear sensitive. She pulled her top over her chest, didn't bother with the straps.

He spoke first, his words more hurt than accusing. "Are you proving your point about not using your sex appeal? Drivin' it home where it stings the most. If you are, I'm not impressed or amused." He turned away.

"To be honest..." Delaina reached for his arm.

He faced her, full of humility. "That's all I've been." She gazed into his diamond-blue eyes. They revealed rejection. She gave in and kissed his lips. His mouth gave way easily. She slid her tongue in.

He quit. "Cabot or me. Time to choose. And as much as I like kissing you, I'm not a puppet on a string. It doesn't have to happen today, but either you will, or you won't."

She studied him. "Then I won't. Not now. Maybe not ever."

"I'm not sure I understand."

"I was willing 'til you started undressing me like a pro, and I was reminded of your..." She pondered the right word. "Reputation. I don't wanna be a trophy of yours." Delaina offered a smile.

Hell's angels! Did he have to spell it out on a chalkboard for her? Couldn't she see it? Feel it? Jed could. *A trophy?* Cabot had willing women stashed everywhere. An insult came back to pester him. *Unfeeling.* He fired off using reliable defensiveness. "I won't be your scapegoat."

"Scapegoat?"

"Yeah, when things don't work out between you and Cabot."

"This has nothing to do with Cabot."

"It should. It would if you loved him."

"I've never known love, Jed. I'm not sure I would know it if I did love Cabot."

"You don't have to know love, Delaina. When it's there, it knows you."

Delaina looked into his eyes. She saw longing. She saw... Laureth. "Sounds like the voice of experience."

Jed looked into her eyes. He saw a lifetime. What he wanted and hadn't known until her. "It is."

"I guess my standards for you are higher than you're accustomed to. See, I don't want you to want me. I want you to...need me."

An uninvited visitor named realization set in. Minutes ago, Jed offered to marry her, and she laughed. Now she wanted him to say he needed her. Need was an uncomfortable term to use with someone who used insulting words like trophy and unfeeling. What about Fain Kendall's secret and threats? Delaina's SUV parked outside was enough to bring those threats to fruition. Best not to say more. To do something to get her out of there. Making her mad never worked; she hunted for a fight. He'd have to hurt her. Better to hurt her now, rather than after having sex with her. "Delaina, apparently, you need me. You came to me, remember? I absolutely don't mind helping you with Cash Way issues." Jed gathered a suitcase of confidence because she was about to go packing. "Don't be disillusioned by what just happened between us or what we shared at the river. I don't need anyone, and nothing will change that."

From the distress on her face, she took the bait. "How stupid of me," she said lowly. "I forgot the standards you have set for yourself. Such good ones, aren't they? I guess asking for faithfulness would have been comical."

Jed winced.

"And makin' love? A far cry in the distance. Right?" Jed winced again. "In fact, I should consider myself the lucky one. You actually conversed with me today." Delaina yelled furiously, "When I think about it, it's almost, *almost* flattering! You were about to screw...is that a fitting term...a blonde. Your first since your beloved, perfect Laureth." Jed turned away. The gal had a temper and a tongue to match. A knife stabbed in his heart would have felt better.

Delaina pulled her straps onto her shoulders, slipped into her blazer, and stepped into her shoes. "I'm glad you spared yourself before you lowered your standards to a normal human emotional level. God forbid you do anything that takes feelings. On behalf of *Lainey Cash?* Don't worry; you'll never be tempted again. Never!" The door crashed shut behind her. She opened it and stuck her head in. "By the way, I was at the ballgames and have the whole collection. Bottles are much more valuable as a set, you know?" She stormed out.

Jed could have handled her fit. He deserved it, and she'd thank him one day soon for turning her away. Then she mentioned the bottle collection. The greedy little snot. Probably the only other set in Mississippi. He picked up a bottle. *She had the complete set intact.* He crashed it against the door and grabbed the remaining bottle. He pulled his arm back and slammed it against the wall. Debris scattered like pigeons in a park.

~ ~ ~

"It'll be official Thursday night, huh?"

"I hope so," Cabot replied to his caller, also his partner and informant.

"I'll be impressed if you snag her. She's a handful of dynamite."

"The way I plan to handle her, she'll be putty in my hands."

"Good luck," was the grim reply.

"Who believes in luck? This is about power." Cabot paused. "Do you have your end of the deal secured?"

"Finished the nighttime work."

"Anything new?" Cabot asked.

"Yeah, definitely developments today to discuss."

"Seven o'clock. Same place," Cabot confirmed.

~ ~ ~

Delaina went straight home and took a midday shower, thinking she could wash off Jed McCrae. Too late, she realized he stamped his well-known mark on her heart, her dreams, her sexuality. She felt stupid for almost becoming a Jed McCrae has-been. Yet, she believed he was genuine in giving her advice about Cash Way and respected her aptitude for business and farming.

Cabot sent nice flowers with a silly-sweet message. His bank ties were a necessity to Cash Way. She had to mend their relationship soon. She dressed in work clothes as the grandfather clock chimed three times. An afternoon in the dirt, like a bottle of wine for her.

She found Moll in a field, checking the crop stand. First step in making a bountiful harvest, a certain amount of planted seed had to sprout in order to get a good stand. He remarked, "It's comin' up."

"I see."

Moll stood. "How are you today?"

"Better. I've talked to Attorney Gage."

He nodded. "Do I still have a job?"

"As long as you want. Heck, you might get a promotion." Delaina remembered Jed's words. Keep *everyone* guessing. "We'll talk more later."

Moll grasped the brim of his cap and scraped it on his forehead. "Lainey, I heard you got nice flowers from Jed McCrae when your daddy died, and Dale Barlow stopped me yesterday to say y'all would handle the Farm 130 irrigation system from now on." Delaina nodded. "Jed is a threat to you."

"Jed and I aren't James Ed and Tory. We see where it might be easier to get along rather than avoid each other."

They weren't having trouble getting along at the river. Moll had seen for himself. "Watch your step and don't get hurt." Delaina turned toward her car. "Thank you for caring, Moll. I'm going to the Talton Place to check cattle."

Delaina returned home at dark, losing track of time. She walked into her father's walnut-paneled study. She hadn't been in there much since his stroke. The room offered no solace, a sore reminder of violent outbursts. Tory liked to drink hard liquor while he sat in his leather desk chair. The least thing, the phone ringing, a debt notice, anything set him off. It was the room in which he called her mother a whore the first time. "Hey Cabot," Delaina said when he answered.

"Hello, beautiful. How are you?"

"I'm better. I've been outside. I needed to work."

"I miss those pretty green eyes, Lain...Delaina. I'm ready to see you, dear."

"I apologize for my behavior this morning. Thank you for the nice flowers."

"Darling, you're forgiven, and you're welcome for the flowers." Uncomfortable silence. "I'd like to take you out for dinner tomorrow night."

"Exactly what I need. Where will we go?"

"A nice surprise. Wear a dress; you look pretty when you do. Be ready at six at Cash Way."

"Sounds great." Delaina didn't feel much. She'd work on getting excited for their night out. "Cabot?"

"What is it, gorgeous?"

"Thank you for everything."

"Sweetheart, you're very, very welcome."

~ ~ ~

"You are certain Jed was in there. She couldn't have been there to see anyone else?"

"No, sir, Mr. Kendall," Boone Barlow answered. "I saw her come out. She slammed the door. She looked angry."

Fain sighed. "Anything else?"

"Yeah, an employee asked Jed what she was doing there. He seemed irritated but answered that they had a disagreement over Farm 130."

"For two hours and twenty minutes?"

"Mr. Kendall, I don't think she would consider a physical relationship with Jed McCrae. She's sly in business. I think Jed told the truth. Lainey's the type of gal who'd get mad if Jed wanted to do something as simple as grease the unit before she did."

"Thanks, Boone. Continue to keep an eye on him. Both, when necessary. Your check is in the box."

Twelve

April Fool's Day

Holland hurried toward Delaina like long-lost friends. "Hi!" Shirt open, with her hair, nails and makeup detailed to perfection, her large breasts were on display atop her frilly bra.

Delania had taken off work after lunch to go to downtown *Salon Doreen* for a pedicure. What was Holland doing there in the middle of a workday? "Hi, Holland. I'm surprised to see you." *Why don't you take another hour off and go to bed with Jed?* Delaina couldn't stop her wicked thoughts.

"My day off. I'm going to the cow auction in Meridian with Eli!"

"Like that?"

Holland scanned herself as she buttoned. "Oh, I didn't think about it."

"Yeah, well, the place smells like cows, know what I mean? The auction is dirty. You're seeing Eli?"

"He's a doll! An absolute doll. I love the country boy appeal."

Delaina smiled a little too sweetly. "I bet." She judged her pale blue linen shirtdress. "Stop by Crossroads. The boots and blue jeans store."

"Good thinking. Isn't it out by the stables?"

"Yeah, by the red barn." Holland scooted up and gave Delaina a one-sided hug. Her gigantic breasts mashed into Delaina's chest. "Thanks. We should go out for lunch soon or dart to Jackson for shopping! Bye!"

Delaina watched Holland as she went to the reception area. The kind of woman men lust after. Shopping? They didn't have similar taste. Well, there was one exception. Delaina chewed her lip in jealousy, a new emotion, and she didn't care for it. She overheard the receptionist say, "Cabot called to confirm you could put today's services on his charge account. Have a nice day, Ms. Sommers." Oddly, that statement brought about no bad feeling.

After her pedicure, Delaina asked the stylist about her hair. She could never look as fascinating as Holland Sommers. Glamorous was what she asked for. They did her hair and face and oohed over the finished product, pretty in a way she'd never been. Hair bluntly straight and parted, slicked behind her ears, Delaina wore red lipstick and black eyeliner and mascara. "Wow!" one lady said. "You look like a star." Delaina didn't feel like a star. She didn't feel anything. Maybe a new dress would lift her spirits. She shopped at the local boutique and bought the first dress she saw with a lackadaisical attitude. Black satin, column-style, and halter-neck with a high slit up both sides of the skirt, it had a plunging, open neckline. Delaina didn't have the cleavage for it, no way to wear a bra because the back was bare to the waist. She decided it molded to her breasts decently.

Dressed with time to spare, sitting on a chaise lounge in her bedroom, she viewed the back acreage of Cash Way through the window. Gauzy curtains billowed. Late afternoon sun slumped in the sky, pale orange across pastureland. Green grass rolled like a bolt of fine silk, rolling, rolling, until it met an azure velvet sky. As azure as Jed's eyes. Her phone startled her. *Jed* flashed on the screen. "Hello?"

"Where are you?" She'd recognize his voice inside a Texas tornado. "Have you seen 130?"

"No, what's wrong?"

"Out here checkin' my crop stand. Got a good one. You too except the acres planted while you were in New Orleans."

"What's wrong with it?"

"Beats me. Maybe a different seed lot? It's skippy. Looks bad, Delaina."

"You're kidding."

"It is April Fool's Day, but I'm not foolin' you. I called because I thought you might need to get your planters ready. Later, it's supposed to be stormy. Moll and the guys are in Meridian for the auction probably, right?"

Delaina interrupted, "Radar is showin' hellacious rain in about forty-eight damn hours. Holy freakin' crap."

"You need to find a new Sunday School teacher."

"Oh, go to hell," she said. She would break his hot body in half if she could get her hands on it. "Where are you?"

"Out here. Lookin' at your pathetic rows." He chuckled. "Should've taken my advice, Lainey Cash."

"About what?"

"Staying home from New Orleans to plant it yourself."

"Screw you."

"You say when."

"I'm on my way." Delaina cursed the double meaning. "Stay there."

"Don't know if you're worth it. I'm ready to call it a day and get a beer at Mac's."

Delaina hung up. That trash-minded bully. She'd choke him into oblivion when she finished surveying the plants. She went downstairs, impeded by her tight dress and shaky shoes, and grabbed one of Moll's ice-cold beers from the fridge. She took off like a scalded dog, not giving thought to her pending date with Cabot.

"The queen in her carriage," Jed mumbled, bracing for her anticipated attack. Delaina raced her SUV down the middle path at rocket speed. Dust and rocks shot from the ground like they'd been blasted from a launchpad.

He was propped against his truck. She had started looking for him before she turned off the main road. What a sight. Sweaty T-shirt, jeans, and work boots. Baseball cap smashed down on his head. She envied the two-day stubble across his chin; she'd like to be as close to his face. *Strictly business, strictly business, strictly business,* she repeated. Delaina scanned the pitiful rows, grabbed the beer and dove out, stumbling as she landed on her wobbly high heels. She clenched her car door for support and threw her hand out toward the field. "What the hell is this?"

Jed studied her sophisticated image. "Yeah, what the hell is this?" He pushed away from the truck and stalked through the grass to the field's edge. "I was expecting Lainey dirty-boots-and-jeans Cash, not...a VS model."

Delaina tossed the beer at him. "What do you know about VS models?"

"Not as much as I'd like to." Jed popped open the top. Never mind VS models. He was seeing nude Delaina swaying in the night. The dirty little tease. "To my future crop." Jed gulped beer. Delaina glared, crossing her arms at the waist, and stared down another row. "Not a great stand. I can live with it."

Jed frowned. "Gets worse." He motioned toward a dip. "Beyond the bottom."

"I need to see it." He looked her over from head to toe. Heat surged through her scantily clad body. "Gonna be a rough walk in your costume, cupcake."

"You interrupted a hot date, but I'm glad you did. I needed to know today." She examined the field. "I'm going out there." Delaina tentatively stepped onto the soil with her strappy shoe. "Dang it! I'm not made for high heels." She kicked off her shoes and touched the dirt with her foot squeamishly. Jed couldn't hold his laughter. She tried to walk in soft dirt without her toes touching. "Damn, now I'm ruining this pedicure. Who am I foolin'? I can't walk out there." Jed snickered. Her look toward him would freeze Florida.

"Delaina, darlin', you can't walk in that slinky excuse for a dress anyway."

"Shut your mouth." She stomped in the grass.

"Why don't you take it off? No one's here except me, and I've seen you. All of you." He whistled.

The arrogant ass. "What time is it?" she asked to ignore what his suggestion did to the vee between her thighs. *Strictly business, strictly business, strictly business.*

"Ten minutes 'til six," Jed replied casually, like he had all the time in the world. He did, with her.

Delaina cast eyes at him deductively. She looked like someone lit a candle inside her pretty head. "Jed?"

"Yep?" He took the last swallow of beer, crushed the can with his boot, tossed it in back of his truck.

"Carry me out there. It's not too far."

Jed cut his eyes. "April Fool's, right? Except, I'm no fool." Delaina's face was impudent. He stared at her rigidly. "Ah, hell, you're serious." His resistance had long been transported elsewhere to seek medical attention. In swift motion, he pulled his dirty shirt over his head, tossed it on the hood of his truck, lifted her effortlessly into his arms. He looked down at Delaina's upturned face. The unpredictable urgency that overtook them was insatiable. The act of carrying her brought thoughts of carrying her to bed to both minds. The skin of his arms brushed against the smooth skin of her back. His nipples pressed into her shoulder blades. The neckline of her dress crunched open revealing her right breast. She did nothing to conceal it; Jed did nothing to conceal his gaze upon it. Deep slits in her skirt had folded apart in the upsweeping. His left arm held her thighs beneath her bottom. She took it all in, every brush of skin, every look, every sensation, every everything. Jed made himself appear unaware. Holding his emotions, like holding dynamite. He hadn't died from his debilitating need for her at the river because God, or the devil, saved death for now. What a way to go, holding nearly naked Lainey Cash in the middle of a fresh-planted field.

Silence spoke to Delaina in an indisputable way. The swishing of his jeans, rubbing against her bare legs; the sinking soil, giving their bodies a rocking ride; the steady pace of his breathing, his chest rising and falling against her back; jagged skips in her breathing, moist against his neck. Every sound, every movement, was a soft note in this suggestive song, their symphony of foreplay. Delaina didn't think she could keep it in. He'd laugh at the only words she could think of, the only words her mind would allow. Jed stirred with arousal and fought with shreds of willpower telling her what he wanted to do. To carry her in his arms all the way to the cabin, lay her across his bed, and carry her all the way to heaven. Neither spoke since they recognized four words from the English language: *Make love to me.*

They reached the shallow dip in the field. He mumbled, "Hold on to me tight." Delaina gripped his muscles as he lowered her. Her bottom rubbed against his crotch. He was hard. At least he felt something for her. Jed moaned as he set her bare feet on his boots. "Don't want those fancy toes in the dirt," he managed to say and latched his arms around her waist to hold her back to his chest as she peered over the field. He rested his chin against her shoulder, an inappropriate but desirable move.

"Goodness," she said, calculating the damage. Jed gazed into her dress, her breasts at his disposal. His mouth, hungry for them. "Goodness," he imitated.

"Bad, isn't it?" She turned her head against his collarbone to look at his face.

"Pretty bad." Jed grimaced, thinking of another hellish, sleepless night he would spend alone, drinking and smoking. If he didn't die first... No, he wasn't going to die. God was a god of wrath; he remembered that much from church. This, his lifelong punishment for the times he took what women offered and offered less in return. What a wicked sense of humor the boss in the sky had.

"Definitely get the planters ready," she decided.

"I agree." He relaxed his grip on her.

"It'll be after midnight when Moll and the guys get back, and they'll be tied up with cattle in the morning. Unless I try to do it alone."

Jed cracked a smile. "May have to cut your hot date short. Maybe leave out dessert. You don't have a problem with cutting a man off. Boone and I know firsthand."

Delaina jabbed him in the ribs. He lost his balance. Dust swirled as they crashed into a heap, Jed landing on his back. Delaina fell across his stomach and chest. Her knee accidentally jammed into his crotch. "Ccc...Christ," he stammered, gasping for air.

"That should cut you off for a while!" she yelled, pushing herself up on top of him.

"Ccc..cuh...cut...me...o...off? Mmm...my...kids...flashed before...mm...my eyes."

Straddled over him, Delaina melted. "Oh Jed, you want children?"

"I *did*." She laid her head against his chest. "Oh, how sweet." A sobering thought entered her mind and she spat off, "To have kids, you'd need a wife, and to have a wife, you have to be faithful. Kids are out of the question for you."

"Not necessarily." He grinned. "We're in a nice position for making a baby, so it's possible to have a kid without a wife. Besides, a lot of men have a wife without being f-... Ah, shit! Wh, wh...what the hell? Sweet Christ...ddd...damn." Delaina had jabbed her knee into his baby-making tool. Twice.

Jed clamped her arms. "What did I do to deserve that?" His face scrunched in pain.

"Once for your unfortunate wife and once for your poor children."

"Get up!"

"No, you sit up. I can't get dirty."

Jed pushed himself to a sitting position. "Get off me."

"No! I'm already late. You have to carry me back."

"After those three hits, I'll be lucky to stagger back myself."

"You're tough." She wrapped her legs around his waist and nudged against his crotch. "Let's go." She clutched his shoulders for support.

"I ought to leave your pampered ass out here."

"You won't. You like the way this feels too much." Delaina's eyes glinted sexily.

"For you to say it, you must like the way it feels."

"Jed."

"Don't *Jed* me." He moved his hips. "Is this what feels good, huh? You can't play innocent with me, little girl. In your eyes. In those dazzling jade green eyes of yours. Every time I do this..." He nudged again. "...they spark with specks of gold. They're burnin' like flames now, darlin'." He got to his feet, holding on to her. "I'll take you back since you asked me to. Back to Cabot." He flung her over his shoulder and stomped across the field, tossing her like a backpack. "Put me down!" Delaina yelled and beat on his back. She uselessly attempted to kick him. Unshakable, he hurled her up and down as he strutted, a pillar of masculine strength. They reached the grass. He plopped her down and glued her arms to her sides. "We're going to find Richboy. Do you want me to tell him how you threw yourself at me or are you going to? I mean every sexy detail!"

"No!" Delaina's eyes went stark wild. "No, Jed. We can't." Her voice trembled. "Please. I'll do anything!"

"Anything? I want Farm 130."

"Oh God! Oh, Jesus..." Delaina blinked several times, grasping for a reply.

Jed broke out in a victorious grin and let go of her. "April fool."

Delaina nailed him in the arm. "You really had me going! You seem to get pleasure from my panic."

He admitted in a gravelly voice, "I find pleasure in everything you do, baby doll."

Delaina knew what she wanted to do, and being Delaina, she did it. She pushed him against his truck. "You give me pleasure too, baby doll. Is it in my eyes? 'Cause if you can't see it, I can show you where to find it." She took his hand and rubbed down the middle of her dress. Jed was too shocked to speak. She laughed with amusement then said in her naughtiest voice, "Kiss me, and there'll be no Cabot Hartley."

Jed grabbed her head. Tongues entwined habitually. He gripped her shoulders, pulling back. "Delaina, I..." *I love you,* he wanted to say. Should he? He looked into her eyes for the answer. His cell phone on the truck seat made a sound through the open window, the alert for a text message. She pulled his head to her mouth impatiently for another kiss. He let her. It beeped again. Still they kissed. Jed would tell her when the irritating thing quit interrupting. He would figure out how to tell her the rest of what he knew about Fain later. She had finally said, *'There'll be no Cabot Hartley,'* and her eyes had revealed enough feeling to give him the courage to take the first step. To admit he loved her. He wished the beeping would end so he could stop kissing her and tell her.

It ended. Because Delaina reached through the window. "Here. Someone's persistent," she said breathily, smiling. Then halted. *Nealy.* The name on the panel winked at her as she passed the phone to him. Jed glanced down. *Nealy.* He didn't reach for the phone in Delaina's hand. She tried to act brave, uninterested. "Go ahead," he said. His adrenaline was going now along with assurance of how he felt. He could explain. Nealy had been seven, maybe eight, weeks ago. It happened once, the last woman he'd been with, another eager, fixed-up female.

Delaina touched the screen, punched in their passcode. Her hands might've been visibly shaking. She read to herself with innate defiance, the first one, *Hey cutie!* With kissy face emoji. Number two, *I enjoyed our night together.* Lovey-dovey emojis like hearts, moons, a baby, a high heel. Then a separate line, suggestive emojis like a cherry, a cat, an eggplant, an open red circle... Delaina held out the phone.

Jed read and frowned. What the hell? A baby? Never. A cherry? *Get real.* He closed his eyes for a moment.

Delaina stared at the sky. At clouds. At nothing. Nealy Daniel, local accountant. Beautiful, educated, 28-ish, single. Eggplants and open circles. Jed reached for her hand. "I can explain. I want to explain."

What was there to explain? Yet Delaina had seen the date on Jed's side far above back-to-back *Nealy* messages. Weeks since Jed answered her, no emojis. His look...he wanted to try to explain. She scrolled for them to see the final text. *I'm at Mac's for a repeat. You were (red flames and a farmer emoji) Saturday. Xoxo.* Followed by a hot dog emoji.

A hot dog? Jed would've laughed at the absurdity; he had walked out of MacHenry's without speaking to Nealy that night, same night Delaina spent *overnight* in New Orleans with Cabot. She stood there judging him, dressed for a *date*. He was starting to get for-real mad and opened his mouth to point out these facts but Delaina's face. The anger...no, it was purified anguish.

The hot dog did it for Delaina. "Forget your explanation! No wonder you were in a rush to call it a day and go to Mac's." Delaina drew a breath. "Everyone has told me to stay away from you. I can't seem to get it through my thick skull. Forgive my stupidity! I think I've got it now. Joke's on me, huh?" She fetched her high heels and ran to her car, tears stinging her eyes. She sprayed Jed's boots with sand as she spun off. With a feeling close to impotence, he watched her leave, cursing Nealy and every woman, cursing his name, cursing life. He'd trade for one fair shot at Delaina Cash.

~ ~ ~

Delaina returned to Cash Way, significantly disheveled and twenty minutes late. A black limousine, more like a black leopard waiting to whisk her through another jungle, occupied her driveway. A uniformed driver propped against the car. "Hello, Miss Cash. Mr. Hartley just called to see if we were on the way."

"I'm sorry I'm late. I had a farm problem." She had a farm problem, for sure. In pitiable lust with the enemy. A man who would consider going to bed with her an invasion of Cash Way's most private property. Evidently, nothing would please him more. He got aroused every time they were near each other.

"Mr. Hartley told me not to rush you." The driver opened the door.

Once inside, Delaina found a mirror. Dear God, she looked like she had been coughed out of a windstorm. She tried to smooth her hair. Her lipstick had been kissed off. Oh well, Cabot would have to take what he got.

They crossed town and headed west on the county bridge over Big Sunflower. They rolled toward the Hartley estate, fit for King and Queen of Mallard. Delaina should've felt excitement. Her mind junked up with Jed. She got conflicting vibes. When he touched her, she felt like the only woman he wanted. Everywhere she turned, there were other women, Jed McCrae has-beens. The driver wound the limo on the private drive. A three-story castle stood gracefully. White brick, black shutters, beveled glass front doors. Delaina had been there many times. Still, it held royal charm. The driver led Delaina to the verandah. "Wait here, Miss Cash."

Delaina wrung her fingers. Quiet footsteps caused her to swing around. Cabot came to her, dressed in a white dinner jacket and black pants. "Don't you look splendid?" he gushed. "You have nice hair, Delaina, when it's styled."

"Thank you. You look good, too." She wished he'd stop calling her by her name. It didn't sound the same coming from him. She wished he'd stop complimenting her with every breath. Compliments seemed more genuine when they were rare. Cabot reached for her hand and brushed a kiss across her fingertips.

"You went to a lot of trouble for a dinner date."

"Nothing's too much trouble for you." He guided her body. "You haven't seen anything yet, beautiful. Forgive my behavior at Attorney Gage's office." He smiled apologetically. "Must be difficult to deal with your father's death alone. Let me know when I overstep. When you love someone, you want to be there. Hard to know when to stop." Cabot gave her a quick kiss.

Why had she doubted him? Here, the chance to be happy. Too bad Cabot didn't give her tingles when they touched. Such a feeling wouldn't last longer than a heated night in Jed McCrae's bed. With Cabot, she could build something stronger. Love, she guessed, must take time to develop. Stuck on the ground floor, she would find a way to go higher.

"Follow me." Cabot led her to the back, a trilevel deck and Olympic-size swimming pool. Delaina gasped. "*Cabot.*" Her eyes toured the display. In the grass, a towering cabana had been decorated in twinkling lights and white roses. He escorted her down steps to a table set in china and glimmering crystal. A string quartet played music. A server dressed in black waited. "Good evening." He bowed to Delaina. Soon they were served lobster-stuffed mushrooms and chardonnay. "A toast?" Delaina asked, raising her glass. Cabot stopped his glass in midair, about to take a sip. "I'll do it. I need to put wine tastings and etiquette classes to use. Let's see... May you have in your arms tonight the one you'll love for life."

A thick lump gathered in Delaina's throat. She lifted her glass. She hated mushrooms, forced a couple. Cabot and Delaina ate silently, except comment on food. The main course consisted of orange-glazed veal, au gratin potatoes, and steamed carrots. Delaina couldn't think about the veal's origin, or she'd vomit. Halfway through, Cabot asked, "How am I doing so far?"

"Perfect atmosphere."

"I like your manicure, a first for you." Cabot reached for her hand. "Delaina, I love the way your eyes flicker in the light. There are these little..."

"Flecks of gold," she finished. They continued eating until plates were cleared and the server came with a dessert tray. They took bites. Delaina commented, "Delicious, but I'm full." Cabot motioned to the musicians. "Delaina, dance with me."

And I'll never dance with anyone else again. She could hear it, nearly feel it. It wasn't Cabot. She didn't want to dance with anyone else, only Jed. Despite doubts crammed in her mind, she wanted this dinner and this night to be with him. Her stomach churned. Mushrooms and veal, that was her problem. "I want to finish my chardonnay."

"Sure, the fourth glass does it for you." Cabot grinned.

It'll take ten, she thought miserably, and gulped. When she stood, she had a drunk head. Cabot pulled her close. She avoided being face to face, looking over his shoulder. The light strumming of the violin faded into a guitar bellowing from a truck. Delaina's fancy black evening dress became a dusty white bed sheet. Cool skin on Cabot's cheek became Jed's warm stubble. Delaina's body relaxed. "Much better," Cabot whispered. She recalled the intensity she felt in Jed's presence. "Mmm..." she mumbled, eyes closed, and brain tickled.

"Will you marry me?"

Chardonnay fueled her roller coaster of thoughts, up, down, high, low, twisting and turning, whipping her along the track until she lost orientation altogether. She coasted to the day Jed took her to the funeral home. She prayed for a husband. He was there. His smoky eyes, his silky hair, his tanned arms holding her, taking away her grief with the simple utterance of her name. Marriage? He'd never marry her; he wasn't the marrying type. Nealy, Holland, Laureth, and how many more? She spoke in self-defense, "Yes, I'll marry you." She opened her eyes and swayed. The roller coaster screeched to an abrupt halt and jolted her into Cabot's arms. He opened a blue velvet jewelry box. Delaina gawked at the gaudy ring. "Is it real?" she blurted.

"*Lainey.*" He frowned.

"Sorry. It's huge."

Cabot bragged, "Thousands and thousands of dollars real. The square, there in the center, over two carats. Each of the trillions on the side is a half carat." He slid it on her finger.

"Three-plus carats of diamonds in platinum?" Delaina pressed her hands to her chest. "It's worth more than I am."

"Never. Trust me, never." Cabot had won. Goddamn! It was over. "When?" He exploded inside. "Soon, I hope." He couldn't contain his elation, swooped her up, and twirled her around. "Tonight wouldn't be soon enough!"

Delaina wiggled out of his arms. "Oh goodness. I've had enough emotion for one week. Uhm, when I finish school? Maybe next year." Cabot's smile got snatched from his face faster than a pickpocket to a wallet. He should have known the stubborn bitch wouldn't make it easy. Delaina decided on a test of love appropriate for her new fiancé. "Cabot, I was late arriving because of a farm problem. I didn't want to skip this fantastic evening altogether, but I need to leave and prepare the planters. I need your help."

"Really?" Cabot looked disgusted. "What about Moll?"

"They're in Meridian. Besides, I wanna do it."

"Then I'm not the one to help you."

"You're eager to learn, right? Since we're getting married." Cabot loathed the idea of getting on his hands and knees beneath a dirty tractor. "You don't seem excited."

"We got engaged. I had another way of celebrating in mind."

Delaina understood. Any man would expect her to be more excited, more interested. "It's been a wonderful evening. I owe you an apology for rushing. Let's get this done. It'll take an hour or so." She paused to shield her heart. "Then I'll spend the night with you. We'll make it official."

Cabot's phone buzzed in his pocket. He glanced at a text message. "Excuse me." He disappeared into the house and made a phone call regarding the message.

"Sorry to bother you, but we've got a problem," his partner said.

Cabot remarked, "More than one problem. I'm looking at a long engagement."

"No way."

"I know. I'll do something, if I have to get the girl pregnant."

"Can we meet? It's urgent."

"Uh, yeah. Give me a few minutes."

He stepped out. "Sweetie? This has been great, and I want to learn about the sprayer."

"Planters."

"Yes, excuse me, planters." He attempted a joke. "All the same to me. Anyway, I must meet someone. It's bank stuff, an international issue. It's not nighttime everywhere, you know. Markets and foreign currency," Cabot rambled. "Have the driver take you home. I'll come to Cash Way when I'm done."

"Fine," Delaina answered. "It's not late. Take your time." The longer it took, the less time they'd have for the inevitable sex they would have tonight.

~ ~ ~

The back end of a pickup truck never felt so good, not that she had been on one before. What a supreme Mississippi spring night. He went on about a trip he took to Atlanta. She didn't care what he talked about as long as he kept a sly grin on his face, eyes sparkling, dark hair shining.

Holland Sommers had never been to a cow auction. She liked wearing her snakeskin boots and tight blue jeans. She liked smelly animals and sweaty men. She liked Eli Smith. He would disappear to take care of things, return, and pick up where he left off, entertaining her with stories of crazy things country boys do to pass time. Holland liked that she didn't know much about Eli's lifestyle. All her adult life, she'd been paired with men she knew everything about, men with deals. No deal here. Eli didn't fool with pretense or motivation. "I'm having a great time."

"You gotta love her." Eli kissed her lips. "This place smells like manure and looks like hell. I smell like crap and look like hell, and she says she's havin' a great time." They laughed. "Got a surprise for you."

"What? How could you surprise me?" She patted his leg. "I've learned a lot about you this week, Cowboy."

"Dad and Rhett are taking the trailers back tonight. We're gonna stay in Meridian. Got us a room. That's why I insisted on drivin' separately."

"Eli, perfect! But I don't have clothes or makeup, and I have to be at work at nine in the morning."

Eli kissed her chin. "We'll figure out something." "You've got me. Yours 'til morning."

~ ~ ~

"It's Jed McCrae. I'm certain," Cabot's informant said.

"Well, Christ." Cabot double-checked the photo. From the back, the man looked like Jed.

"You told me to watch for anything suspicious. Led me to this bank in Atlanta."

"He brought Holland here. I should've figured it out before now." Cabot felt flustered.

"Let's try to piece it together and come up with a plan. Rethink. Jed's as private as the CIA."

"And as smart. When was this photo taken?" Cabot asked, studying his informant's phone.

"Tuesday. Day of the funeral."

"Do you know what he did at the bank?"

"All I know is he used the elevator."

"Do you know if Lainey's been near him the past few days?"

"I told you she came yesterday mornin' to ask him a question about Farm 130. They seemed angry. Haven't seen her since."

"Stay on top of everything. Stay with him. Don't let him breathe without knowing it. Let's go over details and look for cracks in our plan."

"Maybe you should incriminate Lainey, too. We wouldn't have to change much."

"It'll work better if I marry her to be sure I get the money from the sale of Cash Way."

~ ~ ~

That gal Lainey Cash wasn't the only one who'd had a ring on her finger.

Dacey Boyd had a ring on her finger once. It was a chip, so tiny the fat woman behind the counter at Diamond-Mart called it a pre-engagement ring. Poor Coby Pollock saved for it. Such a nice guy and, dang it, she thought she loved him. Till she went to work at the bank.

Ooh, then entered Cabot Hartley, her "Butterscotch." She knew she wasn't the only one or prettiest or smartest or richest. She believed she was his favorite. She got herself in a heap of trouble from believin' it.

Her mama had taken a night job as soon as Dacey showed her the engagement ring from Coby Pollock. She wanted her only daughter to have a big wedding. Her daddy had taken Coby over to the Western Wishbone in Greenville for a catfish dinner the night they told them they were getting married. She and her mama had stayed home to plan. But it didn't last. Like something out of Patsy's songs, Dacey was crazy. Months later, she threw away a nice boy, ruined her reputation, and look what it got her. Sure, the presents and secret meetings at the Hartley camp house were exciting, but she sat home most nights. Her dear mama scarcely said a kind word to her.

She didn't have nothin' against Lainey Cash. She better treat her Butterscotch right. If she didn't, Dacey would kick her scrawny rich ass. And that girl better appreciate the rock of a diamond Dacey was sure her Butterscotch had put on her finger by now. Dacey hung her head. Then she remembered. The Elvis special was comin' on at ten. She wouldn't let somethin' as silly as a 'business partnership kind of marriage,' that's what Butterscotch called it, ruin her evening. She dragged herself off the bed and slipped into the living room.

Her mama glanced. "Seein' as you ain't got nothin' better to do, you could get you a night job to help us with them weddin' cancellation fees we're still payin' on."

"I give you part of every other paycheck. The weddin' expenses ought to be paid by now. Turn to channel seven. You'll find somethin' there we can agree on."

Her mama smacked her lips. "If I didn't like Elvis so much myself, I'd keep it on this *Idol* rerun for spite."

"But you ain't, by nature, spiteful, Mama."

"I didn't think you was, by nature, a cheater, but you proved your mama wrong, didn't you?"

"You ain't perfect," Dacey smarted off. "Neither is Daddy. Lay off me or else I'll move out and you can do the cookin' and cleanin' and washin' for Daddy and them boys."

"I do most of it anyhow, missy."

"Yeah, but you hate to starch them Sheriff's uniforms of Daddy's. It would get old quick."

"You're probably right. Hush up. They're tellin' how many folks has been up to Graceland this year."

Thirteen

In Lust

Tingly from wine, Delaina sat in the foyer of Cash Way waiting on Cabot, thinking how good Jed's bare chest felt against her bare back as he jolted her across their land.

Her thoughts were wrong, especially now. She could not help herself. She cupped the ring in her hand, attached to a chain around her neck she found to string it on. Dangerous to wear it on her finger while she worked, yet she knew Cabot would expect her to have it on when he arrived. Wanting to push its significance away, she tucked it beneath her tank top. Delaina felt sort of glad she said yes to Cabot now. To have someone to lean on.

One thing she needed to do first, and she could not help herself. Go to bed with Jed.

Ooh. She liked the way that sounded so much she did a little dance and sang, 'Go to *bed* with *Jed*.' Certainly, her lust would dissipate once she had him. *When* should she go to *bed* with *Jed*? As soon as possible since she was officially an engaged woman, before her engagement became public. It had to be done... tonight. Tonight! At Jed's cabin, if he weren't tangled in Nealy-the-accountant's legs. On impulse, she knew what to do. She and Jed could strike a deal. She didn't have to worry about Cabot finding them. Given his lack of interest in actual farming methods, he probably couldn't find his way past the main drive to her house.

~ ~ ~

Jed rested across the bed facedown. He could feel himself floating into satisfying sleep for the first time in a week. Never mind it took an o-t-c sleep aid to get him there. He had spent the evening contemplating his options, of which he incessantly had two. Tell Delaina everything. Don't tell her anything. He decided to tell her everything. Tomorrow.

Ever so subtly, a torturous dream crept into his drug-induced brain.

Her again. Standing over him, a shadowy form. Wearing a red hoodie over a BC tank top, words *Snow White,* and frayed denim shorts with work boots. Have mercy on the Smith men; how did they work with blonde Snow White working beside them? The vision whispered, "Jed?"

He squeezed his temples. "Go away." These dreams had to stop. At least she wasn't naked and dancing in this one. The stomp of boots jolted him. "What in hell?" He scrambled to sit. "This isn't a dream."

She twirled around, prissy as a cat. "No, darlin', I'm for real."

He grimaced. "You're in my house. In my bedroom. You're..."

"I knocked twice." Delaina shrugged. "Lights in the den are on. I found a key over the door frame." She clucked her tongue. "Very original place to hide it, big guy."

Well...hell. Jed got wide awake.

She began to prowl his room. She touched a souvenir mug on his dresser, from the first beer he ordered inside an Irish pub. Her careless violation of his most private place unsettled Jed's nerves. Watching her strut around in those scant shorts would soon leave him unable to think at all. Delaina's hands landed on her hips. "Where's Nealy? Has she finished eating your hot dog yet?" She made bold eye contact.

Jesus, her mouth. He kept eye contact. "I finished with her about two months ago."

Delaina's insides shook, in contrast to the emboldened persona she attempted to display. The overconsumption of dinner wine helped. This had to work. From the corner of her eye, she watched. Jed sat on the bed's edge wearing his BC boxers and slammed his hands through slept-on, messy hair. His sleepy-grumpy face held darker-than-usual eyes. His lungs rose and fell sharply, enhancing his awesome chest. Delaina murmured aloud intentionally. Jed jumped to his feet. "How many times do I have to tell you? You're gonna get killed sauntering around in the dark."

"Hopefully seduced." Golden fire burned in her eyes. She twisted her ankles in her boots.

Delaina was acting strange. She clearly propositioned him. "Hours ago, you told me not to worry. You learned your lesson about me."

"I've tried to." She crept closer, her hands on his pilot logbook bedside. "I need you for two things."

Jed's eyebrows scrunched. Women were moody but rarely were they unpredictable. Delaina needed sex if she needed anything. He needed to give it to her more than anything. Something wasn't right... He played dumb. "What do you need, Delaina?"

She picked up the log and answered in provocative puffs, "I can't get you out of my head. Out of my dreams. They are dirty dreams, James…Evan…Darrah…McCrae…private pilot for…" Flipping pages. "…seven years."

Something akin to a plane flew through Jed's middle.

She put down the log. "Silly lust." Delaina forced a giggle. "You're used to it. Nealy, Holland, Laureth, who else? Forget it, I don't need to know. A whole lot of eggplant and red circles, I'm sure… Ha! If *I* texted you, it'd be the eggplant and the…tiny doughnut, not a big open circle." Another "Ha!" as she faced him.

How afflicted she made him; her emoji reference seriously turned Jed on. "Are you drunk?"

"Drinking, yes," she bragged with a pretty smile. "Not drunk. Heck, after guzzling vermouth, I still want you." Jed knew the feeling. "I haven't gone to the shed to set the planters. I need you to…"

"What about Cabot? Why isn't he knee-deep in grime right now?"

"Shit, *Cabot*?" She made a terrible face. "He'd be as much help with either of my needs as Spongebob."

That did make Jed smile along with, "You're just about wasted, I think."

"Took four glasses of wine to get through his horribly ostentatious idea of a dinner date. I'm actually feelin'..." She licked her lips. "...nice and warm for our..." She shimmied slowly. "...rendezvous." She rolled her tongue with the word and winked.

Good Lord. Jed nearly abandoned being sensible and tossed her on the bed.

She hitched her shoulder. "Cabot's long gone. *Yayyy*," she dragged out with a girly cheerleader voice and clap. "Business call on international currency or some crap. Who knows? So, yay!" Another clap and quick hip shake.

Whew. Jed thought about suggesting they get rid of Cabot for good, so he could see more clapping and cheering and shimmying and shaking. The suggestion, no, demand would come tonight.

Her index finger trailed his neck to his chest and flicked his nipple. His hot skin sent shivers up her arm. His blue-black eyes penetrated her. Her finger worked its way to hair below his naval. She swallowed a wedge of uncertainty. "What I said in your office was true. A one-night stand isn't my style. I think it's gonna be the only way I forget about you. I accept this on your usual terms. In fact, I don't want it any other way. No conversation and I'm not here to get information. To hell with a relationship or faithfulness."

Jed frowned. "No." Why did she want to forget him? Why be with Cabot if she disliked him? If Jed took her offer, he wanted to know she felt something, more than eggplant, for him. He would seduce her so effectively she would come back for more for the rest of her life. She wouldn't do it if she knew what Fain Kendall told him. He'd get to that first. Somehow.

Delaina yanked at her topaz hair shimmering in faint light. "So, I'm blonde." She ran her fingers over his eyebrows. "Close your eyes. It's all...the kitty cat emoji in the dark."

Jed winced. "Delaina, that's not it." He put on a T-shirt and jeans. "Where are the planters?"

"Shelter at the Denton Place." She looked around his space. "I thought you'd have a different logbook by your bed. Where is it?" With a cutesy nose wrinkle, "I'm ready to..." She jiggled. "...write

Lainey Cash on the next blank line." She scribbled into the air. "Yay." Big smile, tiny cheerleader clap.

He sighed while he grinned. "Let's go, Lainey Cash."

"You wanna do the planters before you do me?" She curled her fingers into her waistband.

Jed swallowed hard. His physical needs were quite obvious. "Workin' on the planters will require concentration and strength. Baby, I'll have neither when I get through with you."

He wanted truth in the open, Cabot Hartley out of the picture, and Delaina naked underneath him. Or on top or side by side or back to front. Whatever she liked. When he finished with her, she'd love him, by God, or he'd kill the exasperating heathen. Virtually no way to have it all without hurting her with what he knew, he determined he would think of something. He hurried downstairs. Delaina followed like two squirrels on a tree.

~ ~ ~

Holland soaked in a Jacuzzi-style bathtub, luxuriating in their spontaneous detour. She could do without a change of clothes for one night. She could even do without her herbal shampoo and coconut facial scrub. She felt like she forgot something. "Holy God!" Birth control pills. When had she last taken one? Days ago. She sprang out of the water and grabbed a towel. She hadn't taken one since...Eli. Stress at work and with Cabot and Jed frazzled her brain.

Eli slipped in wearing his briefs. "I thought I heard you..."

"Eli, something terrible has happened. My God, please forgive me." Her face was stark white.

Eli backed up. "Lord, you're scarin' the cowboy. What?"

"My pills, birth control pills. I haven't taken them in days. I ran out and just remembered."

He looked like he'd been hit by a truck. A big one. He scratched his head. "Oh Lord, are you pregnant?"

"I don't know." Holland leaned against the wall. "What if I am?" She closed her eyes.

"Would it be mine?"

Her eyelids fluttered open. Seconds stretched. "Uh, yes."

Eli whistled, looking like the truck that hit him reversed and backed over what remained. "Have mercy, I should've took care of this myself. I... Good Lord, I thought you had everything under control since you ain't mentioned it. Half my fault."

"I blame my job. So stressful. I haven't had time *to think*."

"Look, ain't nothing we can do about it. I'll be there for you, whatever happens."

"I don't want a baby."

Eli frowned. "I ain't ready for one."

"Maybe there won't be a baby."

"Don't those pills have some kind of overlap? Ain't there an emergency thing?"

She laughed nervously. "Overlap? Emergency birth control for six days?"

Eli scratched his head, disappointed. "We've done all we're gonna do tonight, I guess."

"Yes." Holland smiled weakly. "I can't risk it. I'll find something I can take at the drugstore tomorrow, maybe."

He gazed at her body, appreciating certain features. "Hell, honey, there's a heap of things we ain't done."

~ ~ ~

Only half of his body could be seen. Delaina wasn't quite sure if it was the most desirable half. That remained a toss-up, but right now the lower half had her full attention. Jed was sprawled across the concrete on his back. The fly of his jeans jutted; the muscled mass of his thighs pulled faded denim tight across his legs. His dirty boots weren't tied. She enjoyed this scrumptious view he couldn't see her indulging in, top of him under the metal rack of the planters.

When they got there, she had flipped on overhead work lights and the shop's FM radio set to golden oldies. Apparently, it was a rainy night two states over in Georgia.

In the history of farming, surely planters had not been used as tools of seduction. Tonight, the large, metal implement was worth the thousands Cash Way paid, if it never rolled into a field again. Delaina straddled atop the cobweb of bars in the opposite direction snapping a seed plate in place while Jed adjusted the depth lever underneath. Her head dangled above his crotch.

Only half of her body was visible. For the moment, Jed felt sure the most desirable half, and he had no trouble looking at it in florescent light. Her slick legs dangled over his face. Her position on the bar caused her shorts to bunch up. He could see the crease where her legs met her crotch and no underwear. He had a good idea what he'd enjoy doing in that position. Jed's fingers gripped a tool handle more often than a dinner fork; tonight, he was cumbersome.

"Are you thinking what I'm thinking?"

"I don't think so," he grumbled. "Make sure you snap the plate in tight."

"Then what are you thinking?"

Jed laughed softly. "I'm thinking of a number between one and a hundred."

Whoa. Delaina twisted the lock to make sure it was tight against the plate. "What's it like?"

"Perfect."

"Perfect?"

"The depth is set. Perfect. What's what like?" he called up to her.

"That, uh, number you're thinking about."

"You don't know?" She was only twenty. Jed forgot. Sometimes.

"No, but I'd let you show me."

Another plane crashed in Jed's middle. He decided to ignore her bonus gift for a while. "Let's set the down pressure. I wanna see if you're a genuine farmer." She watched from above as his stomach, his chest, his neck, his face appeared. Hers was above his by inches. Delaina flung herself forward and kissed his lips. Repeatedly, they brushed tongues. He sprang to his feet, cut his eyes, and smiled sardonically. "Show me what you're made of, Miss Cash."

Delaina pulled off her jacket. Her tank top did little to conceal her naked breasts. Jed liked the silver chain dangling inside, its pendant hidden in her shallow crevice. He averted his attention to gears of the planters. They needed to be adjusted to determine how much seed would be fed out of the seed boxes.

Delaina put her hand on the spring-loaded adjustment and changed the gear to disperse the right amount of seed. "We've got a long night ahead of us," she said.

Jed watched her. The night might not last as long as she thought. He felt fifteen as far as control went when he thought of them, of her. Jed reached over and stroked her arm. He watched his hand, big and rough, move over her soft skin and realized he couldn't tell her what he knew from Fain Kendall; it would hurt her, and he'd lose her, and she wasn't his to lose. Selfishly, he could leave the truth unsaid and have her for one night. One night, what she asked for, was better than never. He would deal with the ugly fallout from Fain's will later.

~ ~ ~

"Jed's looking at years in the cell. Attorney Gage won't have a problem nailing him with the evidence we're providing," Cabot said, rehashing plans.

"You really think Attorney Gage will believe he's guilty. He won't figure out it's us?"

"Gage gave me the will, the only wrong thing he's done, but..." Cabot snickered. "I could remind him it was wrong. Besides, he wants an election win this fall. He'll be hungry to nail someone. This'll cause a media frenzy statewide. Free publicity for him to get a conviction quickly."

Cabot's partner nodded. "Sheriff Boyd knows the plan and supports us completely?"

"He and Investigator Raybon Hall are aware of everything. Sheriff Boyd dislikes Jed because he was seeing his daughter Dacey two weeks before her wedding. She's the reason Jed came to the Mill's Pond party. The boy she was engaged to found out after the incident and broke the engagement, leaving Sheriff with wedding expenses and no groom. The sheriff has another motive: He'll look good for busting up a large operation. Plus, I've paid him off. Mallard's had a pot problem for years." Cabot had a smug look.

"The funny part is Fain Kendall's gonna croak about the same time."

"Perfect, man. No one with rights to McCrae land. Jed'll be out of the picture. I'll purchase it with no problem."

His partner probed, "What about Lainey? How are you going to get married fast?"

"I'll figure it out. She accepted the ring. Progress for a cold bitch."

~ ~ ~

Delaina and Jed sat on the concrete floor of the farm shelter, backs against the wall, drinking root beer from the shop's fridge. They had finished working and done away with bright light. Delaina set the sprockets as fast as Jed could. An outside security bulb glowed across the space. Late-night music had been too good to switch off; they found one of Tory's Led Zeppelin CDs in the player. The band had turned romantic.

"When we were workin' on the planters, what were *you* thinking about when you asked me what I was thinking about?" Jed asked.

"That our fathers are probably beatin' their fists into their caskets if they can see us." She slid toward him and got his hand. "Then again, maybe they would be proud of us for tryin' to get along." Delaina kissed his lips. And kissed and kissed.

Jed kissed back. And kissed and kissed. "We're damn good at the kissin' part, at least." Led's serenade didn't help; Jed positively wanted to give her all his love. He'd start below her waistline with the number 69 she knew nothing about. "Tell me, Delaina, what do you really expect from me? After tonight."

"I got it straight earlier. I don't expect anything from you after tonight."

"What if I want you to expect something?"

What could he want? Land, farm details, more sex? She would leave no room for maneuvering. "I'm ready to get this over with and move on."

"Move on, huh?" She wanted to use and be used. Jed scrubbed his stubble against her shoulder while he stroked the small of her back with his fingers. He would do it to her so effectively this would become an easy question: "Is there a particular reason why what I've got in my pants is different from any other man?"

Delaina's eyes lowered to his jeans. She quivered. "It's bigger than the ones I've seen."

"You haven't seen it." His voice seemed stormy. "Do I need to pull it out so you can measure and compare?"

Delaina bypassed his mockery. "Not important to me. Uh, I don't think it is." She still looked at it through his jeans. He watched her study him, his eyes glazed. She attempted explanation, "I have a theory. You're a drug."

"A drug."

"Or a tornado."

"A tornado?"

"Yeah, a woman gets swept in, and that's it. One kiss and she must see it to completion regardless of consequences. That's got to be it, no other explanation. I mean, I've never felt like this."

"No other explanation for why you've never felt like this, huh?" He ran his tongue down her arm to her fingers, sucked each one.

Delaina's being flew to the other side of the moon. "I'm definitely caught in a storm." The way he licked, bit, scrubbed her skin -with his tongue, teeth, stubble. She held out her hands to get her balance though she was sitting down. He or the perfect song had to go. She was about to *come,* hard and vocally. "*Jed,* you and that song. I'm ready to give all my...woo, something."

"Yeah, this song's giving "Thank You" a run for the money right now. I'm plannin' on saving it for the wedding," he said between rubbing her back and kissing her neck.

Huh? "*Thank You?*" His hand felt rough on her ribs under her tank top, like a man's should. "Wedding?" She couldn't think clearly about what he meant with his touch so slow and right.

His eyes shone like diamonds in the dark. "Their song "Thank You," even better. For my wife. First dance at our wedding. I guess it's you and this for now."

Delaina's head was pudding. He talked, moved, and kissed like she would want a lover to. 'This for now...' Fine with her, swept in utterly and hopelessly. "I'm ready."

"Do you think you'll ever love, or heck, like Cabot?" Jed continued his mouth thing on her skin.

Delaina's brain had to search to find the name Cabot. Her privates were screaming Jed. "Uh, Cabot. I sort of, whoa God, like him, uh, sometimes. Oh God." Jed's tongue and teeth behind her ear, down the nape of her neck. What else did he ask? "Uh, love and Cabot. Uhm. I'm getting there." Heavens, she was about to take her shorts off and get there. "He's a..." Her breathing became embarrassing in its neediness. "A building."

"A building?"

Delaina slid her hair upward with her forearm, encouraging his mouth to move over the front of her shoulder and collarbone. "Yeah, I'm on, uh, the ground floor, but I found the, uh, elevator tonight. Ooh oh, *Jed.*" Mouth on her breast, wet, hot, biting through the thin tank top

"Could you use plain English?" He sat up and stopped his seduction.

"I'll...fall ...in love with Cabot slowly...with a lot of work. It's gonna help move me to the next level to massage this sore spot."

"Now I'm a sore spot." Jed sighed. It got worse each second. "Tell me something, Delaina. You've explained why you're here. Why am I?"

"Easy." She patted his head. "I'm a bigger challenge than most. The ultimate thrill for you." "The ultimate thrill?" "Yeah, a chance to vandalize Cash Way as personally as possible and prove to yourself that you really can have anything you want. Even the twenty-year-old daughter of the man your family despised. I happen to also be involved with the local banker you don't like and won't do business with." She smiled. "*Jed,* let's go to *bed.* I want more of your mouth and your..."

Damn, her reasoning for him was brutal. Jed kissed her lips hard. He cupped her shoulders and pulled her onto his lap impatiently. "You're wrong."

"Which part?" She straddled him, clothes on, and sensed the thickness of him through his jeans.

"I can do it with you, but I don't have what I really want from you."

Delaina's heart squeezed like an orange. Laureth, his ex-fiancé. He didn't have Laureth. Well, she asked for this callus treatment, actually begged for it. At least he was man enough to let her know beforehand she didn't mean a thing to him. "At least you're honest."

Jed all but told Delaina he loved her, admitted he wanted more. She offered nothing. He gave up. "I am honest as much as possible."

What a fate. The one he loved, begging him to take her to bed and leave her alone. He dove in and kissed her with the brutality she thought him capable of. "Don't say I didn't warn you, little girl. I'll show you the ultimate thrill. Is here good enough? I can take you to my bed." He crushed her lips with his.

"Here's good." Delaina, enveloped in heat, felt disappointed with his sudden harshness. Jed plundered her mouth while his hand toyed with the silver chain around her neck. All at once, she bolted. The ring! Caught up in her seduction plans, she forgot. Too late, the gaudy diamond escaped his grip, its facets flickering. A glinting jewel, like a dagger raised through nightlight. "I can explain!"

Jed's eyes speared in an un-glittering navy blue. "You are your father's daughter. That explains it." He got up and went toward the door.

"Jed, the ring shouldn't matter! What's the difference?"

He spun around, a gunpowder outline in an ebony world. "The ring *should* matter, Delaina. After you thoroughly seduced me at the field, you ran off and got engaged to Cabot Hartley then came running back to seduce me again. What am I supposed to think? Act like there's no difference!" He slowed his words so their clarity and insult would not be mistaken. "I don't flaunt or use women like your fiancé does, but I have more females in my phone contacts than the population of Mallard County. I'm not desperate. I have no interest in Cabot Hartley's bride."

Delaina darted into the crisp air. The wind took her breath. A moonless, starless night. "My car is at 130."

"Is that your biggest concern?"

"No, you are. You act hurt."

Jed's head dropped. "I'm not acting."

"I'm sorry."

"You owe him an explanation. Apologize to him." Jed pointed at distant headlights.

"Oh God! Take me, please. Please! I can't face Cabot." She jumped in as Jed slammed the truck in reverse. The air choked life out of Delaina. She didn't mean to hurt him. Why was he hurt? What did he want?

Inside the field row at 130, Jed parked. Lights on the dashboard reflected on Delaina's tears. "Is it the blonde hair that does it?" he asked.

She felt horrible. He didn't have to say more. It hadn't been her intention to use Jed. She fumbled with the decadent ring then ripped it from her neck. "I don't want it."

Jed let his gaze fall over her body. "Neither do I."

Fourteen

In Love

What a whirlwind! Grandest wedding they would *ever* live to see. The Topic all over Mallard, core of gossip at the bank, the salon, MacHenry's, church. Eight hundred invitations, hundreds of white roses, dozens of bottles of wine, and an abundant supply of Alaskan salmon, Maine lobster, and Texas steak had been procured. The cake, a mind-blowing rendition of her homeplace with the bride and groom on the front steps, created by Divine Designs in Manhattan, would be flown in and assembled on site the day of. A week of travel in Sweden had been reserved. Eight tuxedos were being fastidiously tailored for the groom and his attendants, no father of the bride's tuxedo. Three bridesmaids' dresses were custom. The groom's sister and the bride's closest high school friends, Mary Beth Bell at Florida State University now and Waverly Wallace at Mississippi State, were her attendants.

Rumor had it, the wedding dress, designed by world-renowned Holly Lacey from Nashville, had been fashioned after a dress in the bride's recurring dream. Only the bride had seen it. No one else would see it until six o'clock in the evening on May first. The groom conferred with his partner-in-crime at their secret meeting place, up to their ears in complex maneuvering. The bride baked at home alone in her kitchen, pitching a tantrum, up to her ears in cookie dough.

The engaged couple had spent time together three times in nineteen days.

~ ~ ~

"Eli-motherfuckin-Smith married to Holland Sommers. Who would've guessed? She's a smart one, especially with McCrae. This is slick." Cabot slapped a tree trunk. "I know mine, but what's your theory?"

"You've been playin' along with Holland since we got the picture of Jed in Atlanta, right?" his partner asked.

"Yeah. She doesn't know we now realize she came to Mallard to help Jed. Been stringing her along in hopes she'll slip up and tell me something useful."

Cabot's partner scratched his head. "Holland started seeing Eli so Jed would have an inside track on Cash Way. Eli told Holland that he is Lainey's top choice for the farm manager. Holland told Jed. Jed encouraged her to marry Eli."

"You've got it, and Eli's such a dumb, pussy-whipped country boy he can't see it." Cabot smoked and rolled his eyes.

"Why don't you turn in Eli for selling marijuana to college kids? Get him out of the way."

"We made a deal. He'd get me the plants, and I'd overlook his dealing. I'd be walking a fine line. I've bought my personal stash from him in the past. He would do his best to incriminate me, and Holland would be willing to help him produce evidence. Their word against mine, and I think they have Jed on their side. Could get ugly." Cabot sighed wearily. "Let's do the drug bust Saturday as planned. To get Jed out of the way. Fain Kendall has told me he'd sell McCrae Farms to me first if it's ever a possibility. Since he's about to die anyway, I know he'll sell to me after Jed's arrested. Go ahead and make the calls. Confirm for this Saturday around three o'clock."

"Are you sure? This won't impede the wedding?"

Cabot buried doubts. "Time to act. We're playing with a big dog. Time to make him choke on a bad bone."

~ ~ ~

Holland and Eli took the day off work on Wednesday to honeymoon overnight in Memphis. They had married on the courthouse steps in Mallard.

There was no plan or scheme with Jed McCrae. Delaina had not told Eli that she might make him her farm manager. She only told Cabot because he hounded her about it. She had taken Jed's advice and kept everyone, including Cabot, guessing.

Later the same night Jed saw Delaina's engagement ring, Cabot found Delaina crying on the creekbank and questioned her. Delaina reluctantly admitted Jed helped her with the planters. She and Cabot became embroiled in an ongoing argument that ended days later when Delaina apologized, asked forgiveness, and offered to marry Cabot immediately.

Attorney Warren Gage had been put in a tough position because of the wedding date Delaina wanted to use: May first, the same deadline she had to choose a farm manager. He and Delaina came to an agreement. Cabot wasn't overly thrilled, but he had his other plan, *creating fear in Delaina*, to rely on. She chose May first because she could name a farm manager before the ceremony, and it wouldn't have to be Cabot. Her wedding date she used as another way to keep everyone guessing. If she didn't name anyone before they were pronounced man and wife, Cabot automatically became manager because he was marrying her before she turned twenty-one.

Holland and Eli were casual lovers expecting a baby. In the past, they each preferred noncommittal relationships, communicating unknown to them. Neither mentioned what they knew about Cabot because neither knew to whom the other gave allegiance. Eli feared Holland's involvement in a crooked scheme with Cabot and vice versa. Both were paid not to talk. Instead, they married on a whim to covertly obligate the other. They'd worry about the rest later. But not much later.

~ ~ ~

Jed McCrae had a problem. He had several. He concentrated on the biggest one. Cabot Hartley. Jed knew he used Delaina but had no proof. Cabot kept his coconspirators local, a town full of people indebted to him financially and otherwise. Locals, under those conditions, were as tight-lipped as a whore's blow job. Over and over, day after day, and deep into most nights, Jed talked himself in and out of an attempted reconciliation with Delaina. Hours slipped through his hands. He had to come up with proof not only because he counted the days to her marrying Cabot Hartley but also because his stepfather Fain Kendall deteriorated in a hospital in New Orleans. Any day now, that harrowing truth would come. Thereafter, Delaina would never forgive Jed or consider trusting him.

Jed could admit, only to himself, for the first time in his adult life living alone seemed lonely. He wanted one more day, one more night, one more anything with her. Would Cabot kill her? Cash Way would be his. Jed thought Cabot might wait for Fain to die and try to kill them. Everything they owned would be his. Jed and Delaina didn't have anyone to will their land to who wouldn't sell it at a Cabot Hartley price. Or maybe Cabot and Delaina planned to kill him. Who knew? All Jed knew, he had an ominous feeling. Decades of competition along the banks of Big Sunflower River were about to come to a tragic blow.

~ ~ ~

"To heck with the chocolate chips!" Delaina threw the opened bag of morsels across the room. They flew like a flock of birds then scattered on the floor like poisoned ants. She couldn't remember how many cups she put in the bowl. The recipe called for three eggs; she had two. She sent Miss Maydell to town to buy more. She started picking up the chips and decided to put all of them in the dang bowl. If he liked chocolate chip cookies so much, the more the merrier. One by one she flicked them into the mixture. He'd never know they were on the floor.

Depleted, Delaina had been to three cities in less than three weeks securing the boring details of the ridiculously expensive, ridiculously extravagant wedding. Her home buzzed with a wedding planner, a decorator, a florist, gardeners, and handymen sent by Claudia Hartley and billed to Delaina.

She hadn't talked to Jed since April first, since the horrid incident with her ring. They met head-on driving down Cash-McCrae

Road two days later. He waved first casually. Delaina waved in return and cried like a baby.

With nuclear explosiveness, pieces of their last night together had appeared inside the vehicle with her:

I got it straight earlier. I don't expect anything from you after tonight, Jed.

From him, *What if I want you to expect something?* And, *Led's song "Thank You," even better. For my wife. First dance at our wedding. I guess it's you and this for now.*

She had pulled over, downloaded the song, and listened. She did not feel for Cabot any emotion within the same hemisphere of the loving words of that song.

Jed McCrae wanted a wedding, wanted to feel that way about his bride, wanted to dance with his wife to those ideal words. But he promised ALL his dances to Delaina.

More of his words had come to her:

I can do it with you, but I don't have what I really want from you. And *The ring should matter, Delaina.*

Was there any way she could be that person to anyone? To Jed. Was there a chance in hell she *was already* that person to him?

Pointless to cry or wonder. Cash Way came first.

Delaina stirred cookie dough. ...She missed a lot of things about Jed. Mostly she missed talking to him although they argued half the time. She never realized physical attraction could run so strong and cut so deep. Sometimes she wondered if it was...

"Lainey, I've got eggs." Miss Maydell peeked in the bowl. "My goodness, sweetie, you used a lot of chips." She sniffed authoritatively. "I know you wanna learn for yourself. Don't bake too long. They're gonna harden more after they cool."

"Thanks. I'll get dressed while they bake before I deliver them to my sick friend in town." She didn't look back, afraid Maydell Smith would recognize a lie.

~ ~ ~

Summer Lynn Moss had always been flirtatious. A known fact countywide, she had the hots for Jed for years. Fortunately, she was Cabot's personal assistant at the bank before Holland

Sommers moved to town, still employed as front desk receptionist. Jed's best shot and his last good idea, he did what was necessary today.

He waltzed into the bank around ten o'clock dressed like a celebrity and figured he could have, in one short night, wined and dined Summer Lynn Moss into his bed for half the money the stone-colored pants cost him. He hated to think about what kind of elegant, sassy woman he could have wooed for the cost of his shoes. In the Miss Mississippi league, no doubt. Maybe one more ritzy date with the Houston Channel Five News anchorwoman he dallied with not too long ago.

The instant the heavy glass doors closed behind him, the usual murmur of morning business fell silent. Jed McCrae at Mallard First Financial Bank? Such a rarity, some never remembered seeing him there. Summer Lynn Moss remembered. He had been two times since she worked there.

She flashed a dentist-bleached smile from her chair. Short brunette hair tucked behind her ears in a sleek bob styled impeccably paired with sky blue eyes accented by heavy mascara. Her lips were meticulously outlined fire engine red to heighten their heart shape. She wore a pastel pink suit and white blouse one button too many unfastened revealing full breasts. Apples, Jed thought instinctively and suppressed a grin, thinking he could've almost paid for the plastic surgeon who put them there for the cost of the cornflower blue dress shirt and tweed sports coat he wore this morning.

"Good morning, Jed, eh, Mr. McCrae. How can I, uh, we assist you?" she chirped out cheerfully, reminding him of a caged canary ready to be set free.

Jed leaned across her desk and let his eyes peek in her blouse. He caught wind of familiar expensive perfume. She smelled like a rose. Like Holland. Like Cabots' others. "Hey, Summer Lynn. I realized after I got to town, I've misplaced my debit card. I need quick cash." His face had *Come and get it* plastered over it frosted in an air of good manners. Summer Lynn's fluttery eyelashes, attentive smile, and nervous fingers insinuated, *I'm putty in your hands.* "Will Mallard First cash Jed McCrae's check, ma'am?"

"Absolutely," she cooed. Her breasts jutted farther as she pointed to tellers. "Danielle's available..."

"You can't do it?" Jed flashed a killer grin.

Summer Lynn closed in and mouthed, "Do it?"

"Uh, huh."

"I can't cash your check if that's what you mean." She fumbled through papers. Jed knew her type, the moves she'd use to weasel her way into a more intimate setting, precisely what he aimed for. "You look like you're dressed for a lunch date, Jed."

"I do?"

"A farmer has never come in here dressed like you, and none would look like you if they did." Summer Lynn smiled. "I get a lunch break at eleven. Do I dare hope you might accompany me to Harper's?"

"Meet me on the patio." Jed sauntered away and approached a teller to cash a check.

~ ~ ~

Summer Lynn Moss didn't know much. She knew Cabot went in and out more than usual at the bank and seemed overly stressed. She heard Cabot talking in a muffled voice on his cell phone about something major to take place this Saturday. He cussed, lost his temper, hung up.

Jed didn't like that. He hated to leave town and leave Delaina there for the weekend. He had plans in Houston. Summer Lynn claimed she knew nothing else. Jed believed her. The way she carried on throughout their meal, no doubt she would've spilled her guts if she knew more. He bought her lunch and kissed her mouth thoroughly when they parted, promising to call.

Summer Lynn was a pretty woman, and Jed liked kissing pretty women.

She wasn't fresh and natural and down-to-earth and petite and bitchy and opinionated and hotheaded and stubborn; she would never strip on the riverbank or kiss like a snake; she didn't smell like peppermint candy and ocean breezes or laugh contagiously and flirt unintentionally. Jed was certain Summer Lynn Moss already knew what that number between one and a hundred felt like, and she wouldn't know how to lock a seed plate into a planter box or shuck an oyster. Her lips weren't soft as clouds. Her breasts didn't have a sexy little barely detectable sway when she walked.

She wasn't Delaina.

~ ~ ~

It was a tiny baby step. It was the only thing Delaina could come up with.

She wore a lilac knit slip dress, fitted and flared above the knee. She wore a bra and perfume, styled her hair, and applied more makeup than normal. She wrapped the cookies in cellophane and put them in a brown paper bag.

She had mailed Jed an invitation to her wedding, her offer to truce. The cookies would be her token of peace. Jed had sent a bottle of wine from Florence...*Italy*...with a pair of intricately colored, handblown wineglasses as a wedding gift by delivery to Cash Way yesterday. A good sign, she thought, or a nice gesture.

She chose to go to his cabin in broad daylight at high noon. To prevent herself from touching him or worse. He'd be there for lunch, hopefully. The cookies could be his dessert. She slipped her engagement ring on and off her finger apprehensively as she drove down the dirt path and decided to wear it.

His truck was parked in front. Her limbs went slack at the sight. For God's sake, why did she miss him so much? A roller coaster did inverted spirals in her stomach. She got out and walked uneasily to the door. Should she knock? Had he seen her through the window? He might not come to the door. Please God, he had to. She had to see him. One more time. She had to touch him. One more time. No, she couldn't touch him, Delaina harshly reminded herself. Funny, she had thought daylight and wearing the ring would help dispel her desire. She stood gripping the doorknob, releasing, gripping, and decided not to knock. She would barge in, so he had no choice but to face her. In final preparation, she smoothed her free hand through her hair and down her dress. No, now she probably looked fixed up and overdone. She bent and shook her hair over her head, licked her painted lips, and tugged on her dress. Now she probably looked like she just had wild sex. She sighed and backed away from the door.

She was going to leave. Maybe he hadn't seen or heard her.

Delaina took two steps backward and stopped like she ran into a brick wall. He was there. Somewhere. Watching her. Behind her? *Say something.* He didn't, making her go first. She twirled around. Her skirt fanned out to expose her naked thighs.

Jed. Propped against the porch rail. His blue eyes sparkled silver and revealed amusement. He had seen the whole thing. All her preparations to open the door. "Did you bring me tequila?"

She couldn't look at him. He looked at all of her. "I'm not legal, remember."

"Legal never mattered to a Cash." Jed shrugged. "I have an impression of you that causes me to forget you're a little girl sometimes anyway." He paused. "What's in the brown bag? A concealed weapon? The Murano wineglasses smashed to smithereens?"

"The glasses are far too incredible to smash," she said and omitted that she made a vow to herself yesterday to never open the bottle of wine, or use the glasses, unless it was him, them, getting tipsy together at a water hole. Delaina raised her shoulder to her chin, tossed her head back, and stomped past him. "Doesn't matter what's in the bag. I've decided not to give it to you." Jed wore a good-looking blue shirt and flat front pants. He had not eaten lunch at the cabin; her heart sank.

"Since when did you start wearin' the flower crap?"

She wrinkled her face. "What?"

"The rose-scented perfume."

"Since Cabot gave it to me."

Jed waved his hand in front of his face. "Well, don't. You smell like the others."

Delaina fumed. "What're you talkin' about?"

"Cabot's girls. Jenna Lee, Dacey, Danielle, Summer Lynn and on and on." Jed scanned her critically. "Floral perfume, prissy purple dress, pink lips. A hundred bucks says I can guess what your panties look like."

"A hundred bucks?"

Jed looked into her eyes. "Yeah, a hundred bucks."

"Deal."

Jed let his eyes fall to her crotch. For a moment, he didn't see anything except what he saw at the river. For a moment, Delaina felt it. His eyes, they had been like fingers stroking her. Did he remember, or had her image blended in with countless others who stripped for him? "Purple lace...no, pink...thongs...a hot pink lace dollar-store thong." He reached in his shirt pocket for a cigarette.

What a dumb ass. He knew she would *not* wear a hot pink lace dollar-store thong. It jarred her a little that he guessed so freakin' close. "Don't smoke."

He gripped the stick. "Why?"

"You can't afford it." Delaina's eyes glinted victoriously.

"Any other reason?" Jed moved in on her, bracing her without touching her, against the front door.

Delaina felt suffocated, not from his closeness, from his lack of it. She dropped her head to relieve the tension. "No."

He lit his cigarette. "How do I know you won the bet?"

"Trust me."

Jed backed up and blew his smoke. "Never."

"Then find out for yourself." Delaina held out the hem of her dress.

Jed reached out reflexively, dropped his hand to his side. "Never."

Delaina assessed, "You're dressed up."

"Uh, huh."

"Have you been to lunch?"

"Yep." He put out his cigarette.

"Did you have dessert?"

"No." He broke into a bad grin. "Depends on what you define as delicious."

Delaina knew how to play his game. "I owe you about seventy-five dollars."

"For what?" He watched her. Even with her face made up and her skin smelling like a marketplace rose, she was the loveliest package of dynamite he'd ever seen.

Delaina smiled slightly. "My *VS* underwear *are* lace and pale pink but..."

Jed hit a wall. Life without her had been dismal. Delaina in lace, pale pink, VS... "Bikini cut," he finished and nodded. "Men like Cabot keep predictable women."

She huffed and puffed. "I'm not *kept* by anyone."

Jed gave her ring a bold stare. "Really? Your ring suggests..."

She threw her hand in the air. "I don't care what it suggests! I didn't choose it, Jed."

Jed watched her eyes. "I know." He turned the doorknob. "Do you dare come in?"

"Yeah, I'll take the risk." She stepped toward him, catching a whiff of his erotic, outdoorsy, hellion aphrodisiac. "On second thought, I don't think so. It's a sunny day. Let's, uh, sit by the river."

He checked his watch. "I don't have much time."

"Hurry inside and get milk. Meet me over there." She pointed to a clearing in the grass on the bank.

Breeze danced across Delaina's skin while the sun napped behind a cloud, the kind of day she had in her dream, the wedding one. She heard Jed coming out. He carried a jug of milk and two glasses, had shed his dress shirt and shoes, and looked so kissable, barefoot in his pants with white undershirt. It got better the more she watched from her hiding place behind a fat tree. He did the unthinkable. He went to the truck and retrieved the bed sheet, her favorite dress in the world, except for her wedding gown.

He walked to the spot she had picked out. She stepped in front of him. "So, I've become predictable?" Jed's mouth fell open. He had seen Delaina dressed in less, never wanted her more. With her hair tucked behind her ears and her lips licked shiny, she wore a strapless white satin bra and the pretty pink panties. "A nice metamorphosis, but put your dress on, Lainey." He said her nickname with annoyed authority as a father might.

She looked herself over and shrugged. "Why? This is no different than wearing my swimsuit."

"Your swimsuit has a lace crotch?" He spread out the sheet.

"You know what I mean." She had made her point, put on her dress, and sat. He sat beside her and began to gaze securely upon the river. She held out her hand, wiggling her ring finger. "What does it suggest, Jed?"

"Cabot thinks the price of true love can be measured in dollars and cents. He will control you, and he wants every man to see you're untouchable."

Delaina leaned in close enough to breathe on his cheek. "Untouchable. Are you sure?"

Jed moved his hand, his fingertips, toward her lips. He hadn't touched her in nineteen days. Resistance wobbled. He held his fingers as close to her lips as he could without caressing her mouth. Delaina felt energy radiating from his hand. Reciprocating heat radiated through her body. If he didn't hurry up and touch her, she would throw herself on top of him.

Seconds passed.

Resistance found a crutch. Its name was impossible. "I'm sure," he said.

Delaina's shoulders slumped on a weary exhale. She wore a regretful smile. They watched the river. Quietly, she admitted, "I would have preferred a simple ring. Just a wedding band, with... hmm, maybe a modest sprinkling of diamonds. And a simple wedding..."

"This is Cabot's wedding," Jed interrupted. "You're Cabot's girl. What kind of wedding did you want, Delaina?" Resistance and impossibility were both curious dreamers.

Her name swirled off Jed's lips like the smoke of a pipe and soothed. She closed her eyes, smiling and imagining. "I've had a wedding in my dreams at night for weeks. In a garden park, a day like today, with only the bride, groom, and pastor. Bubbles blowing and lots of laughter." She giggled at her girlish fantasy. "I do, at least, have the dress. I had it tailored to match my dream." She shrugged and opened her eyes.

Sunlight struck Jed's hair a chestnut-chocolate color. His lips were pressed together in a subdued smile. His eyes had narrowed into slits of silver dotted with a rich blue ink pen, focused solely on her. He had never, no one had ever, looked at her like that before. She should remember something. He looked at her like...she was... the bride. He was...the groom. In her dreams, it was Jed.

Delaina slid the cookies toward him without losing eye contact. "A token of peace." There were tears in her eyes. Jed reached for the bag. His eyes left hers and peeked inside. "Are they..."

"Chocolate chip. Homemade. I don't cook or bake."

"Maydell made them?"

"No, I did. My first effort." Each breath going in and out hurt her lungs.

"So, they're seasoned with arsenic or carbon tetrachloride..."

She smiled. "No."

Jed reached in and pulled one out, grinning like a kid with a candy apple at the county fair. He bit into it and chewed then reached for the milk. "They're a box mix?"

"Made from scratch," she said tentatively.

Jed dug in for a second one. If he had ever doubted he loved her, he wouldn't again. A little heavy on the chips but damned good. "Where's the honeymoon?"

Delaina watched him chew the cookie instead of watching his eyes. "Sweden."

"Sweden? In the countryside, I assume. You'll like it."

"Stockholm." Delaina looked at a breezy willow tree and shivered with it. "I've never been outside the U.S., except my high school graduation cruise. *How worldly.*" She sighed. "In twelve days, I'll be seeing the hubbub of a foreign city." With each word, her voice flattened. "Cabot has business scheduled before we set the date. We're staying at a famous renovated hotel. An absolute must, he said." Her eyes went downcast.

Jed pointed out the obvious. "You could stay at a ritzy hotel in New Orleans, Atlanta, any big city." He cracked his knuckles. "I've been to Europe a few times. Spent a summer there after med school."

"Business?"

He handed her a cookie. "Stayed the first two weeks on the French Riviera. I don't mix business with pleasure."

"You could've fooled me," she retorted with a mouthful of cookie. *He had a girlfriend there.*

"It's extraordinary."

"What? Travel in Europe or the sophisticated Parisian?"

He chuckled and glanced. "She was rural Irish. Keely." His face went back to the river. "Anyway, after I turned twenty-five, I quit med school to start farming. Mama supported my decision but encouraged me to spend the summer traveling before the grind of adulthood. I started in France, spent time on English and Irish farmland. Did some work there." He looked over. "Irish farmland is more your style. You'd love it, Delaina. Some might call it backwards. I understood their way of life. They maintain their land and their land sustains them."

Delaina saw a different side of Jed, the same one she caught a glimpse of the last time they sat on the riverbank and ate together.

He kept his eyes steady where they were. "I witnessed a wedding there. In Scotland." The conversation headed where he wanted. To make his point. "Between neighbors, a daughter named Chloe and a son named Ty. Archaic by our standards. Chloe was very young. Ty, not much older. Neither family had money to spare. Ty came to me one night and confessed she was pregnant. They wanted to elope. He asked me to take them to a nearby town the next day." Jed's eyes narrowed. "We found a clergyman." Delaina listened, captivated. "I witnessed the wedding. A humbling experience. I was full of myself and hung up on the supply of beautiful women everywhere."

Delaina was not too captivated to point out, "Some things never change."

He glared halfheartedly. "Anyway, the preacher, Ty, Chloe, and me in the churchyard." Jed knew he shouldn't say more. Delaina's life, her choice. "Chloe cried, and Ty got choked up during the vows. They got off to a rocky start, but they're together. We stay in touch. It impacted me. They meant their vows."

Delaina refused to let him see the stab. "A touching story, Jed, and like the wedding in my dream, it's unrealistic."

Jed paid attention to her ring. "Yeah, I guess."

They watched the river somberly. She asked, "Are you comin' to my wedding?"

Jed had known the question would arise. "No one knows this, but I go to Houston on weekends when the Astros play at home. Sometimes I make it a long weekend if they have a Monday game.

My personal time away. They're playing at home this weekend, and next weekend they also have a Monday game. So, no, I won't be there."

"Houston?"

"Yeah, but please Delaina, it's my only hideaway or reprieve. Keep it to yourself." "I will." Somehow, he didn't doubt her. Not for a minute.

With a smile, she admitted, "I love baseball."

"I know. You have the bottle collection."

"My daddy took me to those games with his buddies. Rough company. I only cared about seein' the games and getting the bottles." She shrugged. "Impressive I have the set, huh?"

"I'm impressed." Jed picked up a rock and hurled it into the river begrudgingly. "I know it takes patience to acquire." He chewed down on cookie number four or five. Then a notion struck him. Summer Lynn suspected something unusual would happen with Cabot this Saturday. Perhaps Jed could protect Delaina one more time. "Do you wanna go to Houston this weekend?"

Delaina heard the question, assumed it to be a mean trick her mind played, and gabbed, "Cabot leaves to go to Biloxi for his bachelor party Friday. There are unfinished details for the wedding, I haven't made the farm management decision, and I don't have a veil." She took a big breath. "My dress designer offered to create my veil, but through this wedding thing, I wanted to make one decision by myself. I'm making a trip to Jackson this weekend to shop for it."

Jed made a small nod. "I see."

"Houston would have more veils," she shyly tested.

"Lots and lots of veils."

Delaina's head jerked toward him. "You did ask me to go to Houston? When? How? With you?"

"No, not with me, in case we're being followed."

"We're being followed?" Delaina's eyes darted over their surroundings.

"I'm not sure. I think I am."

"Yeah, by me!" She grabbed his arm and smiled gleefully. "'Cause I'm going to Houston with you!"

Jed looked down at her fingers resting on his arm. Desire coiled inside him like a roll of copper wire that needed to be stretched. Badly. "Not with me. I'll meet you there. For the baseball game, remember?"

"How will I get around?"

"I'll take care of it. I'll take care of you. Do *not* tell anyone. Let them think if you can't find the veil in Jackson, you'll travel elsewhere on a whim. Don't bring your phone. Pretend to accidentally leave it at home. Get trip details from the old toolbox on the Denton Farm. I'll leave a note in there for you."

Delaina nodded. Her whole face smiled. "When will I see you?"

Jed stood up, as did she. "This is not about me. It's about going to a baseball game in the middle of the afternoon. Sort of a...parting gift so we stay on good terms. Gonna be interesting. I don't think I've taken a girl who knew much about the game."

"You've taken girls there?" Delaina glared jealously.

"Hell yeah. Nothin' better than a fine woman, cold beer, and good baseball on Saturday afternoon."

"Yeah, there is." Her smile was bashful.

"What?"

"A kind of pretty girl who likes cold beer and good baseball."

Jed nodded. "You might be right. We'll see."

"Jed?"

"Hmm?"

"I've missed you."

He looked at the passionate priss, hands on her hips, in a skimpy purple dress, barefoot with wild hair, smiling into his face. "Delaina, I..." he started.

She replayed his comment about his delicious lunch date and interrupted, "Don't say anything. Let a good moment between us...stay good."

It would've been better. Jed chose to leave her standing when he heard her words of protest.

~ ~ ~

What a mistake. Jed knew it. Delaina had to know it.

First-class plane ticket bought, room at Calla Hotel reserved (She better hold on to her horses; he probably should've given her a heads-up about the hotel).

A major part of Jed's trip to Houston included seeing his best friend Meggie Henderson. If anyone could make him feel better, Meggie could. They met in med school in Atlanta. She settled in her hometown of Houston as a successful obstetrician. Smart. Beautiful. True. Theirs was an odd relationship. They spent countless hours together. Sometimes in Houston he'd see her, spend days with her. Sometimes he'd see someone else or no one. This time he called Meggie in advance to go to dinner on Friday night. Now, for Christ's sake, he was sending *Delaina* to Houston. Jed drove the work truck down the field row. He had been neglecting the farm. He reached for his bag of cookies, two left. If he could get her to Houston safely, Delaina would be safe there with him, at least. He had hired someone to follow her to Jackson and see that she got on the plane. Someone else to get her to the hotel in Houston. From there, she was on her own, staying in the newest, most secure, poshest hotel in the city. Only the best for her. Her safety. It's all that mattered. All in the world that mattered to Jed McCrae.

~ ~ ~

"You're sure you don't wanna take a friend or my mom?" Cabot and Delaina stood in front of his car on the driveway at Cash Way.

"I'm certain. I've had a lot of togetherness lately."

"Whatever the bride says. I'll see you when I get home from Biloxi." Cabot glanced at his watch. "We should ease up to your bedroom, so you can say goodbye to me properly."

Delaina frowned. "It's eight o'clock in the morning, and Miss Maydell's in the house."

"We need a lot of practice," Cabot said bluntly.

She shoved him. "Goodbye, have fun in Biloxi, and be careful."

Cabot climbed in his car. "Call my cell if you need me."

"I'm not plannin' to contact you since it's bachelor weekend." Delaina winked. She would also pretend she forgot her phone in the rush to leave. She felt no guilt about Houston. She told Cabot and Miss Maydell she would drive to Jackson and she'd shop for a veil. Both were true.

Cabot left, and she felt fantastic relief. She hadn't seen Jed since he invited her. She found the note in the toolbox the first time she checked. Simple instructions printed on white paper:

Leave at nine on Friday morning. Drive to airport city. A man named Pete will be waiting; he'll have your plane and hotel info.

Land at airport in game city. Ted the Driver will be waiting to drive you to the hotel; he'll have a phone for you to use to get in touch with me only. His shuttle service is available to you 24/7. Call or text me every time you leave, no exceptions. He'll take you to bridal shops on Friday afternoon and/or Saturday morning.

See ya at the hotel at one Saturday for the game. No phones.

No salutation. No name. Essentially being kidnapped by her fiercest competitor, vanishing without a trace, Lainey Cash had never been more excited. She rushed in the house to get her bags and leave. For the next forty-eight hours, she would entrust her life to Jed McCrae.

Fifteen

Novelty

Just how much money did James Evan Darrah McCrae have? Good grief. More importantly, how much was he willing to spend *on her*...uhm, and why? She would absolutely pay him back for this! Not that material items or money mattered much to Delaina. She had plenty of things and could buy plenty more. Still, *holy cow.* When Ted the Driver conferred with a uniformed bellboy at the entryway, Delaina was 100% positive they got it wrong escorting her to Calla Hotel. Her jaw hadn't closed since. The smartphone Jed left for her, thankfully, had internet access. While they talked, she sat in the car and searched her destination.

Calla Hotel, originally another name/chain which deteriorated downtown in the last decade, had been, in the words of the website, "marvelously reinvented and joyfully reopened" last Christmas.

Lainey Cash had never visited a palace.

She assumed this is what the outside of a palace looked like. A current-day city castle, more appropriately. Creamy stone exterior, high but not skyscraper high, bedecked in Jacuzzi-size pots with the tallest dark green plants ever. The whole place, elegant and sprawling, hip yet graceful, accommodating but old-spirited. The website's words to describe it, not hers, and dead on. Internationally acclaimed architects and designers were listed with their untranslatable credentials above anything else on the main page, from San Francisco, Atlanta, Rome, and Singapore. Good heavens. The only trips/hotels she had for comparison, period, were: 1. One night in New Orleans with Cabot 2. Three economy class flights she'd taken in the last month before today's first-class ticket to get her to three wedding-shopping overnighters in regular hotels with Claudia Hartley 3. A high school graduation cruise to the Caribbean 4. A few vacations to Memphis or Gulf Shores or flights/stays in Tampa Bay to see baseball games, growing up.

 She checked the base price for a lower level room correctly called wings. Gulp. $$$. Lower Wings of Calla, 100 rooms on the first three levels per website- *For the world-class conventions-Champagne clique.* People in this world were proud to be called cliques? Wings are layered with painstakingly detailed reinvigoration by Calla Nests, 25 perching quarters on levels four and five. $$$$. *For comfortably sophisticated celebration-stays.* Delaina assumed but wasn't positive, a "celebration-stay" was better known as a weekend getaway to a Mallard girl. Nests are bird-caged softly with poise (Who wrote this stuff?) by Calla Contemporaries, condos on level six where it appeared these cliquish human beings could sequester for months, $$$$$, from the listing price. *Chic cohabitation feathered in Cognac-to-coffee carousing.* If Jed put her any higher than Lower Wings of Calla, she would protest loudly and proudly in her rural Mississippi accent by loaned phone to him in the next five minutes and use her own credit card with the staff.

 Good God, she might have to sell something to pay him back if she stayed in Calla Nests. Her dying-to-be-further-impressed crotch suggested selling her body. To him.

 Calla Contemporaries, the condos, out of the question! Those were for…a jet-setting executive's birdbrained ho…to hang out in and chirp about first world problems with her fellow swanlike supermodels, waiting in a silk robe and high heels on the balcony, bird-caged precisely until the next sex-capade with her Sugar Daddy.

Damn Jed. She was not his next ho. Was she? *Those rumors about Jed and New Orleans.*

Oh Lord.

She looked out the car window at the elaborate hotel and tried to remember how he presented it, about her going to Houston, when he asked casually and cutely by the river in sunlight. She could not reproduce what he said exactly or if he implied anything sexual since she currently found herself in the middle of the situation she accepted eagerly and naively from a farm boy by the water eating cookies at noon. Her current situation being another world, beautifully beleaguering her with lovely lavishness, provided privately by handsome Jed.

She quite likely was his next ho. But hell, to be honest, she would do it with Jed at Motel 7 on the Houston beltway in a dollar-store thong if that's what he preferred.

Staring, Delaina flipped automatically head over heels into city nestling and newness and awe and possibility and *kind of* Jed for offering her a glimpse of this side of life. And she hadn't even stepped out yet.

Then she did step out, with gentlemanly help, and felt instantly underdressed. She wore jeans, for crying out loud, Bleu Cotton at least, with a white T-shirt, a navy cardigan, red sneakers, and a ponytail. She felt like an outside-the-Pennsylvania-Avenue fence, Fourth of July fireworks observer mistakenly allowed permission into the Oval Office during the State of the Union. Everyone around her wore heels and black, neutrals and good jewelry, designer sleek.

She comprehended the name immediately. Calla Hotel, admittedly fashionable even if slightly showy in a flawless way, a flowery while unfussy adult experience. Not for the average weekender, not for the guy who gave hotel reservations minimal thought like ordering red roses on Valentine's Day. This was white and cream and marble and whispery and absolute and expressive and thought out. The calla lily of celebration-stays.

A thought fluttered as she walked with her noble attendant. This was a Ms. Cass Kendall kind of place.

On their oyster/river date when Jed talked openly to her, he said that his mama gave him 'an appreciation for good stuff, for traveling other places.' Maybe, just maybe, Delaina wasn't his next ho. Maybe she could be...a teeny-weeny likeness to his revered mother. Worthy in his eyes. Any chance? Another adult thought fell like a Calla Contemporaries' feather through her blown mind.

If she wanted to be worthy, she had to make herself worth it, and *Jed and Delaina* were worth trying. Whoa. Is that what *he* thought when he booked it? Shut up. *Any chance?*

Or *was* this place the new go-to spot for his next ho?

No. She stuck to her belief of being classy-deserving even if it seemed incredibly never-really-left-Mississippi mindset of her.

The bellboy, who had introduced himself by name and if she were Cass Kendall-level she would remember, walked with a bright smile through airy illustriousness as if he accompanied executives' canaries to birdcages every hour. Walked right past the check-in tucked under a marble, bridge-size arch with no signs denoting it. Delaina would not have realized it was the check-in, except for the line of discreet computers and matching black suits on insanely attractive attendants behind the counter. They stood, no chairs anywhere.

Garrett, his name was Garrett. Ha! She felt so classy. "Excuse me, Garrett, I haven't checked in."

"No check-in required for you, Miss Cash. You're an esteemed guest of the house."

Who the hell was 'the house?' 'On the house' was a term Delaina knew. Why the heck would this be on the house unless Jed was...oh holy hell...*the house*. He did not own this place. No way. She knew better than that from bits and pieces she got from Cabot about Jed's finances and from her and Jed's earnest conversation in his office about farming. He might be comfortably affluent; he didn't roll around in money.

A garish thought came. *Gal, this is rolling around in money! Wink. He could swing buying a Calla Contemporary condo, and you're going up to the sixth, baby. On the house.*

Delaina's mouth stood agape. More views of the hotel opened wide in front of her and caused her to ponder additional notions, which had never crossed her unseasoned mind. Would Jed be waiting? Did he live *here* when he came to Houston? Might he step out at any moment and take her the rest of the way? Where *did* he stay or go in this city? Why and with whom?

Her eyes toured quiet richness laced in generous comfort as they walked toward tubular glass elevators. Balconies were stacked skyward from the rooms, *inside* the hotel, into cosmic middle openness of more tall, dark, handsome plants in enormous pots. Loud, toppling fountains seemed to fall from the center of God. She viewed a glass roof to Texas, blue-bonnet-hued skies and puffy clouds.

Delaina felt...twenty-five-ish and maybe capable of doing this well if she put her mind to it. This would never be how she wanted to live every day, but...

She stepped into a Cinderella-shoe lift and elevated into Calla clouds with the ineffectuality of Garrett the Bellboy.

~ ~ ~

All pilots, alive or dead, felt a cryptic connection to one another. Any living two could sit and watch planes in the sky indefinitely and have a conversation without words. Jed became his father, and every pilot who had ever flown, each time he ascended. The aeronautically universal emotion: Exhilaration. Every safe landing was a tribute to his father and every other pilot who ever landed, or never landed. The aeronautically universal emotion: Satisfaction. Flying was a thrill like no other he'd experienced.

That might change.

He hadn't spent the night with Delaina Cash yet. He might never.

He wanted to make love to her *one day*. He hadn't given up completely.

Short of taking her himself, he'd done everything he could to ensure her security in Houston. It would take all his strength and patience to wait twenty-four hours to see her. What was he doing in Texas with Lainey Cash anyway? "Hey, Jeffrey." He spoke to the private airport/hangar manager.

"Jed. Smooth flight?"

"Yeah, good."

"Here are the keys to your jeep. Enjoy your weekend."

Jed had a full day ahead. A meeting with his lawyer and with his accountant. Dinner at seven with his best friend Meggie Henderson. He got in and left, optimistic his hectic schedule would keep his mind off the sexy, sneaky girl stashed in her haute hotel room known only to him minutes away.

~ ~ ~

Making notes about her wedding, Delaina sat in her hotel room, eh, mini house in a comfy chaise lounge facing the balcony's French doors (she supposed they were still called French doors when they spanned twelve feet high and swerved and beveled and introduced an ivory-plastered ledge view of heaven above and down to indoors Hawaii). She had the doors open with the tops of cascading sky-lit fountains as her guest.

Finally, she had overcome her initial undoing upon seeing her uppity cage.

This was how the other half lived. Not half. Maybe 1% of 1% of the world population had seen anything like this in person, much less lounged in it. She willingly relaxed in a dreamy scene now, playing star of Jed's show for a weekend, perched prestigiously in perhaps the most palatial life a Houstonian could buy. When Jed texted her earlier, she nearly gave him a blistering piece of her mind. Ms. Cass Kendall's feather of a soul dusted upon her and whispered, 'Wait and see. Have patience. Act normal. Be appreciative but unaltered.' So, she trusted newfound inner maturity in its budding stage and played it cool.

From a payphone in the lobby, she had called Miss Maydell on the Cash Way home phone and told her she accidentally forgot her cell phone and didn't have a veil yet. She would stay overnight somewhere (Ha! This was somewhere!) and let her know more later. She didn't contact Cabot, up to his eyelids in bachelorhood. Tonight in Biloxi with former fraternity brothers would be a raging theme of women, alcohol, and gambling. For some reason, she didn't feel worried about his safety or jealous of his lap dancers.

~ ~ ~

The worrisome brat got tucked away safely in her room according to Jed's hired driver. Soon after he landed, Jed also texted her, *It's me. Everything good so far?*

She answered promptly, *Hey me. It's me.* with a thumb's up emoji. How her reply, along with anything about her, turned him on instantly, he chose not to think about too long.

Now if the brazen hussy would stay put. Fat chance. Ah, what the hell? Jed decided to go by and check on her after dinner. It couldn't hurt. He, the only person in the world who knew her location, hopefully. She was his responsibility.

~ ~ ~

Bull's Alley. The local bar and grill where they met many times. Immediately, Jed spotted Meggie Henderson sitting on an iron bench and looking as fine as new money, a lingerie model in a business suit. She wore her trademark tortoise shell glasses; they accentuated, rather than hid, her whiskey-colored eyes. Her twenty-inch black mane shone as polished onyx in the evening sunlight. She wore a pencil skirt and thin blouse. Every man within a twenty-foot radius panted after her like a caged dog. She stood when she saw Jed. "I'm sorry. I didn't have time to change clothes. I came from the office."

Jed nodded, keenly aware of men who looked like they'd been shot in the heart, or testicles, when he greeted her with a kiss on the cheek. "Good thing you work on women. Men would never hold up for the exam."

She laughed. "Good thing you changed your line of work." Jed laughed. They met in obstetrics class at Emory. She always joked women would be uncomfortable using a doctor as drop-dead gorgeous as Jed.

"Haven't seen you lately. How've you been?" Jed asked when they settled in a booth.

"Since I came to your mother's funeral. How are you?"

"I'm fine."

"Astros game tomorrow?" Meggie struggled to catch his gaze.

"Uh, huh." Jed sipped on his water.

"Are you okay?"

"Yeah, why?" *Was his misery that obvious?*

"You're worlds away. You can fool a lot of people, Jed McCrae, but not Margaret Anne Henderson." She smiled.

"Problems in Mallard."

"The farm?"

"The farm is part of it."

"Is this about your broken engagement to Laureth?"

"No. She doesn't mean anything anymore. Maybe she never did."

"What is it?"

"I don't know. Let's talk about something else." A waiter brought two beers and a plate of nachos.

"Okay. Here's a revelation for you. I'm engaged!"

Jed looked at her. *"What?* Really?" His navy eyes gleamed. "When? Who's the lucky guy?"

Meggie smiled so hard Jed thought her face would break. He'd seen her kind of smile somewhere before. Delaina, when he asked her to go to Houston. "Now, don't laugh. He's a pastor. We've been dating three months, engaged about a week. I decided to tell you in person." She flashed a ring and another big smile.

"Very nice, Meggie. A pastor? You mean like in a church?" Jed made a surprised face.

"Yes, and he's close to fifty. His wife died last year. His name is Lewis. We're getting married in September."

"Do you go to church now?" Jed laughed then.

"I do. Three times a week." Her chin went to her chest with humility. "I know I ribbed you about church with your mom." She looked at her ring with that smile. Delaina never looked at her engagement ring with a face like that. "I love his church."

"Meggie Henderson, off the market." Jed grinned broadly. "A shame for the male population. As choosy as you are, Lewis must be great. This is fast. I never would've thought…"

"I can't explain it." She flashed another I'm-in-love grin. "Love knows no creed or manners. People create those boundaries. Reality is when true love happens, there's not much you can do about…surely more than you want to hear of my sappy philosophy."

"It's okay. I understand."

Meggie watched his eyes, the way they smoked over. She started shaking her head and could've fallen out of the booth. "Oh! James Evan Darrah McCrae! You're in love. Your lost puppy look, I get it now!"

"Lost puppy?"

Meggie whispered like she gossiped with a female, "Are you getting married?"

"No." He grimaced. "Not soon."

Meggie reached for his hand, pulling it to make him look at her. "Why not? You'd make a super husband. What's she like?"

"She's..." Jed could think of things he wanted to say about his Delaina. He wanted to share her with the entire world, and yet he wanted her to be his little secret. "...engaged to be married next week."

"Whoa." Meggie dropped his hand and reached for her beer.

"But she's here with me this weekend."

Meggie missed her mouth completely. Beer ran down her chin. She dabbed it. Her eyes remained on his. Jed looked away. "It gets better. She's...it's...I... she's Delaina Cash."

"As in *The Cashes* you've told me about?"

"The one and only heiress to the throne, and she's twenty."

Astonished, Meggie said, "I didn't think you could tell me anything more unbelievable than what I told you, but you did." She laughed. "Leave it to you, sweetheart. Never to be outdone."

"It's a crock of crap, Meg."

"But you love her."

Jed shrugged. "Love means different things to different people."

"You love her."

"She doesn't love me."

Meggie crinkled her nose. "*How* could she not love you? I've never seen a female who didn't chase you, want you, try to snag you, stalk you." She winked, kidding him about the women who went after him back in the day. "Then why did she come to Houston with you? Are you that good in bed?"

"She wouldn't know the answer."

Meggie's eyes widened. She laughed sympathetically. "Oh my. Honey, you're definitely in love." She waited for his response, realized he finished revealing details. They stopped talking long enough to eat nachos then moved to other subjects, the comfortable conversation of old friends. After a pause, he raked his hands through his hair and sighed. "Meggie, thanks for everything." He smiled genuinely. "Congrats to you and Lewis. You deserve all the happiness in the world. Maybe I can meet him when I'm in town again. Call him here for coffee and dessert." Jed laid bills on the table. "My treat."

She grabbed his hand. "Jed, you've been my best friend for eight years. I don't want to see you let this one get away. So what, it's Delaina Cash. If she makes you happy, if she makes you feel how Lewis makes me feel." She smiled. "I'll have to ask the waiter to clear the beer, and I'll cover up with my blazer before he arrives. Everyone makes concessions for the sake of love. Make yours."

He kissed her on the cheek. "Keep in touch."

"Where are you going?"

"Where do you think?"

Meggie watched him, the best-looking man she'd ever seen, the most trustworthy man she'd ever known, the most determined man she'd ever encountered, until he disappeared. Soon, she thought, female hearts would break in Mallard County and beyond. Jed McCrae would get Delaina Cash. He never failed to get what he wanted. Never.

~ ~ ~

Mallard County's Chief of Police Raybon Hall had known love. Once.

Thirty-three years ago, she rode a pony at the county fair on a windy spring night. He, the pony's owner. A dozen times, she paid fifty cents, and he led her around the dusty circle. Her name was Cassandra Jane Darrah, a rich, eighteen-year-old beauty from Baton Rouge who came to Mallard for the weekend to visit a cousin. Raybon and Cassie Jane began to meet regularly. She filled his heart and soul and body and spirit with a love he never imagined could feel so good and hurt so bad. He sold his motorcycle to buy her engagement ring and gave it to her for her nineteenth birthday.

A month later, she came to him in the middle of a rainy night. Dripping wet and sobbing, she confessed she was pregnant. Raybon knew it wasn't his child. He'd never been with her. It was James Ed McCrae's baby. They married and she bore their only son.

Raybon Hall finished his gin and tonic and rammed his fist into his desk. 'Your drinking's going to kill you,' the doc had told him. Something would kill him. Might as well be something he enjoyed.

He had waited over thirty years to exact revenge. The time had come. James Evan Darrah McCrae would pay for his mother's betrayal. If possible, Raybon Hall hated Jed more than he had hated Jed's father. The two resembled heavily and held the same attributes, character traits women couldn't resist at any cost.

Three months after James Ed's death, Raybon approached Cassie Jane again. He surrendered his pride and asked her to marry him again offering to adopt Jed. She said no. She had grown up and needed someone more socially accepted, more financially suited. Essentially, her Baby Jed was too good for Raybon Hall. Weeks later, she married Fain Kendall.

Jed McCrae would pay. His very conception ended Raybon Hall's life as he envisioned it. Cabot Hartley had the right idea. Raybon's sweet revenge.

Mallard Sheriff Dan Boyd watched his friend's eyes. "Ray, I know what you're thinking." He drained his own gin and tonic. "The problem with them McCrae men is they have something women can't resist, especially women engaged to other men." Raybon threw up his hand. He didn't want to hear it.

"Let me finish. Look at my daughter Dacey. Her mama's been two steps from the nuthouse since the Mill's Pond incident because Dacey threw away a nice boy for a chance at Jed McCrae's dick. We've got bills to pay for a wedding that ain't never gonna happen. Jed McCrae wouldn't give my girl the time of day. I could kill the son of a bitch if we don't convict him."

"Let me." Raybon Hall poured himself another drink. "I've got nothing to lose. The only thing better than hearing James Ed got killed in a plane crash thirty years ago would be watching his only son suffer. Let me."

~ ~ ~

Jed paced in the hotel lobby. He should leave. Did she need anything? In a strange city, alone, and knowing her, Delaina wanted to get out and mill around. "Excuse me, mister?" Jed looked up to a pleasant smile on the face of a young desk receptionist. "May I help you?"

"Yeah, uh, could you ring room 600? Delaina Cash."

"Certainly, what's your message?"

"Tell her someone's here to see her."

"Does someone have a name?" the receptionist asked, a please-the-patron smile pasted to her face.

"Call her first, please."

"I'm sorry. It's Calla Hotel security policy."

And Jed wanted Delaina secure. "Jed. J-E-D." He acted disappointed and flashed his best smile. She didn't seem to be budging, and it wasn't his nature, yet he slid out his wallet, showed her a special card, and added, "James *Darrah* McCrae. I wanted to surprise her." He thought about texting Delaina to come downstairs, but this seemed more, heck, romantic.

The desk receptionist looked from side to side. No one saw them. "You *know* we pride ourselves on top security. Welcome, Mr. McCrae. I don't think we've met."

No, they hadn't. His mother died the day of the Grand Reopening in December, and he hadn't taken time to swing by and see the hotel since.

"I'll call her for you. I'm a hopeless romantic."

The phone rang as Delaina pulled her athletic bra down over her chest. "Hello?"

"Hi, Miss Cash. Someone's at the front desk to see you."

Delaina's heart leaped out of her body. "Who?"

"I can't tell you," the receptionist answered in a playful voice.

"Is he the sexiest man you've ever laid eyes on?"

"God bless my boyfriend, but yes."

"Tell him I'll be there in five minutes."

Delaina the Disney princess twirled around the room, smiling and glowing. She thought to check herself in the mirror. Terrible, travel weary. She ran into the bathroom to apply lip gloss and yank her hair into a higher ponytail. She added mascara. Better, but she wore a white tank bra and low-slung, worn-out yoga pants. She had no business walking through Ridiculously Rich People Perches wearing such. She refused to take time to change and scurried to slip on her red sneakers. Had it been only two days since she saw Jed? Seemed like...eternity. She almost tore the bulky door off its hinges and ran for the stairs. She couldn't wait on the elevator. She took the cruise-ship-ballroom-style, staggered staircase two steps at a time and reached the lobby, out of breath and red-faced.

She saw him, and her knees went weak. She grabbed hold of a beige balustrade.

He was...*everything*. Bent over an inconspicuous luxury water fountain gulping, dressed in worn-out khakis and a polo shirt untucked in places. "I've missed you!"

Jed's head jerked. Water missed his mouth, soaking his shirt. Delaina laughed as he glowered at her. Heads turned. Eyes stared. He broke into a grin and gave her body a nice overview. "I should ram your head under this fountain." He seemed shy when he whispered, "Surprise."

She smiled. "What a surprise!" She did a hip jiggle in second-skin pants. "I was thinkin' about winding through this maze of a place to a corner café. It advertises homemade peach ice cream and sugar cookies. I'm also going to exercise. Treadmill and kickboxing."

"You shouldn't roam around. I told you to stay put."

"It's nearby. Inside bird villas." She used a dab of sarcasm and winked. "Wanna go?"

"The cookies sound good, but I don't like peaches." He shrugged. He couldn't stay with her dressed like that; he'd make more of a drooling fool of himself than he already had.

"How 'bout going with me to work out?"

"Okay." Resistance abandoned him, on a hunt for impossible.

"That was easy."

"I'm too tired to fight." Jed followed her. Who was he kidding? He wanted to be around her. In eight days, private contact with Delaina Cash would be unthinkable. Curvy, beveled, house-high French doors led to a regal roomful of superior equipment, artsy and empty of people. Somebody soft voiced, fast-paced, coffee shop cool bellowed through the sound system. Like exercising in a glassy gallery. Good heavens. Delaina rolled her eyes.

Jed saw Delaina roll her eyes for some reason. Obviously staying in Calla Hotel did nothing for her. Huh. This place went really, really over the top. Way more than Jed realized. *Far* more majestic than early sketches and graphic presentations in the investors' meetings appeared.

Remarkable by any earthling's standards, it should be reserved for the very best of the very best special occasions, which made it embarrassingly suggestive and too seductively stirring given the state of their relationship. Oops.

Yet she walked around like *she* owned the place, only more casual than that. How? He wanted to haul her yoga-pants-wearing ass up six flights of ridiculousness and see what Calla carousing meant. All weekend.

A heavy door marked Snowy Banks Sauna teased. Maybe Delaina would need a good steam in the snow after her workout. In downtown Houston, Texas, in April. *Christ Jesus*, the elaboration and enticement of this place.

"They have a snow sauna," Delaina said, shrugging a shoulder. She gave him a sincere look. "Calla has everything. Thanks." She mounted the treadmill, clicked on the timer. "I'd rather run."

Calla has everything. Thanks. His capricious Lainey Cash, unaffected. Okay, then... Perhaps in their days apart, she committed herself to making it work with Cabot and took Jed at face value when he peace-offered the ballgame. "Yeah, you've got running mastered." She glared lightly and turned her attention to machine adjustments. He sat on a bench and focused on a mirror against the wall so he could watch Delaina without looking at her, reflected in glass infinitely.

"I'm surprised you're not at a bar with a girl."

"I was. An old friend. Your stay is good so far then, huh?" *Give me something.* Jed wanted Cabot eliminated, Delaina accountable to him in Mallard until they got ominous possibilities sorted, and a chance to speak the truth about Fain. They had to start somewhere.

Delaina moved steadily despite unsteady thoughts. At a bar with an old friend while she waited in an outlandish birdcage. He apparently meant what he said about taking her to a ballgame.

Nothing more. "Yes, good stay. Impressive, uh, caging. Thank you again."

Caging? What did she think he was? "For your safety, you know. Something's...awry in Mallard." Shadowed eyes, she already had. Jed wouldn't scare her too much. "You look tired, Delaina."

"Awry? I must be wanted by a foreign government, tucked away this extremely." But she smiled, really smiled at him. Then it evaporated. "I am tired, Jed. It's this wedding that's gonna kill me."

Those words pierced Jed's conscience. "If it doesn't, being married to Cabot Hartley will."

Delaina judged him cautiously, couldn't interpret his expression, and resumed her pace. "You think you'll ever get married?"

Jed turned his head from the glass Delaina to the one in the flesh. Much better. The swishing of her pants, flouncing of her hair, jiggle of her breasts. Too much better. He stood to leave. "A lot of things would have to fall into place first. Most of them impossible."

She stepped off the treadmill and grasped his arm. "Like what?"

"You tell me."

"You mean, tell you what falls into place to make a person get married."

"Yeah, Delaina. Why do people get married? Why should you? Why should I?" He spoke acrimoniously.

Delaina pictured Cabot's marriage proposal. Her mind became a blank tablet, her mouth a dried-up ink pen. "Well, first, you...uh...have...companionship, so it seems...more convenient to, uh, get married. And to have kids and stuff."

Jed reached for the door handle. He smirked. "That's convincing. I like companionship, and the last time I checked, my sex organs worked. I'll stop the next pretty woman I see and ask her if she wants convenience and kids."

"Oh, shut up! Everyone gets married. A part of life." Delaina tossed her ponytail and smarted off, "You were engaged to Laureth. See if you can explain it better."

His arms laced around her bare waist and roped her to him in one swift current. He began without a breath or flinch or thought. "You go through life doing things that are normal and expected, like grade school, college, jobs. Knowing one day you'll get married, never really thinking about when or who or why until you meet her." His eyes met Delaina's unabashedly. "Suddenly, you just know." He let her go. She assumed he finished, and she felt relieved. She didn't want to hear how much he had loved Laureth.

He grabbed her naked shoulders. "You start believing in ridiculous things like fate and destiny. The more you know of her," Jed stopped to look in her eyes. "...the more you want things like romance and...faithfulness." Delaina swallowed tears. "When keeping those feelings inside is no longer possible, you begin saying downright unbelievable things like..." Jed touched her cheek. "...I'll love you forever." He gave her body a sensually seductive tour. "Make love to me now." Delaina tried to swallow, tried to speak. He continued without waver. "You're believing in some pretty deep possibilities like being soul mates and spending eternity together. Your heart is..."

"*Stop.*"

"No." Jed wrapped his arms under hers, shaking her gently. "Your heart is sitting on your sleeve, waving at her, begging to be trampled on and crushed." Tears leaked out of Delaina's eyes. Her ragged breath tore at his cool facade. He faltered then jacked her up to his face and whispered in a cracked voice, "You say to yourself: I have nothing left to lose and everything to gain here..."

Delaina shook her head violently. She couldn't bear more.

He quit and dropped her with a thud. "I don't know, Delaina, I kind of hoped you'd answer that way."

"How could I?" she cried. "I've never felt like that. Tell me the rest."

Jed clutched her quivering hand with the monstrous diamond. "You'll never know." He stalked through the door.

Delaina lashed out, "Neither will you, Jed! Neither will you! Laureth Stevens found it elsewhere."

"So did I," he said. Delaina didn't hear him over her violent sobs.

~ ~ ~

Boone Barlow sometimes bet hard-earned money on football games and won. He played his share of rowdy Saturday night camp house poker and staggered out with cash in his pockets. He would've lost every dime to his name, which was becoming a heap, had he bet on whom Jed McCrae would see tonight. For Jed to arrive at an uppity hotel in Houston, not surprising. Probably had an extra-fine gal shacked up in there. Whoever she was, she made Jed pace and fidget before he went to the front desk.

Lainey Cash? Couldn't be! She slipped up behind Jed, and he sprayed water on himself clumsily, ogling her like a junior high kid on the brink of puberty who'd seen his first set of tits.

No small feat to follow Jed, Boone knew he went out of town and assumed he'd fly his own plane. On a whim, and abusing technology and financial persuasion, he discovered through another pilot that Jed's frequent jaunts most often led to Houston. He tried online tricks to find an address, came up with none. He caught a last-minute flight and, once there, went into upscale hotels until he found a J.D. McCrae reservation. Being related, being named Boone McCrae Barlow, persuaded. They wouldn't give him a room number. He sat and waited. Bingo! Jed drove up in a gunpowder gray jeep at eight o'clock.

Unfortunately for Cabot Hartley, who paid him as an informant, Boone wouldn't call and tell Cabot where he found Jed. This information deemed a pay raise.

Fain Kendall paid him to keep track of Jed's every move, too, but he was about dead.

Boone did more than catch them in a casual hookup, which would've been plenty shocking. He saw an unprecedented, forbidden love story complete with Cinderella's castle, in-love looks and smiles, a huge fight, and tears. He had fuzzy but identifiable pictures on his phone for proof. He'd catch his flight to Jackson, drive to Mallard in time for the bust, and see if he couldn't ante up the going rate for such priceless dirt.

A big dog now, he had the prize bone.

Sixteen

Privacy

Jed drove on the road in front of the stadium. He patted his pants pocket. "Damn. I left my wallet on the chest of drawers." He started in another direction.

"I have money. I owe you for this," Delaina stated.

"No. We have time. We might miss pregame stuff."

Delaina didn't care if they missed pregame or the whole game when she was with him. Sleep-deprived and emotionally devastated, she had stopped caring about why that was true. It just was.

Jed hadn't slept more than an hour and felt like someone beat him with a baseball bat then dragged him through a muddy field. Last night's argument hung over them like a menacing storm, anger and regret its threatening torrents.

He wove in and out of traffic. "My apartment's near the stadium."

"You have an apartment here? There's so much I don't know about you." He shrugged obnoxiously and pulled into a high-end complex. "Nice," Delaina remarked.

"Yeah. I come here a lot."

"Of course. Your break from sluts caged up in hotels wearing dollar-store thongs."

Such a smart ass. Jed wanted more from a woman than hookups in dollar-store thongs; hadn't she figured that out by now? "Yep," he answered as he parked. Temper misted Delaina. The unscrupulous jerk didn't try to hide his flagrant ways. He motioned to her. "Come in. I wanna show you something."

"Sure. You wanna add me to your Houston ho list."

Jed sighed. "I'm gonna let that slide. Come on."

He led her to his one bed, one bath high-rise apartment. Delaina noticed aspects of sleek, urban living all around her. Inside, Jed disappeared through a hallway. Delaina stepped into a nicely decorated den, open to his kitchen. Modern amenities, good art, nice floors, swell views. The decade spanning their ages had never been more obvious. He came out with his wallet and a picture frame. "Have you seen my father?"

"No," she answered, attempting to ignore a framed photo of a mostly nude brunette holding one arm over her nipples and a baseball glove over her crotch, words Grand Slam! Love, Sophie written across it.

Jed made a sniffing sound. "Meet Sophie. Former Miss Louisiana."

"I'd rather not."

He turned her body around and pointed to the sofa. "Have a seat." He sat close beside her. He smelled woodsy and looked like dreamland. His face partly shaved, hair parted to the side, he wore BC jeans molded like a coffee cup to his generous sex. He handed her the picture.

"Oh God, you look identical." She ran her finger around the edge of the frame.

"We look a lot alike. There I am." Jed's father had him scooped in his arms, candidly posing in front of a small plane. "I was too young to remember, not a year old. According to Mama, when I started pointing at his plane flying over the house a lot, he surprised us one day and took us to watch him take off. He made two circles then..." Jed's father's plane crash had been from a massive early-onset fatal heart attack called a widow maker, not related to the plane or pilot error.

Delaina reached for his arm. "The day he died."

Jed nodded. She laid her head against his shoulder. "I suppose there are pictures of me with my mother. I've never seen them." She sat up and smiled with glassy eyes. "Do you miss him?" "Yeah." "Hard to believe, isn't it? You miss someone you never knew, and the older I get..."

Jed finished, "...the more you miss your mother. Or maybe the fact you never had one. I know, Delaina."

She slid away. "In some ways, you're lucky. There's more emotion in this one picture than I felt in twenty years of living with my father. While you coped with what might've been, I coped with what never was."

The underlying significance of her words jolted Jed to reality. He came to his feet. "Want a drink?"

"Water, please." He went to the kitchen. When he returned, Delaina was looking at pictures on a desk in the corner. A vivacious, black-haired model-type with very big breasts and very long legs curled like an eel on Jed.

"Who's she?" Delaina asked, unable to conceal her disdain.

"Meggie Henderson."

"Maggie Henderson," she mocked icily, swinging her hips. "Is she your Houston girl, 'cause she certainly has the qualifications."

"*Meggie with a e-*. What qualifications?"

"*Sorry, Meggie with an -e.*" She made the correction bitchily. "Tall and curvy. She wears flashy clothes. She's not blonde, and her boobs are at least as big as Laureth's or Holland's."

"Grapefruit," he said, grinning.

"What?" She spun around and squinted. "Forget it. I don't need to know what you and *Meggie* Henderson did with a grapefruit." Jed laughed aloud, amused at her irritation.

"How many women have you been with?"

His laughter curled into a punched-in-the-stomach grunt. Delaina faced him evenly, unashamed of her candor.

"You first. How many men?"

"None of your business," she remarked curtly, stamping her foot on the floor.

"Yet it's your business how many women I've had sex with."

"That's different. You men, you testosterone-pumped beasts, enjoy bragging about numbers. So, ten? Twenty-five? One hundred? More?"

"Hmm. Been a while since I counted."

Delaina made his words a death sentence. "A while since you counted?" The threatening storm unleashed its fury. She threw her hands up in the air. "Last night you surprised me, Jed, and came to see *me* at hedonistic Calla after you stashed me away there. You proceeded to tell me that, what should I call it? That *fairy tale* about fate and romance and makin' love and soul mates and..." She stormed across the room and pushed his chest. "You make a girl feel special." She puffed up, imitating him. 'This is fate, honey. Come on over here and make love to me, my darling soul mate. I'm not sure how many women I've said that to, but...'"

Jed yanked her up to his mouth and kissed her so hard she wasn't sure if he kissed her or hit her. He grabbed her face between his hands and stopped himself. "The only way I know to shut you up."

Delaina's head swirled and she breathed heavily. "Well, buddy boy, it felt good. You kiss better than anybody. Didn't work, though! I wanna know about the women. When did you lose your virginity? Sixteen-ish?"

"Fifteen. Why do you wanna know?"

"*Fifteen.* Before you could drive, my God." She got highly bitchy on his clarification again. "Who? If you can *remember*..." Delaina pulled at her own hair. "Not a blonde. We know that much."

"She was blonde and seventeen, so she did the driving. More like parking." He winked. "I know you think they're all sluts." He made a click sound. "I admit we acted kind of slutty together."

"Bless you, I really *don't* wanna know your parameters for kind of slutty."

Jed laughed genuinely. "Miss Crandall Holloway with the MINI Cooper from Clarksdale." He enjoyed his trip down memory lane far too much.

Openly agitated, Delaina scanned him. "Aren't you a little too big to do it in her MINI Cooper?" There came her haughty voice with a meany-ass head jiggle this time.

He did that male sniffing thing again. "Nah. She had plenty of room, and I wasn't full-grown."

Delaina's mouth opened. How...geez, totally uncalled for.

"A blonde babe with boobs the size of cantalo...excuse me. I didn't develop a dislike for blondes until..."

"After your lifetime love Laureth. How could I forget?" She pointed at the pageant girl in the frame, outwardly steaming. "You're too old for this...immature, insensitive...ego-boosting, obnoxious display of...female degradation. It blatantly proves your inability to...commit to a relationship that might actually require the use of a vital organ like your brain or heart."

Shrugging, Jed acted jerky. "Why do you care? Have you given Richboy a lecture like this? He's the one who's piled up a collection of cheap thongs, you know."

"Who, Cabot?" Delaina rolled her eyes. "Why would I ask him who he's been with?"

"Why are you asking me?" he challenged, a grin on his face.

"Because, because..." Delaina blew her breath out and evaded the question. "You know, I heard the part about Kkk...Kendall's breasts being like cantaloupes."

"*Crandall.* Sorry." He corrected and apologized with a smile of pure amusement.

Delaina boiled. She refused to correct herself again, crossed her arms over her chest, and puckered her lips. "Do you always do that?"

"Do what?"

"Compare a woman's breasts to something inanimate. Most asshole chauvinists do."

A month of fighting what they felt got ready to explode before their eyes. Jed fired back, "Yeah, I do. Fruit, it's always fruit."

"How disgusting and appropriate. Tell me about the women."

"What, you want me to list them for you?"

With humility, she nodded yes. She flicked her hand. "And some of those tidbits." Her voice had taken on a quality, honestly way too appealing, like, *Little boy, you will eat all the peas on your plate.*

Jed stood watching her, not believing what he was about to do. "I know who I've been with. You help me tally." He assumed that would shut up her hot-mama voice. Delaina held out her hands to count on her fingers. Jed smarted off, "You need to take off your shoes, cupcake."

She glanced down. "Huh?"

"You'll run out of fingers."

Implication setting in, Delaina's chin lifted a notch.

"Hell, Lainey, what's this gonna prove?" Her face didn't change. Never in his life had Jed swerved. "I've been with Sophie." She wanted tidbits. Okay. "Best was a hut in Jamaica. Her boobs remind me of coconuts."

Delaina swallowed visibly. "You've been with her? Grand slam pageant girl? In a hut?"

"You wanted to know." Jed didn't look at her. "First, Crandall. Second, my high school girlfriend Shay Morris, the cheerleader captain." Tidbits... "She'd been hookin' up with a rival running back 'til Mallard County High School's pretty damn good quarterback started winnin' every game his senior year." Jed paused with a reminiscent smile. "That would be me."

Delaina's mind did its flash card rewind. Her daddy never missed Friday night home football games, the only place he let her go with him; it's what small-town Southerners did. She *heard* clearly their rides to the stadium and home- "The boy's got an arm." "He could play ball somewhere." And once, Tory admitted, "James Ed should've seen this." A single image, blurry, games rolled into one. Jed behind the line of scrimmage, helmet on, passing the ball, cheering, touchdowns. Blurrier, Senior Night, last home game, halftime, crowning the Homecoming Queen...Shay Morris wearing long, straight...white dress. Long, straight...brown hair. Beside her, Jed. Delaina could hardly make it out. Tall with buzzed hair, looking distracted in bright blue home jersey with bright white number???

"So, she started dating big number 7." A shrug. "Begged me to do it every chance we got senior year. I broke up with her graduation week." He shrugged again. "Shay practically stalked me on our senior trip to Disney World. I introduced myself to Lola Ell...Ellis? Ellers, from Tampa, no, Tallahassee, on her senior trip, too. Wanna hear about her? Boobs like honeydew. We did it against a life-size statue of Snow White ten minutes after we met." Big badass sniff. "I guess that's kind of slutty."

Delaina's eyes widened. She held up a fourth finger.

"Aw hell, my college girlfriend. Started off great. She was smart, premed." He had a different face. "All females are sometimes, you know..." He smiled harmlessly, did a circular motion with his hand to his temple. "Morley had nothing but snakes in her head. I got tangled up, manipulated, yelled at, lied to, tied down, tied up (sniff), bitten (wink), slapped (shrug), and *stuck* the whole time at Baylor. She..."

"Shut up, just shut up! I don't wanna hear about fifty shades of Molly. What are mine?"

"Fifty shades of *Morley*," he corrected, chuckling at Delaina's sly reference. His boasting fell from his throat into the well of his stomach like a pail had been cut from its string. "Huh?"

"You heard me. What are mine?"

He faked disinterest. "I don't know."

"Liar. Why can't you treat me like you treat them?"

He looked at her boobs. At her trendy gray T-shirt with black-glittered vinyl baseball field outlined across her chest and words *Give Me Dirty Diamonds*. Second and third base centered on her tits. What premium fruit. "Peaches."

Her mouth flew open. "Peaches?"

"Yeah. I pegged 'em as peaches the day you came to get the wrench and confirmed it when you, uh, stripped down to your skin for me at the river."

She fisted his arm. "I ought to jam one in your slick mouth and force it down your throat! Peaches? Last night when I asked you to go to the corner café and eat peach ice cream, you specifically said you don't like peaches." She flared her nostrils.

"I don't like, uh, pea...well, not to eat, but, uh, peaches, when referring to a woman's tttuh...anatomy, they're..."

"They're what, Jed?"

He shook his head, defeated. "Why does it matter?" He jerked her hand in front of her face. "You're engaged to be married."

"That's not the point!" Her eyes burned like a pasture set afire.

Jed kept his voice conversational. "I don't care if your tits are the size of watermelons and taste as good as those chocolate chip cookies you made me. You're engaged to be married...and that... is precisely...the point, Delaina." He walked out the door. Delaina walked out and closed it. Jed stood at the top of the outdoor stairwell, smoking a cigarette.

"Don't smoke," she said softly. "Because I...care about you."

He put out the cigarette and skipped down steps. "You want me to take you to the hotel or call the driver?"

"Neither."

"I'm not takin' you to the ballgame."

"Why not?"

Jed climbed in his jeep and called back, "Because you're a pistol always loaded and ready to shoot, and I'm forever the target."

Delaina sprinted toward the jeep, past guys loading luggage into a car. She yelled, "You're the target? *You?* No, Jed, I'm the target. You told such a beautiful speech about makin' love and getting married last night at that..." She looked for a description. "Glorious sex dungeon of a hotel." The college boys halted their loading and watched. "Then you called my wedding a fluke and walked out! Now you've lured me to your apartment..."

One guy yelled, "Dang, this is good stuff." Delaina continued, "...where you have pictures of girls with breasts the size of...of... soccer balls plastered everywhere! Knowin' you saw mine during that strip show, knowin' they aren't like that."

"You're a stripper?" the other guy yelled.

She plunged on, "You called my boobs peaches, a fruit you despise!"

"Hey, honey, I like peaches," the first guy called out and laughed.

"Damn it!" Jed roared, losing his temper. He shot the boys a look that would flip heaven and hell. "Get in, little girl. *Now.*"

"No!" she yelled and smiled daringly. "They like peaches and they're cute enough. Maybe they'll..."

Jed hoisted Delaina onto his lap like an empty sack. He pressed his mouth to hers. "Baby, I'm sorry about the hotel. I didn't know it was so..." He didn't know what word described Calla Hotel other than perfectly perfect for their first time together, which he wouldn't say. Unintentional; he would swear it was unintentional until his grave. "I wanted you safe." He kissed her, drew back an inch, grazed second base with his knuckles. "They're perfect. You're perfect. Perfect, Delaina. Is that what you wanna hear?" He pushed her toward the passenger's seat.

She slumped into the seat and stared at him, searching. "Is it the truth?"

"I swear, you don't quit." He cursed. "You cannot be satisfied." He drove down the road at racetrack speed.

She threw another dart. "Not by you, anyway."

"Oh, and I guess Mr. Whore-Lovin', Slick-Dick Hartley satisfies you."

"He likes peaches, particularly peach pie."

"Good. Why don't you bake one for him, instead of cookies for me? *He'll* be your husband soon." Jed was three weeks beyond controlling what he said.

"Another chauvinistic remark. I'll never feel the need to *cook for my man.*"

"My wife will enjoy cooking for me and with me."

"Oh really? Well, I'm glad I'll never be your wife!" Jed flew down the road, radically compromising their safety and that of others. "In fact, I wouldn't ever marry you." She pointed her finger and shouted, "If you were the last man on earth and the continuation of the human race depended on it, the world would go to hell because *I* would not marry *you!*"

Jed screeched his jeep to a park in the stadium lot, jolting them forward. "Great. I can respectfully scratch the name Lainey Cash from my growing list of candidates." He gave her a contemptuous look. "Most do have tits the size of melons." He slid out and stomped toward the stadium entrance.

Hostile tears burned Delaina's eyes. She felt startled, hurt, and completely in awe of his profile from behind.

~ ~ ~

Sheriff Dan Boyd, a heavyset, gray-haired man in his fifties, watched the scene with evident pride. As if executed with an edited script and a practiced director, the Saturday afternoon drug bust on Cash-McCrae Road was off to a start as dramatic as a Hollywood blockbuster. Sheriff Boyd's men swarmed like flies around spoiled meat. A laser-equipped helicopter swarmed above. Townspeople gathered and swapped speculations.

The words Jed McCrae and Mill's Pond surfaced frequently.

A public spectacle yet Dan Boyd reveled in it, hero of the hour, hero of Mallard County. They had a marijuana problem for a long time; today everyone believed the culprit had been discovered. A Jackson channel news van arrived and set up near the Sheriff's car. He jumped at the chance to speak. "I'd like to make a statement." He had been practicing for this. A reporter motioned to the camera operator. "Over here."

Sheriff Boyd started, "What I can say at this time is we've had a strong suspicion for over a year. Today we were finally given the opportunity to capitalize on previous investigations. Mallard has a marijuana problem. I feel certain we're witnessing the beginning of its demise."

"Sheriff, whose land is involved? Do you have suspects?"

"We have warrants for this entire area, but none of the landowners are available for questioning at this time. I refuse to speculate."

"You said landowners in the plural form?"

"I won't speculate." Lord, he hadn't meant to rope Lainey into it. "No further questions. Let me say Mallard County will not tolerate illegal drugs in the hands of children. We'll carry this investigation through regardless of consequences for any individual. Justice will be swift and severe."

"Thank you for your time, Sheriff." The reporter turned to the camera. "An impressive interview with Sheriff Daniel Boyd here in Mallard County. Stay tuned for more."

Impressive interview. Dan Boyd strutted toward important officials. He could get used to this.

~ ~ ~

Holland and Eli Smith stood on opposite sides of the balcony at Cash Way and watched in utter dismay. The latest payoff in Eli's pocket, a bonus from Cabot on Friday morning, proved a measly and inadequate reward for keeping quiet about supplying plants in what *he now knew* to be Cabot's plan.

His mama sobbed uncontrollably repeating, "You're not involved? Please tell me you didn't know about this." Eli beat himself up every time Maydell made him promise. His father aged ten years in ten minutes when Sheriff Boyd explained the discoveries.

All Moll Smith could think about was seeing Jed and Lainey at the river. He had a bad feeling the poor girl involved herself in something more than sinful with the man, something illegal. He didn't tell the Sheriff; the guilt of knowing ate him alive. Why had Eli married Holland Sommers three days ago? Moll watched Rhett furtively. Rhett acted guilty as hell, pacing and sweating, making eyes at Eli.

Eli watched his father rub his cap into his scalp like he could rub away fear or rub in truth. Eli received questionable glances from Rhett. He knew why. Rhett must still have pot plants at their house; Eli didn't know for certain because he hadn't stayed at home in weeks. He had been smart enough to quit growing marijuana, like Cabot told him to, when Cabot asked for a huge supply of plants. Eli had told Rhett he needed to quit growing, too. At the time, Eli couldn't give him reasons why, and Rhett apparently didn't take him seriously. Eli couldn't bear it if his baby brother were falsely implicated for Cabot Hartley's crimes.

Eli hadn't mentally prepared himself for any of it. He felt clammy and sick. His head spun as fast as the chopper spun overhead in its heady pursuit. Cash Way's legend, Tory Cash, may have been an accomplice to illegal acts. Never had Cash Way been visibly compromised. Until now. Until Eli, however unintentionally, allowed it.

He gripped the banisters. He hurt his family, sold whatever moral fiber he had for a meager sum, and betrayed his employer. It would get worse with Holland undoubtedly involved. He understood the significance of the maps he saw in her apartment their first night.

Fate hammered down. Maybe she got pregnant to rope him in, Cabot Hartley's way of ensuring a silence money couldn't buy. Eli couldn't bust Cabot without implicating Holland, his wife, mother of his child.

Holland watched Eli. She longed to go to him and tell him everything would be okay. Everything would not be okay. She had put it together in her mind. She assumed Eli obtained and planted the marijuana for Cabot. The same marijuana they would blame on Jed. She could free an innocent man or implicate her husband, father of her child. Eli's eyes found hers, the eyes of two strangers who shared the most intimate bond on earth.

~ ~ ~

Jed rushed through the crowded stadium to his seat. Delaina scrambled to keep pace. People in matching purple T-shirts lined across the turf's edge for Survivors of Cancer Day. Jed motioned for Delaina to scoot in first. She surveyed her surroundings, the laughter, candy-faced children, and cozy couples, the smell of pretzels and iced coke. In the seat next to her, an attractive, gray-haired lady stroked her husband's hand in her lap, their eyes fixed on the conclusion of pregame. Jed bought a beer and popcorn from a vendor. He sat, draped his arm over Delaina's seat, and tipped his beer. She offered him a truce smile; he looked away, positively still angry. Her words had been strong. She raised her hand to get popcorn. Light filtered through the large diamond on her slender finger.

Drawn to it, the lady beside her said, "Your ring is unbelievable. When's the wedding?" Delaina gulped and looked at the ring like she forgot. She *did* forget. She opened her mouth, having no idea what to say. "Nice, isn't it?" Jed butted in. "The wedding's next week." His fingers grazed her arm possessively.

Delaina spun around questionably. He grinned like the cat who swallowed the canary. She started to, somehow, explain. That Jed was her affectionate brother? The lady simultaneously spoke to her husband, "Felton, they're gettin' married next week." Felton chimed in, "Congratulations! She's an awfully pretty girl and willin' to sit through the games with you."

"Yeah, isn't she pretty?" Jed jolted Delaina with madness only she could detect and kissed a tendril of hair on her forehead. "I knew she was the one for me when I discovered she loved baseball, not to mention the talents of her tongue." He put a get-even kiss on her lips and took a swallow of his beer.

Delaina's face stained cherry red. The lady laughed. "Oh honey, don't be embarrassed. Enjoy it. He adores you. Besides, I like the morals of your generation. Marriage partners need to be compatible. Right, Felton?" She squeezed her husband's hand with a sneaky smile.

Delaina couldn't hold in her laughter.

Jed laughed. "I agree." She gave him a sideways go-to-hell look. She had a feeling he hadn't finished his charade.

The old man smirked at Jed. "I knew immediately Gwen was the one for me. In the back end of my old truck, she did the hanky-panky on our first date." Gwen tapped him on the arm in reprimand. "My goodness, Felton." Glowing, she looked at Jed and Delaina. "He loves to tell our story."

"Aw, it's okay." Jed hunched Delaina up to him. "She stripped naked and begged on our first date, but I held her off." Mortified beyond speech, she sank in her seat. "Delaina, *sweetheart*, maybe this great couple is a lucky charm..." He gleamed when he looked into her horrified eyes. "...for a long and happy marriage."

"Forty-seven years," Felton confirmed. "Six children," Gwen finished.

"Whew." Jed drained his beer. He patted Delaina's thigh with an amazingly convincing look of intimate lover's knowledge. "It'll be fun workin' on it."

Delaina jabbed him imperceptibly. His insides shook with contained laughter. She whispered against his ear, "I'll kill you." He squeezed her. His scent blew like an orchard breeze. "I love you too, darlin'." The words suspended in the air between them. Delaina's heart stopped, and not from the lovely version of "The Star-Spangled Banner" a decadent lady crooned. The older couple and Jed focused on the field while Delaina sat frozen in the past. She desperately wanted to play the scene again, only this time to gladly play along. She gazed into Jed's face. He chewed on a kernel of popcorn and watched the first pitch.

~ ~ ~

"Where's Lainey?"

Moll Smith grimaced. "We're not sure exactly."'

Boone Barlow shook Moll's hand. "Hell of a mess, isn't it?"

"Gonna get worse, I'm 'fraid." Moll's jaw jutted.

"You haven't got a clue where Lainey is?"

Maydell spoke up, "She's out of town shopping for a bridal veil. She accidentally left her phone here, so we can't contact her or tell her what's going on 'til she calls us."

For believability, Boone commented, "Huh, well, Jed's disappeared. He does that a lot, leaves my father and me and my brothers in charge for the weekend. His plane's gone, but hell if we know where he took off to. We usually get a hold of him within hours. So far, no luck."

Moll Smith shuffled his feet in the dirt. His thoughts weren't good. Did Jed McCrae have Lainey somewhere? He needed to tell someone in authority what he saw at the river. Might be all that saved her life.

~ ~ ~

"Best game they've played so far this season," Jed said, standing up.

Delaina jiggled her hips. "Awesome! Down by two, the ninth, two outs, three-run homer. Doesn't get better." She squeezed his hand and slyly added, "Not to mention the kind of pretty girl and cold beer."

Fabulous woman and lukewarm beer, Jed thought. Their anger disappeared with the first home run in the second inning. He had twirled Delaina around while she howled with laughter. They loved baseball too much to spoil a good game. They clapped and cussed and kissed and cheered. And when the music started in the seventh-inning stretch- a country megastar Okie bragging about having friends in near-to-the-ground places- they danced a slow twist and sang to each other. Everyone around them admired their show without their notice.

Now they walked among people drunk on beer, drunk on love, drunk on victory. Jed cupped her arm and veered toward an exit. A shabbily dressed mother and her scraggly twin boys cut in front of them. Delaina spotted a man selling cotton candy. "I love cotton candy," she said into the air, not for Jed's sake but to fill the silence. The sandy-haired twins had seen it. "Mama, can we have a bag of..."

"No." The mother sighed. "I struggled to buy tickets. Be satisfied."

"Excuse me, two cotton candies for these boys," Jed said to the vendor then smiled sinfully at Delaina. "And one for my wife." Delaina melted like chocolate in the summertime watching Jed talk to the boys. "Did you guys enjoy the game?"

"Yes, sir," the one who asked for cotton candy answered. The other one fixed his eyes on the bags. "Are you God? Can I put this on IG?" Jed chuckled. "I tell you what, if your mother says it's okay, you can have these." The second boy took a picture with his phone.

Their mom shrugged her shoulders. "I don't know what to say. It's your birthday, okay. Thank you so much, sir."

"Happy Birthday. What're your names?"

"Hunt."

"Hunt who?" Jed asked, extending his hand to shake.

"Hunt Jackson, and this is our mom Cricket and my brother Beck."

"Jed McCrae. Nice to meet you, Hunt and Beck Jackson. You guys be good." He draped his arm over Delaina's shoulder. "Gotta hurry home. First time we've left the baby with a sitter." Oh, why not, Delaina thought. Jed enjoyed using every opportunity he could to smear her hateful words in her face. She reached for his hand and smiled her best smile. They began to walk. Devotedly, she answered, "Yes, sweetie, let's hurry. Time to feed the baby."

Jed's eyes widened in surprise. Glimpsing her chest, he whispered, "And Daddy."

Delaina squeezed his fingers as tight as she could yet managed to comment sweetly, "Daddy doesn't like peaches." Jed reached for a piece of cotton candy. They went hand in hand to the jeep.

~ ~ ~

As soon as he crossed the county line, returning from Biloxi, Cabot met Boone Barlow, at his insistence, in their usual spot on a deserted road outside Mallard.

"What the hell are you talking about? Houston?" Cabot exploded.

"I saw her."

"That bitch. Why were you there?"

"I followed her. It's part of what you pay me for. To know what she's up to." Boone was unwilling to inform Cabot that he was also paid to follow Jed by Fain. He had figured out Jed didn't stay at the hotel with Lainey, certain Jed would pay him more to keep the pictures to himself.

"She's there shopping for her veil, I guess," Cabot concluded. "I thought she'd be home in time for the bust. Damn. Do you know where she's staying?"

"Yeah, I do. She forgot her phone, you know."

No, Cabot didn't know. He hadn't thought about Lainey since he left her driveway Friday morning. Considering possibilities, he chewed on the end of a cigar. "I'm going to show up, get her stubborn ass, and bring her back."

Boone hadn't predicted Cabot would want to go to Houston. Yikes. "She'll probably be home tomorrow, right?"

"Who the fuck knows? She doesn't even have a goddamned phone on her... I need time alone with her. Lainey is making things more suspicious not being around during these proceedings. Law needs to clear her." Cabot didn't need anything to go wrong with his perfect plan.

"I think I deserve a bonus. I'm the only person in the world who knows where Lainey Cash is." *Almost.* Boone's stomach felt uneasy. What a debacle it would cause if Cabot happened to catch Lainey with Jed. Christ, the entire conspiracy had become unbelievably complicated.

"Tell me where she's staying. And get me on a late-night flight to Houston. The little cunt."

Boone said nothing for seconds, trying to decide. Trying to choose between right and wrong. "For a hefty payment, I will tell you."

Cabot paid, and Boone told her location. He did not admit that Jed was with her.

Seventeen

Realization

Jed and Delaina were thinking the same thing. Their thoughts left no room for words, as there were not any to bridge the gap.

Their agreed-upon time together was over.

He sped along watching for the road to Calla Hotel. Delaina, as usual, broke silence when they neared the entrance. "I'm sorry about how I acted earlier."

He didn't acknowledge her apology, weighing options. He made up his mind as he parked at the curb. "Do you like Japanese food?"

"Don't think I've ever had any. Why?"

"I'm hungry. How 'bout dinner?"

"I'm not dressed for it, am I?"

"Not at all. It's an uptown joint. Mega-swanky. There are boutiques in the hotel. I'll leave you here and come back at eight."

A spontaneous dinner date with Jed. My, my, my. "Sure." Gold sparks in Delaina's eyes didn't go unchecked by him.

"On one condition."

"What?" she asked disapprovingly.

Jed stroked her jawbone. "Don't open that smart-ass, kissable mouth of yours tonight. For anything."

"I have to open it to eat, you fool. I'm hungry."

"I'd like to enjoy this night and you." He stared at her. "Every time you say something, we get into a full-blown argument."

"Oh, this is good. The only way you enjoy being together is when I don't talk?"

"It could be worth a try," he joked.

"Well, if you wouldn't compare me to Miss-damn-Alabama..."

"*Louisiana*. See, there you go. I didn't compare you to anybody. You compared yourself to them. Forget it. Order room service and charge it to me."

Delaina slid out of the jeep onto pavement among prim and proper passersby. If he corrected her on his trashy hookups one more time, she would straddle him in his jeep with their pants pulled down in front of every wealthy soul at Calla so he'd be unforgettably clear who came to Houston with him *this time*. "I'm going to dinner with you! One day you'll learn not to challenge me, Jed McCrae. Fuck Miss *Louisiana*." She bobbed her head.

Jed could've acted like a giant prick. He valued staying alive too much to point out he *had* fucked Miss Louisiana.

Delaina had her hands on her hips, foot jutted, pretty breasts rising and falling inside her *Dirty Diamonds* shirt. "You'll be beggin' me to talk in five minutes or less." She stamped to the hotel entrance. "I'll see you at eight, and I won't utter a single word to you 'til dinner's over! Miss Louisiana, huh, you wait. I'll give you a night to put all those bitches to shame." She vanished inside palatial-size paradise.

Tory Cash raised that gal, for sure... Jed would've laughed his butt off completely if she hadn't somehow astonished and irked him to the highest degree. They absolutely would have the dinner date of their lives followed by the hottest sex ever, and he *knew* she would put the rest to shame. He stepped on the accelerator and drove recklessly to his apartment.

~ ~ ~

"I got your ticket reserved. You need to leave now to make it," Boone told Cabot by phone.

"I'm already driving. By the way, have you found Jed?" Cabot asked.

"I still haven't," he lied. At some point, it went beyond being paid by Fain or that Jed would pay more. Jed was his first cousin. The sudden guilt, he supposed, came from working on the land, now seeing it compromised publicly and illegally. "He took his plane somewhere, probably Atlanta."

"Are you ready to lower your bomb?" Cabot asked.

Could he really do it? Implicate Jed unfairly. ...Boone had gone too far in to get out. "Yeah, when do you think?"

"As soon as I'm gone," Cabot replied. "Everyone is playing along expertly. They need your testimony. I want Lainey's name out of it by the time I get back with her."

"Go on. I'll handle Mallard County. You'll land in Houston before midnight. I sent you the address."

"Excellent work. You're getting better at the major leagues, pal. I guess you've finally figured out, if you're going to make something of your life, you can't sit around bass fishing."

~ ~ ~

Delaina panicked inside the hotel. She wanted to look so beautiful, lovable, and sexy that Jed would beg her to talk all night long. Ten minutes after seven. "Shoot!" She appealed to concierge, "Where's the very best dress shop?"

"At the end of the mini mall in the courtyard down there," a woman drawled in Texas twang. "They're apt to have a little somethin'..." Delaina dashed through glass corridors and doors, scanning shop windows. "Books. Toys. Shoes. Sorrel's?" She barged in, forgetting her casual attire. A snooty lady chose not to acknowledge her. "Excuse me."

"Yes, excuse you."

"I need help." Tensely, she slipped her ring on and off then on her right hand.

"Yes, you do. You're lost, I presume."

"I need the prettiest, sexiest dress in this store in the smallest size."

"It'll be very expensive."

"I don't care what it costs."

The lady judged Delaina's appearance. "You have a nice figure and a lovely face..."

"Save the snobby overview. I'm in a hurry. I have money."

"Follow me." They walked through a plush corridor into a plusher fitting room. "Undress while I get a few for you to try." She went to a glassed-in closet and came out holding cocktail dresses on satin hangers. "Blue, black, white or red?"

"Black, yes, black." Delaina eyed the classic cocktail dress and changed her mind. "Too predictable. I need something unexpected. Something to make him say *whoa*." She gulped thinking of that reaction from Jed. "How in the world do you make Jed McCrae stop dead in his tracks?" She giggled. "Maybe red?" She held out the bareback dress. "Too obvious. Maybe the blue one." With eyes as round as quarters, Delaina stared at the woman. "Help me." She pressed her palm into her abdomen and swallowed. "Oh God, I can't mess this up. I usually fly off the handle over a comment he's made or pull a sensational stunt and ruin it. Tonight has to be good. I wanna show him with one look..." Delaina concentrated on the dresses. "I have to convince him without saying a word that I..." She felt the world slipping out of her hands. "You see, I have this tendency to rant. He only speaks when he knows what he's talking about. He's brutally honest." She paused. "Things about him drive me crazy. He has a history of romantic entanglements he doesn't deny." Delaina narrowed her choices to blue or white. She held out the hangers. "He'll look perfect, if he shows up in boxers with his head shaved." Delaina gave her the blue dress and gripped the hanger of a long, halter, white dress, feeling close to tears. "This is too virtuous. Oh, I don't know. God help me." She turned on her feet. "What do you think?"

The lady smiled thinly. "Honey, you're so in love."

Delaina's arm went slack. She gripped a velvet chair. Her other hand flew to her mouth. Truth swept through her with the force of a gale wind. "Oh my, I... I am." Dressed in a gray cotton panty set, she spun around slowly on her feet. "Oh God. You're right." She ran around the room like a frenzied psycho. "I love him. I love Jed McCrae! I love him so much. Eee!" She stopped and stared. "Oh my. Help me, please." Dramatically, she emphasized, "I want him defenseless, breathless, speechless, and hard. Very hard! Oh lord, excuse me, Miss, Miss who?"

"Helen," the salesclerk answered demurely. "It's Helen, and I think I have the dress."

"Eee! You do?" Delaina jogged in place and squeaked, "Get it! Get it! Get it!"

"It's foolishly expensive."

"I'll take it!"

Helen disappeared and reappeared holding it out. "Oh hell, Miss He*ll*en! That's it!" Delaina jerked it from her and hurriedly slipped it over her hips. Helen zipped and turned her toward a wall of mirrors. They gasped as she pulled Delaina's hair out of the rubber band.

A wonderfully simple and undeniably sexy dress. Pale gold soft silk chemise with intertwined straps thinner than spaghetti noodles over each shoulder and a scooped neckline. Straight hemmed and tight, it fell at Delaina's midthigh. "I have thirty minutes! I need good underwear. Simple. Like a nude, strapless..."

"Push-up bra and thong panties."

"Yes, yes." Delaina smiled. "Definitely a push-up 'cause I have peaches!" She threw her head back in ecstatic laughter. "Do you have it?"

"I stock a vast selection of lingerie. I'll look. You go to the employee break room and freshen up." She pointed down the hall.

"Great! What about makeup?"

Helen reached behind a counter. "We get samples." She handed Delaina a basketful of cosmetics. "Help yourself."

Delaina ran around the corner singing, "I love Jed. I love Jed," and took a sponge bath in the employee restroom. She rummaged through samples, tested packets of interest, and applied subtle makeup. Glistening powder, black eyeliner and mascara, pale lipstick and gloss. Helen stuck a shimmery flesh bra and panty set through the door.

Dressed, Delaina dashed out yelling, "Shoes?"

"There's a shoe shop you passed. Good gracious, that coal-black liner on your eyes is to die for. Honey, you've been transformed! Here's an evening bag for your lipstick and phone.'"

"Thanks! Here's my card." Delaina tossed lip gloss into the purse. They hadn't had phones all day, and it was *fabulous*. "Keep my other clothes."

"Wait! Wait!" Helen yelled, losing her composure in the excitement. "Your hair needs to be pulled away from your face."

"You're right. Ooh! I can't believe I love Jed!" Helen scanned a glass case and retrieved an elegant hair clip while Delaina sang an off-key tune of her own design, "*I love Jed. It's not in my head. We're going to bed. Lah, dee, dah. I love Jed and I will 'til I'm dead.*" In a rapid upsweeping motion, Helen put Delaina's hair into a loose twist. The lack of hairspray or pins made it seductively messy. Delaina grabbed her charge card. "Have a wonderful life!"

She scurried into the hifalutin shoe store barefoot, searched the rack, and saw strappy high heels. She slid them on and jabbed her card at an older man. As he charged her card, she said, "Guess what? I'm in love," signed, then "Thank you! Bye!" Delaina sprinted. Perfect people stared because she was striking or because she barged into them. She neither knew nor cared. She fled to the hotel lobby and spun around. An enormous clock revealed two minutes before eight.

"Oh God! Oh, my heavenly God. I love Jed." Her stomach spun like a slow-motion Ferris wheel. Her clammy hands trembled. "Okay." She talked through heavily oxygenated breaths. "Calm down, Delaina. Okay. Breathe. Ooh!" She paced the marbled floor, shoes resonating like broken glass. She inhaled deeply, fumbling for a mask for her emotions. She found none. She wrung her hands, felt the ring on the wrong hand. She choked on the truth, put the ring on her left hand, and stumbled to a leather sofa situated between gigantic decorative trees.

A small-framed Asian lady sat watching her. "Are you fine?"

"No! Can't you see?" Delaina scrambled to her feet. "I'm nervous as a fairy in hell! God, help me relax."

"You, dear, should not be nervous. You are beautiful. A lucky man is coming for you?" Delaina beamed with happiness. Boldly, she turned to the woman and declared, "No, I'm the lucky one! I'm going to dinner with the love of my life."

Jed couldn't stop his steps echoing across the tile, realizing what his Delaina said one moment too late.

~ ~ ~

Boone tried to settle down and carry on as planned after Cabot left. He *would* play the role in the drug bust he had agreed to play. Too late to do otherwise. But he was concerned about the possibility of Cabot catching Lainey with Jed. He couldn't explain it; he just didn't like it.

He surprised himself by texting Jed. *Hey. Fain's been paying me to know what you're doing because of the will. I know where you are and who you're with. Major problems in Mallard. Very important. Call ASAP.*

To verify, Boone sent Jed a photo from his spying trip last night in Houston: Smiling like hopeless fools, Jed and Lainey stood face-to-face at the bottom of an extensive staircase in Calla Hotel's luxurious atrium.

Jed would never believe Boone was in cahoots with Cabot Hartley after he read that message.

~ ~ ~

Delaina swung around and looked at Jed like she swallowed her tongue. His shining sapphire eyes glued to her burning emerald ones; he halted in his spot. Whether from her shocking admission of love or golden graceful image, Delaina would never know. The clock chimed eight times across the dignified hotel. She searched for words and found them. "It's eight o'clock. I've officially turned into a pumpkin." She sauntered sexily past Jed. "Or should I say...a peach?"

She slithered toward the main doorway. Jed wasn't coming, transfixed in the same spot, vividly impressed. Delaina pranced up to him and circled her fingers around the arm of his dinner jacket. Caught up in her drama, she hadn't taken notice of the looks of him. Until now.

He smelled crisp as a pine tree. His hair shone like scorched oil, brushed back and damp from a shower. His eyes sparkled silver-blue with...delight? Yes, delight. She couldn't just imagine such a look. He gazed down on her adoringly. He wore a fine black suit, jacket with two-button front unbuttoned, and his broad shoulders and chest filled it perfectly. He had the collar of his tailored white shirt undone, no tie. Matching black pants fit marvelously. He looked more incredible than ever, his presence as commanding as a military general and equally humbling.

Delaina gasped aloud when she finished scrutinizing him. "Isn't he breathtaking?" she said to the Asian lady. "A minute after eight and already you've broken the rule," Jed inserted. Delaina continued, "If my memory serves me correctly, and it usually does, I'm not supposed to talk to him, and only him, until we finish dinner."

Jed eased toward Delaina and looked into her eyes. "You are... the most...stunning female I have ever...taken anywhere."

Delaina smiled tenderly then jerked her head toward the lady, who gawked. "I guess I should be flattered. You see, he doesn't compliment women. Too bad he's not faithful. In fact, I'm really out of luck. He won't even hook up with a blonde!" She marched to the entranceway.

The woman clasped her hands on top of her head. "Crazy Americans!"

Jed stammered for an apology. "I'm so sorry about her. She... was raised on a farm, and...she's going to be returned there." He stormed toward the door. "Immediately."

Delaina approached the jeep on the sidewalk.

"Wait, little girl! What a fiasco. Why in hell did I deserve such a scene?" He pressed his hand in the small of her back. She turned. Downtown Houston on Saturday night, traffic and tragedy, people and celebrations framed by corporate buildings and luxury hideaways, surrounded them. Their eyes locked in love and hate and regret and spite and awe. The same feelings holding them back urged them to give in. The Ferris wheel in Delaina's stomach turned to butterflies. Radiant butterflies. There was no world beyond Jed McCrae.

Jed recalled their funny charades at the stadium, banked on that, and spoke first, with words diced by feelings. "Please...tell me you weren't serious...tell me you were...making up a story for the woman's amusement when you said...I'm the love of your life."

Delaina held his gaze. Come hell or heaven, she wouldn't break her silence. She climbed in the jeep. Jed lifted his head toward the clouds. If Delaina didn't know better, she would have sworn he prayed.

God, if you're up there and I'm worthy, give me patience and strength.

They rode along.

"You'll like this place. Great view of the city, the lights. They cook food on a hibachi, you know, from an exposed cooktop in front of the table. We're in the private lookout tower tonight. Owner is a longtime friend, Pate Hendricks. Built this restaurant into a multimillion-dollar franchise in major cities across the map. Started with one hole-in-the-wall..." Jed talked on. Delaina admired his face, his hair, his skin, his hands. And laughed aloud. Jed McCrae rambled endlessly. "You're not listening." She smiled. "Okay. I give up. Talk to me," he begged unashamed. "What can I do to make you talk?" She smiled again. He gripped the steering wheel. "Fine. Have it your way." Delaina looked at him doubtfully. "I see what you're saying. This was my idea." Jed screeched to a stop at the curbside valet. "I'll fix you. We won't eat. Dinner's officially over. To hell with it, as hungry as I am. Now open your mouth and say any-damn-thing." She grinned. "You think this is funny?" Delaina burst with more laughter. He gritted his teeth. "I've never in my life known a woman I could argue with when she hadn't opened her mouth, but I'm a son of a bitch if this is not the most irritated that I've been with you."

He stepped aside for a waiting valet, barreled toward Delaina, and reached for her arm. "I'll play along." He rolled his shoulders. "Maybe I'm not using the proper approach." He ducked and kissed Delaina's hand. "Right this way, beautiful."

Her stomach flipped. She made up her mind without hesitation. As soon as the server brought the dinner check, she'd open her mouth to tell Jed: Her wedding to Cabot was off. Cash Way could burn in hell for all she cared. At the hotel, Jed seemed undone by her untimely admission of love. He didn't love her. Of course, he didn't. He liked her; he wanted to be around her; they laughed; they kissed a lot. He would love her. He needed her to go first. To show him how.

In a matter of moments, Jed transformed into gentleman, a tactic to make her talk, certainly. He stood at the sidewalk curb, arm extended, waiting. She stopped to admire the place, Calla of the restaurant variety. The name Bonnou shimmered in gold lights across intricate doors. The building stood at an angle on a man-made hilltop overlooking city night. A matching glass lookout tower straddled the roof. Couples poured in dressed for dining. "Wow." Delaina spoke to the place.

Jed gave her an openly sexual once-over. "Wow." Desire burned Delaina to the core. He draped his arm around her waist as they entered.

"Good evening, Mr. McCrae. We welcome you and your guest. Mr. Hendricks informed me of your reservation." An attractive woman in a black dress greeted them.

"How are ya, Maria? This is my, uh, friend, Delaina Cash. Delaina, this is Maria Broughton, best hostess in the place." Jed smiled with familiarity. Maria Broughton returned it.

"Hello, Maria. Nice to meet you. Jed talked about this lovely place *all the way here*."

"He is a frequent and most enjoyable patron."

"Oh, I'm sure," Delaina answered through slightly gritted teeth.

Maria escorted them to the elevator. "Watch your step."

The elevator lifted, offering a wondrous view of first-floor dining. On the second floor, sunken private rooms awaited. Decked in Japanese lanterns, which created an unmistakably romantic ambiance, the entire level was glass including the roof. Divine fountains adorned two corners trimmed in vibrant plants. Off to the side, their chef prepared a hibachi with oil. Asian acoustics filled the air. Jed led Delaina to a black lacquer table for two placed auspiciously, deep in a corner hidden by greenery. He pulled out her chair and blew his breath on the nape of her neck. "I love...your hair like that." Her skin tickled. Jed smirked at the look on her face then kissed her mouth, mumbling casually, "Your eyes are burnin' gold, sweetheart." He went to his seat.

Delaina quit breathing and thought she might, forthrightly, die. Her love for Jed swelled inside her, consuming every fiber, while he unflappably viewed the menu. He told her a rundown of sushi

Realization

choices and ended with, "Order whatever your little heart desires." He smiled his most chivalrous smile.

Oh my goodness, Delaina thought in exasperation. What had she done to deserve this? She overflowed with joy and love and happiness and passion. "Jed, how ya doin', buddy?" Then she almost collapsed seeing a dimpled, dirty-blond-haired, firmly muscled, cowboy-hatted demigod smiling at her. "Ooh, you must be Miss Cash." He sucked air through his teeth with a wide smile.

Jed spoke up, "This is Delaina. This is my best friend Pate, and I can guarantee you, the only Japanese restaurant owner in America who greets his patrons in a cowboy hat."

Pate returned the warm smile of long-running friendship. "Jed, you've outdone yourself with this one, good buddy. Pleasure to meet ya, Miss Delaina."

Outdone himself *with this one?* "Ooh," she cooed. "No, a pleasure to meet *you*, Pate." She flashed a deadly smile and leaned forward extending her hand. Pate kissed it and winked. His eyes slipped to the low-cut neckline of her dress. Air went through his teeth again. Jed glared undetectably at Delaina.

"I believe you're robbin' the cradle." Pate glanced at Jed. "Listen, miniature darlin', my buddy here knows how to use good manners, so..."

"What manners?" Delaina interrupted.

"Jed, man, you didn't tell me! You snagged her!" Pate held up her hand and checked out the diamond ring. "What a rock! Engaged when?'"

"No, you see, Pate..." Jed gave Delaina the payback-is-hell look. "That's the kicker. I can't take credit for this little hottie. She's about to marry a real scumbag. Here with me last minute."

Pate raised his eyebrows. "Well, honey, if you're interested in Round Two, last minute." He laughed loudly.

Delaina glowered at Jed. "No, actually, your good buddy here is going to be surprised to find out Round One is only his wet dream."

"Whoa, now. There's my cue, y'all." Pate rubbed his hand against the back of his neck and chuckled. "I believe you've met your match, cuz. Really had to finagle to get you in but my pleasure.

Oh, Jed, that reminds me." Pate tapped his arm. "What ya think of Calla?"

"Uhm, I'm, uh, not there, but what I've seen of it is better than preliminary sketches. I've heard it called a glorious sex dungeon and hedonistic…" Jed joked, and because payback is hell, he asked, "Lainey? Thoughts on Calla?"

She had tried to follow their conversation. Did Pate and Jed typically share drinks, good times, and paying for women in hotels? "Mmm. It's…" She felt a featherlike wave of daring and maturity. "Positively a hedonistic, glorious sex dungeon. Yet, it's also…" She said the first thing that came, from the first time she saw it, "admittedly fashionable, even if slightly…showy in a flawless way, a flowery while unfussy…adult experience. Not for the average weekender, not for the guy…who gives hotel reservations minimal thought, like ordering red roses on Valentine's Day. Calla is…white and cream and marble and whispery and absolute and expressive and thought out. The calla lily of celebration-stays."

The guys' mouths went -o. "Too bad we can't market her. Wow." Pate whistled. "Your monologue would sell sex to monks, darlin'."

Jed tapped Pate on the shoulder. "Who'd we have to bump? Hopefully not anyone too important." Delaina paid close attention. Who was *supposed to* stay in Calla 600? Khloe, Ivanka, Duchess Meghan? Pate shrugged looking toward enchanting Delaina. "Emilia won't move in 'til May first." He had a broad smile. "Looks like it was…" He winked at Jed. "Meant to be. Enjoy dinner. If we can do anything to make it more enjoyable, holler."

"Good to see you, Pate. How 'bout a bottle of your best Riesling?"

"No problem. Miss Delaina, pleasure was mine."

Images of dark, dazzling international beauties tortured Delaina's mind. *Em-meely-ya?* How would one spell it? 'Meant to be' that Jed slid Delaina into the condo in time? Before Em-meely-ya. What were he and Pate, joint pimps? She wanted to flip the table, crash the orchid centerpiece, sling food.

Something stopped her…

This was Jed's life. Jed's best friend. In their thirties. If she loved him, she had to know him. Get to know him. Accept him. Attempt to fit into his life, or at least understand it, pre-her.

Jed sighed. "I swear, we haven't been here five minutes. Already you're hitting on my best friend. You talk about my morals." Delaina stamped on his foot. "Ow! Damn, little girl." He mentally counted to ten and changed his facial expression and bodily posture. "Let's order, cupcake."

~ ~ ~

"Monday mornin' at nine o'clock, we'll be in the doctor's office, you hear me?"

Holland sobbed and laid her head against the truck seat. "Why?"

"You know why, Holland! Is there really a baby?" Eli shouted.

"Yes!"

"Well, I ain't seen the positive test results. How early can they do paternity?"

"Eli!" she cried, her Hershey eyes defenseless. "Please! Don't put a wedge between us. You're all I have."

"Then you don't got much, honey." He swerved into the apartment complex and squalled his tires. "Get out!"

"What do you know about Cabot? Tell me! You're my husband." She grabbed on to his arm and screamed, "Eli, look at me!"

He jerked his arm away. His dark eyes met hers. She grabbed his face in her hands, her long fingernail scraping his cheek. "I love you. We can work this out. Whatever it is."

He shook his head. "I'm only sure of one thing. That country song was right. If you're gonna ride, you gotta learn to fall. Get out, Miss Holland."

Eighteen

Straight Talk

Their bottle of wine arrived with the fanfare of presentation and opening and sniffing and pouring and twirling and testing. Something Delaina had never seen, she appeared enthralled. Jed soaked in her joy then held out his glass. "Here's a good one…" He watched bubbles dart through golden liquid. "Let's forget what is best forgotten and remember what is worth remembering." Their rims touched as their eyes locked.

He led her, glasses in hand, to their personal perch overlooking the nightlife horizon of Houston. They sat on barstools. Delaina enjoyed the busy, sparkly view. Jed never afforded a glance to the city. Tuned to her, he touched unusual places. A brush of fingers on the inside of her wrist, rim of her shoulder, line of her spine. He stopped long enough to feed her the first bites of sushi. Caught up in the exotic flavor, the exotic surroundings, the unbelievable man, she chewed each bite like manna. She reached for Jed's tray and fed him. He let her. They returned to their table, sipped wine, and watched the preparation of their meal in open firelight. The authentic Japanese chef performed an entertaining show, juggling utensils, flipping food, playing with flames. Jed absently toyed with tendrils of Delaina's hair while she watched the chef in a trance. Jed chuckled, as if he were watching, each time she shared an amused glance. They feasted on a scrumptious meal, laughed over Delaina's clumsy use of chopsticks, smiled and touched. Jed said, "This is the way things should be, Delaina. This is a dinner date." He patted his empty pants pocket. "I haven't thought about not having my phone or the farm." They had closed themselves in an ocean shell, ensconced in their couple's realm. The world was theirs. Raging seas reduced to soothing echoes against a dense wall.

A server came with dessert. Jed said, "What if I told you..." He served a bite between her lips. "...there are no terms or rules or ridiculous standards with you? You got it wrong from the beginning. I was trying to warn you about Cabot and...hold myself back." He gave her a shaky smile. "No defenses tonight." Delaina's eyes widened. She shrugged.

Jed swallowed ragged breath and tried again. "Okay, what if I told you I want you to remove that ring so I can pretend you're mine without being reminded of whose you really are?"

Delaina slid the ring off her finger and dropped it in his lapel pocket. Before she could sit, he pulled her to him and stood up. "What if I told you..." He gazed over her body and shook his head in steadfast assurance. "I love you, Delaina Cash, and I do need you. I've needed you since the first day." Delaina didn't fight tears glistening in her eyes.

"My God, sweetheart, please talk to me. I'm dying to hear your voice. Dying to hear you say you love me too."

Delaina's eyes searched the deserted area for a server with their check. Jed slapped bills on the table. "Dinner's over." Delaina wrapped her arms around his neck and pulled his face to hers. Her eyes sparkled. "I am so in love with you, Jed."

Jed tipped her chin and kissed her lips then delicately slid his tongue in her mouth. They engaged in deliciously sweet, overwhelmingly hungry kisses. As strong as Jed's love for Delaina was, ironic truth conquered it. For days he thought he wanted to tell her what he knew so he could have her, selfishly. Now he loved her enough not to tell her, to let her go, selflessly. He pulled away. "I do love you, Delaina, so much it scares the hell out of me. I don't know how you did it, but you roped me in, and I'll never be the same. I don't want one speck of dirt that belongs to Cash Way. I never did. Look at me."

She did. She could not have imagined what came next.

"I would never intentionally hurt you, but I cannot and will not be able to have you. Not now. Maybe ever."

"If it's Cabot..."

"No, baby." He shook his head and pulled her fingers to his mouth, kissing them. "It's not Cabot."

"Please," she sobbed. "Is it...Lll...Laureth? Nealy or... another woman?"

"No. God, no. There's no comparison."

Delaina held on to him. "Jed, you *are* involved in a scheme meant to hurt me." Her tears wet the sleeve of his jacket.

"Delaina, please. I can't stand this. You'll never forgive me. Come on." He wiped her tears with his fingertips.

Elevator doors split open, a passageway to what could never be. Delaina grabbed him and leveled with him bluntly. "I want tonight with you, Jed McCrae, and I don't care if you're scheduled to stab me with a knife in the morning. Whatever it is, I'll bear it if you'll stay with me." Jed let out a string of expletives not fit for a pirate's ears. They arrived on the first floor.

Maria Broughton waited to escort them to the door. "Enjoy your meal?"

"Yes. Thank you," Jed managed to answer. Delaina managed a nod.

Delaina held on to him as they waited for the valet to appear. She didn't care and couldn't worry about what Jed was involved in. Her body ached with a need for him alone, its origin deep within her sexuality. Like nothing she'd known in sickness or in health, she hurt from the ends of her fingers to the tips of her toes. She hopelessly struggled with a way to convince him to stay. That was all that mattered.

They arrived at Calla in what seemed the blink of an eye. Jed pulled up to the curb, his emotions indiscernible in darkness. Their hands were linked. "Delaina..."

"I love the way you say my name, my full name," she blurted. "It rolls off your tongue like velvet, like melted ice cream."

He pushed a strand of hair from her face. "Delaina. Delaina. Delaina." They watched each other quietly until he stated, "I'll walk you to your room to make sure you get there safely. Stay inside all night, I mean it." Delaina nodded, buying time, counting every breath as her last.

They walked along. Purposely, Jed didn't touch her. He knew he played with fire; he already said volumes more than he should have. He repeated his stepfather Fain Kendall's secrets and threats in his mind as motivation to do the right thing. To leave. Although nothing about it felt right.

They entered. Desk receptionists smiled as Delaina and Jed walked into the wide middle opening splattered with fountain sounds and racy night lighting. The elevator door, twinkling in lights, opened. When it closed, she cornered him in a slow-motion game of chase viewable to any pretentious body on floor 1-5's balconies. She eventually had him backed against the glass. Streams and shadows fell behind him as they rose. Jed gave up and kissed her lips, her tongue, her chin, her forehead, tasting her skin with unforgivable greediness. He gripped her shoulders and flipped them around, sliding her against moving glass impatiently. She moaned and cried. He kissed away salty tears. Trapping her, he pressed hard against her and sucked her mouth into his. She shook with an unquenchable desire to be filled with his body. "Jed, I love so many things about you." Her voice trembled.

The elevator opened. Jed stepped out pulling her with him. The door to her hotel room hovered over them like the gates of hell, their passion burning as hot. "I love everything about you." Jed's eyes glazed with tears as he turned away. "Everything, and don't you ever forget it."

~ ~ ~

"Investigator Hall, I know what I saw on Cash land, and it's worth checking out."

After eleven p.m., Raybon Hall had stood all he could stand. He cussed the young man's insistence. The last thing they needed was an overly anxious helicopter pilot. "Listen, your crew's done enough for today. I'll contact you if we need more information."

"But that'll leave someone time to destroy the other plants."

"We've got a prime suspect, boy!" Raybon Hall yelled. "Leave it alone unless you hear from me."

The young man walked out, replaced by Boone Barlow. "I came to tell you what I know as planned." Jed had not called or texted Boone. He chose to proceed. "Sorry it's so late. Seems like everything has taken longer than it should've."

"Tell me about it." Raybon sucked on a cigar and hollered out, "Men, in my office, ASAP."

Once everyone convened, Boone Barlow began. "Jed McCrae disappears from the farm in his private plane a lot on weekends. No one knows where. He doesn't answer his phone unless we have a major problem. He returns on Sundays. I hate to do this to my cousin, but I mean, I believe in justice. I've been suspicious. I see him a lot at night around the farm, particularly Farm 130." Boone faked nervousness. "I hope I'm doing the right thing."

"You are," Attorney Warren Gage spoke up. "Have you seen Jed with marijuana in his possession?"

"Lately, he's been edgy. He's neglected work, which is out of character, and he's smokin' more and been drinkin' hard liquor. Lainey Cash came to see him at the office about a month ago. You know, Farm 130 is subdivided. When she left, she was upset. Later, Jed told me they disagreed over the farm. He had a look on his face like he'd get revenge." Boone shook his head in disbelief. "Can't believe this. I always thought Jed was a good ole boy, you know?" The men listened, nodded. "My cousin sure does have nice things. He's funny that way. He keeps his money to himself, doesn't bank in Mallard. I hope he's not trafficking drugs with his plane..." Boone shrugged his shoulders.

He was in now, all the way.

"Damn, the more I think about it, I should've figured it out a long time ago."

Investigator Raybon Hall nodded. Attorney Gage chewed on the side of his mouth. "Have you seen marijuana in the field?"

"No, sir, but Jed has me workin' a few plots a couple days a week. None where plants were found... I'm feeling bad about this. Family and all. If y'all will excuse me, I want a cup of coffee."

When Boone disappeared, Raybon Hall said, "Men, what do you think? I think we need to issue a statement that we're searchin' for Jed McCrae, our lead suspect."

Attorney Gage spoke up. "Hold your horses. I'll have to get a conviction out of this. Let's keep quiet until we speak with Lainey. I'd like to talk with her before we proceed."

Raybon Hall disagreed out of respect for Cabot's plans. "We don't have to question her."

"Yes, we do. Landowners are liable for anything on their land, and ignorance is no defense. Excuse us," Attorney Gage said to the men. When they filed out, he said to Raybon, "Hear me out. It's my job, not to hear what someone says but what he doesn't say. Y'all need Jed and Lainey in here together if they'll agree, ASAP. I'll explain."

~ ~ ~

Moll and Maydell Smith couldn't sleep. Moll didn't like withholding what he saw between Jed and Lainey at the riverbank from the sheriff's department but felt he should let Lainey explain herself first. If he ever saw her again. God only knew what she was doing, more than likely with Jed McCrae. Maydell, convinced Lainey shopped for a veil, added to keeping his mouth shut, so far. They hadn't heard from Rhett or Eli since late afternoon. Close to midnight, Moll pulled on overalls, kissed Maydell's cheek, and left.

He rode and rode and rode looking for his sons. He found Eli sitting on the bank of Carr's Creek, drinking whiskey and smoking cigars. "Boy, we're gonna get things straight." Eli didn't comment. Moll sat beside him. "Why'd you marry Holland?"

"She's pregnant. Don't tell Mama yet. It may not be mine."

Moll grimaced. "Why do you think it's not yours?"

"I can't talk about it."

Moll jerked him by the front of his shirt. "You'll never be too old for me to turn your ass over my knee. What do you know about this marijuana bust?"

"Nothing," Eli said, jerking away. "I grew a little grass in the past. Not lately."

"Your brother's nervous as a blanched worm."

"'Cause he's still growin' in containers at the rental house. For them college students. Nothing like what the sheriff's department found."

Moll sighed. "I ought to kick y'all's asses. We raised you better. Do you care about that slut of a wife you've knocked up? To my knowin', you ain't been seeing her more than a month."

"Holland means as much as to me as any woman has, for what it's worth. It's not gonna work even if the baby is mine. If there is a baby..."

"Are you dumb as a brick, son? You're not sure there's a baby, but you married her?"

Eli stood up. "To hell with you and this godforsaken farm! I've worked for over twenty years in this hell, and what do I have to show? A father who says I'm dumb as a brick. Don't call me son again!" Eli slugged his father in the jaw and stumbled away. He climbed in his truck and gunned it, plowing down the field row in a drunken frenzy.

By the time Moll got on his feet, Eli's truck had disappeared. Eli was too intoxicated and enraged to drive. Moll soared in his own truck down the field row. When he reached the main road, his headlights flashed across a morbid scene. He let out a pained yell. Eli's truck was flipped over in the ditch, tires spinning. Patches of blood and guts glowed scarlet red against the narrow strip of black.

~ ~ ~

"Jed McCrae and Lainey Cash doing anything together for any reason is preposterous," Chief Raybon Hall exclaimed. Damn, where was Cabot Hartley? He should've been back from Biloxi by now to guide them on what he wanted done next.

"Thus, the perfect alibi. Jed McCrae's wickedly smart. Boone Barlow said both own land on the impacted farm," Attorney Warren Gage observed.

Raybon didn't think Cabot would want him to tell Attorney Gage the truth without him there. Raybon attempted to put it off.

"It's late. We might as well go home. Jed McCrae will be back from wherever probably tomorrow."

Attorney Gage continued, "I'm not saying anyone wants to incriminate Lainey. Her father and I were close friends. It's a way to protect her. Here's how: You men approach them together, call it an informative interview of sorts. She adamantly denies involvement, and with her age and reputation, her name is cleared. She's too young to pull off an operation this size without help anyway."

Raybon Hall considered Gage's theory. Might be the best approach yet. "You're sayin' you don't think Lainey's involved, but others might speculate, especially since she and Jed are missin'. We bring her in with Jed; she'll be so offended it'll be obvious she's not involved. That leaves Jed."

"Exactly. Unconventional, I realize. The less people you involve, the better. They could refuse to talk." Gage rubbed his chin. "Emphasize if they cooperate how much better it'll be and hopefully clear Lainey in the process."

"Okay, we shoot for tomorrow." Raybon made the decision. Cabot would have to accept it or tell Gage otherwise.

Nineteen

Sweet Talk

D elaina had one card left in her deck, the queen of hearts. She might be forced to play it.

"*Wait.*" Her voice was imperative. "Jed, I wanna hear what you love about me. Who says we can't talk? All night if we want." She stepped in front of him.

"It would be harder to leave you then, Delaina."

"There's nothing harder than this. It can't get worse."

"It can and it will."

Trembling to the bone from his menacing words, Delaina typed the code on her hotel door. She looked up and saw tears in his eyes. It crushed her. "One more time, please come inside. There's so much I wanna know about you."

Jed followed her and lit a small lamp, tossing his jacket negligently. "There's so much I already know about you." The condo *was* a glorious sex dungeon. *What* must Delaina think of him? They sat on the stretch limo of ivory sofas and faced an imposing white-linens bed front and center, turned down with a single calla lily on a plumped-up pillow among mounds of precisely placed pillows. The emptiness of the bed attracted heavily. Deluxe doors on the other side with blinking elevators below and flowing fountains above them created pale, graceful waves over the room. Every place Jed tried to avert his gaze presented an opportunity for hedonistic lovemaking. Delaina, supremely golden, took off her high heels, tucked her legs, and twisted toward him with her sweetest smile and dangling cross earrings. A night here, what would it be like, *with her*? "What do you know about me?" she asked in dazed contentment.

Jed made himself look at her and, unwillingly, smiled. "I know you kiss like a dragon, cuss like a sailor, work like a slave, dance like smoke, and smell like peppermint and oceans." He shook his head, mystified, then pulled her face to his, his voice strained. "I know you are the most intelligent, strong-willed, fascinating female. I know you have the strength and determination to do anything. I know if you were mine, I would make love to you every night and a lot during the day." Delaina laughed shyly. Jed smiled easily at the thought then became serious. "I'd be faithful to you 'til death, Delaina." He watched her face, kissed her lips. "'Til death."

He plunged ten shaking fingers across his face and into his hair. His eyes went mercury silver and his hair tar black. "I know I haven't been with a woman since the day you borrowed the wrench, actually a couple months before that, actually once since Thanksgiving, since I saw you with Cabot the first time. I know it's your fault all I think about now is touching you, only you." Delaina was shocked, embarrassed, impressed. She squeezed his hand. Jed got up and put on his jacket. His voice became brittle. "I also know something...that will turn your world upside down, tear our lives into...tiny irreparable pieces, and that's why I know...I cannot stay." He reached for the door handle.

"Stay." Delaina said it with utter plainness.

Jed turned as her dress slid to the floor.

"Because there's one thing you do not know about me."

Jed watched her face. His mouth went as dry as a towel. His heart beat like the wings of a hummingbird in his chest. But his eyes were calm-seas blue; Delaina's were charred gold.

"I'm still a virgin." She let the words sink in, her last card played.

Jed looked downward at the floor. His chin touched his chest. He never saw it coming.

"Look at me. Look at all of me."

He wouldn't.

"Whatever you're involved in, I can forget it for tonight. I want it to be you, Jed." He didn't move or speak. Delaina gathered the strength required to survive a loveless life and came forward, stopping arm's length from him. She held out her hand. It trembled.

Surrendering to her was more valiant than sacrifice. Jed swept her into his arms, carried her to bed, and put her down softly. He walked through a hallway and turned on a light, ensuring dim illumination seeped their way. He wanted to see her face, her eyes, her body. He took off his shoes, socks, jacket, and shirt, went to the bedside table, took off his watch, and laid it there. He faced her. "This wasn't on purpose." He motioned. The bang of the space took a lot of getting used to, without her lethal declaration of innocence. "I'm a…an investor here, I wanted you safe, and…"

"Shh. Jed, I know you didn't do this on purpose." Delaina smiled and whispered, "God did."

Jed took in the sight of Delaina, surrounded by white and cream and marble, all whispery and absolute and expressive and thought out. "You're an angel."

Delaina shook, not from fear but from her love for him. Jed shook too, because he loved her and mostly because their future was too bleak to describe. He held her hand and spoke in a tight whisper. "Is this how you want it?"

Delaina reached around his waist and pulled him over her. "No, this is how I want it."

"Christ," he muttered, settling on top of her, burying his head against her chest. Her heart beat rapidly. Either way he was going to break it. This way, they would go down together in flames. He offered her a way out one more time. "I can't promise you anything."

Delaina clutched his face in her hands. "I do not care."

"Christ," he muttered again. He slid his arms behind her shoulders and scooped her. He kissed her lips and talked in a loving voice. "Since our night at the river, visions of your bare body have tormented me. I've had a long time to think about how I want to do this."

She admitted, "In my dreams, it's been wonderful. Night after night." Her eyes were shining. "Jed, we've done this every way, everywhere." She giggled. "Not here, though."

He grinned. Water whispered; lights lulled; sheets soothed. Jed twirled the calla lily, touched her nose with the petals. "Tell me what you want. This night is for you." He placed it beside her head on the pillow.

"I want...whatever you want, Jed. You know me. You just know." He nudged her head to one side and kissed her neck, nipping teeth across her skin. Delaina moaned and arched against him. He moaned and stumbled over his next words. "And you...know me. Without any effort, you're...everything I need, everything I want." His hands moved to her chest. His fingers grazed the shimmering transparent fabric. "Take this. So simple, so pretty, so..." He stroked his hair against her cheek. "...easy to take off." He unlatched the hook, slid the fabric aside, and buried his face against her. "God, Delaina." His fingers gripped her shoulders to keep his hands from shaking. He lifted his head, grinned unsteadily at her with sterling eyes, and let his tongue slice over her left breast. His wet mouth sent shivers through her body, into his, back to hers. He moved to her right breast and began again. Over and over, he took turns, enthralled. "You're perfect. Perfect," he whispered against her moist skin. She struggled to maintain any decency, struggled not to beg for more, as he moved downward. "Here. So tiny, so tight and tan." He slid his tongue horizontally across her middle from rib to rib, down, down, down, until he reached the waistband of her sheer underwear.

She grabbed his wrist and whimpered, "I'll never survive this."

He tripped over the words, "I'll die if I do; I'll die if I don't."

Delaina reached between their bodies and unfastened his pants. She unzipped them and pushed his clothes as far as she could reach. "Since our night at the river, visions of your clothed body have tormented me. I've had a long time to think about how I want to do this." She shoved him onto his back. "Say my name, Jed."

"Delaina."

She bent to his waist. "My name is Delaina Tory Cash." Her breath fanned across his most sensitive skin.

Jed's fingers dug into the mattress. "Delaina Tory Cash, I love you." It came out quivery and strained.

She shivered at the delicacy of his words. Raking her tongue down the line of hair on his abdomen, Delaina shook her hair out of the twist and let it fall across his hard shaft.

"Delaina, baby, I wanna...I'm gonna...I can't." He reached to push her onto her back. She caught his arms and pushed him down again.

"Shh, you can." She laid her tongue on him, sliding up and down. Jed's head spun. The feel of her around him, all over him, on him. His world went black with heat. Familiar shivers crept down his spine. He closed his eyes tight, clenching his teeth. Black went white with restraint. He propped up on his elbows and sucked in, for sure, his last breath as he caught a glimpse of her golden hair spilling over her face and felt the brush of her tongue.

"As your fiercest competitor, I'll teach you turnabout is fair play, Miss Cash." Jed pushed her onto her back and jerked her panties off. He scraped his stubbled chin against the skin of one thigh then the other nudging them open. For a moment his most intimate caress was to look. Then he put his mouth on her, pulling his tongue up and down the folds of her body voraciously. Delaina grabbed handfuls of his onyx hair and groaned uninhibited; she bit her lip until she drew blood. Jed looked up and licked his lips, smirking indulgently. She blushed. "More?" She pushed his head down. He lowered his mouth and laughed against her. She burned until her body became a pile of forsaken ashes with a single flame beneath his tongue. Her stomach grew tight. Delaina felt herself swirling away from the tautness and grabbed uselessly at the wad of sheets damp with sweat from her palms. Jed wouldn't let up to let her catch her breath. He tasted deeper and harder with an intimacy too tender for words. She let go of the sheets to reach out. Their hands interlocked. Delaina whimpered and let him take her, allowing herself the freedom from a life full of rejection, empty of love. She tumbled headfirst into a life of her own. "Thank you," she stammered through shallow breaths afterward.

Coming down offered as much glory as going up had because Jed brought her down effortlessly with his hands and mouth everywhere. Delaina couldn't feel her limbs, her body made into a mound of ashen bones. "Thank you," she said again.

"This is the beginning." No sooner were the words out, Jed remembered Cabot Hartley and Fain Kendall. This was the end. The finale of life with Delaina Cash. An elementally male possessiveness overcame him. He lashed out, "I'm selfish, Delaina. I'm warning you."

"Go ahead," she said, spreading her legs underneath him.

Jed's mouth and hands had been everywhere on purpose, make-out sessions on fast forward. This would not be the hottest sex ever like he had in his mind when he left her in front of the hotel four hours ago. The only real-life scenarios he knew about this came from the locker room more than a dozen years ago, so he put a millionaire's silky pillow under her hips and bent her legs up, like high school sports jocks and country boys had talked about. Then he looked at her angel face, his Delaina, and gave her lips-on-lips kissing, being so sweet she felt apologized to. When he spoke again, his voice sounded alarmingly tight. "Don't hold tonight against me." He gulped and kissed her harder. "Do you understand?" His face sought hers vitally. "It would get better and better for you, better for us beyond belief if I could have you for a week, for a month, for..." Jed paused so significantly, it hurt Delaina to watch. "...life." He studied her face, studied her eyes, and chastised her in a voice too soft to punish. "Damn you, you're too young for me. You've had this comin' a long time, for twenty years, Lainey, and I'll strangle you if you lied about being a virgin to get me here."

"For once, trust someone. Trust me."

His head heavy against her shoulder, his hands splayed on her back. "Then trust me." Delaina understood. There had been so much between their families. Tonight, his flesh on hers, as close as two bodies get. He edged closer. "No protection," he confirmed. She nodded. No such protection existed for her heart anyway. Braced above her, Jed watched her eyes for a sign. It came from her lips. "I love you."

He mouthed *I love you* as he pushed into her powerfully. In direct synchrony, he realized what she was about to do. His hand came down over her mouth to stop the sound. Her teeth bit into his hand bone, tearing through his skin, and muffled her pain. The impact, the severity, shocked them. Her jaw slackened as his blood trickled, and she sucked her breath in a loud gasp. It took everything in Jed to stop. Took strength he didn't know he had to pull back. Peeling his skin off with his fingernails would have been easier. But he did pull back, and he waited. Delaina's eyes focused on a faraway wall. Her hands clenched his shoulders.

Jed's hand throbbed. Everything throbbed- their bodies, the room, the fountains, the shadows- with a strange splendid misery. He sucked the blood trickles. "Here, angel." He put his hand to her lips. She looked at him without a hint of movement. "Bite down until you don't need to." His face strained, his voice throaty, his eyes compassionate, the pupils like black pinheads when he whispered, "It hurts me more than it does you..." He shook his head in assurance. "...because..." He pushed deeper into her. "...nothing else will satisfy me again." Delaina clung to him while slowly, deliberately, repeatedly, impulsively, he moved, groaning in a purely masculine brand of ecstasy. She released his hand from her mouth. He kissed her unendingly. "I'm part of you now, Delaina, whether we like it or not." He had branded himself on her body permanently, leaving a mark never to be erased.

Delaina gripped her arms around his back, nearly crushed by his movement and force in the most magnificent way. She wanted to know his body, for him to know hers, without limits. She wanted their first time, probably their only time, to be hedonistic there with him. Water welled in her eyes. Jed felt sudden tension. Neither budged. He watched her unfallen tears. "I don't want to be a virgin."

"You're not." Jed tried to smile. He knew what she meant.

"What if we don't get to do this again?" Her eyes searched his; her body clung tighter.

Her tears falling saved him from a quick ending. Halted his need. "Shh. We will." Fifteen thousand times for fifty years, they would. Somehow.

"I want us to be more. Now." She lifted her hips.

Jed tensed. She lifted again. "God, wait, baby." He could not do this much longer. "You're okay?" How he spoke, he did not know.

She tried twisting. "It's not so bad..."

"Oh hell. Oh God." Jed's head dropped closer to her face. He was about gone. "Here." He pulled the pillow away, bent her legs up more than when they started, and began French kissing her mouth.

"Oh God," from Delaina this time, into his mouth. Jed kept going. "Oh God, Jed." She put her hands on her knees, pulling them up to her chest. That minor ordinary action, the sight of it and her, was the damnedest thing he'd seen, or felt, in his life. Jed didn't know if he was about to come or die. His chest closed too tight to respire. They began an extremely choppy version of the real thing with her knees held high into her chest and their faces locked on each other. She said, "Jed..." "Delaina..." More unrhythmic movement. *"Jed."* *"Delaina,"* he mirrored. She started moving a little more with a little smile, and a lot more with a big smile, and then God and Oh and Oh God, and he might as well have lost his own virginity because Jed had no reference point for this swallowed-up entirety. Every touch, every move, every sound mattered like breath.

Against his will, he went to a place in his mind where he couldn't separate dreams from reality, facts from fiction. Delaina held him on the opened Calla balcony. Treacherous fountains crashed below. Again and again, she pushed him, jolting him to the edge. He reached out to save himself. Only Delaina could bring him back. Over and over, he bordered the edge, saved by Delaina. He pushed her into the sheets, into the mattress of the bed, pushing away from the end. She held her hands out to him. He grabbed tight; their fingers coiled. He pushed her arms above her head and tumbled, no longer spared another chance, into deadliness below.

The plunge, as pleasurable as any man. An erotic freefall, sensually floating, helplessly moaning, breathlessly gasping, heedlessly grasping. Fifteen thousand times for fifty years.

Jed said her name as he broke the jagged plane of cold truth. It cut his skin and pierced his heart. He plunged uncontrollably, fighting for the surface, battling the conclusion. Until he hit bottom, hard and fatal. It was over. Forever.

Twenty

Pillow Talk

Jed collapsed onto Delaina.

His head rested on her chest. Tears streamed into his hair. The moisture caused him to check her face. He wiped her cheeks with the pad of his thumb. "Please don't cry over me."

She shook as she spoke. "I'm not crying over you, Jed. I'm... crying for you."

He lifted himself off her, flat of his back. Seconds passed. They stared at the ceiling, at whispery light waves. Delaina cried quietly. With heavy-lidded eyes, Jed whispered, "Kill me while I sleep, Delaina Cash. I don't wanna live another minute without you. Without this." He closed his eyes and slept.

~ ~ ~

Holland Sommers Smith's scream echoed like the cry of a wolf. "No! No! No!" Her stomach caught in her throat. She gagged on dry air. "Oh God! No!" she yelled and fell down. She clutched her middle in agonized desperation, her body in fetal position. "Someone, please make it stop."

Rhett Smith stared at her, drowning in his sorrow. He reached to touch her.

"No!" she cried out. "You look like, you're so much like, you're... God, help me. Eli, why Eli?"

~ ~ ~

Cabot Hartley laid his head against the stiff economy seat in the airplane headed to Houston, furious at the immature aggravation also known as his fiancé. He stayed up all night in Biloxi. He had planned on a wild bachelor party, more convincing that he wouldn't be involved in the drug bust the next day.

Considering the task he had to pull off when he got home, he hadn't planned on it being as wild as it became.

He and his buddies, plastered drunk and snorting cocaine. Women came to the room. Three strippers. Sisters. He settled into the indecent memory. *Money is everything*, one gal said. He responded, as he dipped his tongue into her naval, "No, honey. Money isn't everything. It's the only thing." He couldn't think of anything he wouldn't do for millions of dollars. He had lied, schemed, blackmailed, cheated, stolen, and victimized. His win was close.

~ ~ ~

Jed slept peacefully.

Delaina planted feathery kisses on his hairline, the skin behind his ear, the crook of his elbow, the bend of his wrist, the curve of his ribs, the ridge of his hip, the joint of his ankle. Inconspicuous places, hoping her lips touched one spot no other woman had ever known. Or ever would. When she believed she had memorized every feature, she put her head on his chest and curled against him. After midnight. She figured he'd either sleep all night or leave inaudibly when he woke. For however long it would last, she clung to him in Calla ecstasy.

Jed woke up when he felt her body embracing his. He squinted drowsily. No, he wasn't dreaming. She was real. He assumed she slept. He would ask her not to marry Cabot, the first step when she woke. If she agreed, he'd tell her what he knew about Fain Kendall. If he lost her, he would lose her honestly. A slim chance, she might forgive him. They would take it one day at a time.

"Is this your normal approach? Bed 'em then go straight to sleep?" She smiled.

"Huh? Oh." He tipped her chin. "I'm sorry I fell asleep. Haven't slept much lately." Concerned, Delaina propped on her elbows. The sheet fell away to expose her breasts. Jed appraised them. "I might never sleep again." He grinned lopsided.

"Why haven't you been able to sleep?"

He pulled her head to his lips. "You. Falling in love mixed with sexual frustration are new things for me."

"Good." She talked, eager to keep him there without begging. "I guess I'm the necessary sedative. You rested."

"No. I dreamed provocative things about you the whole hour."

"Even better. Any fantasies I can fulfill?" She made a coquettish face. "You so graciously fulfilled mine."

"I do have one." Jed led her off the bed. "Take a shower with me." As they stepped onto floor, he stopped, a vivid picture drawn. The imperial bed where they made love. Delaina, naked and marked. Him, naked and marked. Delaina halted, seeing what he saw. Feeling what he felt. *How nature intended it to be.* He squeezed her hand. "Get the warm water going." Jed didn't say he was ordering clean sheets after midnight, and whoever came would get a significant tip on the pillow.

In a minute, he joined her in the bathroom. Not the right name for such a...tempting adult tree house. Delaina in a shower, wide open, no door. Water sprinkled from the ceiling like rainfall. There were *trees* in the tree house. He stepped from the room into the water. Delaina stood in front of Jed under the spraying stream. The water steamed and relaxed. "Is it too hot?" he murmured against her hair.

"Not yet." She curved her face to his. "To do it this way. Now that would be almost too hot." She smiled in embarrassed innocence.

He nudged the back of her thighs. They could tear each other up with unbridled passion soon. "Like this?"

"Yes, sir."

"I'm gonna hold you to that. I'm gonna bring you back here. On purpose."

She laughed. She nudged. "Hold *me* to *that*?"

Jed's resistance had been willingly carted onto a proven foundation. Honesty. He turned her around. "We have a lot to talk about, baby." She nodded. He kissed her hungrily. Hot water rolled down their faces into their mouths. They coughed simultaneously and laughed. They took turns washing each other. Finished, Jed held her in the stream, watching her, something on his mind. "I wish tonight could've been better for you…" Bodies slippery wet, he tightened his hold on her.

Her head tilted back, bright eyes. "I loved tonight." His blue eyes defined intimacy, discerning her face. He needed her to be satisfied, she sensed. This is how he, how they, would be. All the way, always. She glowed. "Can't wait for next time."

Next time. Jed hoped to God so. "I love you. Don't forget it."

Dried off, they climbed into a clean bed. "Come here." She settled halfway across his chest. Jed pulled the coverlet over their bodies. "Why haven't you been with Cabot?"

"Uhm, I don't know. It's been…maybe five dates?"

"It's been since Thanksgiving," Jed clarified. "I've known you four weeks, and we're not exactly dating."

"True." Delaina couldn't physically close her pleased lips. Naked in Jed's arms, clandestine, in another city, in a wickedly right hideaway, after four weeks. She basked in the feeling of being in bed with him. "*Or.*" She began with the purest smile. "You could say, you received a special birthday present when you were ten, the other half of your soul, and I did too, the day I was born, since I've never known life without you. We spent twenty years in nearness, surrounded by *our* land, *our* river, *our* homes, *our* cemetery, *our* road, and nobody else's for five miles, intensifying our bond. Your father's death and my mother's desertion strengthened our compassion. Failed relationships with your exes and your broken engagement, failed attempts to give my virginity to Boone and Cabot led to our destiny. Facets like Lucy, fancy blue jeans, same music, baseball, and so much kissing made it undeniable. Tonight, we fully acknowledged what was always meant to be by admitting how much we love each other. We sealed our fate by celebrating together in the most intimate way." She hitched her shoulder, no big deal. "I'm good with either version of you and me." She glanced. Oh my, were his eyes shining with tears? Yes, they were.

"Very Adam and Eve of you, Mrs. McCrae."

Her eyebrows lifted. How unexpected; Delaina had never said it, or even thought it, before. Mrs. McCrae. Hmm.

"You had a failed attempt with Cabot *too*?" Not important really, Jed had to hear it, being genetically male back to Adam, and she would tell him, Eve that she was.

"I tried to be with him. Crazy. On a rampage to prove to my father, my mother, and you..."

"Me?"

"Yeah, in New Orleans. You told me to go spend the night with Cabot Hartley while I thought about you."

Jed frowned. "Not one of my best moments."

She said, "I don't like Cabot," running her finger along the snake of hair on his abdomen, more interested in where her finger went. "Plus, I'm kind of a good girl." Jed laughed unexpectedly. Yeah, *kind of*. She swished her lips, recalling. "I overdrank at dinner and his house, but no matter what, I felt unsure." Chills ran over her skin. "For one thing, he smelled oddly sweet." Jed played with a strand of hair; her fingers stroked his ribbon of hair. "I got pretty drunk, and he did stuff, you know." Delaina scrunched her face.

"I think I've heard enough if you value Cabot Hartley's life. I don't."

"I need to tell this." She kissed his shoulder. "Guilt is eating me alive."

Jed scanned her face. "Go ahead." The muscles of his chest flexed tight against her skin.

"He turned to put on a condom, and I almost vomited."

"Too much alcohol."

"For sure. Same with Boone, though. I *hate* condoms. Something to do with my mother's prostitution, I think. Who knows? Condoms take intimacy out of the act."

Jed nodded. "I agree, but I'm extremely careful. Saw bad stuff in med school." He also assumed she was on the Pill with her wedding a week away and since he made sure she was okay with no protection earlier. "Now that I know how you feel about them, I'm glad I didn't pull out the foil wrapper in my pants pocket."

She fake-glared. "You had one in your pocket?"

"To be honest, three. You know the whole box belongs to you, cupcake." He enjoyed watching her face. Delaina giggled. Three? Wow. Yes! Wait, a box. Her nose crinkled. "What?" The whole box, he said. A box of condoms? *Oh mercy*, comprehension. Their river date, the box. He thought about her when he bought those? "Oh. Oh goodness." She laughed happily with a tiny cheerleader clap. "I think I love condoms now! I wanna use up my box just because they're mine."

Lord help him. 12 times with a condom in her. Not after tonight. He was gonna need it unsheathed from now on. Jed tapped her. "Go on with your story."

"Uhm, so, when Cabot leaned over me, I envisioned you. You're what made me allow him to continue."

"Should I be flattered?" No sign of a smile. "Will you picture my face to get you through the wedding?"

Delaina shook her head fiercely. "I won't marry him. At the last moment, I asked God to give me a sign that night." Insight punched her. "Oh Lord, I wasn't gonna marry him, Jed... I was gonna leave him at the altar."

"Yep, about the time you tried to say your vows." Her face looked horrified. "Delaina, I know, sweetheart. With most of Mallard watching. Fortunately, I tend to figure out your feelings before you do." He shrugged. "I would've shown up, if other attempts failed, in your bedroom at Cash Way before you went down the stairs, down the aisle, to save you the humiliation and to say, 'I love you. Marry me... Or marry no one yet. You're *twenty*.' I already asked you to marry me one time and you laughed."

Jed would've stolen her in her wedding gown. "In your office? When you asked me to marry you, you were serious?" Many points were coming at Delaina. How much they were capable of, together and apart, in the name of love. Heaven help them.

Jed let her go and rubbed his hands down his face. "One story at a time."

"Okay, the phone rang rewarding me a gut-wrenching trade."

"Tory was dead."

She nodded. "It hurts. It hurts so much not to have a family. Why didn't they love me?"

"We'll get to that. For now, let's get something out of the way." Jed pulled her close for a persistent kiss. "Tell me that preposterous wedding to Cabot is off."

~ ~ ~

"Eli is alive," the doctor said. "The resuscitation took its toll. He has multiple injuries. He's unconscious, heavily sedated, and in critical condition."

"I want to see him," Holland spoke up, sipping coffee.

"Later. We are monitoring him closely. I'll send for you as soon as it's convenient."

Holland turned to look at Eli's family. Her new family. Odd. They huddled together on a sofa. "Eli and I haven't told you. We're going to have a baby. Eli must survive; he'd be a great father. I love him. Please accept me."

Maydell Smith wept. Rhett stared at Holland with eyes as big as cookies. Moll glared.

~ ~ ~

"Do you have to ask?"

"Yes," Jed said stubbornly.

"No," Delaina answered. "I'm not marryin' Cabot." She looked anxious. "I said yes for the same reason I came to get your wrench. I need help. I've tried to be brave."

He stroked her hair. "It's gonna be okay."

Delaina raised up. "What about this terrible information you know?"

"I'm getting there. First, anything you want in the open? Because I want you to know I'm not hiding or holding back from you."

"You said I wouldn't be able to repair the damage from what you know." Delaina had sad eyes.

"Gonna take a lot of effort, patience, and faith, baby girl."

"Jed, do you believe in faith? In God?"

Jed thought about her question, pulled back the covers, looked at her body. "After tonight, I do."

She smiled briefly then probed, "What made you propose to Laureth?"

"Well, she was beautiful and sweet...smart and respectable, which are the actual characteristics I've been lookin' for.

Plus, Laureth had this born-again Christian story." He glanced. "Translation, no sex. She piqued my interest, but deep down I knew our engagement happened too fast. It was about getting her ex back."

Delaina pondered, "You're kind of a good guy, you know that?"

He chuckled. "Yeah, I *kind of* am."

"If it makes you feel better, I'm not a real blonde. See the roots?" Delaina giggled.

Jed didn't laugh as he gazed into her face. "I don't care if your hair is really green or striped or a wig."

Delaina claimed with certainty, "I love you, Jed McCrae. I believe you about the Mill's Pond marijuana incident. Why didn't anything come of it?"

"Give it to you straight or sugar-coated?" "Straight, damn straight." "Okay. Dacey Boyd, Sheriff Boyd's daughter, the redhead at the bank. She got drunk and called me to pick her up at the party. We were friends. She was engaged but acted like she wanted a hookup before the big event. I planned to take her directly home as messy drunk as she sounded. I got there, and police sirens came out of nowhere. Lights shone on suspicious bags in the back end of my truck. Police accused me of comin' to distribute pot and wanted to take me to the station. Anybody could've dropped the bags. I talked to Sheriff and told him about his daughter's proposition and threatened to tell everyone why I was there, so he let me go. Dacey didn't get married. I don't know why. Not because of me."

"Ugh, the women."

"Delaina, you asked." Jed ran his hand down her body. "If you don't believe you're what I want after what's happened between us tonight, I don't know what else I can do to prove it."

"I expect faithfulness."

"So do I." His eyes skittered to a wall. "I've honestly been selective in adulthood. I've had to be."

Delaina got it. "Because of all the women who offer."

"Yes, mainly. Med school, I got this awareness, too." He thought about saying more. Why not? "And my mom. Church every Sunday. Talks about finding the right woman."

Delaina's head jerked around, seeing another part of intriguing Jed McCrae. "You're old-fashioned." She sat up, energized, figuring him out. "Jed, you want what your parents had. That's why you're on guard in the beginning."

"Yeah, what they had was drilled in my head." He smiled. "Look, my mother, she would've blistered my ass up 'til the day she died if she thought I disrespected women. I've been particular and discreet." He did *that* wink.

Delaina did *that* wink at him. "Old-fashioned and a mama's boy, sneakin' around."

He moved his arms out, hands up. "I won't have a shred of manhood left when we finish this conversation. Sort of a mama's boy, yeah. I'd make Mama watch war documentaries and shows about planes. She chose movies, and some were big-time love stories. Rhett and Scarlett, Jack and Rose, the one at Pearl Harbor with super-hot Evelyn…"

"And Rafe and Danny! So hot and way hot." Delaina wiggled under the covers. "They're a good excuse to have lovers #1 *and* #2." She put her hand on her mouth. "Oops."

"Fine, if that's your scenario. I'd have to *die* before you move on to #2, and you'd be stuck with my baby."

Delaina laughed loudly. "Good point." She kissed his shoulder. "How cute you are, talkin' like this."

"I draw the line at pink shirts, seersucker, or bow ties with animals on them."

"Me too. Yuck."

"I've got a number for you."

Delaina watched his face change. "Huh? A number. *Oh.*" It sort of…stung now. She shrugged. "Doesn't matter." It shouldn't, she realized, because she meant the most to him.

"You sure? I came up with it when I left to get dressed for dinner."

Delaina felt an itty-bitty hollow inside. "Uhm, is it really a lot?"

Jed showed sensitivity. "Baby, consider I'm thirty, never married, and I love *you*." He whispered in her ear.

Okay, she got jealous. "Well, lucky me." Borderline mad. "Rounding out the Dirty Dozen."

Jed had a small laugh. The Dirty Dozen. Clever. But actually, no. With a charming smile, he said, "Uh, not exactly. What I mean is..." He sniffed. "You're..." He was probably about to get slapped. "Lucky number thirteen."

"Excuse me, I'm *thirteen*." She sat straight. "Jed, thirteen is the unluckiest number in the universe." She crossed her arms.

He stared at her a long time. "I don't know, Miss Cash. I'd call myself unbelievably lucky." She let him kiss her. "Little girl, you were right. You put every woman before you to shame."

Her face wrinkled. "I'm not done with you." She grinned at his body like a candy bar with her name on it. "A couple more questions. What about Emilia?"

His eyes, so blue. "What? Huh? Em-who?"

"Are you and Pate pimps? ...Em-meely-ya. The international beauty moving in this glorious sex dungeon behind me." She drilled him with eyes so green.

He tried not to laugh. "Pate and I are not pimps." He couldn't hold it. He laughed. "Pate, now, he does love him some women. Of all nationalities. We're kin to each other, kind of. Someone on his daddy's side and my mama's side. We grew up like family, were roommates in Atlanta. We, uh, look, we..." What private stuff. "We invest in things like Calla and Bonnou. Emmy, uh, how'd you say it?"

"Em-meely-ya. That's how Pate, your cousin who is not your cousin who is not a pimp but is your best friend and loves him some women, said it."

She caused Jed to laugh again. "Emilia is probably Emmy Calhoun. Cousin to one or both of us." Delaina deserved more sharing, more knowing. A real relationship did. "Pate and I are involved in legal, money-making opportunities. The Darrah-Hendricks-Calhoun bloodlines in Louisiana and Texas are, uh..." Here goes. "Wealthy. I invest for my grandmother Jane Calhoun Darrah. My grandfather passed away years ago. Mama was an only child. I guess Emmy is Calla 600's occupant on May first."

"Nothing sounds legal about a woman named Emilia. But okay." She smacked his lips. "Hey Jed, is it Calhoun as in Bleu Cotton Calhouns? I'm linked someway on Daddy's side."

That obliterated Jed out of nowhere. Bless her. "Yes, the same family."

"We're not related, are we?" She raised up, all peachy breasts and white sheet. "Our *kids*."

Jed didn't want a bad reminder of Fain yet, with precious her here and now. "What about our kids, Delaina? I'll still love 'em. Our dodo-brained monsters." He grabbed her possessively. *I don't want to hurt you* came into his head, so he tickled her, gobbled her, nestled her. "We're not related, cupcake."

"One more question. What about rumors of you and New Orleans, Mr. Filthy Rich-Not a Pimp? From what I've heard, you should be way past the *Dirty Dozen*."

Jed cleared his throat. "Hope you're ready to hear this. Do you care about Cabot at all?"

Delaina made a strange face. What did Jed's women in New Orleans have to do with Cabot? "I'm not attracted to him. He's been a decent family friend since Daddy's illness."

Jed started, "When I first returned home to Mallard, logical for Cabot and me to become friends. You know, twenty-something, single." He shrugged. "Not many guys, uh..."

"In your league." She followed. "Your and Cabot's league."

"We hung out, played golf, almost bought a boat but the deal caused friction. We weren't..." Jed thought for a word. "Alike in business. He's..."

She compared Jed and Cabot professionally. "All over the place?"

"Exactly. Impulsive. Daddy's money. No responsibility yet."

"Yes," Delaina agreed. Jed clearly knew Cabot.

"You know, or maybe you don't, guys can be crude when we're away from women." Jed made a face. "But Cabot *always* refers to women as whores, sluts, bitches, worse words. *Never* capable of respect."

"Jed, that doesn't seem true. When I met you, you were the most blatant man I'd been around whereas Cabot has been strait-laced and patient. Boring."

"Baby, Cabot is patient because he gets it on the side from women whenever, wherever." She cringed. "Cabot acted the opposite in front of you because you're THE catch of Mallard County.

He wasn't stupid about what it'd take. Had I *really* been trying to catch you instead of fighting it, I would've been well behaved. Think about our dinner date tonight. That was me once I allowed myself to pursue you. Making sense?"

She smiled, thinking of dinner, of sweet and handsome Jed. "Makes sense. THE catch, huh?"

"Yeah, and now you're caught." He squeezed her. "Anyway, Cabot invited me to New Orleans back then. I've..." He glanced. "Been to the Hartley weekend house, the one where you, you know..."

Jed had been to the NOLA house? It shocked. "Gray house, three story, patio kitchen, hanging bar." Yes, he'd been there. "Full of girls from the bank like Danielle, Summer Lynn, Liza. Cabot and guys I didn't know, his associates. Alcohol, pot, other drugs. Uhm, a lot of dollar-store thongs, sweetheart. Casual sex, Delaina. Cabot, the main instigator. He does drugs, and every woman at the bank has been with him."

Her face. Confusion, disgust. Things came together. The stocked bar, towels, robes, drawer of condoms. "I believe you." She stood up, went to her luggage. She wanted clothes on. She wanted dignity and morality and purity. To believe the best about someone even if she believed wrong. She slipped on a T-shirt, sat in a chair. Jed joined her in the other chair, suit pants on. "You okay?"

"I'm tryin' to be. Go ahead."

"I'd gone to some of Cabot's parties at the Hartley camp house. You know, watchin' football games, grilling. Pretty mild. Same basic crowd. You haven't been?"

Parties in Mallard? "Don't think he's had any since we've been together. Who knows? We spend our time apart."

"He has a mini penthouse atop the bank for flings and bank girls. I guess you haven't seen it." *Oh my god.* She shook her head no. "At Mallard parties, Jenna Lee Lester came on to me strongly." He waited to see her reaction. None evident. "In New Orleans, she wasn't doing drugs. She approached me. We talked outside a few minutes. She seemed more interesting and...nicer?"

"Prettier." Delaina went from uneasy to queasy.

"Yeah, prettier. We hooked up that night."

Delaina made a sound. One statement about Jed caused a jab worse than the entire story about Cabot. Jed and Jenna Lee having sex somewhere in Cabot's NOLA house. She wanted to be a big girl. She also wanted to cry. Jenna Lee Lester, who handled Delaina's farm accounts, she saw weekly at the bank; she recently told Delaina the name of her pale pink lip gloss, Kotton Kandy, which Delaina loved to wear now.

"Hey, come here... Come sit here." He patted his lap. "Delaina." She did want to be close to him. To know he belonged to her for tonight. She sat on his lap. He put his arm around her. "Cabot could tell it wasn't my scene. We got back to Mallard, and Jenna Lee acted pushy, showed up around the farm for weeks. She invited me to NOLA again. I declined and broke it off. She got mad." He looked at Delaina. "Cabot and I disintegrated. I think he and Jenna Lee, together or separately, who knows, were afraid I would reveal their New Orleans party house, gossip about it. Hell, I could've nailed him for drugs, I suppose. I stayed mute because I wanted to be on the farm with as few complications as possible, and I don't care what lifestyle Cabot leads if he leaves me out of it. Before I knew it, rumors flew about me and women in New Orleans. Kind of like, they took what they were doing and accused me of doing it instead." They sat for a minute. "Do you believe me?"

"I believe you. Believing and comprehending are...two different things." She looked sad. "This isn't the big information you know about me, right?"

"Something else completely." He looked sad, too. "I'm sorry, Delaina. It must feel like you've had nobody in your life you can count on. I swear you can count on me. Kiss me." She did. Intimately. Possessively. He pulled away with a purpose. "One more thing...in Mallard, as far as women I've been with."

"No, don't."

"If we're gonna be anything, you shouldn't live there without knowing. There's been Jenna Lee, Sam Hensley, and Nealy once. I preferred relationships out of town and had a lengthy one with Sophie anyway, here in Houston."

Samantha Hensley. Delaina quietly accepted it. All three in Mallard, gorgeous and capable. The three best in his age group. "It's over? Sophie, I mean."

"Yes. Into her career, a Houston channel TV anchor. Ended before Laureth."

The hotel phone rang, startling them. Jed reached for it. "Hello?"

"This is the front desk with a message. Mr. Cabot Hartley insisted I call. He wants to come up. An emergency."

"Send him up." Jed slammed down the receiver. "Party's over. I guess I'm the fool. Cabot's on his way up."

"What? Oh God! I didn't *tell* him." Delaina slung her feet on the floor. "How? He doesn't know I'm in Calla Hotel or what city or state!"

"Obviously he's keeping closer tabs than you think. Get dressed."

Delaina grabbed his arm. Jed's muscle flexed, and he gave her a malicious look. "What are we going to do?"

"I'm plannin' on standing beside you, Delaina." He walked around tidying items in the room.

"No!" she exclaimed then softened her harshness. "I should start out talkin' to him by myself. I owe him that."

"I'm not leaving you alone with the bastard. I'll hide in the bathroom." He gathered his clothes. "Tell him I'm here if he doesn't already know. I'll come out, and we'll handle it." Jed scanned the room and grabbed the calla lily off the bed. Delaina, fidgety, put on jeans. The elevator bell rang out. Jed went in the bathroom.

Tap, tap. "Lainey?"

"I'm coming." Delaina opened the door. "Hi." She sensed uneasiness. Did he know? "This is a surprise."

"I wish I could say I'm here for pleasure." Cabot walked into wonderland. "*Goddamn*, Lainey. This place." He studied her with uncensored curiosity. "Are you seeing someone? Everybody's wondering where you are."

How did Cabot find her, Jed wondered. Everything was in his name; he made sure of it.

Delaina spouted off, "You spent last night drunk with strippers in Biloxi. I came to Houston to find a veil for our wedding." She looked around like Calla was ordinary. "My bachelorette party to myself. What the *hell* are you doing here?"

Cabot relented. "I'm sorry. You're trying my patience. Running off without a trace. We must talk." She sat. "Yes, Cabot, we do need to talk. I…" He interrupted, "I got home from Biloxi and discovered serious problems in Mallard." He pretended shock and reached for her hand. "Lainey, there's no easy way to say it. Marijuana plants were discovered in the woods and field edges at Farm 130 this afternoon."

Jed flinched and Delaina cried out, "What? No! Whose part?" She didn't want to hear it. She didn't want confirmation of Jed.

"Primarily yours."

Jed sank. He would've rather heard his own. He could defend himself better than she could. "Some on Jed's," Cabot added.

Jed didn't think he heard correctly. *Ah, someone, most likely Cabot, intended to incriminate both of them.*

Cabot rose to his feet to recite his rehearsed speech. "Let me get something straight with you, girl. It's crazy in Mallard. You're lucky to have me. Damned lucky I tracked you instead of the cops." Jed fisted his hands until his knuckles turned white. Every bodily cell meant to go out and get Delaina. His better judgment knew he needed to stay where he was to overhear as much as Cabot would admit. "Tell me the truth. Are you involved in a drug operation with Jed McCrae?" When Cabot planned the scheme, Lainey and Jed had never crossed paths. That was his assurance- she would be so vehement it would be obvious Jed was the culprit. Here lately, Cabot could not relax since those two developed a sort of… working relationship.

"No, of course I'm not involved in a drug operation with him!"

"Lainey, altogether there are upwards of three tons of marijuana in the woods. There's a small, older patch near Jed's cabin. A hefty operation."

Delaina's head spun. Jed struggled to piece it together. Delaina started crying. "What am I going to do? Oh Cabot, I'm going to lose Cash Way."

Cabot threw the knockout punch. "This could work in our favor. Be thankful I'm close to Sheriff Boyd. We talked. He believes..." Delaina looked up questionably. "Jed McCrae framed you."

"I don't believe it!"

The bastard. As unnatural as it seemed, Jed stayed put to see how Cabot explained.

"Hear me out. He's your competitor, honey. The age of this marijuana comes to within days of your father's death. Men play dirty, Lainey. Jed knew you didn't have anyone. I warned you!"

Delaina's miserable sobs pulled at Jed's heart unmercifully.

"You're naive. He saw a way to overcome you, probably planning to discover marijuana on your land this week, before I could marry you. Your land would be seized, you'd be held in prison, and he'd descend on Cash Way. He got caught first."

Jed had heard enough. He grasped the doorknob. "Cabot, you're right. Jed framed me." Delaina doubled over and shook. She heard Jed's condemning words in her brain *'...I know something that would turn your world upside down, tear our lives into tiny, irreparable pieces...'*

"Hey, it's not so bad. We'll prove what he's doing; he'll go to prison; we'll buy McCrae land from Fain Kendall."

Exactly. The real plot. Jed exploded inside.

"No!" Delaina insisted. "I won't step foot on McCrae land again! I don't want anything to do with him! Do you hear me?" She faced the bathroom door and banged her fist against it. "I don't... want... anything from Jed McCrae."

Cabot had known Lainey would be distraught. He hadn't expected her to react so violently. "Sweetie," he said, putting his arm around her. "Let's talk more rationally."

She shook her head in instant denial. "Doesn't sound like Jed to have any on his place and risk getting caught."

"You'd better not place reasonable doubt on Jed McCrae! You're the other choice or you two together."

Son of a bitch, Jed thought. Trapped any way they turned.

"Why?" Delaina cried in hysteria. "Why Jed? Why did he choose to do it like this?"

She fell against Cabot's chest. He pulled her to the sofa. "Cabot, what should I do?"

What Cabot really wanted. Scare her to death then pounce on her.

"First things first. Jed McCrae's missing. No one knows where."

The bathroom door seemed like the Great Wall. Jed could only wonder what would happen on the other side. He had to leave unnoticed. Cabot evidently didn't realize why Delaina was in Houston. Jed had all but incriminated himself by telling her that he knew something disastrous about her. She'd never believe his innocence. He was, at best, freezing to death in a pot of scalding water.

"You need a farm manager before Jed's found. I'm the best choice."

Don't do it, Delaina. Jed would walk out to save her from that.

"I don't know, Cabot."

"Listen, you can trust me. Put it in writing. I'll protect you. I brought the papers. Gage supports me. Sign it."

"No! I don't trust anyone. I'm innocent, and I know it. I'll prove it."

Cabot frowned. "Not smart, Lainey. Damn you, accept my help." On the verge of losing his temper, he eased up. "Look, we'll talk about it on the plane. We're on the earliest morning flight. Pack your things." He looked around at strewn travel items. "It'll take you a few minutes." He reached for his phone. "I'll let everyone know you're okay." He wanted to make his necessary phone calls away from her. "Hurry. I'll be in the lobby."

"I think I know where Jed McCrae is."

No, Delaina, no.

Cabot paused, turned. She continued, "If I'm right, we'll call Sheriff Boyd and ask him to grant me some leniency if I can find Jed."

"Lainey, I don't want anyone to get the wrong impression and think you're in this with Jed." Hell, Cabot would think it if he didn't know the truth.

"No one would believe I'm involved in anything with Jed McCrae. Our families have hated one another for three decades. My hatred runs deeper than ever. If Mallard doubts it, they won't when I'm finished." Delaina gritted out, "I plan to see Jed McCrae prosecuted to the fullest extent of the law, and my punishment will extend well beyond his jail cell."

Cabot smiled as he turned to leave. "Now you're playing with a full deck of cards, babe. I hope you make up as passionately as you fight."

Twenty-one

Broken

Neither wanted to make the first move.
Delaina stood for a moment then deflated onto the bed. The world seemed to tremble in earthquake proportion. Jed took the initiative, no time to waste. He stepped out wearing his tuxedo pants, same thing he came out in the last time she was on that bed. Sitting, Delaina faced him and lost her composure.

Steely eyes met middle-of-spring green ones. Delaina choked on her words, "You have nine hours to turn yourself in, by noon today, or I'll confess to them everything I know. I'll tell them you admitted to me that you knew something that would destroy me."

Jed scrubbed his fingertips beneath her chin, tilting her head. "Tell me, Delaina, will you include that you were begging me to make love to you when I admitted knowing something? Watch it, little girl. You'll incriminate yourself."

"Go to hell."

"This is hell."

She looked at him wearily. "I committed an unforgivable mistake the day I came to borrow your wrench. We were never meant to look at each other, let alone talk or...touch."

"Delaina, the one thing I'm sure of is what we are together. Hell knows, you can't deny it." He crouched in front of her, eye level.

"I would regret tonight for the rest of my life, only it seems my laughable acquiescence may be what saves Cash Way from your greedy clutches. Get out, Jed McCrae. Now!"

Jed jerked her to standing. "You're going to listen to me." She slapped him with hell's force. Her hand stuck to his skin like a block of ice. She cried out like she had been hit when she realized what she'd done.

Jed dropped her and turned away. "You don't mean it."

"I mean it. Don't you dare touch me again."

"I didn't do it. Any of it."

She yelled, "Don't deny it!"

"I've never lied to you. Open your eyes! He's out to destroy us. Cabot is bent on acquiring our land."

"Stop! You fill my head with loads of passion and seeds of doubt. I won't do it anymore."

"If you choose to fight me, Lainey, I'll be forced to fight back."

A single sob escaped her mouth. "Fight me. I'm strong enough to win this time."

Jed stared into her face. "It's going to get worse. Much worse. Other things, unrelated to this, you have no clue about. You will soon. Do you understand?"

She didn't, couldn't fathom it. She nodded yes anyway.

"You're, for sure, gonna get on a plane with him? I told you what a lowlife he is."

She'd never been more unsure in her life. "Yes."

Jed went to the bathroom and dressed. Returning, he found Delaina standing in the same spot. He took her hands and spoke gently, "Through it all, you can come back to me when you're ready for truth." He cupped her face. "I love you."

Delaina's heart told her to believe him. She let her mind win without a struggle. Her heart lost even when it won. "You have a twisted view of love."

Jed let go and reached in his jacket pocket. He pulled out her diamond engagement ring, lifted her left hand, and slid it on the third finger. "No, Delaina, you do." He left her.

Delaina turned to the rumpled sheets of the bed. *'Come back to me when you're ready for truth.'*

She made love to Jed McCrae. That was the truth.

Then she spit him out like a mouthful of rusty nails. She gripped the sheet to smudge tears and crawled into their bed. Its essence had found her hopeful and left her hopeless.

Like an avalanche, more truth came at her with debilitating force. Her father's last words to her. They stood on the edge of Farm 130, the day before she left for Ole Miss. Drunk, he lectured her on the changes of adulthood. 'Love and hate are flip sides of the same coin.' He tossed a coin into the air. It fell on tails. He flipped it again. It fell on heads. 'Watch out who you love, Lainey. Or hate.'

Resolutely, Delaina stood. She reached deep inside and found a shield for her soul, one of mere survival. It saved her and compelled her to move again.

About the Author

Clare Cinnamon is from a Southern small town. She enjoys reading or writing about almost anything and holds dual college degrees in business and psychology. Happily married to her high school sweetheart with two wonderful grown kids, she regards among her life's best: their large family farm, heralded with various awards including 2015 National Outstanding Farmer winner. When she's not nestled in a book, her passions are yoga, world travel, and outdoors.

Lightning Source UK Ltd.
Milton Keynes UK
UKHW010610230622
404852UK00001B/17